RUNES
AND
RED SAILS

RUNES

AND
RED SAILS

ANDER LEVISAY

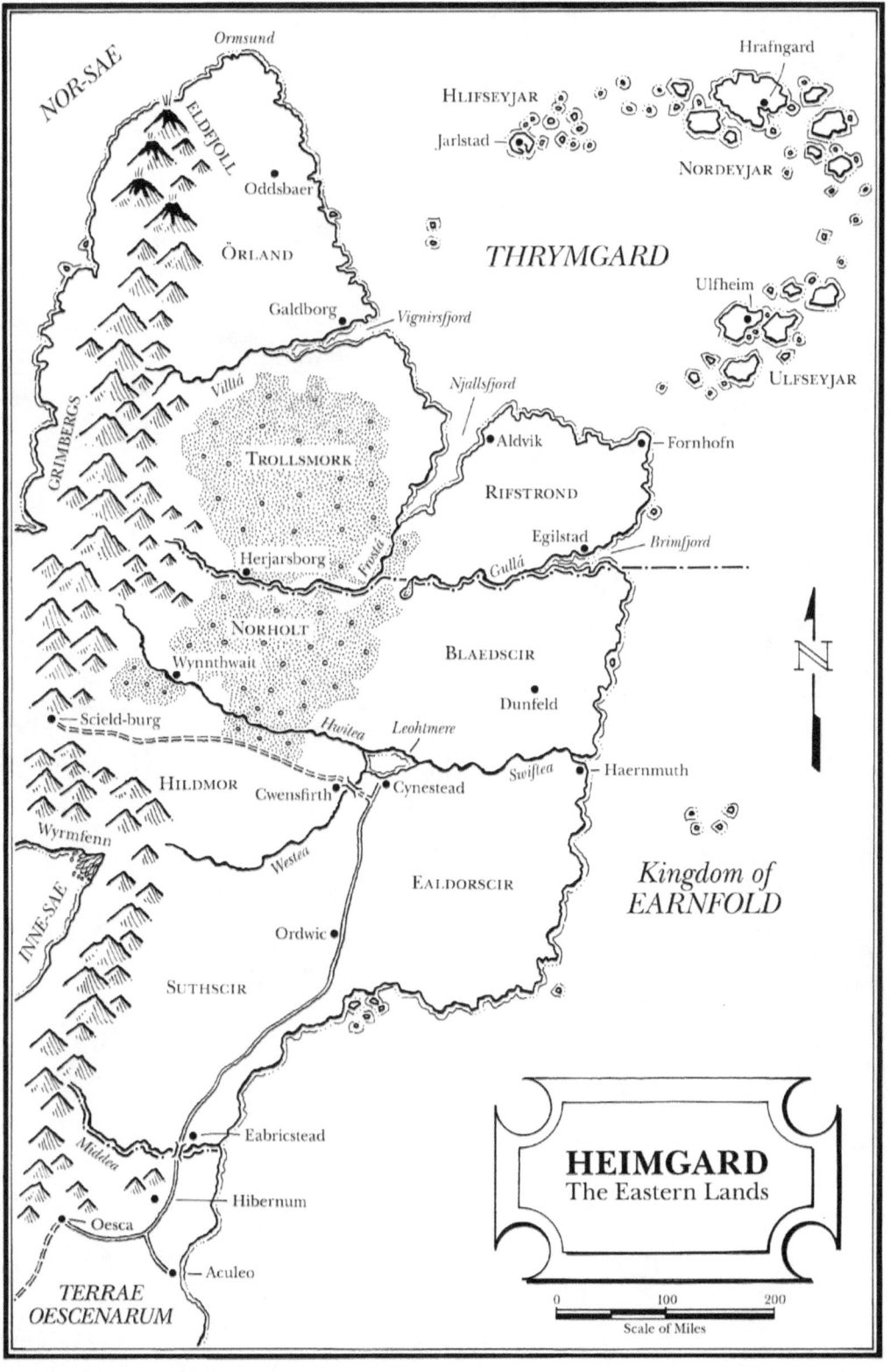

NOR-SAE

Ormsund

ELDFJOLL

Oddsbaer

ÖRLAND

CRIMBERGS

Galdborg

Vignirsfjord

Villá

TROLLSMORK

Herjarsborg

Fnatá

NORHOLT

Wynnthwait

Scield-burg

HILDMOR

Cwensfirth

Hwitea

Westea

Wyrmfenn

INNE-SAE

SUTHSCIR

Ordwic

Midelea

Eabricstead

Hibernum

Oesca

Aculeo

TERRAE
OESCENARUM

HLIFSEYJAR

Jarlstad

Hrafngard

NORDEYJAR

THRYMGARD

Ulfheim

ULFSEYJAR

Njallsfjord

Aldvik

Fornhofn

RIFSTROND

Egilstad

Brimfjord

Gullá

BLAEDSCIR

Dunfeld

Leohtmere

Cynestead

Swiftea

Haernmuth

EALDORSCIR

Kingdom of
EARNFOLD

N

HEIMGARD
The Eastern Lands

0   100   200

Scale of Miles

1

AT THE FAR end of the hall, in darkness broken only by a few shafts of faint candlelight, the King lay dying. Osred, King of Earnfold, was not an old man—he had seen only two score and six summers—but death was coming early to him.

A plague had swept up from the southern reaches of the Kingdom during the depth of winter and laid waste to the villages and towns in its path. With the coming of spring and the return of the sun, the pestilence had lifted, lingering only long enough to claim one last victim. The King was wracked by fits of coughing; he burned with fever, his breath labored and uneven. When he mustered the strength to speak, he raved like a madman.

Aelfhild watched from the rear of the hall with the rest of the servants. Her heart quickened with every spasm and gasp from the King, and each she was sure would be his last. But Osred clung doggedly to life as the evening wore on, just as he had for days.

There was nothing Aelfhild could do for her lord, and nothing anyone could do, so she stood amongst the useless and waited. Her fingers were aflutter, ceaselessly flattening and folding a crease in the front of her dress; her mother had never abided idleness and the dutiful daughter in Aelfhild feared that this impotent dawdling might qualify as such.

Forgive me, mother, she thought, and cast her eyes skyward.

There was a crick in her neck from peering over the rows of shoulders, for the vigil by the King's deathbed was a well-attended event. Waiting in the hush of the darkened hall were an assortment of courtiers, advisors, retainers, and hangers-on, the constant crowd that followed in the wake of royalty. Most were of little import, there only to gawk and to carry gossip to those waiting outside the walls of the keep. Aelfhild had seen more compassion in the eyes of vultures.

The unmistakable hunched shape of Wictred, the King's High Ward, swept by.

And there went the biggest vulture of all. Aelfhild had never trusted the man—he had a habit of toying with the greasy gold chains around his neck whenever he spoke which she found repulsive. A servant of the Gods should not, in her view, show so much wealth, not even one of so high a rank.

The High Ward craned upward to whisper in the ear of a minor courtier who was trying quite hard to look mournful. Aelfhild sighed and turned back to the King.

King Osred had been, as far as she was concerned, a fine king. He kept his hands to himself around the younger girls and had always seemed content to let the servants get on with the real work. Those who knew about such things said he had guarded the boundaries of his kingdom with a firm and fair hand, though Aelfhild could not say one way or the other. The streets of the city bustled with carts these days, sure, and there was more gold on evidence in the hall than she remembered from her youth. Candlelight glinted off jeweled throats and fingers, played across tapestries woven with silver thread and cloths dyed in costly hues.

The King's one weakness had been—still was, she chided herself—his children. He had for years delayed choosing an heir, fearful of driving away one or the other of his offspring, and now was too feverish to speak coherently or even discern the faces of those closest to him.

The King's sudden illness had taken everyone off guard, and now factions moved in the great city of Cynestead to take advantage of this new weakness.

Wictred crossed through Aelfhild's view again. Even in the weakest of light his layered robes glinted, covered as they were in a magpie's hoard of gems, baubles, feathers, and bones. The old man laid a claw on Ceolwen's shoulder.

Aelfhild shuddered for her mistress.

Ceolwen was the oldest of the two Aethlings—heirs to the throne. She sat beside her father, bathing his brow and clasping his hand, as serene as she always took great care to be in public. For two days now she had not left the King, and Aelfhild had waited by her side as she had every day since childhood. Ceolwen's eyes were sunken and ringed with darkness, care lines etched deep in her face. Her clothes and hair were disheveled, and Aelfhild imagined that she herself must look the same. Sleep had been in short supply of late.

The High Ward whispered his platitudes to the girl and swooped off.

The other Aethling, Osric, sat nearer the edge of the room, removed from the crowd of lookers-on. He was deep in council with two of his bondsmen. Osric had stayed close to his father since he fell ill, but kept his distance from Ceolwen—there was little love lost between the two half-siblings.

The Queen, Ceolwen's mother, died bringing her daughter into the world; Aelfhild had only just herself arrived, and was raised alongside Ceolwen, part playmate and part pet. Aelfhild remembered a succession of royal consorts and lovers, but for his daughter's sake the King had not taken another wife. A doting father's kindness, though, proved to be the King's error, for he had put off the question of succession, and now had neither the breath nor the time left to set matters straight.

Aelfhild tried not to retch. Now Wictred was by Osric's side, on his face the rictus of a reassuring smile. She knew the old man would play both sides until a winner emerged. In her mind, there was no question that her mistress was the rightful heir, but the King had not formally chosen either child, and there were some in the court who preferred the idea of an illegitimate king to a legitimate queen. For years, nobles and courtiers had quietly been positioning themselves in one camp or the other, simpering and fawning and waiting.

Of all the things in the King's court, she hated the endless scheming and backbiting the most. Emptying chamberpots was refreshing work by comparison.

The gasping rose to an apex, and all eyes strained for a glimpse. Not a word was spoken. The King sucked at the air, drawing in breath after rasping breath. He strained as if to speak, but no sound came forth; his lips worked furiously but in vain. He could not speak, and so, with a long sigh, he lay still. The silence was total—Aelfhild could hear only the rushing beat of her own heart.

Ceolwen stood and bent over the King's body. Let it be over, Aelfhild prayed, let him be free of it. Muscles in her neck ached as she craned to see her mistress.

Ceolwen stood. "Our King has left us," she said.

She chose the tone well, thought Aelfhild. A touch mournful but without that womanly frailty the nobles so feared in her. But then, Ceolwen always did have more patience for courtly matters.

Greedy eyes in the crowd absorbed every detail, while minds scrambled to find a way to insert themselves into the story when they repeated it later to rapt audiences throughout the city. Whispers rippled through the hall, a breathy susurration that echoed somehow more in the dark than would normal conversation. Aelfhild knew that none there would dare be first to break the studied quiet, but all had to take great pains to have their presence at such an event noted. She sneered, safely ensconced in the darkness.

Wictred emerged from the throng. In his dusty croak of a voice, he spoke the customary words. "The Gods have taken back Osred, son of Ceorl, son of Sighere, of the line of Earn. Let us carry him out and lay him before his forebears."

Servants scattered about to light torches, and the King's guard lifted the contorted body upon a stretcher. There seemed to be no weight to him at all at the end. The crowd parted silently as their lord was carried out; Ceolwen fell in behind the pallbearers, Aelfhild by her side. Osric and his men followed, and the waiting assemblage trailed out after them.

The horizon to the west was still pale, faint tendrils of day clinging to the edge of night, and a few stars were beginning to shine through the purple of the sky. As the procession turned down the path, Aelfhild stole a glance back at the Great Hall—it stood forlorn at the top of the hill, the narrow windows in the rough stone walls dark and empty, its master departed.

The doors of the Hall of the Dead, dug into the hillside atop which the Great Hall sat, swung open on oiled hinges and the King's body was laid on a bier beneath the watchful eyes of the Four. Statues of the Smith, the Weaver, the Skald, and the Huntress, stone faces worn smooth by the touch of plaintive fingers, would watch over the corpse until a burial mound could be raised and offerings gathered for the King's use in the afterlife.

The city would be in black for days. Peasants would come to touch the body and bid farewell to their master. Wictred would see that the old ways were honored, as always.

Ceolwen knelt next to her father's bier as arrangements were made and guards posted, while the mourners filed through the Hall and paid their last respects. Aelfhild lingered behind, waiting for her mistress to give some sign.

"No tears today, Aelfhild?"

It was a voice that made her stomach turn on the best of days, and not one she ever wanted to hear from directly behind her. She turned to face Osric and his lackeys, careful to keep her gaze cast toward his boots. It was his eyes that made her shiver.

"No, lord."

The scuffed leather boots moved slowly to the left, and she turned with them. "Did you not care for your king, then? Come now, girl."

She had not heard his approach. Osric was a quiet one. They had all three played together as children, until Ceolwen had grown old enough to understand the circumstances of his birth. After that, she cast him out and he had kept his distance, watching from the shadows where he had apparently found his calling.

"Your mistress is well?" The boots stopped.

"Yes, lord."

"I worry for her. My sister can be so delicate and these are not easy times. And now with father's death, it could be too much to bear."

"Kind of you, lord."

Her face betrayed nothing and she knew it. Life as a servant had taught her that, at least. Say nothing, mean nothing, hide it away. But always—*always*—listen.

"There are enemies all around us, my girl, within and without.

Earnfold needs a strong king, and I know you want what is best for your mistress. We both do. So think of me as a friend, Aelfhild."

"Lord."

Her tone was one that had to be studied, and carefully—not defiant, that could mean a whipping or worse. Just empty. She was there, and she was listening, and that was the full extent of it.

But the act did have its limits. No amount of honeyed words could conceal Osric's temper, however he tried.

"I would be in your debt," he said through gritted teeth, "if you came to me for council, Aelfhild. A king can give great rewards to loyal friends."

"I will think on it, lord."

"See that you do. It is never too early to think about the great future of our kingdom."

"Lord."

She tensed, but the blow never fell. The boots turned without reply and stalked off, gravel crunching under heel.

Aelfhild glanced after the men and let slip a trembling breath. Leaving aside his eyes, Osric was a fine-looking man. It was his companions that made her feel like she needed a thorough scrubbing. The lank hair and greasy stubble, and the feeling that they had only recently scrubbed the blood from beneath their fingernails.

Kings attracted the kind of men that revel in pain and violence. Aelfhild saw it as a sort of natural law. And kings always found some use for them. Old Osred had put such men to work, beyond a doubt, but seldom and with the greatest distaste; his son, on the other hand, had always seemed drawn to them.

Her hands would shake for the rest of the evening.

The shuffling mourners were nearly through. When all but the King's guard had left, Aelfhild moved to Ceolwen's side. As she drew closer, to her surprise she heard that her mistress was muttering prayers to the Four under her breath. Neither of them was particularly devout; Aelfhild had always assumed that Ceolwen, like the rest of her people, believed in the Four, but she was not given to shows of religious fervor. In trying times, though, the Gods offered some small comfort that could not be found in the world of men.

Standing from prayer, Ceolwen turned to her servant. She offered a feeble half-smile, but she could hide little from Aelfhild; the two had known each other since childhood. They were both exhausted, mind and body, and neither could conceal it from the other.

"Come, my lady, we must get some rest," said Aelfhild. "There is much to be done tomorrow."

"There will be little sleep for me tonight, I fear," Ceolwen replied. "Dark days are coming, Aela." She gazed off into the distance as she spoke.

Though her mistress' face was drawn, her eyes distant, Aelfhild could not hold back a smile—she had not been called Aela since they were children scampering through these same grounds. Happy memories on a grim day.

"So you need your strength. *We* need our strength." Aelfhild did not much care to see more than a single sunset in a waking day. There had been three since she last got any real sleep. "Let us go and find what rest we can."

Ceolwen did not protest as she was led away. Two guards followed them—the Aethling's shadow for the past two days. It was unlikely Osric or his allies would move so soon, but there was no sense in taking risks. The royal court could be an adder's nest at the best of times. And there was much now at stake.

"What did Osric want?"

"Nothing, lady."

Aelfhild hoped Ceolwen had not noticed the pause.

2

THE GREAT HALL was far too exposed and dangerous a place for the Aethling to stay at the moment, so Ceolwen and Aelfhild were guests of Cuthbert, the Eorl of Norholt, in his hall at the heart of Cynestead's merchant district. News of the King's illness, and now his death, had circulated quickly and drawn an oppressive hush over the normally bustling city streets. They walked back from the keep undisturbed by the usual crowd of travelers, drunks, and soldiers that kept the city moving at all hours. Life went on regardless of the King's death, though. There were still a few folk shuffling about on their various errands, cloaks drawn tight against the damp.

Cuthbert's hall was decidedly less grand than the King's Great Hall, but it was far richer than the homes of most men. Walls of red oak rose to a tidy thatch roof, and beams carved in the likeness of a lunging Norholt bear crossed above the ironbound doors. Only wealthy merchants and great warriors could afford as fine a dwelling as the Eorl; most Earnfoldings slept on hard-packed dirt floors under roofs of sod.

Aelfhild had never traveled far, but she knew Norholt from stories. It was a land of huntsmen and woodsmen, a great forest that sat at the kingdom's northern boundaries, stretching from the Leohtmere, the lake which wrapped itself around the northern edge of Cynestead, all the way to the Grimbergs, mountains that guarded the western edge of the kingdom. The stories also made much mention of witches and man-bears, but those were children's tales.

The nobles in Cynestead often said that the only things to come out

of Norholt were "bows, bears, and bastards," but not within earshot of
Cuthbert. The Eorl was counted among the most powerful men in the
realm; his levy of warriors was one of the largest amongst the Earnfolding
lords and his hall the most hospitable. Ceolwen was kin to him on her
mother's side. The two had always gotten on well, and Aelfhild adored
the old man. He had the paunch and the laugh of a man who truly
enjoyed life.

They found him, not unexpectedly, at table with his warriors. As the
guards opened the doors to the Eorl's hall, the assorted smells of a feast
wafted out on the humid air. Food was spread out in abundance there as
it so often was; the Eorl was famous for his insatiable appetite for pleasant
fare and strong drink. As Ceolwen entered, the warriors at the table with
Cuthbert grew silent—someone had brought them the evening's tidings
already.

Cuthbert rose from his seat and wrapped Ceolwen in a bone-crunching hug. The Eorl had obviously been helping himself to generous por-
tions from the mead cask—his bright green eyes glistened with drunken
tears, and the smell of honey hung heavy on his breath.

"My dear child," he lisped as Ceolwen tried in vain to extricate herself
from his embrace, "a sad night, a grave night! For Earnfold, for Norholt,
for... dear Ceolwen." He dropped back onto his bench, nearly bringing
his unfortunate cousin down with him. Gasping for breath, she brushed
crumbs imparted by the Eorl's tunic off the front of her dress.

"Sit! Feast! Drink!" boomed Cuthbert, tears banished for the moment.
Flinging his arms wide over his table, he shouted, "Tonight we remember
your father; tonight we feast for old Osred!"

Ceolwen patted the Eorl's hand and spoke slowly for the benefit of
her drunken host. "I thank you, dear cousin, for your hospitality, but
I am tired and must rest. Tomorrow, we can speak more of my father.
Tomorrow!" Despite his sputtered protests, she retired behind the curtains to the bed prepared for her, leaving Aelfhild with the Eorl and his
men. Cuthbert squinted at Aelfhild as she watched him try to dredge up
her name from the mead-soaked depths of his memory.

"Aelf...," he managed.

She came to his aid. "Aelf*hild*, Eorl Cuthbert. We have met many times."

"Aelfhild!" he exclaimed, overjoyed by the small victory. "Sit, Aelfhild! Feast!"

Although tempted to check on her mistress, Aelfhild could not deny that the aroma of the Eorl's table had reminded her of just how little she had eaten in the past few days. The smell of charred meat and crusty loaves set her stomach to rumbling. She took the offered seat and set about the table. The Eorl resumed whatever story he had been in the midst of telling when Ceolwen and Aelfhild interrupted. His warriors humored him without paying much attention; it was a hunting story which Aelfhild could not possibly have followed even if she had been of a mind to, full as it was of broken spears and charging bears and drunken digressions. The warriors looked unimpressed, and she doubted this was the story's first telling.

Aelfhild ate to bursting. The Eorl seemed to have mostly forgotten about her so she was left in peace. Cuthbert careened from jovial to mournful, booming peals of laughter changing to snuffling tears with little warning. His arms were a constant danger, waving to and fro as he told increasingly tall tales. He did not seem to care that his men had either stopped listening or fallen asleep long ago.

After a sustained attack on the spread, Aelfhild pushed back her plate and looked around the hall. It was a home, unlike the Great Hall. None of the gaudy hangings, the gilding or the jewels, but bare beams carved with whorls and spirals that ran up into the rafters where smoked meats hung to cure. The benches that lined the walls were piled with furs, and dancing light from the hearth filled the hall. It was a place for drinking and dancing, songs and feasts.

If this had been what Osric had offered her, she might have been tempted. But his world was all blood and gold.

There was a brief pang of guilt. She had not told Ceolwen about Osric's offer. Other things weighed on her mistress' mind, no doubt, but that was not the reason. Of course, she had never considered going to Osric. Not even for a moment; this she was sure of. But she had hesitated, and that worried her. Each time she resolved to get up and tell Ceolwen what had happened, her legs were leaden.

A heavy hand fell upon her shoulder, and she jumped. She turned to face Cuthbert's bloodshot eyes.

"No shame in worrying on days like this, girl." The Eorl looked ready to drop. "All will be well, I promise." Cuthbert seemed certain, but Aelfhild struggled to believe him.

The Eorl's warriors had all retired to their benches along the walls where they lay snorting and snuffling amongst piles of furs and blankets, except for one boy whose head rested soundly on the table. Someone had placed a blanket over his shoulders and taken the drinking horn from his hand. A puddle of drool gathered beneath his cheek, but he slept on, oblivious to all.

Cuthbert, hand on Aelfhild's shoulder, squinted at her as though trying to discern which one of several Aelfhilds he ought to address. "Sleep, child; we shall be busy tomorrow." He stumbled off toward his bed at the far end of the hall. A dull thud signaled that he might have found the floor instead, but it would likely be of little difference to him.

Aelfhild went back to the chamber prepared for her and Ceolwen. She hesitated outside the curtain, running through her defense once more in her head.

Ceolwen's back was to her as she entered, the parted curtain allowing in traces of firelight.

"Still awake, lady?"

"I am too tired to sleep."

Aelfhild sat down beside her mistress. "There was something I needed to tell you." She picked at the front of her dress, stalling. "When Osric spoke to me earlier, I told you it was nothing. That was not true."

"He asked you to betray me?"

Aelfhild's face burned. Of course she had known. "Yes."

Ceolwen turned to her. "Did you agree?" It was hard to tell in the dark, but Aelfhild thought she detected a grin.

"Of course not!" She bristled, ready to defend her innocence to the last. Ceolwen laughed, and Aelfhild's chest deflated.

"Aela, I trust you with my life. I know you." She squeezed Aelfhild's hand. "Did he at least offer you something worth your trouble?"

This was not how the talk had gone in Aelfhild's mind, but her stomach began to unknot. "He did not name a price, but he did mention something about a king's favor."

Ceolwen whistled. "Well, that must be worth something." She bumped her shoulder against Aelfhild's and they both giggled.

Then there was silence in the dark for a long while.

"What will happen to us, lady?"

"I do not know, Aela. But I do know that we can trust Cuthbert. We build from there."

"Three of us against the world, lady. For now."

"For now." Ceolwen laughed at that, and said, "Osric had best be careful."

UTHBERT AND HIS warriors were gone long before Aelfhild was up and about, and she had little idea how the old bear had managed it. A fine skill for an Eorl, she thought, to tap the mead cask late into the night and rise early enough for battle. These days the Eorls settled with words what their ancestors had used armies to do; King Osred had often called that his greatest gift to Earnfold. It was neater, certainly, but harder to do with a headache by Aelfhild's estimation.

Ceolwen emerged, scrubbed and bright-eyed, from her chamber. "Why did you not wake me earlier? The day is half gone already."

"You needed it, lady." Aelfhild found a bowl and ladled out a dollop of stew from the cauldron over the hearth. "We both did."

Ceolwen's nose wrinkled. "Fish for breakfast? Stew does not agree with me this early."

"You slept through breakfast, lady. Now it is bread, stew, or nothing."

"But I want porridge."

Aelfhild took a deep breath while mustering her response, but then she noticed that sly glint in her mistress' eye, the look of a spoiled child who had always delighted in winding up her caretakers. She played along.

"You shall eat what you are served, young lady, or get the hard end of my ladle!"

"Yes, matron," replied Ceolwen, grumbling.

Their eyes locked for a moment and they dissolved into giggles.

"Remember her pies? Oh, but I would kill for her boar and kidney pie right now. Even at breakfast." Ceolwen stirred her stew, gazing through the table into years long past.

Matron Sif had ruled the kitchens of the Great Hall for several generations with iron fists and a sturdy ladle. The silver-haired giantess, each fearsome knuckle the size of a walnut, had waged war against the two young girls and their nighttime raids on the kitchen.

"The stewed cherries were my favorite. I cannot say I miss her voice, though," said Aelfhild.

"Her bellow, more like." Ceolwen laughed. "How long has it been, now?"

"Eight years; nine, maybe."

"Well, in memory of the Matron, then." Waving a salute with her spoon, Ceolwen dug into her breakfast. Aelfhild had to refill the bowl three times; the stew agreed with her mistress more than she had at first admitted.

Ceolwen pushed back her bowl and let out a throaty belch. "Cuthbert will be out talking to the other Eorls, looking for support," she began with no preamble. "Osric will be doing the same. Wictred will see to the preparations for the burial. We will…" She trailed off.

"What will we do today, my lady?" asked Aelfhild.

Ceolwen chewed her lip for a moment, then sighed. "There is little we can do," she said. "Cuthbert is dear to me, and I do trust him, but he and the others will do whatever they think is best for their own people, and for themselves. We are pawns in all this. Our task is to fidget and wait and do nothing of use."

That does sound like nobles' work, Aelfhild thought, but decided not to share. She did not like the tone of resignation she heard in her mistress' voice, though. Ceolwen had always had that stormy nature which came with a rich upbringing; her whole life, whenever she spoke people listened and obeyed, or at least feigned obedience, and so her moods had free reign. Now that power was gone, at least for a time, and she clearly felt its absence. She needed a distraction.

"We should walk out in the market, my lady," she said, "let the common folk see your face and know that you are with them. That you are not afraid. As a *queen* should be."

Ceolwen was silent for a moment. "You think I am so easily distracted from my worries, Aela?" she asked with a hint of a smile. There was the old nickname again, and all this talk of the Matron. Aelfhild did not know what to make of this newfound wistfulness from her mistress.

"Very well," said Ceolwen, "let us go out and see what distractions our city has to offer today."

They wrapped themselves in woolen cloaks before leaving the hall, as the chill of winter still clung to the land even with spring's arrival. It was just noon as they ventured out, and the city was abustle with life.

Cuthbert's hall sat in the center of the merchant's district, just a brief walk from the market square, where merchants behind sagging tables hawked goods from every corner of the kingdom. The cries of fishmongers mixed with those of butchers, furriers, coopers, tailors, farmers, and countless others into a wall of sound that was felt as much as heard. Livestock bleated, blacksmiths hammered on their anvils, and the thrum of commerce resonated through the entire square. Aelfhild loved to come here, to merge into the crowd, to soak in the sounds and the smells and the ceaseless cascade of motion.

As she followed Ceolwen through the market, Aelfhild noticed little change from her previous visits. A few of the merchants and peasants wore black bands of cloth around their arms or soot on their foreheads to mark the passing of the King, but for most the day was the same as any other. Kings lived and died with little real effect on these people.

Some of the commoners spared a glance at the two interlopers with their armed guards, but stopped short of staring. Aelfhild had heard stories that staring at one of the touchier nobles might cost a peasant his eye. And besides, there was real work to be done.

Ceolwen and Aelfhild were clearly out of place, marked by their clothing, their faces, their bearing. The peasants wore coarse fabrics, undyed and oft-mended. Their hands were creased, their faces sunburnt, and their backs bent by hard labor and heavy loads. Some of the wealthier merchants wore finer wool or sported brighter dyes, but nothing to match the fur around Ceolwen's collar or the silver around her neck.

Aelfhild knew her hands were rougher than her mistress', for few could be smoother. But they held not a patch on the woman's palms into which Ceolwen pressed a copper coin. Standing a head taller than most folk in the market, and with hair that shimmered in the sun, Ceolwen always drew a crowd of beggars. The guards kept a few of the rougher-looking ones back, but a gaggle of women and children came to get what alms they could from the pale lady. Aelfhild could not say whether it was her appearance or demeanor, but the beggars always ignored her. She tried not to mind. They would disperse as soon as Ceolwen's purse was empty, anyway.

The sun was bright, the sky was clear, and the breeze gentle. Ceolwen turned back to Aelfhild briefly and a smile passed between them. Aelfhild knew Ceolwen loved to come here as much as she did and for mostly the same reasons. That blend of sounds and smells, the pure feeling of life in the place—it was intoxicating. She hoped this would lift her mistress' spirits.

Ceolwen stopped at a stall where a toothless old woman sold herbs and poultices; she sifted through fragrant bundles of mandrake and hyssop while she chatted with the dribbling vendor. Aelfhild waited nearby, looking out over the crowd. Their guards kept back at a respectful distance, looking bored as they watched the peasants shuffle past.

Aelfhild drew the market in deep, and exhaled; her eyes swept the square. Something caught her attention; a hooded face had turned away too fast, retreating back into the press of bodies.

Just a cutpurse, she hoped. Ceolwen had given away her coins and Aelfhild's pockets held a spoon, a darning needle, and some thread, so little threat there. Any other day, it might not have troubled her. He, if it was a he, was gone, though, and she saw no further sign.

They wandered for a while more. Ceolwen seemed to be enjoying the open air and the flow of the market as much as Aelfhild. A pox-ridden man tried to sell them an assortment of potions and ointments from his tray—this one for boils, that one for gout, another one to excite the humors and one to quiet them. He proved persistent, but eventually was discouraged by a kick from one of their guards. He left behind an odor that was even harder to shake.

One stall was selling honeyed sweet rolls, a treat they had frequently stolen from the Great Hall's kitchens in their younger days. The rolls left an inevitable mess on hands and fingers, but the reward was always well worth the price.

An opening in the crowd drew Aelfhild's eye. There was the hood again, pulled low over a man's face, turned toward her and perfectly still amidst the market's swirling currents. Something about the man was off. Aelfhild knew there was no thief alive that would take such pains to be seen. He did not move from his spot, did not interact with the nearby tradesmen or peasants. He stared, and Aelfhild was sure it was Ceolwen who occupied his attention. Their guards had apparently not noticed the man.

Ceolwen was in mid-story. "I always could eat more of these than you, but you never did like sweets as much—"

"Do you see that man?" Aelfhild tried to keep her voice low but urgent.

"What man?" Apparently the urgency had been lost on Ceolwen, because she looked around wide-eyed and made no effort to lower her voice. "What are you on about? Were you not listening to my story?"

"There was someone watching us." Hearing this, the guards swept around but their observer had long since disappeared.

"I saw him before," Aelfhild said, "I think."

"One of Osric's?" Storm clouds brewed on the horizons of Ceolwen's good mood.

But Aelfhild could hardly bear to spoil the afternoon. "Maybe just a thief?" No one seemed convinced, but they moved on.

She snuck looks over her shoulder every now and then but saw nothing, and fell to brooding. What did Osric have in store? Though Cuthbert could have sent the man to watch over them just as easily as Osric. But why spy on his own guards? Or maybe, she reasoned, he had just been a curious traveler staring at a strange, beautiful woman. A foreigner would stand out, and that was no reason to get worked up. But it was her job to worry for her mistress, as it had been since childhood, and she was exceedingly good at it.

They spent a while longer wandering in the warm sun, but the spark was gone. Returning to the hall, they discovered that their host had returned from council with the Eorls, for even from halfway down the street Aelfhild could hear Cuthbert yelling.

OWARDS, THE LOT of them!" shouted Cuthbert, as he hammered the table with a meaty fist. "Never have I seen such a pack of whinging curs, standing by and wringing their hands like old women!" He sent a wooden bowl flying into the nearby wall with a fierce backhand.

"Calm, cousin," said Ceolwen, "Tell us what happened, and spare no detail."

The Eorl seethed, having returned from his meeting with the other lords not long before Aelfhild and Ceolwen arrived. He had the look of a madman: his face flushed a worrying shade of puce beneath his unkempt mane. Things did not look to have gone well.

"For hours they spoke, and for hours not a man there said a word of meaning," he hissed, pausing to take a few gulps of air. He exhaled and straightened his tunic. "They all wait for some sign that will ease their decision—their conscience. They know they have only one chance to cast their lot in this, but are too afraid to put anything at risk."

"Was Osric there today?" asked Ceolwen.

Aelfhild took a seat by the fire to warm her hands and, as it happened, to once again remove herself from range of Cuthbert's arms. The bulging veins in the old man's neck and forehead suggested he might burst at any moment.

"No, but Thrydwulf was, and he argues for Osric. The snake! I should have smothered the life from his puny little body when he was still in the cradle!" His attempts to regain composure had failed. The Eorl sputtered as he mimed just how he would have crushed the infant child.

Thrydwulf, the Eorl of Hildmor, was as young as Aelfhild and Ceolwen—his father, Wulfhere, had died a premature death not long ago under somewhat mysterious circumstances. The city had been filled with rumors about it; Aelfhild could not count the number of grim and gruesome tales of patricide she had heard, none anywhere approaching believeable. But Wulfhere had been an old friend of Cuthbert's, as it turned out, and so the old bear bore a bit of a grudge against the newly-crowned Eorl.

"What of Caelin?" Ceolwen attempted to steer her cousin toward sanity.

The Eorl sighed, and his anger seemed to ebb. "Caelin is a fine man— better than the rest of those mongrels!—but he cannot muster the men to stand up to Thrydwulf and he knows it. The blood of Ealdorscir is not what it once was."

And that was true. The lands around Cynestead and south of the Leohtmere had been particularly hard-hit by the plague that took the king. For weeks they had watched from the Great Hall as smoke rose from the pyres in outlying villages. If Caelin tried to raise the Fyrd now it would be little more than a handful of men with sharp sticks.

"And the others?" asked Ceolwen.

"Hlothere might—I say *might*—fall on our side, but Aethelwald will likely go with Thrydwulf. He fears the Oescans on his southern border. Which reminds me, the Oescans sent a man to the court as envoy. Arrived today. A Maro, he is, one of the fancier families, Lucianus or Lucilius or some such they called him. Lucianus Aulus, I think it was." The foreign name was accompanied by a sneer.

Oesca was a loose confederation of city-states to the south, their people of a different heritage and tradition than that of Earnfold. There was history between the neighboring realms, and the Oescans were known to be meddlers in the affairs of Cynestead.

"He met with Osric today, but only briefly. The boy will say anything to get himself on the throne, there is no telling what kind of deal he would make with the southerners." Cuthbert grimaced and spat once more. "No backbone, that one. He certainly did not get one from his father." He snorted.

"Cousin!" Ceolwen shouted, her voice gone shrill. Aelfhild half rose from her seat to go to her mistress, but Ceolwen waved her away. She settled with directing a withering gaze at Cuthbert.

"Sorry, my dear," the Eorl replied. He raised his hands as a shield. "If only your mother had not been taken from us so early, she could have kept poor Osred on the right path. Avoided all this nonsense." He dropped down upon a nearby bench. His brow remained furrowed, but the lines around his eyes softened.

Even the old bear grows weary, thought Aelfhild.

Ceolwen sat beside him, placing her boney hand atop Cuthbert's clenched paw. "*Ifs* do us little good today, old friend. Not words, but deeds are what is called for. What can we—what must we do?"

"There is little to be done," muttered Cuthbert. "I have said before that—"

"—no," Ceolwen interrupted, pulling back her hand, "there must be another way."

"Deeds you said and deeds I offer, cousin. If you are to be queen, your hands will be bloody one day or another." All eyes turned to Ceolwen in the ensuing silence. She gazed into the fire burning in the hearth.

"How?" Her voice was faint. Aelfhild could hardly blame her. She wanted to be nowhere near this discussion.

"I have men with an eye on him," Cuthbert replied, "He is under guard in Thrydwulf's hall, buttoned up tight. I do not have enough to go at them straight, we would have to lure him out on his own."

Ceolwen pondered this. "Osric will be planning the exact same thing. He will not waste any time."

Aelfhild had stayed quiet up to now, content to sit and listen, but she joined in here. "There was a man, today in the market, he was following us."

Both Cuthbert and Ceolwen seemed to have forgotten she was there. She gulped hard and recounted what she had seen earlier, straining to remember every detail of the hooded stranger. The Eorl listened, stroking his chin.

"I nearly forgot about it," said Ceolwen. "I did not see the man."

"Did my guards do nothing about him?" Cuthbert stirred again, like distant thunder rumbling.

"No, just me." Aelfhild felt like she had to defend herself further. "But I swear I saw it."

"And I trust her completely," Ceolwen added. She smiled and Aelfhild's chest swelled.

Cuthbert seemed satisfied with this. "Must have been one of Osric's or Thrydwulf's; was not mine. They watch you, we watch him. We circle like snarling dogs." He shook his head. "I should give my boys a whipping, if a maid can do their job better."

Though the last comment did sting a bit, Aelfhild continued with what she had been about to say. "Any message we send, any meeting we set, they will suspect a trap."

The conversation paused as a serving girl stepped out from behind a curtain with cups and a jug of mead. She laid them on the table before retreating back to the shadows. Aelfhild recognized the expression; she could get no read on that one. Cuthbert and Ceolwen had not even seen the girl. The Eorl took up the jug, which might have been conjured by magic for all he was concerned, and offered his guests a cup before pouring one for himself.

"What about Caelin?" asked Ceolwen, breaking the silence. "Does Osric trust him?"

"How should I know? And what has he to do with this?"

Ceolwen stood from her seat and set to pacing across the room. "You said Caelin could be trusted, so we go to him tomorrow—"

"—I said Caelin was a fine man, that is not the same thing," the Eorl protested, but Ceolwen silenced him with a raised finger. Aelfhild failed to stifle a giggle at the Eorl's bemused expression; he was not as well versed in Ceolwen's moods. She managed to conceal the giggle in a snorting cough, but a sideways glance from her mistress told her this had not gone unnoticed. There could well be words later.

"We go to him tomorrow, and ask him to meet with Osric. Take demands to him, bargain with him, whatever will make Osric listen. We follow and take Osric, alive if we can," Ceolwen continued.

The Eorl pondered this for a moment, stroking his beard once more. "And how do we get to Caelin without Osric finding out?"

"They cannot follow all of us," Ceolwen said. "You and I both go out with our guards, and Aelfhild sneaks out in secret to Caelin."

A lump rose in Aelfhild's throat. She would serve as best she could in most things, but she was no spy. And Ceolwen had not even bothered to ask. This side of her mistress was usually directed at other people, and Aelfhild squirmed beneath its weight. But perhaps Cuthbert was right—those that sat on the throne did not do so with clean hands or a spotless conscience.

Cuthbert sucked mead from his whiskers. "That leaves a great deal to chance, and the girl may not be—"

"If you have a better idea, cousin, I would hear it gladly," Ceolwen cut in.

The girl may not be *what?* Aelfhild did not appreciate any of the words that might complete that thought, nor the tone, especially since she was sitting within a stone's throw of the man. In truth, she wished Ceolwen had let him finish, but she of course said nothing. There was more at stake here than her pride, such as it was.

The Eorl rose, nodding. "Let me think on it. But I grow tired and hungry! No more talk of plots and sneaking for now; time to sit and eat."

The table was prepared at the Eorl's order, and supper served. It was country fare, the kind that stuck to the ribs: roast lamb and mashed turnips drowned in butter. Less mead was served than on the previous night, and conversation was sparse. Aelfhild felt that she should have been more scared, somehow. None of it seemed real; the plotting was just another story repeated in hushed tones by the maids in the Great Hall kitchens.

Partway through the meal, Cuthbert stood and left the table without a word. He returned with a bundle of old rags under his arm which he spread out on the bench beside him. There were several leaf-bladed daggers on the cloth, and he handed one first to Ceolwen and then one to Aelfhild. The weight of the situation crystallized around that weight of iron as soon as it touched her palm. The hilt was cold and oily to the touch, and Aelfhild dared not draw it from the sheath. This thing had one purpose, and she was now a part of that. She shivered.

"Dangerous times," the Eorl said. "Do not draw the blade unless you are ready to use it."

He retired to his bed not long after, saying little more. Servants came to clear the table, and his warriors went off to their beds as well. Two stayed behind, bolting the doors and sitting by the fire to keep watch. Ceolwen and Aelfhild left them to their duty.

Before they got to their chamber, Ceolwen placed a hand on Aelfhild's shoulder. "Aela, I know I am asking much of you…"

Aelfhild heard the hesitation, the doubt, in that quiet voice. She tried for something reassuring, something confident and powerful, but failed miserably. "I will serve as best I can, my lady," was all she could squeak out.

Ceolwen's voice rose as she leaned in. "We cannot afford to be afraid." But just whom she was trying to convince was unclear.

5

ELFHILD DREAMT OF a hallway. She could feel that it was a dream from the beginning, sense it from the way the colors shifted at the edge of her vision and the sound swirled around her completely decoupled from direction. The hallway itself shifted in size and shape, dwarfing her in one instant as it stretched onward and upward for leagues, then collapsing to just barely allow her passage. There was a doorway at the far end, silhouetted in light and the only fixed point, and she was drawn toward it.

The palm of her right hand itched, a twinge deep below the skin. She flexed her fingers into a fist. She could not look away from the glow ahead.

Beyond the doorway she found a room, or at least a space. There were no walls that she could make out, no ceiling or floor. In the void floated a writhing ball, a tangle of gnarled vines and jutting thorns. The vines were green, but not the fresh hue of spring—they verged on black in places, splotchy and putrid. She glimpsed flashes of white beneath the twisting brambles.

There was a voice. Countless whispers rose around her on every side to form two words.

Wake. Up.

She awoke slick with sweat. Her dress and blanket were soaked through and sucked at her flesh as she tried to peel them back. The darkness in the curtained bedchamber was total, as was the silence. She rubbed her thumb across her right palm, but felt nothing on or below the skin. The itch was fading but not yet gone.

The dream had been all wrong. Not a nightmare, for she had not felt frightened. But she recalled fever dreams brought by childhood illness, and that feeling that the waking world was a hair's breadth away, glimpsed through a gossamer veil, yet utterly unreachable. This dream had been the same: lucid but flat, as though she could peel back the tapestry and glimpse the artifice behind.

The dank air of the hallway lingered in her mouth and nose. The tendrils were seared onto the back of her eyelids. And the voice.

There had been urgency in the voice, a warning. Whether it had bubbled up from within her or had been placed there by the Gods, she was uncertain. The Gods had never before spoken back to Aelfhild, and she had not the faintest idea of how to proceed.

From time to time it happened that a man or a woman would wander, ranting and screaming, through the streets of Cynestead, accosting passersby with incoherent shouting about visions and signs. The commonfolk said they were touched by the Gods and listened for omens; the nobles called them mad and locked them out of sight. Aelfhild had seen one such woman in the market before guards had lifted her withered body from the street and hurried her away. She remembered the sunken face rent by muddy fingernails in a vain attempt to drive out the divine voices, and she shivered.

She prayed for the second time in as many days, and this time for herself: Please, let it not be me.

The air in the room was stale. She needed a drink to wash the taste from her mouth, she needed air and to stretch. Sleep would be far away for a long while, now.

Ceolwen's breathing sounded steady, but Aelfhild still took care not to make noise as she stood. Something stopped her short as she moved to part the curtain. The voice's warning stuck in her head. For a moment she hesitated, then reached out in the dark and found the Eorl's dagger. Grasping it between thumb and forefinger, she dropped it into her pocket.

The fire had burned down to embers in the hearth, casting a flickering half-light over everything nearby. She could hear only the snores of men on the benches along the walls; the two watchmen at the far end of the hall were fast asleep, feet to the fire and backs propped against the door they were meant to be guarding. Smoke was heavy on the air.

At night, the windows were all shut and barred, but she remembered that one had a knothole which might let in some cleaner air. She went to it, careful how she placed each foot. The night watch proved to be heavy sleepers, which was lucky, because she was of little mind to explain herself or her sodden nightdress to anyone.

Peering out into the lane outside, she was surprised at how well she could see. There were a few wispy clouds that night, but the twin moons shone bright in the sky and lit the city. The air proved no better by the knothole, though. The acrid scent of burning pitch drifted in from outside. Aelfhild's neck began to prickle.

Something was wrong.

Sweeping her gaze up and down the street, she saw nothing. There was a flicker of torchlight from around the corner, but that was nothing strange—guards did patrol the streets at night.

Something shifted in the shadows and caught her eye. There were men moving in the lee of the building across the way. Moonlight glinted off metal. Armed men.

She dropped to her knees, and barely stifled the gasp that leapt from her lungs.

Stupid girl. You think they saw your eyeball through a hole in the wall? For the briefest of moments Aelfhild was a child again, under her mother's scolding finger. But there was no time for shame. Think, she commanded herself. What do we need to do?

Find the Eorl first, she decided. He needs to know. Every step, every breath, every heartbeat she was sure the men outside would hear. She wended her way to the back of the hall step by trembling step.

Cuthbert lay face-up on the bed, his mountainous belly rising and falling as he snored. Aelfhild clamped a hand over his mouth as she shook him awake. She pressed down the urge to scream at him as his bleary eyes took an age to focus on her face.

"Men outside," she whispered. He must have heard the fear, because there were no questions.

The Eorl rolled out of his bed with more sprightliness than she would have expected, and squinted through the crack in a nearby window. He gave no sign that he saw anything, but he took her by the arm and shuffled toward the entrance of the hall. As they went, he woke his warriors in the same way she had woken him, a palm over the mouth to keep hold of that one slight advantage: their attackers did not know they were already discovered.

Aelfhild went in to wake her mistress, but Ceolwen was already sitting up in her bower, eyes perfect black circles in the dim. She began to speak as her servant came in. Before the words could emerge, Aelfhild clamped a palm across her lips. "Danger," she whispered, beckoning Ceolwen to follow out into the main hall.

Cuthbert had awoken all his warriors. They crouched silently near their beds, anything resembling a weapon in hand. Every ear strained. Outside there were footsteps, the sound of a heavy weight dragging through dirt.

The smell of burning pitch grew stronger, and there was a soft thump at the door. Ceolwen squeezed Aelfhild's hand until her knuckles popped. Outside the windows, an orange glow started to rise. Fragments of old songs and stories rose unbidden in Aelfhild's mind, bringing with them a grim realization: the roof.

They would burn the roof.

It was a time-honored tactic amongst her people—warriors would block the doors to an enemy's hall from the outside and set fire to the thatch. Anyone not consumed by the blaze would run out, straight into waiting blades. Osric had made his move, and broken the peace in terrible fashion.

Daggers in the dark were one thing, Aelfhild thought, but this does not happen in Cynestead. Not these days. The city was meant to be safe ground for all. The Eorls and Reeves would doubtless be furious with the young upstart, but that was little use to the hall's occupants.

The smoke was overwhelming now, and the raging flames outside shone bright through cracks and holes in the shutters. Aelfhild's eyes watered as the heat began to rise and cinders floated down through gaps in the crackling thatch.

Stealth abandoned, Cuthbert sprinted back to the middle of the hall. Cups and dishes scattered as he cast aside a table and ripped back rugs concealing a chink in the floorboards. With the blade of his sword he pried up the wooden cover to reveal a pit in the hall's foundation.

Two of the Eorl's men dropped down, disappearing into the dark. He pointed at Ceolwen and Aelfhild next, and gestured downwards. Scampering forward on hands and knees below the billowing smoke, Aelfhild half slid, half fell into the hole. It was less than graceful, but a choice between falling and burning was no choice at all.

The drop proved to be hardly any distance; Ceolwen's feet might have touched the bottom from the ledge, but Aelfhild would have dangled. It was pitch black in the hole. Aelfhild moved forward after she landed, and could feel Ceolwen come down behind her. She grabbed her mistress' hand and choked back a scream as unseen fingers grabbed her shoulder from the front.

She struggled to get her careening thoughts back in line. Cuthbert's men had gone first, it had to be one of them. The hand dragged her onward and she followed.

They hobbled forward through the darkness. The tunnel had been dug by someone close to her size; Aelfhild could feel the rough earth on each shoulder, and her hair brushed the ceiling. Grunts and heavy breathing echoed in the close space as they hobbled forward, squeezing around the thick shoring beams set along the tunnel's length. Underfoot the dirt was cold and damp, and more than once Aelfhild's toes sent some unseen, chitinous horror skittering off in the dark.

Small spaces had never agreed with her. Her heart hammered within its cage. She wanted out of this grave, wanted to claw her way up through the earth and back to freedom, regardless of the swords and fire waiting for them above.

Every step took them further down and further away from clean air. She was sure they were lost. The men had gone too far, missed their turning in the dark. Minutes stretched on to hours. Each breath was shallower than the last, each requiring more focus and will.

They came to a stop. She could hear something being shifted up ahead, and saw a faint light appear not far away. The hand led her forward, and she saw the end of the tunnel. A shaft opened over top of them, pale grey against the black of the tunnel, but it might as well have been sunrise to Aelfhild's eyes.

The Eorl's warriors helped her up into what could only have been a barn—the telltale wave of wet hay and manure crested over her and removed any hint of smoke or earth from her nostrils. But she was out. She dropped to her knees, gasping, then turned to help her mistress up from the hole. Ceolwen was caked in mud and bleeding from a scrape on her head, but looked to be just as relieved as Aelfhild to be above ground. They collapsed side by side in the straw, panting.

Two more of Cuthbert's warriors followed behind, then the Eorl himself. How he had managed to squeeze his bulk through that night-marish maze, she would never know.

The last of Cuthbert's men followed along, bringing with them a pair of wide-eyed servants. There were only eight fighting men in the barn—Cuthbert, not expecting any such trouble, had brought only a handful of warriors with him on his visit to Cynestead. Between them they had a few axes and swords, and Aelfhild had her dagger, but no shields or spears or helms or mail. Some were half-dressed, others in nightclothes. This was no army.

Cuthbert and one of his men opened the slightest crack in the door, sending an arc of angry red light across floor and ceiling. As she took a moment to look around, Aelfhild guessed they had come up in the old stable that stood one lane over from the Eorl's hall, a weather-beaten shack with rotting thatch that most folk passed without wasting a glance. They had come, at most, a few hundred paces underground. It had felt much, much longer.

Cuthbert came back over to the group, kneeling in the center as he whispered orders. His calm impressed Aelfhild. Here was a man who kept his head in battle. Mere moments ago, he had been dreaming the pleasant dreams of a rich man. Now his hall was in ruins and his life under threat, but the old bear's voice was steady.

"Bercthun, Ceolwen, Aelfhild, with me. We go east to the wall and then down to the docks. Immin, take Sabert and these two," he said, gesturing at the servants. "Make for the west gate and get clear."

Cuthbert paused. "Where is the other girl? Where is Gyda? Did no one wake her?" His voice rose.

Both of the servants trembled under the Eorl's gaze. One, grey haired and coated with tunnel dirt, stuttered her terrified way through an explanation. "Lord, she never come back home after supper tonight."

The Eorl swelled. His great chest filled with air, his eyes bulged. Aelfhild worried he would start shouting. But with visible strain, he wrestled his temper down. "She *what?*"

Now the old woman was a fountain of pleading words.

"Lord, she has a young man up market way and we thought there were no harm to it and she slips out to see him a-times but I never meant for it, master, to be like this, she is a good girl but young and fool in love…"

She trailed off in tears and shoulder-wracking sobs. Aelfhild's heart broke for the woman. She had failed her master and that guilt would likely go with her to the grave.

But that did explain why Osric had acted so boldly. Servants talked, and that talk had legs faster than the King's own coursers. Aelfhild knew it, they all knew it, but they had wagged their tongues in the open.

I even saw the girl's face when she brought us mead, Aelfhild thought.

Cuthbert looked to be thinking the same thing. His chest sagged. He placed a hand on the servant's quaking shoulder. "You were not to know. All is forgiven. Follow Sabert, now." The calm had returned to his voice.

The Eorl turned to the remaining men and continued. "Eadbald, take the rest and head south into the square. Give us a short lead, then do what you can to draw them away. Set fires, make noise, whatever you can manage."

Then to all assembled, he said, "Do not throw your lives away. Run if you can, but take some of the bastards with you if you are caught—buy the rest of us time. Now go!"

Keeping low, quiet but swift as could be, they left the stable in groups. As Aelfhild followed the Eorl out she could see tongues of fire rising in the distance, silhouetting men waiting around the ruined hall. Anger rose within her. These cowards had come in the night and set them to flight like animals. They were hunted, chased from their nest like vermin.

But there was no time for any of it. As soon as they were far enough gone from the stables to be out of sight of unfriendly eyes, they ran.

The city was starting to wake as the light and smoke from the fire spread. They heard a few cries of "Fire!" as they went, but stopped for nothing. Sprinting flat-out, they reached the western wall of the central keep with little delay.

Breath came in rapid gasps, and Ceolwen clutched at a stitch in her side. Aelfhild had not let go of her mistress' hand since they left the tunnel.

Leaning against the wall for a moment to catch his breath, Cuthbert motioned for them to follow. He pressed a finger to his lips, calling for quiet. They followed the wall north, wending their way through the dark alleys behind houses and huts on their way to the docks. Cuthbert made each turn through the dim, narrow streets without hesitation or rest; the old warrior's muscles seemed to have forgotten none of their former strength. Aelfhild's legs burned, and she could feel Ceolwen flagging as they went. The other warrior, Bercthun, loped along behind and did not seem at all winded.

We live soft lives. There was a touch of shame at the thought, but Aelfhild was sure nobody could see her cheeks grow even redder in the dark.

The ground began to slope down as they came closer to the harbor on the lake, easing their passage. They stayed in the shadows, darting from one building to the next. The warehouses that loomed over the waterfront provided ample cover for them as they snuck alley to alley.

From the part of the city they had left behind came a rising din; whatever distractions Cuthbert's men had managed mixed in with the clamoring of the commoners on their way to stop the blaze before it spread to other houses. With any luck, Aelfhild hoped, the merchant district would be in such chaos that searchers would not be able to pick up their trail.

Cuthbert leaned out from an alleyway to look up and down the street, then flattened himself against the wall at his back. He waved at Aelfhild, who dragged herself and Ceolwen along behind her into the deepest shadows.

The glow of torches played across the mouth of the alley as two men strode down the lane. Aelfhild could see axes in their belts, but the pair did not seem to be in any hurry. She could hear a fragment of their conversation.

"Did you hear that? What do you think is happening?"

"Not our worry. He said watch the docks. So we watch the docks."

A pause.

"Hardly seems right working with the Oescans," said the first, picking up what must have been the previous topic. The voice was reedy and nervous, its owner barely yet a man. "The King would not care for it."

But someone had taken care to pair the boy with a real warrior. The second voice had no youthful uncertainty. "The old King, maybe. He says he just wants to set her straight, and send her off."

"You believe that?"

"Watch your gabbing. You live longer if you ask no questions. Shut it now, and keep your eyes open."

The pair wandered out of earshot.

Cuthbert hefted his sword and motioned for Bercthun to follow with axe in hand. Part of Aelfhild cried out for the boy's life. He was caught up in something bigger than he could understand. She sympathized, now more than ever.

So, it seemed, did Ceolwen. She put a hand on Cuthbert's arm before he could step out of the alley. "Not tonight," she whispered.

The cousins locked eyes for a moment. Neither gave ground. Then Cuthbert sighed and nodded. Aelfhild nearly melted in relief.

"One day, girl," Cuthbert replied. He motioned again to Bercthun.

The Eorl and his man vanished around the corner. Aelfhild stayed with her mistress, back pressed against the wall, and strained to hear every sound. Her palms dripped with sweat which she rubbed against her dress.

Mist was rising off the lake, the first moonlit wisps drifting up along the streets closest to the water. The Leohtmere was famous for it—by morning, the fog would be thick enough to bathe in.

Maybe the Gods are on our side tonight, thought Aelfhild.

There was a thump, and a body hit the ground. A scuffle followed, grunting and kicking. The street grew dark again as the torch went out. Aelfhild chanced a look around the corner, but saw nothing in the darkened lane.

Ceolwen pulled at her shoulder from behind. "Get back, before they see you," she pleaded.

Cuthbert's unmistakable frame leaned out around the next corner, and he waved for them to come over.

"I see Cuthbert. Come on!" Aelfhild dragged her mistress out into the street.

They found Bercthun and the Eorl standing over two bodies. The younger warrior was busy stripping the foes of gear, while Cuthbert wiped down the blade of his sword.

Ceolwen gaped at the men. She opened her mouth to speak, but her cousin beat her to it.

"The boy will live; Bercthun gave him a good crack across the head. The other one was faster. Too fast for his own good," he said, sheathing the sword.

They left the bodies in the shadows for the mist to cover, one bound at the wrists and ankles, the other facedown in the mud.

Cuthbert led them to a stone boathouse along the shore of the lake, nestled up against the central keep's high wall. He waved to Bercthun, who pushed the handle of his axe in between the door and frame, splintering the bolt and levering the flimsy wood open with a pop. Aelfhild glanced over her shoulder, but not a soul was around to hear them. She shuddered as she looked back up the street and thought of what they had left in the alley.

Moonlight reflecting off the lake illuminated the sleek contours of a rowboat inside the building. Cuthbert bustled around, lifting oars from racks on the wall and a bulging sack from a nearby table. Bercthun pushed the boat down to the water's edge and helped Ceolwen aboard. He extended a hand to Aelfhild.

She huddled with her mistress in the prow for warmth against the lake's chill and to balance out the Eorl in the stern. She could feel Ceolwen's heartbeat against her arms. In that fact, she could take some small solace. So long as the Aethling lived, she had a purpose. Smoke rose in a column over the city behind them, over the ashes of her old life. Now there was only one task in front of her: keeping Ceolwen safe.

With a heave, Cuthbert pushed them off the bank and out onto the waters of the Leohtmere.

6

"WHAT HAPPENED?" CEOLWEN was the first to break the silence. They were well out onto the lake now, and her voice cut through the still air. The splash of Bercthun's rowing had been the only sound since they left Cynestead.

It was part question, part accusation. Aelfhild suspected her mistress' words were directed as much at the Gods as the Eorl or the rest of them. Since the Gods would not answer, Cuthbert did.

"We..." He paused. "*I* underestimated Osric. I misjudged the Oescans. I misread all the signs. I thought, or maybe I hoped, that we could get through this without a war. And I was wrong."

Ceolwen stared out across the water. "As was I. I thought I could play the game and have a seat at the table. We both should have known better, cousin."

"We were betrayed!" The Eorl's voice shifted to a growl. "May the Gods curse her name and all her line, may they rain death upon all betrayers and oath breakers!" He spat.

Poor Gyda, thought Aelfhild. She had known the girl for not but a moment, but her heart went out to her. Gyda had been in Aelfhild's thoughts since they pushed off from shore.

"Do you think she is still alive?" As soon as the words left her mouth, she wanted to yank them back in. Both Cuthbert and Ceolwen turned baleful stares her way, neither prepared to hear sympathy for a betrayer.

There was venom in the old bear's voice. "She will get no less than she deserves. If she went to Osric, well, even he knows what to do with traitors."

Ceolwen was subtler. She laid a hand on her servant's shoulder and spoke in the stern yet benevolent voice practiced in the court for just such occasions. "Aelfhild." There were no nicknames now. "She broke faith with her master. Even servants have to know better than that. There is no honor to it."

"Yes, lady," Aelfhild answered. She stared at her feet.

Ceolwen snorted, but pursued the matter no further. Aelfhild knew her mistress recognized the tone of that answer; it was master and servant now, not bosom childhood friends. And so Aelfhild stared at her feet to hide the anger in her eyes.

It was all well and good for nobles to talk about honor and broken oaths. They did not know the life Gyda lived. Aelfhild did. Honor was an indulgence that servants could scarce afford. Theirs was a world of necessity. Maybe Gyda had spoken careless words in the wrong place, ignorant of any consequence. Or maybe she had seen a way out. Aelfhild could not fault her for that, no matter how foolish it had been. She remembered her own brief pause when Osric had made his offer. Hope had a mighty grip once its fingers found even the slightest purchase.

And if the girl had gone to Osric, Aelfhild did not envy her future. Gods help you, Gyda, she thought.

Cuthbert reached down below his bench to root around in the sack he had grabbed before they left. He came up with a blanket, which he tossed forward to his cousin. Ceolwen wrapped it around her shoulders, lifted her arm and motioned for Aelfhild to join her.

Weighing her anger against the cold, the cold won out. Aelfhild shifted over. It was raspy, coarse wool that still smelled strongly of the sheep from which it had been shorn, but it was a welcome comfort.

"Sorry," Ceolwen whispered next to her.

Aelfhild did not believe that her mistress understood what she was apologizing for, but this was not the time nor the place for lecturing. She nodded and shivered.

"Dawn ahead," called Cuthbert from the stern. He hitched up the cloak, taken from the slain warrior, around his shoulders.

To the east, the mist was turning little by little to shades of purple, still bruised and midnight blue at the bottom but spectral pink high above.

"Anyway," he said, "we would be in a good deal worse shape if young Aelfhild there had not got up when she did. Lucky you drank that last glass of mead, eh, girl?"

It was a paltry thing as far as jokes went, but the bowstring had been drawn too tight for too long and finally snapped. Ceolwen started giggling. Bercthun followed, and soon they were all sighing and wiping away tears.

We have our lives, and that is worth a laugh, Aelfhild thought. Better not to mention the dream.

The sun was well into the sky by the time it had managed to burn away the fog. Light glinted off dewdrops left atop the cliffs running along Leohtmere's southern shores, down from Cynestead and into the grazelands to the east.

Two rivers, the Hwitea and the Westea, rushed down from the mountains and poured their glacial waters into the Leohtmere from the west. To the east, the mighty Swiftea drained out of the lake and wound down all the way to the seacoast. The Eorl steered them that way now, toward the dawn and the headwaters of the Swiftea.

With Bercthun at the oars, they made good time across the lake, and as they neared the eastern edge the current began to help the little boat along.

"I cannot be the only one who is starving," said Ceolwen. "And you are all so quiet."

Aelfhild grinned. Some things never changed. Ceolwen would always be the Aethling, even without gilded halls or any of the trappings of royalty. And Aelfhild would always be a servant. There was more to life than immediate circumstance.

"Trail rations," Cuthbert called as he tossed them a greasy bundle. There was jerky of uncertain provenance and hard bread. Chewing it was a job, but Aelfhild applied herself. Her stomach had set to rumbling even before Ceolwen spoke up.

"How did you come to have all this, cousin?" Ceolwen asked between mouthfuls.

"A wise man leaves himself more than one way out of danger."

"Do you plan like this every time you come to Cynestead?"

"Take no chances in the city, girl. It is a foul place even when nobody is plotting to burn down a man's hall."

Aelfhild felt obliged to speak up for her home. "I grew up there. It is beautiful in summer."

Cuthbert laughed. "You are too good for that place, Aelfhild, my dear. You should come live with us in Norholt. The forest does not plot behind your back. The trees do not lie to you. A body needs peace and quiet to grow old and fat like me."

"Now that you mention it, where are we going, Cuthbert?" Ceolwen asked. "Norholt?"

"No, no," the Eorl replied, "We cannot go where they expect us to. You heard those two at the docks. If the Oescans are in on this, there is no telling what snares they have set. We will head past the rapids, then down-river a ways. That way, we throw any that are following off our trail."

Aelfhild and Ceolwen spoke as one. "Rapids?"

Where Leohtmere's deep waters swirled up into the waiting Swiftea, rapids roared. They could hear the sound as they approached, water tearing down through narrow chutes between pulverizing boulders, crashing in sheets against jagged rocks, whipping around tree-trunks eager to snag the hulls of fragile little boats. True to its name, the river flowed fast here.

Cuthbert stood in the stern, looking out over the whitecaps and waves. "Lucky the water is so high this season. I have seen it a fair bit worse than this."

That was less comfort to Aelfhild than he likely intended. She watched as breakers slammed up against stone with thunderous fury. Her mouth went dry.

"Allow me, my lord?" Bercthun asked. He and the Eorl switched places, the young man taking up the steering oar.

Cuthbert called forward to Aelfhild and Ceolwen. "Young Bercthun is a sure hand at this sort of thing. Trust him to get you through here without a hitch."

Ceolwen seized Aelfhild's hand. "I do not like boats, Aela."

"Yes, lady." In that moment, Aelfhild did not disagree. And she was not a keen swimmer.

The bottom fell out from beneath them as they entered the first chute. Aelfhild was glad breakfast had been light, otherwise it might have made a hasty return. The boat rocked and pitched from side to side, threatening to buck them out at any moment. With the hand that was not being crushed by Ceolwen's clammy grip, Aelfhild held fast to the hull.

Bercthun cut a dashing figure at the rear of the boat, his feet locked against the bench ahead of him and arms wrestling the steering oar. His hair was damp from the spray, his face serene in concentration. Cuthbert's thick arms pumped at the oars, knotted muscles in his back bulging beneath the nightshirt.

Ceolwen looked miserable. Her eyes were shut tight, her hand a vice around Aelfhild's. "What have you done to me, Cuthbert?" she screamed. The Eorl did not bother to answer.

Aelfhild, on the other hand, felt her initial fear ebbing. The roar of the water, the play of wind in her hair, the bouncing and racing of the boat; this was a rush she had never known. The sun beat down on her, warming limbs numbed by icy spray, and she threw back her head and laughed.

"And now Aelfhild has gone mad!" Ceolwen shouted.

Maybe, Aelfhild thought. The Gods had touched her once already. But she was alive and there had been too much fear in this day already. So she squealed, and not from fright, as the boat dropped again.

"We shall make a wild one out of her yet!" Cuthbert The river evened out after giving their little craft a thorough drubbing. Bercthun relaxed in the stern, and Cuthbert eased off the oars. The boat drifted out into the broad channel of the Swiftea, bruised but intact.

Ceolwen's voice was shaky, but Aelfhild suspected exaggeration. "Can we walk from here?" The Eorl just laughed.

Greystone cliffs, their constant companion since Cynestead, hemmed them in along the southern edge of the river. The north bank opened up into thickets of fern and briar, punctuated by the odd larch or oak rising stark and proud from the undergrowth.

"That is Blaedscir to our north, is it not, Cuthbert?" Ceolwen seemed to have recovered. Cuthbert nodded. "We could go to Eorl Hlothere," she continued. "He was always a friend to my father and he will hate what Osric did in Cynestead. You said before he might join us; now he most certainly will."

The old bear sucked at his whiskers. "Hlothere, Lord of the Cows." He grunted at his own joke. "I do not share your certainty, cousin. Hlothere thinks of gold before all else. He trades his grain to the Thrym, he trades his cattle to the Oescans, then he sells whatever is left on to us. There is no trusting a man so eager for gold. And now Osric has the royal coffers, and we have only what is in our pockets. Unless you snuck some treasure out with you, we need other plans."

Ceolwen snorted. "My father should have done something about him while he had the chance."

"It is no small thing to boss about a man whose lands feed half your kingdom. Your father was wise enough not to push. If you want to be a queen, remember: knowing when to fight is the biggest part of winning."

Though she let the matter lie, Ceolwen did not look overly pleased by the lesson.

"Back to Norholt then?" Aelfhild asked.

"It seems the wisest course," said the Eorl. "But for now, downriver. There is a place I know we can spend a safe night. But keep those eyes open," he continued. "Who knows what deal Osric has or has not made with Hlothere? We want to keep clear of his men and avoid his notice if we can. Besides, there are brigands in Blaedscir same as everywhere."

"The joys never cease," said Ceolwen. Aelfhild, again, did not disagree.

7

HEY TRAVELED ON for the rest of the afternoon. Both Aelfhild and Ceolwen took a turn at the oars, giving the men time to rest, but the rushing Swiftea did most of the work for them. Bercthun seemed to be in his element at the steersman's oar, dancing around rocks and through eddies, riding the swiftest currents.

All the while, Cuthbert kept his eyes on the northern banks. Aelfhild remembered the Eorl's warning and stared out into the thickets as well. She saw not a soul. From her seat, deer and rabbits seemed to be the sole occupants of Blaedscir. But tracking and woodcraft had not been considered important in Cynestead's court.

"Did you spot them, lord?" Bercthun asked as they rounded a bend in the river. He kept his eyes straight ahead and his voice flat.

"Aye," the Eorl answered. "Two so far."

Aelfhild scoured the riverbank. The trees had grown thicker as they went downriver, oaks crowding the bank to dip their knobbly knees into Swiftea's green waters. There was no sign of life that she could make out.

"You have to learn to listen as well as look, girl," Cuthbert said from beside her. "Do you hear any birds?"

"No."

"Right. They have all left because there are men tramping about. If there is silence where there ought to be noise—or the other way about—something is amiss."

"How do you know there are two?"

"One is light and good at his work; he hardly makes a sound but the birds gave him away first. The other joined later. He crashes about like a rutting boar—we could have heard him from Cynestead."

Ceolwen had been dozing in the prow but joined the whispered conversation. "Who are they?"

The Eorl shook his head. "I cannot believe Osric's men got out here so quick. My guess is either brigands or villagers. Hlothere's guardsmen would not bother hiding in their own lands."

Aelfhild strained to listen, but the sounds of the forest ran together. Water lapped against the boat and burbled through the tree roots; leaves rustled above them, and her own breath drowned out any footfalls. Moss, bramble, and fern screened movement along the riverbank.

"What do we do?" asked Ceolwen.

"Wait. If they are villagers they will leave us be if we do not make any hostile moves. And brigands will wait till we land to make any move. Though we may disappoint them if they are looking for loot." Cuthbert chortled. Even when nobody else cared for them, he always did seem to love his own jokes.

The sun dipped ever lower toward the horizon, dusk creeping up along the river. Aelfhild yawned and stretched; they had been cooped up in the tiny craft for too long. Her limbs were all bent out of shape, her back was beginning to pang, and the dark promised deeper cold. She wanted piping hot soup and a bed piled with furs and blankets.

She still had not spotted the watchers in the wood. At one point, she fancied that there was a face, pale and bearded, in a gap in the tree line, but as the river carried them past she saw it to be a trick of the light through the hanging moss. There was work yet to be done before she could become one of Cuthbert's scouts.

The Eorl drove them on downriver as the shadows lengthened. He seemed to be searching for a particular spot. Another bend in the river brought them out to a broad stretch of flatwater. The setting sun, drowsy and red, shimmered across the river's surface ahead of them.

"Northwards here, lad, to the shore," Cuthbert said to Bercthun.

On the northern riverbank, atop a barren, sandy point, Aelfhild saw three tall standing stones, each one engraved with lines of runes weathered to the point of illegibility.

Runestones. This must be the place, she thought.

Such markers were a common sight throughout the kingdom; some loomed over the sites of storied battles or the barrows of great warriors, others stood at the boundaries of fiefs or at busy crossroads. Most, though, were mysteries, placed long ago for some arcane ritual since lost to memory. Aelfhild guessed these three to be the latter kind, raised by unknown hands for forgotten purpose. Local people had scrubbed most of the lichen off the windbeaten and waterworn surface. The same was true of stones she had seen near Cynestead—even though no one could say for certain why, they respected such sites. There was a pull, a connection to the past and the ancient works of their ancestors.

Cuthbert hopped into the shallow water at the river's edge as Bercthun ran the prow ashore. Aelfhild and Ceolwen dropped down and helped drag the craft up onto shore, feet squelching in the muck. After so long in the boat, it was a mercy to stand on firm ground once more. The muscles in Aelfhild's legs unfurled in a burst of pins and needles as she stretched over and again, relishing the freedom. Her feet felt wobbly on the unmoving ground after growing accustomed to the water's incessant bobbing.

Turning inland, she peered into the murk beyond the beach, past the shadows of the tree line. The evening light revealed no secrets, so she used her other senses. She drew in a deep breath. The smell of loam, earthy and sweet, was thick on the air, with a tinge of something manmade: woodsmoke.

She mentioned it to Cuthbert, and the old bear flashed a toothy grin. "Well done, you are getting the hang of it," he said. "And what do you hear?"

"Birdsong," she replied, after cocking an ear toward the trees.

The Eorl nodded. "I think we left our friends behind some way back. But still, no reason to take chances. They might have gone to fetch more friends."

They carried the boat up from the water's edge, each lending a shoulder, and set it amongst a patch of ferns. Fronds and branches from the surrounding copse further concealed the hull. When Cuthbert seemed satisfied that the boat was well enough hidden, he slung his linen sack over his shoulder and turned to the others.

"There is a safe spot, not far from here, where we can rest for a while. Watch your footing—there are no cobblestones on these streets." He paused, but no one laughed. Aelfhild knew the comment had been pointed at her and her mistress, and was more offended than amused. True, they were born and bred in the capital, but they had both in fact walked in the woods before.

Bercthun and the Eorl led them through the trees in the dying light, making even, quiet progress through the spring ferns and branches heavy with early growth. Aelfhild and Ceolwen followed behind, tripping, stumbling, slipping, and muttering choice phrases.

The snarl of a protruding root hooked Aelfhild's foot, and she flailed out ahead of her. She grunted as her palms scraped against bark, coming away raw and throbbing. In her mind, she willed Cuthbert not to turn around. In part, she did not want to show him he was right, but she also worried that any smug words on his part might cause her mistress to say something they would both later regret. Ceolwen was faring no better herself.

After a fair hike, they stepped—or stumbled, according to their ability—onto a dirt path, two ruts worn deep into the dark soil with patches of anemic grass in between. Cuthbert took them north along it. The track meandered through thicket and forest, leading them to a clearing where a cottage stood.

A sod roof rose directly from the ground to a peak in the middle, and a ring of limewashed stones was spread about to mark out the edges. Smoke rose in lazy wisps from a hole in the eaves, and cracks in the shutters over the lone window hinted at warmth within.

Past a stretch of split rail, Aelfhild could see a yard swept painstakingly clean. At one end was a chicken coop, shuttered for the night. At the other, rows of firewood stacked with somewhat alarming precision and arranged according to size. She liked these folk already. Good order was the key to keeping any house, be it a hut or a hall. Bercthun opened the gate, allowing the others to pass through and taking care to fasten it again behind them. An aged, rheumy-eyed wolfhound looked up from the bone it was gnawing as they crossed the yard. The dog watched them pass without much interest, then returned to its work.

The entrance to the cottage was sunken into the earth at the foot of a few dirt steps. Cuthbert rapped on the flimsy wooden door with his knuckles.

There was a commotion inside, something clattered to the floor amidst muffled oaths. "Who knocks? I told you already we got nothing for you little bastards to steal!" came a rasp from within.

"Open this door, you old brigand!" shouted Cuthbert, mirth in his voice belying the harsh words, "Or have you forgotten your old friend Cuthbert?"

After a moment of scraping and fumbling with the latch, the door opened to reveal a hobbled old man beneath a crown of unruly white hair. He beamed at the Eorl in his doorway, his eyes wide and watery with surprise.

"My lord Cuthbert!" he said, hobbling out of the doorway to greet his visitors. "It has been an age!"

The old man made as if to hug the Eorl, a task complicated by the fact that he had only a single arm. Aelfhild noticed with a start that his left arm ended in a nub just below the shoulder. She tried not to stare but failed. Cuthbert returned the gesture with a sort of ginger affection, not insincere but clearly trying to hold back his accustomed bone-crushing squeeze.

"Good to see you, old friend," the Eorl said. "I bring guests, Swidhelm, and come to you for shelter on a cold night."

"Of course, of course," said the old man, peering past Cuthbert at the other travelers. "All are welcome, get yourselves inside." He waved them in over the threshold.

They introduced themselves as they passed into the cottage, Swidhelm offering a short bow to each in return. As he went to close the door, Aelfhild heard his last comment to the wolfhound.

"Some watchdog!" he muttered and slammed the door.

Swidhelm's home was not the King's Great Hall. No, Aelfhild thought, it is better. They had to duck beneath herbs, fish heads, and dried game that hung from the rafters as they entered. Boxes, sacks, and barrels filled every corner and nook, hemming in a living space just large enough for two people, provided the pair got on well enough. A rickety table and two benches stood in front of the hearth where an iron cauldron hung from the spit, bubbling over the embers. Aelfhild smelled soup—cabbage and a hint of leek. Her mouth watered.

There was only one piece of decoration. A sword in its scabbard hung over top of a shield above the mantle, and they were the only items in the house that did not show the withering of age. The leather of the scabbard was dark with oil, the boss of the shield polished to a ghostly gleam in the firelight.

Swidhelm introduced them to his wife Wilflaed, a spindly, snow-haired woman who bustled about, shoving crates to the side and grumbling under her breath about the troublesomeness of guests who arrived at so late an hour. She pushed some wooden bowls into Ceolwen's hands.

"Make yourself useful, lass, set the table," she muttered, passing right by the young royal who stood with her mouth open in shock. Her gaze met Aelfhild's, and they stifled fits of giggling as they laid the bowls out on the table. That voice carried her back a decade to the Matron's kitchen.

Cuthbert sat in quiet council with Swidhelm, telling the tale of their flight from Cynestead. The old man rubbed his jaw as he listened, breaking in occasionally to ask a question. Wilflaed took immediate charge of a bemused Bercthun, sending him out with a bucket to fetch water from the well. From the cauldron on the hearth, the source of the cabbage smell, she ladled out thin soup into each bowl on the table.

"Eat up, but if you want more, get it yourself," she called as she wrapped herself in a blanket and curled up near the hearth.

Bercthun returned with water, and the travelers washed the dirt from their hands and faces before sitting down to eat. Frigid on Aelfhild's face, the water pushed back her drowsiness. The close air of the cottage was like a smith's furnace after a day spent on the open river, and she could feel her eyelids drooping. She wanted to get some soup in before bed.

Swidhelm watched his guests eat with a broad smile on his face, and Wilflaed's muttering waned as they all returned to the pot for second or third helpings. After a few bowls, Aelfhild sat back and patted her belly. Conversation had been sparse as they ate, and the room was quiet now save for the crackling of the fire.

Wilflaed jabbed a boney finger into Ceolwen's ribs, making her jump. "Clear the table, girl," she ordered. When Aelfhild stood to obey instead, Wilflaed waved her off. "Not you, sit!"

Swidhelm cut in. "That is King Osred's daughter, woman, watch your tone! These are our *guests*."

His wife hooted. "Swidhelm Swidbertsunu, do not push your luck with me! If old Sigurd hisself walked through that door he would still have to pull his weight in my house! It is not much of a queen that cannot so much as lift a bowl." Under her withering stare, Swidhelm closed his mouth as quickly as he had opened it, and the matter seemed settled. Aelfhild helped her mistress clear the table as Wilflaed sat back, chuckling as she repeated her husband's objection in a whisper meant for the whole room to hear.

Cuthbert and Bercthun fell back into hushed conversation with Swidhelm. Wilflaed disappeared out into the yard while the men conferred, returning with a bale of straw that she directed Aelfhild and Ceolwen to spread out on the floor. This was their bed, and at that point Aelfhild was glad of even the smallest comfort.

Swidhelm had said something about people stealing before he opened the door. It had slipped her mind amidst everything else. She caught Wilflaed's attention.

"There were men watching us on the river today, then Master Swidhelm said something about thieves. Are they the same men?"

Wilflaed spat. "Some of the local toughs put together a little fyrd of their own, since Hlothere's men hardly come down this way these days. Came by a couple days back looking for, what did they call it, a *tithe*." Scorn dripped off the word. "Said it was for all our good but I know brigands when I sees them. We told them where to go and no mistake, but they made off with one of our piglets before Swidhelm could fetch that knife of his."

"Will they return?"

"Not if they have any sense between them. I know all the mothers and grandmothers around these parts, see." Wilflaed's lips parted in an impish, toothless grin.

Aelfhild smiled back, and slept better for the knowledge.

8

ELFHILD WOKE ONCE again to the smell of smoke, and rocked up from her bed, scattering straw. *No, no, no!* the screams echoed inside her head.

And there was Wilflaed, bent over the hearth, kindling the day's fire. Aelfhild's pulse began to slow. It was going to take her a while not to fear that smell. Pale morning light poured in through the open window, illuminating the old woman at her work. Aelfhild rolled out of her bedding and shook loose strands of hay from her dress and her hair. She left Ceolwen under their blanket to sleep, and set out to help however she could with the morning's chores.

Wilflaed spared her a nod and beckoned for Aelfhild to follow as she set off into the morning mist. They opened the chicken coop, sending out the pent-up fowl to peck in the yard while they gathered up any eggs left over from the previous day. They drew water from the well and carried it back to the house, then took buckets around the cottage to a small, weather-beaten barn, which Aelfhild had not noticed last night as they came up in the dark. A great fat sow stood steaming in the morning air, knee deep in the mud of her pen and watching the two women with interest.

"Oh, where are the other piglets?" asked Aelfhild. "You said the men only took one."

Wilflaed did not reply, but smacked her lips as though savoring a tasty morsel. She hooted with laughter, and scampered off into the barn.

There *had* been a hint of pork in the soup the night before.

Inside the barn was a brown mare that nuzzled the front of Aelfhild's robe, round, wise eyes begging for a treat. Wilflaed handed Aelfhild some oats, which the horse gobbled from her open palm. The mare's ears were warm and silken smooth to the touch.

Back at the house they found Swidhelm adding wood to the fire, while the others were only beginning to stir. For the morning meal, Wilflaed simmered coarse-chopped oats into a simple porridge, sparing a pinch of precious salt before squirreling the container away out of sight.

Crowded shoulder to shoulder around the small table, they scraped at their bowls while Cuthbert detailed the plans for the day.

"I must return to Norholt," he began, "to gather my warriors and safeguard my lands. There is no telling what mischief Osric will get up to now that he moves freely in Cynestead. But the roads are not safe, and I fear we cannot risk traveling all together. Ceolwen, you and Aelfhild must go with Bercthun to Haernmuth, and then sail north to our kin in Thrymgard."

Thrymgard. Aelfhild savored the word. It was the realm north of Earnfold, a land of fjords, glaciers, and countless islands dotted with the strongholds of the savage warrior-lords, the Jarls. The Thrym were a seafaring people, and most of the stories that came back to Cynestead were of their longships raiding villages up and down the coast. Ceolwen and Cuthbert had distant family ties to the northerners, sharing a great-great-great-granduncle or some such long-dead, distant relative with the current Jarl of Trollsmork.

"There is little to tie us to those people, cousin," Ceolwen said, taking no pains to mask the doubt in her voice. "What would make them willing to take us in?"

"I know old Harald," said Cuthbert, referring to their relative the Jarl, "and there is nothing he hates more than the Oescans—if he hears that they support Osric, and that you have an equal claim to the throne, he just might agree that it is in Thrymgard's interest that you be crowned."

Ceolwen fell quiet for a moment, fidgeting with her spoon. Aelfhild could see indecision written across her lady's face, could almost hear the internal argument. She took it upon herself to break the silence.

"How would we get there?" she asked.

"Bercthun will take you downriver to Haernmuth," answered Cuthbert, "you can find passage north from there. Traders sail up to Fornhofn and on to Jarlstad all times of year. I reckon it ought not be hard to find a ship, as little as the pair of you weigh."

"But we cannot pay," Aelfhild said. Their hurried flight from Cynestead had left them with nothing save for some dried meat and blankets—certainly no gold or silver with which they might buy safe passage north.

"I think we can fetch a small price for the boat, and if that does not cover it, we pay our way with work," Bercthun answered.

"Work" in that context made Aelfhild nervous, but not out of laziness; she was accustomed to thankless chores and filthy jobs. She knew that Bercthun could easily find a place at sea, with his broad shoulders and strong back, but she was less optimistic about the sort of use two young women might be put to on a trader's ship. The thought unsettled her. Ceolwen chose this moment to rejoin the conversation, leaving Aelfhild to brood.

"Would you go back to Norholt on your own, Cuthbert?" she asked, brow furrowed.

"Swidhelm has agreed to take me by road to the western bounds, and I can make my own way from there." The Eorl sounded confident. "I know my lands well, and my people are loyal." He nodded to Swidhelm, who beamed.

Ceolwen shook her head. "So we are just to flee north like thieves in the night, and then what? Return at the head of a Thrym army to conquer our own people?"

Cuthbert's response was terse. "We have few choices, and there are some who have risked much for you, girl." The two cousins stared one another down, and a leaden hush fell over the room.

The pause stretched on longer than was comfortable.

Swidhelm cleared his throat and turned to Aelfhild. "Your face has a familiar cast to it, lass. I marked it last night but cannot place it. Who was your father?"

Deep in thought as she was, Aelfhild was caught off guard. She blinked in confusion before stammering, "Alaric, master, Alaric was my father's name. Son of Hereric."

The old man chuckled. "I knew I had seen those eyes before! I fought under Alaric at Eabricstead, when the southerners marched up into Suthscir." His eyes shifted up to the sword and shield hanging over the hearth, reminders of days gone by.

Aelfhild remembered the morning her father left. She remembered the mist, that heavy Cynestead fog, gathering on the roof and falling in icy droplets down the back of her neck as she stood beside mother, watching men bid farewell to their families. Years later, she learned why. The Oescans had sent warriors across the southern border, part of some petty little dispute between farmers over grazing land that ended in blood. King Osred had raised the Fyrd and sent warriors to make sure Earnfold's bounds were not infringed upon, and the Patricians in Oesca had done the same. She had understood none of that at the time. He had just disappeared into the mist and never returned.

"Long ago, that was, shortly before I came into our lord Cuthbert's service," Swidhelm continued. His eyes were unfocused, gazing back through the veil of years. "He was a good man, your father. Always fair to us, and brave in the shield wall! I remember he always said to us, 'men, you honor the Gods when you do—'"

"'—your duty to the King,'" she finished. That had been one of his favorites. She struggled to return the old man's smile.

Swidhelm patted her hand. "There is strength in your blood, girl. Never doubt it." He stood from the table, leaving his bowl behind.

The others had finished their breakfasts and gone outside, leaving Aelfhild alone with her thoughts. Swidhelm had stirred up more than he could have guessed. Father had been her favorite, the warmer of the two by far. He had doted on his little girl. After he left, mother had faded further away, becoming little more than a judging voice far in the background. Little by little, Ceolwen had become everything.

Wilflaed startled her from the reverie with a hand on the shoulder.

"Enough of that, child. Time to get moving," the old woman said. Aelfhild got the distinct feeling that with a single glance of those wizened eyes, Wilflaed had learned more about her past than words could reveal in an entire evening around the fire.

The others were outside. Cuthbert and Bercthun were helping Swidhelm harness the mare that Aelfhild had befriended earlier to a ramshackle haywain loaded down with bundles of straw.

Ceolwen stood apart, leaning against the fence and staring out over the glistening grass of the clearing. She cut a remarkably different figure in this setting than she had in Cynestead's market just two days prior; her fair hair was now tangled with straw, her fur-trimmed cloak traded for a raspy wool blanket over a nightdress with a hem torn and muddy. We have come a long way in two days, Aelfhild thought. And we have leagues yet to go.

Thrymgard! Her mind turned to the future. We trade assassins in the south for savages in the north. But what have we to lose?

A week ago, she had spared barely a thought for the world outside Cynestead. There had been chores to do, gossip to catch up on, and a warm bed at the end of the day. She had known where life would take her, which was to say nowhere fast. Just three days past, life had still been, in a word, boring. Boring did have its advantages, and no doubt about it. The weight of the dagger in her pocket reminded her of that. She still shuddered to touch the thing.

But before this she had not known Bercthun, or Swidhelm, or Wilflaed. That was worth a smile.

How quickly our fortunes change, thought Aelfhild.

9

HE BID FAREWELL to Cuthbert and Swidhelm with a heavy heart.

It was a whimsical sight, the enormous Eorl perched atop the brittle-looking haywain in his nightshirt and muddied breeches, dwarfing old Swidhelm beside him, but there were few smiles that morning. Bercthun clasped his lord's hand, taking leave of his master and swearing to keep the Eorl's cousin safe at all costs. On the other side of the cart, Wilflaed patted her husband's leg, and he cracked the slightest of grins back at her, words long since unnecessary between the two.

Cuthbert's face looked older, greyer, the creases deeper; all trace of his usual humor and good cheer had departed. To Ceolwen, he said, "Go safely, cousin, and we will see each other again soon."

"Go safely, old friend," Ceolwen replied, offering a wan smile. The Eorl nodded to her and to Aelfhild standing at her mistress' side.

"And you, Aelfhild, remember what I told you. Listen as well as look, and keep the Aethling safe, whatever the cost."

Swidhelm flicked the reins, and the haywain set off across the field. The four of them stood silently, watching the little wagon until it was out of sight. Wilflaed was the first to turn, going back to the house without a word. Bercthun followed, leaving Ceolwen and Aelfhild standing side by side in the dew-laden grass.

"He was right, I know. We do not have many choices," Ceolwen's voice was soft. She spoke as much to herself as her servant. "There is so much that can go wrong. We walk a narrow ledge—one wrong step…"

The same worries hung heavy over Aelfhild's thoughts, but she tried to give her lady some comfort. "So now we focus on our next step and worry about the others later." She gave Ceolwen's hand a squeeze. "We keep going and we survive. Together."

Ceolwen turned toward Aelfhild, eyes brightening as a smile played at the corners of her mouth. She nodded and squeezed Aelfhild's hand in return. "Together. I am glad to have you here with me."

Wilflaed had gathered together what supplies the old couple could spare for the travelers, wrapping some dried fish, a few hard loaves of bread, and two skins of water in a blanket. She gave each of the women an old traveling cloak and linen wraps for their feet, bound with rawhide cords. The gifts were plain, but dearly given. It broke Aelfhild's heart that she had nothing to give back.

Ceolwen and Bercthun received a curt nod and a "farewell" from the old woman, but Aelfhild was shocked when she was pulled in to a tight embrace.

"You keep an eye on those two, my girl," Wilflaed whispered in her ear, "and you stay alive." Releasing her wiry arms, Wilflaed squinted at Aelfhild's face. "My Swidhelm was right about you."

Aelfhild smiled and nodded. "Thank you. For everything."

She left with her companions, looking back over her shoulder as they walked down the path to the river. The grey-haired woman stood at the cottage's open door, her frail form silhouetted by the glow from within. She watched them go, unmoving, without a wave or a sigh, then turned back into the house and closed the door behind her.

Before they passed from the path back into the wood, Aelfhild stole one last look back at the cottage. She was loath to leave it behind. But there was a long way yet to go, and no time to linger.

The thickets of Blaedscir to the north were pleasant to look upon in the morning sun, but paled in comparison to the grasslands of Ealdorscir that opened up along the south bank of the river. Fields of tall, pale green grass stretched as far as the eye could see, broken only occasionally by the sod roof of a farmer's hut. A light easterly breeze kissed the fields, sending cascading ripples through the top-heavy stalks.

Bercthun whistled and said, "Look at that. Reminds me of whitecaps off the lake."

"See?" said Ceolwen, "Norholt is not the only land worth seeing. Cuthbert does not know everything about everything, after all."

The young warrior laughed. "As you say, lady."

He hardly spoke in the presence of his lord. This was as many words as Aelfhild had heard from him in the whole journey. His voice was as earnest as his face; she did not imagine he was much of a gambler. One look at those eyes and even a child could call his bluff.

The wind carried with it the smells of spring, heavy with cloying pollen that set their throats to itching. Pale dust gathered in eddies on the river and left a yellow-gold stain on the sides of the boat as they passed.

Ceolwen took the chance to ask questions of Bercthun. They knew nothing of his life. He was reticent to speak at first, but none alive could withstand Ceolwen for long. She did not stop until she got her way.

"My father is an *ealdor*, lady, he has fought for lord Cuthbert for many a year. He is back in Wynnthwait at the Eorl's hall now. I promised not to let him down, and Gods help me but I do not plan to."

"We are all just folk here, Bercthun. You may call me Ceolwen."

"Yes, lady."

Aelfhild held back a laugh. The poor boy was clearly out of his depth, sweat beading on his forehead as he avoided Ceolwen's eyes. She came to his aid.

"Are you an *ealdor*, too?"

"No, still a *dreng*, until I stand in the shield-wall. There have been no proper battles since the Eorl took me in. But I am ready." He looked crestfallen. "I did kill a bear, though," he added, attempting to make it sound like an afterthought.

Aelfhild and Ceolwen spoke at the same time. "What?"

Bercthun lifted a necklace of hooked claws out from under his shirt. "It was taking sheep from one of the Eorl's villages. Da and I tracked it down with spears, he pinned it and I put one through the roof of its mouth." His chest looked to be in danger of bursting.

They passed the claws around. Ceolwen nodded and smiled, but Aelfhild could tell when her mistress was feigning interest. Life amongst the nobles in Cynestead afforded ample opportunity to practice that skill. Aelfhild's interest was more genuine. The claws were glossy and still warm from Bercthun's chest. She could get a sense of the power in those bestial paws just from the weight on her palm.

Something twinged inside her; pity or a sadness akin to it. Here was a beast that had lived, truly lived—running down prey, rending flesh, roaring over its domain—reduced to a jangling totem on a string. It reminded her of Ceolwen, sitting there in her dirty nightdress. And of all of them, to a certain extent.

She handed it back and was glad to be rid of the thing.

Floating down the broad waterway, Bercthun set about teaching them how to read the lay of the river. Aelfhild took the steering oar and Ceolwen sat atop the rowing bench, while Bercthun crouched in the prow, pointing out the way the water split around submerged snags or flattened out over hidden rocks, showing them where the water sped along and where it flowed slowest. They met only one other soul on the river. An old man in a frayed tunic and broad-brimmed cap poled a barge of freshly hewn timbers down the river, pushing off the muddy bank with his pole in leisurely sweeps. Drifting past, they could hear the man humming softly to himself. He never so much as glanced their way.

There were few other signs of life on the water, save for ducks and sparrows, or the occasional splash as a fish jumped and broke the surface.

As dusk fell, they made camp on a hillock near the water's edge. They hid their boat in the reeds not far from the water and camped atop a broad knoll, beneath willow trees heavy with the golden flowers of spring.

Dinner was meager and eaten cold. Dried fish, Aelfhild grumbled to herself. She was happy to have it, and she had been happy to have it earlier in the afternoon, but the stuff was hard to enjoy. Its pungency was matched by its general resistance to teeth, so chewing it provided ample time to reflect on the flavor and texture, which she found less than satisfying. But chew she did.

The night sky was cloudless, and as they ate, Aelfhild and Ceolwen took turns pointing out the constellations in the stars they remembered from their childhood lessons. The Smith's Anvil spun high in the north, its tip an eternally fixed point by which sailors and wanderers found true north. The Wolf rose above the horizon to the west, locked in eternal pursuit of its quarry, the Boar, which was already well into its great eastwards arc through the mottled sky. Directly above their searching eyes was the Spindle, where the Weaver sat as she spun the threads of fate. Swans, crows, shields, and sickles mixed together with shapes and outlines the names of which neither could recall.

The two moons floated next to one another just above the distant line of the horizon, pale half-orbs of blue and white light in the darkness.

Bercthun cleared his throat. "Do you know the story of how the moons came to be?" he asked.

Aelfhild had heard the story countless times as a child, but she loved the old tales. Each one was customized to the teller and differed in the details or the phrasing. Ceolwen must have felt the same. "We would be glad to hear your telling of it, Bercthun," she said.

Their fire had died down to barely glowing embers, crackling gently within its ring of stones. An owl hooted across the river, and Aelfhild imagined the bird leaning in to listen to the story.

"Long ago, years beyond reckoning," Bercthun began, "when the gods created the world from the Void, they were lonely. They yearned for children to share in the beauty of their creation, children who could help them shape the newborn lands. So Ivar, the Smith, went to his starry forge and stoked the fires high, hammering and bending the raw ether to his will. Two new creatures he made there, one giant and one little. The giant one they called Rymr, first of the Jotnir, Giantkind, and the small one they named Valr, first of the humans, Mankind.

"The gods were greatly pleased by their new children, and each one gave gifts. Ivar gave them the gift of fire and the art of smithing, that Man and Jotunn might shape the world alongside their creators. Solveig, the Weaver, gave to them the gift of speech and song, that the halls of Man and Jotunn alike might never fall silent. Halla, the Huntress, gave to them the gift of mastery over beasts, that Man and Jotunn alike be ever nourished and clothed. And Hakon, the Skald, gave them the gift of runes and rune-magic, that Man and Jotunn alike might mark the deeds of their ancestors and cast the lots of fate.

"Rymr and Valr, first of their kind, led the two peoples as they labored side by side with the gods, setting the newly formed world to order. The Jotnir made a home for their race, and called it Jotunheim; the humans likewise made a home for themselves, and it was called Mannaheim. Both thrived and multiplied, and there was peace between their realms.

"Over time, envy grew between them. The Jotnir were tall and mighty, longer in life but fewer in number. Humans were small and weak and short-lived, but they were many. Humans saw the long lives and the boundless strength of the Jotnir, while Jotnir saw the joy humans took from their many children and their great clans. Envy turned to anger, and blood was spilled.

"Rymr and Valr, the first-made, tried to turn back the rage of their peoples, but blood called for blood, and the vengeance wreaked by Man and Jotunn upon one another was terrible to behold. Rymr and Valr, reluctant foes, met in battle at the front of their great armies, but neither could overcome the other. Valr's speed and guile was even match for Rymr's size and might, and both were unshakeable of courage and of will unbreakable. They battled until the gods could stand to see it no more.

"Sickened by the sight of their children spilling one another's blood, the Gods turned away from their young world, but not before they lifted Valr and Rymr, first and favored, up into the heavens. There they circle eternally, the light glinting off their shields—Rymr's larger and pale blue, Valr's smaller and bone white. Twice in every month, just as now, they come together in the sky to fight anew, and the tides rise high and fall low with the fury of their blows."

The story took Aelfhild back to bonfires beneath dark skies, to the whispers and laughter of two young girls. They had lain there beneath the blanket of stars, just as now, and watched Valr and Rymr in the throes of that endless battle.

Ceolwen spoke. "Well told, Bercthun. Thank you."

"It is my honor, lady." Ceolwen sighed at this, but the young boy seemed determined to keep hold of propriety. He continued, "I will sit watch, while you two sleep. We should make Haernmuth tomorrow if we get underway early enough."

"Wake me when it is my turn for watching," Ceolwen ordered. Aelfhild and Bercthun glanced at one another. It was kind of her to offer, but they all knew that it was not going to happen.

1 0

THE RIVER GREW busier as they drew nearer to the mouth of the Swiftea, closer to the sea and the port-town of Haernmuth.

Aelfhild yawned. The sun had barely cleared the horizon, and they were already afloat.

A hamlet drifted by on the northern bank; a few thatch-roofed houses crowded together in a clearing amongst the oaks. Cows called out for the first milking of the day while sheep bleated in the paddocks, eager to be sent out to graze. Smoke sprouted up from a few roofs as the day's fires were lit within.

Further down the river, she watched farmers walking along a path on the riverbank, headed out into the fields with their rakes and scythes perched on sturdy shoulders. Their feet were wrapped in tattered linen, and their tunics were rough thread mended and resewn countless times. But they joked, shoved, and called out merrily on the way to their day of back-breaking work.

Watching them go, Aelfhild thought of how little of the kingdom she had seen. Her mistress would be queen of these lands one day—she refused to believe otherwise—and yet neither of them had ever been amongst such people. Would they even know the woman in the boat? She doubted it. And would they care? More doubtful still.

Then she spotted a horse along the bank, far downriver. Its tar-black coat glimmered in the morning light. No farmer kept his draft horse that clean. She looked closer, marking the elegant legs and proud, sweeping lines. It was a courser. The whole village together was worth less than a single courser. Only the rich kept them. And the King.

Osric.

"Ceolwen, I think you ought to get down," Aelfhild whispered over her shoulder. Ceolwen did not seem to hear her the first time.

Bercthun spotted it too. "Down, lady, now! Get beneath the blankets."

Ceolwen did not argue. She wriggled down between the benches, pressing her thin body against the hull. Aelfhild pushed what supplies they had down into the gaps and spread a blanket overtop, but the row-boat gave precious little cover.

"Keep to the center of the water," Aelfhild hissed, pulling her hood up over her face. She cursed herself. The warm sun, the fields, the bobbing of the river, all had lulled her into a pleasant mood. She had forgotten what they were up against, and now they were exposed.

A figure appeared beside the horse, tossing down a blanket and hoisting a saddle atop the beast's back. The man crouched at the shore and splashed water on his hands and face.

Aelfhild watched him from beneath her hood, confident he could not see her face. Do not let him notice us, she prayed. She could hear Ceolwen breathing beneath her. Do not let him notice us.

The Gods did not seem to be listening.

Looking up from the riverbank, the rider spotted the boat. He stared out across the water. Aelfhild expected the man to bolt to his horse at any moment. Her chest tightened, heart hammering.

But the man called out to them in cheery tones. "Hail, brother! Fair morning to you." He had a Cynestead accent, but so would most folk rich enough to afford such a horse.

Aelfhild nearly choked on her dry tongue. Bercthun was caught off guard as well, and took a moment to muster a response.

"Fine morning, master," he shouted across the water.

And that seemed to be the end of it. Maybe the man had nothing to do with Osric, Aelfhild dared to hope, and was just a nobleman out for a ride. Maybe they were jumping at shadows.

The man waved and swung into the saddle. Aelfhild's eyes were poised to fall from her head if she stared any harder.

"Is that it?" came Ceolwen's whisper from below. Aelfhild shushed her. This was no time to take chances.

Sitting atop his courser, the rider called out once more. "Tell me, brother, have you seen two noblewomen on the river? One tall and fair—a real beauty!—the other shorter, plain. Maybe with a fat man?"

Plain. Aelfhild frowned at that.

"No, master, begging your pardon," Bercthun cried back. "Seen nought but the fish since the lake."

"No bother, friend!" A pause. "Last one to Haernmuth buys the ale!" Booming laughter, the stranger galloped off.

The boat was silent. A trail of dust rose along the bank, as horse and rider disappeared into the fields.

So, he was one of Osric's, thought Aelfhild.

Ceolwen sat up from beneath the bench. "If that is the best Osric has, I am not worried. The man was a ti—"

But Bercthun did not let her finish. "Better you stay hidden for now, lady. We cannot know who else is watching. Forgive me being forward, but the Eorl said to keep you safe and I aim to do so."

"But—" Ceolwen began. Aelfhild could see the argument brewing.

"I agree, lady," she said. "We were careless before and almost paid for it. And we should hide away that hair, you heard what he said." She tore off a strip of blanket and motioned for her mistress to lay forward.

Leaning back, Ceolwen allowed her servant to gather up her tangled locks. "I heard him call me a real beauty, if you mean that," she jeered. "Ouch! Aela, that pulls."

"Beg your pardon, lady." Aelfhild spotted Bercthun's grin from the corner of her eye. She hid as much of the flaxen hair as she could beneath the cloth. "Keep your hood up when we get to Haernmuth."

There was grumbling, but Ceolwen stayed out of sight for the rest of the journey. Relaxing was out of the question after the morning's encounter, but they did not seem to under imminent threat of attack. Regardless, Aelfhild kept a wary eye on the south bank. They floated past fishermen perched atop long skiffs, untangling and spreading spindly nets. Herdsmen drove cattle down into the river, stirring up muddy sediment and turning the waters a murky brown. Cows and sheep jostled one another for position at the water's edge, and the young calves and lambs played up along the bank.

Aelfhild assumed each one to be a spy, but none of them paid the little boat any mind.

By late afternoon they had arrived at the outskirts of Haernmuth. The grasslands to the south began to grow sparser, replaced by broad, sandy dunes as they drew near the coast. The Swiftea grew so wide near its mouth that they could scarcely see the northern side.

Buildings cropped up on the south bank; first a few peasant huts and fishermen's sheds, then the high thatched roofs of sawmills with their great churning waterwheels. The boatyards of Haernmuth were famous throughout the kingdom, and much of the timber felled in Norholt and Blaedscir was floated downriver to the mills near the sea.

A brisk wind rising out of the east made the water of the river increasingly rough, and Bercthun had to look for a place for them to land their small boat, unsuited as it was to the waves. He found a spot not far from a shipwright's dock, marked by half-built or stripped-down vessels up on frames near the beach, their arched backs and curved ribs exposed to the sky.

Aelfhild and Ceolwen helped drag the boat up onto the sandy bank. The sea breeze carried a chill with it, and Aelfhild pulled the coarse wool of her cloak tighter around her shoulders.

"Lady, if you please, wait here while I find out what we can get for our boat," said Bercthun. "We have to keep from drawing too many eyes, so please, no wandering." He looked nervous, and Aelfhild could not blame him.

She looked out over masts and furled sails, stretching down the beach and out of sight. Haernmuth was a center of trade and travel on the eastern shore, a gathering place for the people of Earnfold, Thrymgard, and Oesca. Oescans dared not sail further up the coast than the mouth of the Swiftea—they feared not only the harsh seas in the north, but Thrym raiders keen to seize their cargo. The infamous longships of Thrymgard came to Earnfold to trade, but seldom went further south unless they were set on raiding villages and cities along the Oescan coast. The folk of Earnfold in turn gathered here to trade their harvests of grain, lumber, and wool with northern and southern neighbor alike, bringing their cargo downriver from the Leohtmere by barge and boat.

The crowds were thick, and there were countless nooks to hide in, but that cut both ways. As Aelfhild saw it, that meant there were plenty of vantage points from which Osric's men might watch them.

The town sprawled up and down the south bank, docks and jetties jutting into the river filled with boats of every imaginable shape and size. Warehouses, market stalls, inns, and taverns crowded along the beaches, walls pressed closely together to keep out the wind, streets and alleys an unnavigable jumble. The city proper was a walled citadel not far from the dune line of the eastern sea, a high wooden palisade ringing the great hall of the lord and the halls of his warriors and nobles. Caelin, Hauld of Ealdorscir, held his court here when he was not away in Cynestead.

Bercthun returned with a gangly young man in a leather apron, wood shavings in his beard and a chisel in his belt. He turned out to be the shipwright's apprentice.

The tradesman walked around their little craft, knocking on the boards and peering under the benches, then set to haggling. It was hard to hide their desperation; their clothes and faces betrayed them. Bercthun did what he could.

Two silver pieces and a handful of copper coins was the final price, and in Aelfhild's estimation it was a paltry offering for the boat that had saved the life of the future queen. Bercthun kicked at the sand as the apprentice went to fetch his master's purse, while Aelfhild wrapped their few possessions in a blanket. She slung it over her shoulder as they set off into town.

Haernmuth bustled with the sounds and smells of a thriving port. Traders shouted over one another, each one offering the best, the freshest, the rarest, the most exotic of goods while heaping scorn on competitors. From one booth they passed wafted the tang of cumin and honeyed dates from the southern coast; from another poured the dog-muck stench of freshly tanned leather. Flocks of chickens and geese squawked and flapped in pens lining the street, while merchants led donkeys and oxen through the narrow lanes.

From the doors of inns, flung open to entice passersby, came the smell of roasting meat and stale beer along with the clamor of men unwinding after days or weeks at sea. As they passed a particularly raucous tavern, a slender fellow of Oescan countenance came hurtling out the door, followed closely by a furious-looking Thrym with fists thick enough to hammer iron. Like a wolf set upon a hare, the Northman sprinted down an alleyway in close pursuit of his prey.

Aelfhild and Ceolwen stood stunned in their wake, staring after the pair; Bercthun shooed the two women onward. As they went, Aelfhild noticed that he kept a hand on the handle of his axe, ready for trouble.

No one can spot us in this mess, she thought as they flattened themselves against a wall to allow a mule team past.

The drovers hollered at anyone fool enough to stand in the way, brandishing their sticks as much at passersby as the braying animals.

Further up from the docks, the buildings began to spread out, a break from the press of wood and thatch near the shore. Sunlight strained over the eaves of the buildings, dappling the muddy lane. Near the walls of the inner city, they found an almost-respectable inn. Inside was smoky but free of fighting drunks, so they parted with two of their copper coins for food and lodging. It would be another night spent on beds of straw with a supper of thin porridge, but they could hardly even afford that level of comfort.

They sat around a table in the inn, warming their backs by the fire. Bercthun slurped at his bowl of mushy oats. The man seemed to eat anything put in front of him, regardless of smell or color.

There were weevils in the bread, and Aelfhild focused her attention on picking out the wriggling larvae and flicking them into the fire, where they ended with a satisfying pop.

Ceolwen stirred her gruel back and forth with a grimace.

Scraping at the bottom of his bowl, Bercthun broke the silence. "We will make the rounds of the taverns tonight…if we can find a captain who is a happy drunk, striking a good price should not be hard," he said with what Aelfhild suspected was heavily forced cheer.

"And if that fails," responded Ceolwen, pushing her bowl back, "We get him dead drunk and steal his ship, then sail it north ourselves."

Her voice was serious, but a grin played at the corners of her mouth and her eyes were merry.

Nodding along, Bercthun said, "How hard could it be to sail to Thrymgard with a crew of three? Just point the boat north and..." He waved his hand in a vague thataway direction, shrugging his shoulders.

"I can row if you can steer," Aelfhild added, turning her attention from the weevils. "And Ceolwen can be our cook." Bercthun barked a short, sudden laugh, and Ceolwen's grin broadened into a smile.

"It is settled, then," Ceolwen said, "we have a crew."

1 1

"I WILL NEVER GET the stench of these places washed off," said Ceolwen, pushing away a drunk in stained breeches who had sidled over to check on the welfare of the two lonely-looking young women. Her shove served more to adjust the course of his inebriated journey than halt it, and he went careening off to spread joy elsewhere.

"No decent woman would dare be seen in such a place."

The Aethling was in a huff. Throughout the evening they had been groped, serenaded, pinched, and drooled on in a parade of indistinguishable taverns, each one filled with damp hay and the reek of spilled beer with all the effluent that followed.

"I think there is a woman over there," Aelfhild ventured.

Ceolwen peered through the smoke-filled gloom. "Where? By the Gods, is that a woman? How can you tell?"

Aelfhild waited for her mistress to take a sip from her cup before replying.

"Less stubble."

It took Ceolwen a while to regain her breath as she coughed, laughed, and dribbled ale.

Bercthun rejoined them, his expression peeved.

"Lady," he whispered, "I did say not to stare at folk. Someone may get suspicious. Even if they are not looking for you, the last thing we want is trouble."

"These drunks would not notice if a team of oxen burst through that wall," Ceolwen protested.

"No luck finding a ship?" Aelfhild asked. The young man shook his head, rubbing at the bridge of his nose.

"On to the next one, then," she said.

The door of the inn closed behind them, muting the clatter and roar within. They stepped over a pair of what Aelfhild assumed to be men wrestling in the gutter—mud covered them to the point that she could hardly tell if they were human. It was unclear which man was winning.

The air outside was cold and blessedly fresh, rich with the tang of saltwater. Strains of singing drifted out of an open door across the way. Another jaunty sailor's ditty, from the sound of it. The one thing she enjoyed were the songs. Each tavern had a mood to it and singers to fit— boisterous sea-chants rang from the walls of one alehouse, soulful keening in another. And what the dancers lacked in form or grace they made up for in pure, unapologetic spirit. Aelfhild found it an improvement over the haughty plucking of strings in the King's court.

They wandered, looking for a drinking hole yet untested. The remaining options were few.

Bercthun led them down a quieter alleyway and into a squat, wood-shingled building. Inside they found the same haze of smoke, but without the humid press of humanity. This was no place for merry crowds and catchy songs, but a place to eat and drink in undisturbed solitude.

After a short conversation, the innkeeper directed Bercthun to a table against the far wall of the inn, near the glowing coals in the hearth. There they found two men, one thin with haggard features that hinted at recent illness, the other clearly descended from the giants in Bercthun's campfire stories. Even sitting down, the man's golden-brown beard was at Aelfhild's eye level.

The sickly one was dozing, head nestled on his forearms, while the giant stared without expression into his mug. He turned his stolid gaze to the three intruders as they approached.

"Hail, friend," Bercthun greeted him, bowing his head, "I was told you are the men to see about passage north."

Their new "friend" stared back unblinking for a moment before he turned and elbowed his sleeping companion. Waking with a snort, the man sat back and peered at them from beneath his tangled hair.

"Whassit?" he rasped, voice still heavy with sleep.

"Hail, friend," repeated Bercthun, "We seek passage north and were told to speak to you. Bercthun is my name."

"Leofstan," the little man said, introducing himself, and gestured for them to be seated across the table. As they took their seats on the other bench, he patted his cheeks and drained the last of whatever had been sitting in his mug. He burped and pointed to his silent friend. "Sigfus."

It took Leofstan some time to regain his bearings, but he seemed to be the man in charge. Sigfus stared into his mug as before, unperturbed by conversation.

"The three of us are headed north to Jarlstad," Bercthun said, "and hoped to buy passage aboard your ship."

"Jarlstad?" asked Leofstan, shaking his head, "We are not sailing that far west. Tomorrow we set out for Ulfheim in the north. The closest I can take you is Fornhofn, but three folk is heavy cargo." He scratched at the scraggly growth on his chin as he passed an appraising eye over all three. "You can row," he added, pointing at Bercthun, "but those two are dead weight." He gestured to the girls.

Bercthun nodded, "I can work for my share, and we can pay. But Fornhofn is only part of the way on our journey, and we will not pay a full price for only half the distance."

Leofstan named his price. "Four silver crowns."

It would have been a pittance for the daughter of the King on any normal day, but then and there he might as well have asked them for a wyrm's horde. Bercthun scoffed. "One silver crown, and even that is too much."

"You pain me, friend, you pain me," Leofstan pointed to his companion. "You see how big Sigfus is? It costs more than a crown to feed him. Three crowns."

Back and forth they went for a while, the captain feigning poverty and Aelfhild's eyes watering as Bercthun's offers crept higher.

They concluded on two silver and four copper pieces. It was the full extent of their wealth, and left them nothing for the remaining leg of their journey.

Focus on this step now, she chided herself. The others come later.

"You drive a hard bargain, stranger," Leofstan concluded, bowing his head and spreading his hands in a show of mock defeat. "Half now, half on arrival—and you provide your own food. I have enough hungry bellies to feed as it is. Agreed?"

He spat in his palm and extended his hand to Bercthun, who nodded and did the same. They clasped hands, and the deal was made. Bercthun handed over half of their coins.

Aelfhild could feel the tightening in her throat as she watched the coins pass across the table. She hated the jolly, reassuring look in the man's eyes. She hated the way his grubby fingers slid the coins into his purse. She hated feeling so trapped. Her fists clenched beneath the table. Part of her mind knew that there was nothing for to do but wait and see how things turned out, but another part raged against passivity, screaming not to trust the men.

They will laugh and walk away and steal our money.

They will find Osric's men and betray us.

She was sure that her seething must have shown, try as she might to keep her face serene, but nobody seemed to be paying her any mind.

"When do we depart?" asked Bercthun, "And what is the cargo?"

"Tomorrow morning, just after dawn. There is a warehouse at the west edge of town by the mills, we load from there. We carry barrels of barley up north, malt for beer and bread and whatnot. Thrym are not smart enough to grow it themselves, so they need us!" He grinned at Sigfus, who had not lifted his eyes from his now-empty beer mug for the entire conversation. The mention of the Thrym seemed to have sparked his interest, and he turned toward his partner. Watching him move was like seeing a mountain rearrange itself boulder by boulder.

Leofstan waved him away, saying something dismissive in the northern tongue. Sigfus shrugged, and the bench beneath him jiggled with the rise and fall of his titanic shoulders.

Turning to his new customers, Leofstan confided in a dramatic whisper, "Big bastard speaks not a word of Earnfolding. Let us just say, if I had hired him for his brains, I would not have to pay him at all." He broke into fits of giggling.

They took their leave of the two, leaving Leofstan to carry on chuckling to himself. As the three turned to go, Leofstan called out, all traces of mirth gone from his voice, "Dawn tomorrow, west docks. If you are not there, we leave with your coins."

Aelfhild's fingernails bit into her palms.

Ceolwen fussed with her cloak as they walked back to the inn, pulling it close against the night's cold. Her face was laid bare for Aelfhild to read, given the long years they had spent together, and Aelfhild saw there the same anger and the same fears that troubled her own mind.

And Bercthun's earnest face concealed nothing. His jaw was rigid, his stare fixed straight ahead.

The night's revelries were winding down, and the taverns had grown dark. A few stragglers remained out and about, heading to their beds or looking for a place to get one last drink. It was gloomy and still, clouds pressing in overhead lit from behind by the light of the moons; torches flickered in iron stands along the main street.

Aelfhild jumped as Ceolwen spat into the mud. Such an unrefined gesture from her mistress marked trouble.

"He is a foul little man."

She did not need to name the target of her ire. Leofstan was on all their minds.

"He is," Aelfhild agreed.

Bercthun grunted.

Aelfhild decided not to press him. He had his own reasons for silence. The Eorl had laid a heavy burden on him in Ceolwen's life. This could not have been how the young warrior pictured his path to glory, of that she was sure.

The door of their inn was still unlatched, and they found a fire burning low in the hearth. Behind a curtain at the far end of the hall they made beds in piles of straw, wrapping themselves in their cloaks.

Settling in, Aelfhild lay and listened to the noises of the house—the snoring of other travelers, the shuffling feet of the innkeeper as she barred and locked the door, the gentle rustle of bedding as someone or other shifted in their sleep.

Bercthun broke the silence with a whisper. "I know it is hard, but we have no choice but to trust them. When we reach Fornhofn…we can figure our next move from there."

"It irks us all not to have a better way. You are right, though, we have little choice." Ceolwen replied. "None of this is your fault, Bercthun," she added, "You have done more than we ever could have asked. Thank you." Her words were soothing. There was a balm in that voice, the tone of a mother coaxing a smile from her crestfallen son.

She sounds like a queen, Aelfhild thought to herself. It was a challenge to reconcile her memories of a mischievous and often petulant child with this calm, confident voice in the darkness. She had heard it said before that hardship showed the true nature of a person, but had not really understood the meaning of the words until now. Perhaps there was something to it, after all.

Rolling on to her side, she settled down into the straw. She could hear Bercthun and Ceolwen breathing, neither one yet asleep. Unbidden, a proverb popped into her mind, a fragment of some long-forgotten song. It seemed fitting, so she shared it with her companions: "A foolish man lies awake at night, worrying of many things. He rises care-worn in the morning, and his troubles are just as they were."

"Thank you for that, Aela," replied Ceolwen with a sigh that hinted strongly at tested patience. Straw rustled as the she wriggled into her bedding.

Aelfhild grinned to herself in the darkness, and closed her eyes to find what sleep she could.

1 2

PITCH-STAINED WAREHOUSE WALLS hemmed in a maze of footpaths and muddy lanes by the western docks. Dusk still clung to the buildings, and Aelfhild's imagination filled every shadowed doorway or alley with dead-eyed rogues and poisoned swords.

The churning in her stomach had not faded since waking.

We made this turn before, a voice screamed in her head. *We will not make it in time. The ship will leave without us.*

Any wood left for long in the salty sea air weathered to the same pitted grey sheen, making all the walls around her identical. How men got any work done in this snarl remained a mystery.

Or, even worse, we will *make it in time*, the voice continued, *and Osric's spies will be there. Not many witnesses around here.*

That phrase repeated itself, over and again: *not many witnesses.* Aelfhild clenched at each turning, expecting Bercthun to come hurtling back around the corner screaming of ambushes.

Ahead of her, Ceolwen trudged through the mud, wrapped tight in her cloak and hood. Bercthun led the way out of some unfathomable sense of direction.

Or maybe he is as lost as we are, and is too proud to admit it.

They rounded a corner and spotted Sigfus' distinct frame beside a warehouse, one which she would have sworn they had passed by at least once before. He was perched atop a barrel, feet crossed in front of him and hands clasped on his belly.

Then came that insidious voice again. *Of course they are still here. Why would the hunter leave without his quarry?*

The massive Thrym stared as Bercthun, Ceolwen, and Aelfhild approached. He rose, stretching, and gestured for them to follow. Around the side of the building were arched double-doors, wide enough to accommodate a wagon or cart; Sigfus knocked twice, and one of the doors was unlatched and opened from within. The giantling led the way, while Aelfhild brought up the rear.

It was dark inside, a single sconce hanging from one of the wooden columns that ran down the central line of the building. Aelfhild could make out nothing past the crates and bails of straw stacked to the roof. She recognized Leofstan by his boney frame, standing in the torchlight with his back to the door, talking to another figure whose face was hidden in the darkness.

The sound of the door closing—and a bolt sliding into place—made her jump, and she pressed closer to Ceolwen's side. Bercthun moved his hand toward his right hip, she noticed, where the axe hung in his belt.

She still had the dagger given to her by Cuthbert in the front pocket of her robe. It had been dead weight since they left Cynestead, unused and untouched. But now the feeling of cold iron, which had made her recoil days before, steadied her hand.

Sigfus stooped to whisper in his master's ear. Leofstan turned to the three newcomers, his eyes bright in the torchlight.

"So, you found us. Good! Welcome! We are almost ready to set sail, just one more thing to see to." He stepped aside to reveal his companion. Aelfhild placed the face at once—it was the rider, the man they had seen along the Swiftea.

"Hail, friend," the horseman spoke to Bercthun. "Ill luck meeting like this."

It was a relief to know. That was a surprise for Aelfhild. Not that Leofstan had betrayed them, she had feared that from the moment they handed over coins—so had the others. The uncertainty, the un-know-ing, had been torment, and as it departed there was the briefest window of serenity.

Then fear rushed in to fill the gap.

Cuthbert's last words to her rang clear in her mind. "Keep the Aethling safe, whatever the cost," he had said. She gripped the hilt of her dagger tight.

Whatever the cost.

Leofstan took a step back. "The new King asks us to take care of you lot, and we always obey our king. Is that not right, lads?"

With the sound of clinking metal, two men stepped out of the shadows with chains in hand. Bercthun drew his axe, but it looked a paltry weapon in the torchlight. Behind them, Aelfhild noticed two other men had left the shadows and circled around by the door, blocking their exit. They hefted wooden clubs.

She could not swallow. Her tongue cleft to the roof of her parched mouth. Blood hammered in her ears.

Sigfus towered over them, seeming to unfold toward the ceiling in a column of flexing muscle. Leofstan, still smiling, spoke from behind his henchmen. "This will go much easier for you," he said, "if you do not fight."

Bercthun gave no answer, but pressed his back to Ceolwen as Aelfhild did the same, drawing her little blade from its sheath. The two men behind them advanced a step, and Aelfhild brandished the wavering tip of her dagger at them.

A wisp of red, like a drop of dye spreading tendrils through clear water, drifted through her vision. She shook her head to clear it from her eyes, but another blood-colored thread snaked inward from the edge of sight. She tried to look past the spots, focus on her assailants.

There were no wasted words, no threats or begging or pleading. Their choice, fight or submit, had been made quite clear. In silence, their attackers circled, looking for an opening. Leofstan looked on from afar with Osric's messenger beside him. Sigfus moved forward, swinging a length of wrist-thick knotted rope in slow circles.

One of the club-wielding men advanced on Aelfhild. Her breath came in ragged gasps now. She could only make out a partial shape through the haze in her eyes; the tendrils twisted together in ever increasing number. A wild, uneven swing of her dagger and the man danced back out of reach, laughing.

His laughter was interrupted by an ear-rending scream from one of his compatriots, who had evidently met with Bercthun's axe. The two men wrestled, blood spattering the floor, as Bercthun attempted to free the axe from his attacker. Sigfus was upon them before he could manage it.

With a bestial howl, the great bearded Northman slammed his body into Bercthun's side, knocking him to the floor. Sigfus set about with the rope, laying into Bercthun and Ceolwen with unbridled savagery. Ceolwen raised her arms to ward off the blows, bent low, and threw herself against the Thrym's broad stomach, but her weight was nowhere near enough to bring him down. Sigfus' battering ram of an elbow hammered the back of her head and left her sprawled on the floor beside Bercthun.

"Do not kill them!" Leofstan's shouting was mute, distant through the pounding in Aelfhild's ears. She was blind.

There were stories she had heard of men going insane in battle, frothing and rending their garments, but those were warriors. She was a servant. And surely those men were not close to soiling themselves with fear.

The Gods were punishing her again. They hated her. Why, she did not even bother to ask. But in that moment she hated them back. And Leofstan. And Sigfus. And the rider.

Osric's face flickered in front of her, silhouetted against the blood. Here was the true enemy. Here was the source from which all her pain flowed. The air tore at her throat as she roared.

She lunged, swinging her blade from side to side. Her shoulder struck up against something soft, and she stabbed into it. Searing liquid poured out onto her hands.

The space around her was a cacophony of sound, but in her reeling mind it was impossible to sort her own shouting from that of the others.

A man tried to get an arm around her, and she bit down hard on flesh. She clawed, kicked, and howled as she was grabbed and pulled from all directions.

Something heavy struck the back of her head, and then there was darkness.

There was the sensation of being carried, then dragged, then dropped.

The pain was distant, but it lingered, waiting for opportunity.

She heard wood groaning, and the call of seagulls on the wing.

Thoughts came back little by little, shifting and slippery and jumbled together.

Someone was humming nearby. It was not a song she could recognize, in fact there seemed to be no rhythm or pattern to it at all.

With immense effort, Aelfhild cracked her eyelids. Light rushed in, searing white and razor sharp against the back of her head. She squeezed her eyes shut, but the pain had woken with her and would not retreat.

She raised her head. Her eyes took time to adjust to the harsh sunlight.

She was wedged against the hard wood of what looked to be the hull of a ship; the groaning was the boards flexing in the waves, and she could hear the splash and feel the rolling crests against the sides of the boat. The fog was clearing from her mind, but slowly, and the world still spun.

The humming continued, and she saw that she was not alone. There were women in the boat, several women, and she recognized none of them. A pair of mismatched eyes appeared over her head—one blue as summer sky, the other a dull, milky white. Their owner was a girl, maybe five or six years of age, who sat braiding strands of Aelfhild's hair, humming away. The girl smiled down on Aelfhild from above.

Aelfhild tried to speak, but her mouth was bound with strips of cloth. Wriggling her hands and feet told her they were also tied fast, and sent fresh currents of pain writhing up her back and through her skull.

"Easy now, lady," came an unfamiliar voice. A new face loomed over her, a woman with crow's feet beginning to show around the eyes and grey edging into the hair at her temples. "They near did you in with that beating. You stay still and let me sort you out. Come away, Sola, leave the lady be." The child retreated from view.

Lady. Aelfhild still felt drunk, but that was not right. She was not the lady. She needed to know where the real lady was.

The woman returned, brandishing a cloth. "You are all filthy with blood, here." She began scrubbing at Aelfhild's face, and the rag came away rust brown.

"I fear there is nought I can do about the ropes, lady," she continued, and glanced over her shoulder, "until they say otherwise."

The damp cloth soothed Aelfhild's skin, but she yearned most for a drink. Her mouth was bone dry, and the fetid gag stuck to her cracking lips and cheeks.

"My name is Runild, lady," said her new friend. "Though I wish we were not meeting like this. That is my daughter, Sola. She took quite a shine to you, even with all the blood." Runild spoke softly, and Aelfhild could not ask whether it was for the benefit of her own aching head or out of fear of listeners. Her fingers twinged as she imagined Leofstan nearby.

"Gods forgive me, but I near forgot." The woman bent low to whisper. "Your friend is here, too, and she is alive."

Aelfhild wriggled against her bonds, mindless of the pain, as tears beaded in her eyes.

"Hush, lady!" Runild hissed.

No words could make it past the bindings in her mouth, but Aelfhild mewed her pleas anyway.

I need to see her. Please, just let me see her, she tried to say.

Runild hesistated; she threw another glance over her shoulder, then stared back down at her patient with watery eyes. Sighing, she put a hand behind Aelfhild's back and lifted her up.

Aelfhild grunted as the pain swelled and crested. White splotches danced in and out of her vision as Runild steadied her.

But there lay Ceolwen. Filthy, tattered, face down in the straw that lined the hull, but breathing.

Tears streaked Aelfhild's cheeks as she lay back down.

I have not failed yet! No pain in the world could stop her exaltations.

1 3

ELFHILD DID NOT know why or how, but she had made a fast friend in Sola. The little girl sat and unwound the tangles in Aelfhild's hair, braiding as she went. She hummed her disjointed little ditties but never spoke. Runild stayed close to her daughter. The woman did not appear to fully trust the strangers around her child, and as far as Aelfhild was concerned it was mutual.

Leofstan was not the sort of man that women would be around willingly; or, rather, Aelfhild refused to believe that such women existed. But she had been wrong before, and watched Runild for signs of treachery.

What such signs looked like, she was far from sure. The bindings permitted little aside from watching, though, so watch she did.

There were two other women in the hold with them. The pair had the snow-pale skin and high cheekbones that marked them as Thrym, and they did not engage with each other or Runild, let alone the newcomers.

Coarse breeches, tunics, and foot-wraps were the uniform in the hold. All the other women wore them; even Sola had her own miniature version. There were no adornments and no color, only patches of mismatched fabric around knees and elbows.

Slowly, Aelfhild's strength returned. She wormed her way upright, back to the boards of the hull, scraping at the hay with her bound feet.

"Come, Sola." Runild called her daughter back and clutched her tight. The woman glowered at Aelfhild, before returning her stare to the aft platform of the boat.

The ship they were on was a wide-bellied cargo hauler, with platforms fore and aft for rowers. From her perch in the depths of the hold, Aelfhild could see no activity on either side. The only thing visible was the mast, braced against the foreward platform and fitted with billowing sails, and a patch of bruised sky directly overhead.

Leofstan was somewhere above, she guessed, from the scowl Runild gave her. As much as she did not want to attract the serpent's attention, she needed to see.

Ceolwen's back rose and fell evenly as Aelfhild dragged herself over.

Leave it to the nobles to sleep in, she thought.

Whoever had bound their hands had at least had the mercy to tie them in front. Aelfhild reached out and pulled at her mistress' shoulder. Ceolwen's eyes were puffy and red; it looked as though she had already woken and cried herself back to sleep in the time it took Aelfhild to get moving.

I should have been faster, Aelfhild thought. She needed me.

There was another thought, but she squelched it down before it was more than a whisper.

She could have checked on you.

Ceolwen opened her eyes. When she spotted Aelfhild, she rocked forward, grasping at her servant. Her hands were bound as well, but she could still touch Aelfhild's face. New tears ran down the grimy tracks left by the previous set.

Aelfhild had never felt such a tender gesture from her mistress, and her own tears stained what was left of her dress.

They sat, foreheads pressed together, sobbing through their gags.

"Well, what a sight that is. Friends reunited."

It had only been a matter of time before he appeared. The voice was as gloating as Aelfhild had expected it would be. He would be enjoying this more than anything else in the world. This moment was surely what men like him lived for.

She turned toward Leofstan, who sat with his legs dangling over the edge of the aft platform. Beside her, Runild cowered, shielding Sola with her body.

"You three cost me two men back in that warehouse, I will have you know. I never expected the maid to be such a troublemaker," he said.

Ceolwen looked confused, and Leofstan explained.

"Look at her hands. See that stain? She stuck one of my boys but good with her little breadknife. And your man killed one, too, but that was more a fair fight. He is pulling an oar now to make up for that." He jerked a thumb over his shoulder.

So Bercthun yet lived; that was an increasingly uncommon kindness on the part of the Gods. They toyed with her dreams, they sent her battle-madness and made a killer of her, but they spared her friend. She almost felt remorse for hating them in the midst of battle.

"I can see in your eyes that you think me a bad one, young queen," Leofstan was saying to Ceolwen. Her expression was untempered venom. She looked ready to bite the man, given half a chance. The man on the other end of the stare did not appear concerned, though. He continued, "I did you a great favor. I gave you a gift worth more than the coins you gave me."

Aelfhild snorted.

"Gods' truth. Osric's man, he said the King wanted you *dealt with*, his words. But I hardly got to be the man you see before you," he gestured to the boat around them, basking in the depth of his achievement, "by passing up a chance to turn a profit. So I thought to myself, the Thrym do love highborn Earnfolding lasses like yourselves. They will pay me a fine bounty, and old Osric will be none the wiser. I was running a load north as it was, so it seems fate brought us together.

"Besides, the less the King knows about my affairs, the better, as I see it. So Osric's man took one last swim after we left port." From Leofstan's grin, Aelfhild assumed that this dip in the ocean had not been voluntary. "So I saved your life, rightly so. And you never know, I heard some of the Thrym treat their slaves quite…tenderly. If your life is not enough, I give you the gift of hope, too."

He laughed and stood stretching above them.

"Cause no trouble and you will have none from us. Be grateful things are not a fair sight worse. Bones line the bottom of these waters and you would be among them right now, if not for my giving nature."

Pointing at the two Thrym women, he said something in the northern tongue. The pair stood, each lifting a sack from behind them, and climbed up onto the fore platform.

Leofstan turned to Runild, who quailed under his stare.

"Well?" he asked.

The woman tucked Sola into a nest of hay scraped into the corner, then filled a bucket with water from a barrel tied to the lower section of the mast. She followed the Thrym women out of sight. Aelfhild and her mistress were alone again in the hold.

Ceolwen rested her head on Aelfhild's shoulder, and they sat hand in hand.

Aelfhild looked down at the blood that covered her sleeves and bound hands. In one day—one single morning—she had become a slave and a killer. It felt no different than before.

What she had expected, she did not know. Guilt, grief, or possibly even a sense of triumph over the evil men, but she felt none of that. She remembered only fragments. Most vivid was the feeling of impact, then sticky, burning hot blood on her hands. She had not even seen the face of the man she killed. But Ceolwen was alive, and Bercthun. And she had her own life, as Leofstan said. More time for the Gods to torment her, drive her mad. And the fool dared to call it a gift.

Night fell, cold and clear. Two of Leofstan's men climbed up from the ship's foreward section to furl the sail, speaking to each other in the language of Thrymgard. Sigfus was not the only Northman amongst the crew, as it turned out.

Aelfhild huddled together with Ceolwen, Runild, and Sola beneath a blanket big enough for only one of them. Neither Aelfhild or her mistress had eaten, and the chill left them both shivering.

A man dropped down into the hold from Leofstan's platform. There was a brand on his cheek, long since healed to a tarry hue still visible beneath his beard. Someone took offense to the man, Aelfhild thought. Maybe the Thrym burn their outlaws. Good.

The man's paunch covered a belt from which he drew a wide-bladed knife. Runild gasped and bent over her daughter, covering the girl's face. Aelfhild could do little but shift herself in front of Ceolwen with a clumsy hop. She glared up at the man as he approached.

He put a boot to Aelfhild's shoulder and pushed her aside without so much as a grunt. As she fell into the straw, Aelfhild could hear Runild whimpering beside her.

Ceolwen struggled as her feet were hoisted into the air, squealing beneath her gag. The slaver reached around the back of her head and fumbled with the knot of her bindings. As the cloth pulled away, Ceolwen spat in the man's face.

A swift backhand sent her sprawling into the hay beside Aelfhild.

"Stop!" shouted Leofstan from above. "Lay another hand on her and you lose it! Those two are worth more than all the rest. That goes for all of you—hands off!"

Then to the women, he said, "If you want to be rid of those ties, be still. But if you want to lose some fingers to the cold, go ahead and keep fighting."

The branded man cut off Ceolwen's ropes then freed Aelfhild of hers. As he worked, she got a better look at his face. It was blank, his eyes hollow and absent of any spark of light or life. There was no place where a laugh or a smile or a tear might linger, even briefly.

Aelfhild could not fathom the sort of stain slaving would leave on a soul, but she caught a glimpse in that man. She wanted to weep, if only to show him that one of them was still human.

He left as quietly as he had arrived, returning to what she could only imagine were nightmares of his own making. The thought sent chills down her spine. But he chose to serve with Leofstan and that was his to bear, not hers.

Ceolwen rubbed the life back into her legs and hands, and Aelfhild did the same. She spat to clear the grime from her mouth and winced at the pain from her raw lips.

"My lady Ceolwen, this is Runild and her daughter, Sola," she croaked her way through the introductions. "Runild, Sola, may I present to you the lady Ceolwen, Queen of Earnfold. I am her maidservant, Aelfhild."

Runild was as silent as her daughter, gaping at the two strangers.

She must think us mad. Aelfhild smiled.

"Good day, Runild. Hail, Sola," Ceolwen caressed the girl's face. "You can just call me Ceolwen. And I would trade being queen for just one sip of water."

1 4

"N O LOUNGING ABOUT today, my pretty ladies," shouted Leofstan, feigning what he must have assumed was a courtly bow. "Today you pull your weight!"

Aelfhild peered out from under the blanket she was sharing with the others. The slaver's breath hung in a white cloud on the frosty morning air. Her toes and fingers were numb, her neck and back contorted into unholy shapes by the hard floor and tiny blanket, and filthy straw coated her hair and face. A sack of something hard and lumpy hit her in the stomach as she hoisted herself up on creaking knees.

"Pick it up, girl, and get to feeding the foreward rowers. And silently, too," Leofstan ordered. He tossed a similar bag at Ceolwen's feet.

"And if you decide to try to swim for it, shore is that way," he said, pointing over the port side. "The water here is powerful cold, though, so you had better be quick about it."

With that, he stalked off.

Runild was already filling her water bucket, while Sola slumbered on in the warm space left by the others, pulling the blanket close. The Thrym women were moving, too.

Aelfhild glanced inside her sack. It was filled with knots of bread or some sort of tack, stale and rock-solid. Her empty stomach gurgled at even that pitiful sight.

She hoisted herself onto the fore platform and helped Aelfhild up.

Benches ran along both sides of the fore and aft platforms, with an aisle down the middle for the slavers to patrol. Men were chained, two to a bench, to metal hoops driven into the wooden deck.

Aelfhild saw ribs, scars, and welts through the tatters of the rowers' tunics as she handed out bread. The men did not look up but held a palm skyward and waited in silence for their meal.

Ceolwen followed behind and doled out some sort of jerky from her sack. Aelfhild saw the shine of tears in her mistress' eyes as they made their round.

Slavers watched over their ship from an alcove in the prow. They lounged, waiting for rations as well. Not all of them had the same dead eyes as the branded man; some of their eyes were much livelier and betrayed dark appetites.

But Leofstan's warning from the previous night apparently still held, and the slavers let Aelfhild and Ceolwen pass untouched. The leering brought out a cold sweat on Aelfhild's back, but the alternatives were far worse.

She hurried back to the platform's edge and dropped into the hold. She breathed deep, away from the stares.

Sola sat up beneath her blanket wearing a smile that gave no hint of being forced, and held out a palm.

Ceolwen dropped down beside them, toting her bag of what turned out to be dried fish. They all took a share of the rations, and saved out pieces for Runild and the Thrym women, who were returning.

Aelfhild was not sure how to tackle the bread. Her teeth could find no purchase on the stuff.

"Like this, lady," said Runild. She still seemed to think Aelfhild was a noble, even after learning her identity. Runild and Sola dunked their bread into the bowl of water, leaving a cloud of dust and debris behind but softening the morsel enough for chewing.

Aelfhild chewed. There was no flavor to speak of, either of the fish or the bread, but it was food and her belly was empty.

At the risk of agreeing with Leofstan, she thought, it could be worse.

Ceolwen tried striking up a conversation with Sola. "And how old are you, Sola?" she cooed.

The girl stared back without a word, chewing her fish. Her uneven stare with the one milky eye obviously unsettled Ceolwen, who coughed and looked away.

"She does not speak, your highness," Runild pulled her daughter close, kissing the top of the girl's head. "Not a word, I fear, begging your pardon."

"For how long?" Aelfhild asked.

"Forever, lady. Not since she was born."

"I am sorry," said Ceolwen.

For the first time, Aelfhild saw Runild bristle. The woman seemed to peek out of her shell, no longer cowed by royalty or by Leofstan, to defend her daughter. "There is nought wrong with her to be sorry for. The folk in our village feared her, too, with her eyes the way they are and her being so quiet. But my little girl is nought but good. She smiles and brings only joy to this world. More folk should do the same."

Ceolwen stammered, but Runild had already withdrawn back inside herself. The woman's eyes were cast back down toward her feet.

"She is beautiful," Ceolwen said, her gaze imploring Aelfhild to help.

Aelfhild saw a chance to learn something about their captors. "What village was that, Runild?"

"Wyrtun, lady. But it is no place that you would have heard of in Cynestead. Just a small village on the coast south of Haernmuth."

It would have been nice to say that she had indeed heard of Wyrtun, but that would have been a lie. There were countless such places in the kingdom, villages with a handful of families that fell and rose faster than maps could be made. Caelin might know about Wyrtun, since it lay within his lands in Ealdorscir, but that was as far as the name traveled.

The next question was delicate, and Aelfhild did not know how to phrase it.

"How…" she started, searching for the right words.

"They took a few of us while the men were in the fields. Three other women they took off in Haernmuth and sold, I suppose." Runild's voice betrayed no emotion, as though she were just rattling off facts that did not affect her. Her knuckles whitened around Sola's shoulder, though, and the little girl turned her smile up toward her mother. Runild smiled back but the lines around her eyes looked deeper.

"I am so sorry, Runild," said Ceolwen. "One day, I will be Queen, and I promise you I will make this right."

The woman only nodded. Aelfhild could not blame her. It was a ridiculous claim, even from where Aelfhild herself was sitting. And she believed that Ceolwen might still be Queen. She had to. But that Queen Ceolwen would save the poor folk of Wyrtun, or any other village like it? Some fantasies were not even worth countenancing. No King ever had or would take care of those men and women. They could only rely on themselves, and Runild had to know that by now.

Sola was back to her humming.

"What about the crew? The men on board?" Aelfhild asked. Answers were more useful than hollow promises at that moment. And maybe not just this moment, she mused.

"One or two from Oesca, a few from Thrymgard, but most Earnfolding. The slaves, too, I think they go up and down the coast taking them." Runild remembered herself after a pause. "Lady."

Aelfhild wanted to shout, "I am not a noble!" But Runild had been kind to her, and Sola was beside her, beaming, and they were all just barely clutching at sanity. And, even more irritating, Runild was right. There was a bigger difference between Runild and Aelfhild than between Aelfhild and her mistress.

"So they are taking us to Thrymgard, Aela," said Ceolwen. "We are not lost yet."

It felt wrong talking about that future in front of Runild. The same hope did not wait for the mother and daughter in the north. Instead, Aelfhild reached out and grasped the older woman's hand. She shook her head, hoping Ceolwen might take the hint.

All three sat in silence, waiting, while Sola hummed her nonsense songs.

15

THEY FELL INTO a new routine. At meal time, they carried food and water to the men; for the rest of the day they languished.

Sola was the only comfort. Unperturbed by her surroundings, the girl played in the hay, scampered through the nooks and crannies in the hold, and traced the flight of birds through their thin patch of sky with insistent enthusiasm.

Aelfhild had never much cared for children, but she tried her best to play along. Ceolwen was lost in her own royal thoughts, which she did not deign to share.

Sola's mother turned greyer by the day. The pain Runild must have been feeling, watching her child walk back and forth in the belly of a slave ship, was something Aelfhild could not begin to fathom. She tried not to judge, and always made sure to smile back at Sola, even when Leofstan was at his worst.

A week passed, or more—or less, it was hard to tell the days apart, but it felt a lifetime. Bursts of activity under the sordid stares of the slavers, punctuated by hours of silent, featureless boredom, stretched each day to torturous length. This morning, though, following mealtime, Leofstan broke the pattern.

"Run out the oars!" Aelfhild heard their captor's voice from the aft platform. "Time to row, you useless sons of whores! We have work to do!"

Wood scraped against wood as the oars were pushed out. So far they had gone mostly under sail and the slaves had been spared, but Leofstan sounded as though he had other plans. Men swung forward across the gap of the cargo hold, clutching ropes tied to the masthead. The slavers were preparing for something.

Ceolwen leaned close to Runild and asked, "What are they doing?"

"I do not know, your highness. Maybe we have come to Thrymgard and the selling place." It was the tone of resignation in Runild's voice that broke Aelfhild's heart. Fear or anger she would have understood, but the woman seemed to have simply surrendered.

At least fight for your daughter, she thought. At least be strong for her.

And what do you know of that? It was her own mother's voice in her ears once more, eager as ever to correct. *Nothing. Your life is a dream next to hers. You know nothing of her struggle.*

And that was true. Aelfhild sighed. Nothing was simple anymore.

"Hard ashore! Row now, bastards!" Leofstan shouted. "Ready in the fore!" His boney frame arced across the gap above them.

There was a grinding impact as the ship's keel hit sand. Everything in the boat pitched forward, and Aelfhild steadied herself against the hull.

"We ran aground," she said to Ceolwen. "Maybe we have a chance to get ashore now."

Sounds of splashing and shouting in both Thrym and Earnfolding carried back over the prow. Aelfhild went to the edge of the foreward platform and lifted herself above.

The deck listed at an angle as the keel settled into the wet sand below. Over one side Aelfhild could make out dunes running out into the distance, kissed by breaking waves. Smoke rose to the other side.

"I can see land. And all of Leofstan's men are gone. They must be raiding another village," Aelfhild whispered over her shoulder. "Come, lady, now is our chance!"

Someone tugged at her dress from behind. "Aela. Aela!" Ceolwen's voice was insistent. Aelfhild turned and saw Sigfus behind them. He stood atop the aft platform, in his hand a quarterstaff, notched at both ends. With his strength, it might as well have been a broadsword. Aelfhild swallowed hard and lowered herself back into the hold.

The giant did not speak, nor did he bother to frown or even shake his head. His presence was enough to tell them all that they needed to know. Any attempt to escape would be met with pain and plenty of it.

"Are you trying to get us killed?" Ceolwen hissed.

Cheeks burning, Aelfhild hung her head.

At least I tried, she thought.

The shouting drew closer to the boat again. Leofstan was returning.

"Get them aboard! These two to a bench, and get him down to the hold," the slaver shouted.

Two slavers lowered a body into the hold, a man with dark stains spreading across his tunic and breeches. Aelfhild recognized him as one of Leofstan's men, of the wandering-eyed variety, whose darker skin marked him as having Oescan forebears. Someone had sliced into his ribs, and deep from the look of it.

No less than he deserves. Aelfhild smirked.

"All oars, pull back! Get us back out to sea!" Leofstan was shouting. "Pull!"

He swung back to the rear platform, and spoke to Sigfus before turning to the women in the hold.

"Still with us, then? You have a new job, now. Some villager took an axe to one of my boys before we could finish our work, and now you can patch him up for me." He panted as he spoke, still winded from whatever exertions had taken place ashore. "It is your penance for thinking of escaping, girl."

Ceolwen stood, eyes blazing defiance. "And why should we help you, worm? You and your men can rot for all we care."

Aelfhild could have cheered. There is my Queen!

In the space of a heartbeat, Leofstan had dropped into the hold and driven a fist into Ceolwen's stomach. She dropped, doubled over in pain, and wretched up her meager breakfast onto the deck.

"No more games." Leofstan winced as he shook out his fist. "It is as simple as this; if my man lives, the little girl lives. If he dies, so does she. Get to work."

Aelfhild gasped, and Runild dissolved into tears.

Turning back toward his roost, the slaver kicked Ceolwen's inert form.

Reasoning, arguing, pleading would be of no avail; there was nothing to do but get to work. Aelfhild bent over the body and stared at the wound. At the edge of her vision she could see Sola's frail outline. The girl was as tranquil as ever.

Tears loomed on the horizon.

Do something. Do anything.

She shook her head to clear the haze and focused.

Blood bubbled from the gash in the man's side with each wheezing breath. His forehead was clammy to the touch, and his heartbeat faint. She tore a strip of cloth from her sleeve, and turned to Runild.

"Runild, fetch some water." The woman did not stir from her weeping, so Aelfhild shouted, "Runild, water, now!"

Ceolwen limped over and collapsed beside the body. "What can I do, Aela?"

"I do not even know what I can do. Tear some cloth for me; we can at least stem the bleeding."

Runild returned with a bucket, and Aelfhild rinsed the wound. Blood kept flowing, though, no matter how hard she pressed. The man gurgled in agony, eyes bulging. Panic was written bold across Runild's face, so Aelfhild kept yelling. There would be time for apologies later.

"Runild, hands here!"

Ceolwen handed over more torn pieces of dress, which they layered over the wound. Dripping tears, Runild shook visibly as she pushed with both arms against the compress.

"What else?" Ceolwen asked, staring at Aelfhild.

But Aelfhild could only shake her head. She knew nothing of this sort of thing. She had never been on a battlefield.

"Sniff it, maybe," her mistress suggested.

"What?"

"I heard one of the women say once that if a wound smells rotten, the man will die. If it smells clean, he will live. I think."

Aelfhild bent down and sniffed at the bandages. They stank like a midden, she flinched away, gagging.

Across from her, Ceolwen lowered her head.

No. Not like this. Not Sola. Aelfhild raged. She strode over to the aft platform and lifted herself up. Her hands left bloody prints on the deckboards. She spotted Bercthun chained to one of the benches, but he did not look up as she passed by. He looked alive, and that was all the worry she could spare for him.

Leofstan reclined in the stern near the rudder, Sigfus beside him. As Aelfhild approached, the towering Thrym spun and lashed out with his staff at neck level.

"No!" called his master. The end of the stick hovered in the air above Aelfhild's shoulder. "What?" the slaver asked.

"We need pitch and fire, or boiling water and herbs. Otherwise your man will die."

"You will get neither." Leofstan sounded perfectly at ease. His head lolled to one side as he spoke. "Surely you nobles learn all the healing arts in the King's court."

She could hear the sneer on the last two words. Even though he had them entirely under his power, he still envied them. Aelfhild fought back the urge to gag once more at his pettiness.

"Your men have lanterns, and you must have pitch for the boat. Give us some, or your man will die."

Her insistence seemed to ruffle his calm. He stood and strutted up to her until they were eye to eye.

"I could have Sigfus beat you again." His breath was foul on her face. "And not go as easy as last time."

"And your man would still die." She matched his gaze, mirroring the ice in his eyes with her own. Every sinew in her body vibrated, every nerve tingled. She knew her limbs were trembling, but took no pains to hide it. She had but one advantage—he had let slip that she, too, was valuable, not just her mistress. Her hope was that he valued his purse more than his pride.

He blinked, then called out to one of his men. "Take your lantern below and fetch a dollop of pitch from the bucket. The slaves need it."

"Remember my price, girl," he hissed. "Save him or I will kill her myself."

It was an idea born of desperation. Aelfhild thought that she might have once heard about such a process, maybe, but could not say where or when. But doing nothing was not an option.

One of the slavers had brought them a brick of sticky-hard pitch and an iron bowl for melting. Ceolwen held it over the lantern's flame, watching the black ooze spread across the dish's surface.

"Will this work, Aela?" she whispered, leaning close to her servant's ear.

Aelfhild shook her head. Leofstan watched from above, appearing genuinely curious, and she did not want him to see a moment's hesitation.

She put a hand on the wounded man's pale forehead. The skin was dry and burning hot.

"Hold his shoulders," she said to Runild.

With a wick of rolled cloth, she dabbed up some of the flowing pitch. Her fingers shook as the blood rushed through them. She took a deep breath.

As soon as the molten tar touched his skin, the man convulsed. Pink bubbles spumed from his mouth as he strained under Runild's grasp. Aelfhild tried to work fast, dabbing and smearing the pitch, layering it with bandages.

At last, she sat back, and exhaled. Runild sagged, and Ceolwen handed the pitch and lantern back to the waiting slaver.

Clucking to himself, Leofstan stepped back from his ledge and left them alone in the hold.

"Do you think that will save him?" asked Ceolwen.

"No." Aelfhild could not bring herself to even stretch the truth. "But he may live long enough for us to come up with another plan."

Runild gathered Sola into her arms. The girl had been watching birds while they worked. None of the strife on the ship seemed to touch her.

"I am sorry I yelled at you, Runild," Aelfhild said. She wiped the cold sweat from her brow with a sleeve.

"You were looking out for my little girl, lady," the woman responded. "The Gods will smile on you for that."

Perhaps the Gods could smile on us by crushing Leofstan where he stands. Aelfhild savored the image. That would make up for a great deal.

"I will kill him before he can lay a hand on her," she said instead. The words sprang out of her, unplanned and unbidden. Though she was not sure where the thought had come from, she was not ashamed.

Both women stared at her. Ceolwen looked surprised. Runild did not.

"I believe you, lady," Runild replied. There was not a hint of doubt in her voice.

1 6

"REDSAILS! REDSAILS TO the west!"

Aelfhild snorted as she rocked forward. Her vigil over the wounded man had lasted long into the night, but at some point she must have fallen asleep.

Men scampered overhead, swinging from platform to platform as they shouted.

Runild and Sola slept in their nook in the corner, and Ceolwen was bent over their patient. Aelfhild went to her.

Dark rings around Ceolwen's eyes hinted at her state. They had agreed to take shifts, but Aelfhild guessed she had been left to sleep longer than discussed.

"How is he?" she rasped.

Ceolwen sighed. "Feverish, still. His pulse is all but gone. Not long now, I think."

"What are they shouting about?" Aelfhild asked.

"I have not the faintest idea." Ceolwen shook her head. "I am too tired to listen. But something spooked them."

"Get some sleep, my lady," said Aelfhild, patting her mistress' hand, "I will see what is happening."

She braced her feet against the curve of the hull and lifted herself as far up as she could. Leofstan and his men were looking out over the port side of the ship, but Aelfhild could not see above the lip of the hold. The slavers looked to be sweating despite the chill of the morning.

And they seemed not to be paying any attention to her. Both were good things.

"Run out the oars! We need all speed!" she heard Leofstan call. She dropped down before he could spot her, as the wood of the oars scraped against oarlocks.

The noise had awakened Runild, who stared up bleary-eyed at Aelfhild. "What is that noise, lady?"

"The oars. We are running from something. I heard them say red sails, I suppose that means another ship."

Runild gasped. "Red sails means Thrym, lady!" She exclaimed. "Gods save us, we are doomed if those savages come for us. Our men back home say the raiders wear the ears of the folk they slaughter about their necks, and they eat the rest!"

Thrym. Aelfhild smiled at the thought. If it was a Thrym village Leofstan and his men had burned, that would certainly explain their instinct to run. The ear necklaces sounded fanciful, though she had to admit that seeing Leofstan's ears removed did hold a certain attraction. Maybe the peasants were right.

"But there are Thrym on the crew," Ceolwen said. With all the noise, she had not gotten back to sleep.

"They are beasts, not men. They kill each other as easy as breathing!" The fear in Runild's voice was infectious. Aelfhild started to consider what could go wrong.

They might think we were with the slavers. They might not care who we are. They might take Sola away.

Leofstan appeared at the edge of his platform. "You two, get him out of there and over the side," he waved some of his men down into the hold. "We need to shed all the weight we can."

Two of the slavers dropped down with rope, which they tied around the wounded man's shoulders. Aelfhild gaped as they used it to pull the limp form up onto the foreward platform.

"But he is one of theirs." Ceolwen sounded as stunned as she was.

Then there was a splash.

He was going to die anyway. And he was a slaver. Aelfhild tried to convince herself it was no better than the scum deserved, but struggled.

Sigfus lowered himself into the hold. Positioning herself in front of Sola, Aelfhild stood shoulder to shoulder with her mistress and Runild.

"You monsters will not touch her," she shouted.

But the big Thrym paid them no attention. He lifted crates and barrels from the hold, tossing some over the side and levering the heavier ones onto the platforms for others to dispose of. The women seemed to be forgotten.

The mast creaked under the strain of the sail, and the hull flexed in the waves. As the ship shed its weight, and the rowers pulled, the deck began to rise and fall sharply with each wave. Spray whipped over the prow and splattered down into the hold.

Aelfhild stood up again to spy on the slavers.

Leofstan stood at the rudder, whence he yelled at his men. They all threw terrified glances over the stern of the ship. Their fear felt like sunshine on a summer day, and Aelfhild basked in it. She was not quick enough, though, and he spotted her. Screaming abuse, the slaver kicked a nearby bucket toward her raised head. With an undignified squawk, she dropped into the hay, the bucket clattering down after.

Ceolwen and Runild watched her with wide eyes.

"I think we may be losing ground," Aelfhild answered their silent question.

The slavers had to yell over the sound of waves and the tortured groans of the ship's frame. A cargo ship was not built for this kind of use, and the wooden beams made their complaints known.

"If we row them any harder, they will not be able to fight!"

Aelfhild could hear the men shouting to one another above; they were talking about the slaves.

"If it comes to a fight we are all dead anyway! The only chance is that they get tired of chasing!"

"We will not get paid if the slaves all die!"

"If the redsails catch us, we will not get paid at all, fool!"

She could hear the occasional clatter of oars, as the rowers tired and lost rhythm. Leofstan had grown hoarse from shouting in the stern.

Ditching the cargo had opened up hiding spots under each platform. Runild and Sola crawled back into an opening between the beams, wrapping themselves in the blanket. Ceolwen and Aelfhild piled what little was left of the ship's supplies around the entrance to the hole. The raiders would have a hard time finding them, at least. The two Thrym women had the same idea, it seemed, and had disappeared from sight.

"We should get you hidden, too, lady," Aelfhild said to her mistress. "I want to watch, though, in case something happens."

"Aela, you have gone mad!" Ceolwen cried. "Just mad! All this talk of killing and battle, what can you do against armed men? Hide with me, you are not a warrior."

Aelfhild nodded. She did not want to argue. She helped Ceolwen find a spot to hide, but stayed close to the edge so she could see.

A slaver swung across the gap, shouting, "Arm yourselves! Hands to the starboard beam!"

She edged back out in to the light. Looking back and over the starboard side of the ship, she could see the top of another mast. A rectangular sail, crimson striped with gold, billowed in the breeze.

"Gangways! Push them back!" Leofstan shouted. There was screaming, both Earnfolding and Thrym. Aelfhild thought she heard prayers over the roaring waves.

Planks of wood, barbed at the ends with metal hooks, hovered in the air over the hull. The raiders were close.

Ceolwen pulled at her from behind. "Get back, Aela! Hide!"

She wanted to see. The boards drifted down, almost lazily, then shot back to dig their talons into the lip of the hull. The slaver's ship jerked in the water, listing violently.

Aelfhild saw the first man cross. The faceplate of his helmet hid everything above the mouth, which was opened in a roar. Arms daubed with dark warpaint hefted a battleaxe over his head. His wordless howl rent the air as he leapt aboard.

That was enough. Aelfhild ducked back under cover. The boards above them shuddered under heavy footfalls, clanking chains, and collapsing bodies. Ceolwen clutched at the back of her dress.

Two men came tumbling down into the hold in front of them. Sigfus and the raider she had just seen rolled overtop one another, punching and choking. The massive slaver had the advantage of size, and pinned his war-painted assailant to the deck.

I should help, Aelfhild thought. I should do something.

But she froze. Sweat beaded on her forehead and soaked her dress. She was rooted to the spot.

A ragged form dropped from the deck above into the fray, a man bound at wrists and ankles with chains. Bercthun lifted himself from the hay and sprang onto Sigfus' back, looping his manacles around the pulsing sinews of the giant's throat. The slaver reeled backwards, wheezing and clawing at the biting links.

At once the raider was on his feet and pulled a knife from his belt. Blade flashing in the sun, he stabbed over and over into his foe's exposed chest.

With a last, dribbling gasp, Sigfus toppled back overtop his former captive. The armored Northman leapt back up and into the fray.

Aelfhild ran out from her hiding spot to help Bercthun, Ceolwen at her heels. They shoved at the corpse crushing their friend, but Sigfus had grown no smaller since their last encounter.

She looked up to see Leofstan vault over the port side of the boat. There was a splash as he landed in the water below.

"Get back, Aela! Help me!" Ceolwen hissed, as Aelfhild lifted herself onto the foreward platform.

"I have to see," Aelfhild felt herself muttering. "I have to see."

Armored raiders lined the port side. One held a spear to his shoulder, training the point on the figure splashing in the waves.

The Thrym chanted and slapped their knees as he took aim, then let fly.

The first throw flew wide, missing by a few paces, much to the amusement of the other raiders. They whooped and jeered at their companion. To Aelfhild's surprise, the spearman threw back his head and barked laughter.

He called out, and the man to his left handed over another short spear.

The current was fighting Leofstan, and he seemed to be gaining no ground. His sodden clothes weighed him down in the water as well, and his strokes looked to be growing increasingly labored.

Shore was nowhere in sight, so he had been a dead man from the time he jumped off the boat. Looking at the raiders, Aelfhild corrected herself—he had been a dead man before that, too.

The spearman inhaled and let fly again. This time, the spear found its mark.

Any sound was drowned out by the waves and the groaning wood, but Aelfhild saw the spear shaft sprout from Leofstan's back. He went limp in the water, face down. She smiled.

"You deserved worse," she whispered.

The warriors howled. It was a bestial exaltation, putting Aelfhild in mind of the King's hounds baying at the moons.

It made her feel like prey.

She dropped back into the hold, where Ceolwen and Bercthun had managed to shift Sigfus' bulk.

Aelfhild put her back to her mistress, and Bercthun did the same. They all turned their eyes to the platforms above.

THE DARK-PAINTED NORTHMAN was the first one down into the hold. Faceplate and helmet still obscured most of his features, so he appeared an inhuman apparition, silver-faced and splattered with gore. He gave Sigfus' corpse a resounding kick before removing his mask.

Aelfhild blinked, worried her eyes had played a trick. She had been wrong about the warpaint; it was lines of white overtop his skin, which was dark as polished walnut. His hair was deep brown to match, a mass of curls. This was not the snow-skinned Thrym she had expected.

The battleaxe in his hands, still dripping blood, clashed with the broad smile on his face. Bercthun's shoulder pressed against Aelfhild's as they edged in front of their mistress.

Gesturing toward Bercthun, the raider spoke in the northern tongue. He sounded friendly enough, but the axe blade held Aelfhild's gaze.

Bercthun raised his palms and shook his head. "We want no trouble, friend, we are not your enemy," he said.

The Northman, or Southman, as it were—Aelfhild was still reeling—spread his wrists apart.

Broken chains, she thought, and said so to Bercthun. The young warrior spread his manacles against the hull. A mighty blow of the axe and his arms were free again.

"Jarngrim," their new friend pointed at himself. He repeated the word slowly and carefully for them, as though teaching an obstinate child her first words. "Jarngrim."

Bercthun introduced himself as well, and was pulled into a bearhug for his efforts. Aelfhild could hear his spine crackling beneath the embrace.

Jarngrim laughed as he thumped the young Earnfolding on the back, then threw back his head.

"Eyvind! Rolf!" he shouted.

Two new men appeared atop the aft platform. Aelfhild recognized the spearman who had slain Leofstan, taller and lean, beside a squat, grey-bearded companion. The tall man dropped down into the blood-spattered hay.

Rings of silver and iron jangled about his arms as he moved. Jarngrim only had one ring on each arm, these others both had a greater collection. It seemed a mark of rank amongst them.

Jarngrim and the spearman whispered briefly in Thrym before the newcomer removed his helmet and tossed it back to his waiting companion. Sweat had slicked down his short hair and stained a face that might once have been handsome, but it was hard to tell. A nose broken on more than one occasion and a scar from temple to jaw dominated the man's features. His skin was starkly pale next to Jarngrim's.

Shouldering Aelfhild and Bercthun aside, he grabbed Ceolwen's hand and ran his fingers across her palm. He pushed a knuckle under her chin to lift her head, examining her eyes and face.

Aelfhild's breath caught in her throat, and she could feel Bercthun's muscles tensing beside her. We traded one set of slavers for another, she thought. There was no escape, so she looked around for a weapon; Sigfus' staff had rolled into the hold during the fight, but Jarngrim stood overtop of it.

The man finally stepped back, releasing his grip on Ceolwen's arm.

"The others on this ship are poor fishermen and peasants," he began without preamble. His Earnfolding was accented but understandable, and his tone suggested that obedience was the wisest course. "You are not. Who are you?"

Ceolwen made as if to speak, but Bercthun broke in before she could say a word. "We are members of the king's court in Cynestead, taken captive by these curs in Haernmuth," he said.

Aelfhild nodded along. He bent the truth without breaking it, which was wise in dealing with these unknown men.

Bercthun continued, "We thank you for saving us, lord, and beg your mercy." He bowed his head, a gesture Aelfhild and Ceolwen imitated.

The tall man threw back his head, the barking laugh ringing out once more. "I am no lord. Eyvind, I am called, and you will have mercy only if you give me truth. Who are you? And who is she?" He pointed a finger sternly at Ceolwen, eyes hard. "And why would a slave fight armed men to save her?"

This Thrym is no fool, thought Aelfhild; he saw how we acted. We will have to tread carefully indeed.

Bercthun paused for a moment, doubtless mustering the right words.

But Ceolwen chose to speak for herself, squaring her shoulders and raising herself up to full height. She mustered all of the haughty force of her royal training, belied though it was by her unwashed face, knotted hair, and ragged clothing. "I am Ceolwen, daughter of Osred, King of Earnfold. These are my servants, Bercthun and Aelfhild," she nodded to either side. "We seek passage to Jarl Harald, my cousin, in Jarlstad."

There was silence in the hold.

Eyvind stared. Bercthun stared.

The words echoed, deafening, in Aelfhild's ears. She has rolled the dice, Aelfhild thought, but if she rolled them wrong, then the damn fool girl has killed us.

The other warriors awaited orders without hint of boredom. Jarngrim and Rolf stood poised, hands on weapons.

Then Eyvind spoke. "Then you go with me to Jarlstad, under my guard. You are not slaves, but you are not yet free. The Jarl will judge you." He spoke to his underlings in their native tongue.

Aelfhild let slip the breath she had been holding and looked to Ceolwen. Relief was writ large on her mistress' face. She, too, had been far from certain of the outcome of her little gambit, it seemed.

Jarngrim and Rolf lifted Ceolwen out of the hold. Bercthun's strength appeared to be flagging after his long ordeal, and his arms gave out as he attempted to help Aelfhild up.

She patted his shoulder and smiled. "You did well," she whispered.

Then she remembered—Sola and Runild. So much had happened, one thought had driven out the last. Crossing the hold, she called them out of their hiding place. Runild emerged with Sola in her arms, squinting against the glare and looking miserable.

"Leofstan is dead, Runild, we are saved!" Aelfhild cried, embracing the woman and daughter. "We are saved, Sola!"

Sola beamed right back, but her mother looked unconvinced. She stared at the raiders.

"More of you?" came Eyvind's voice from behind.

Aelfhild turned to face him. "The man you killed threatened to kill this little girl. They have been through more horrors than you can imagine. You must let them come with us."

The Thrym captain looked her up and down. "Must?"

The tone of that one word reined in Aelfhild's galloping spirits. His cocked eyebrow hinted at jest, but there was a note of challenge in the voice as if to say, *push it further, and see what happens.*

Ceolwen stared down from above, eyes wide with disbelief.

Swallowing hard, Aelfhild lowered her eyes. She had grown too bold, forgotten to keep her head down and voice low. "If it please you, master," she said. "They deserve fair treatment."

Eyvind snorted. It might have been a trick of the scar along his cheek, but Aelfhild thought—or hoped—that she detected the ghost of a smile. "They are under my guard, this I say to you. This boat is also going to Jarlstad, and they go with it."

She took Runild's hand in hers. "I will see you in Jarlstad, I promise. But I must go with my mistress."

Runild squeezed back and at long last smiled. "The Gods love you for all you have done, lady. We will remember you."

Aelfhild swept Sola up in a hug. The girl grabbed her hand as they parted and kissed the palm. It was an odd gesture, but Sola was an odd child. "Farewell, Sola. I will see you again, I promise," she said, then turned to join Ceolwen and Bercthun.

Her heart sang and her steps felt light, as though she might drift away in the breeze. Leofstan would never know it, and had never meant it as more than a cruel jest, but he had given her a gift. With his death, her hope returned, hope that there was some justice in the world, however small, and that the Gods had more in store for her than murk and madness.

Humming one of Sola's tunes, she vaulted onto the upper deck.

1 8

EYVIND'S MEN WERE hard at work making the slave ship sailable once more. The boards of the deck were sticky with rust-brown blood, the oars were scattered, the sails a tangle of loose ropes and billowing cloth. Some of the raiders carried barrels and sacks across the gangways from the longship, replacing supplies ditched during the pursuit—Eyvind had said that they would take the slave ship to Jarlstad, so the warriors and slaves needed fresh provisions for the journey.

Aelfhild got her first look at the longship as they crossed the deck. The sleek, overlapping boards of the hull lent the ship a predatory air alongside the squat bulges of the cargo hauler, an impression deepened by the contorted wyrm-head carvings at the prow and stern.

Bracing his booted foot against the corpse's shoulder, one of the Thrym removed his axe from the ribs of a former slaver. The damp sucking noise as blade parted flesh made Aelfhild wretch into her mouth.

More bodies disappeared over the side of the ship, splashing in the sea below.

The Northmen laughed and called to one another as they worked. Most had removed their helmets, revealing close-cropped hair and beards layered in plaits and braids. Aelfhild could not understand the words of their merry cries, but needed no translation—it was the trifling nonsense of those too proud to show relief that they had survived a battle. Men were men, all the world over, and she had not yet met one that would gladly admit to fearing anything.

The slaves were no longer in chains but still on their benches. The two Thrym women who had shared the cargo hold with Aelfhild and Ceolwen were back to carrying water and food to the rowers, but Aelfhild could see a light in their eyes that had been absent before.

"What will happen to them?" she asked of no one in particular.

Rolf gave no indication he had heard; he did not seem much of a talker. Jarngrim spoke no Earnfolding and just shook his head.

"They will work. Some will earn their way back home." It was a woman's voice, and came from what Aelfhild had at first glance taken to be a man.

"Built for breeding" was a term Aelfhild had once heard a midwife use, and it sprang to mind. The woman was no taller than Aelfhild herself, but broad shouldered and with hips to match. Her arms, poking out from beneath her leather jerkin, were knotty as aged oak. Short hair, combined with that silhouette, had tricked Aelfhild's eyes into believing they saw a beardless man.

Jarngrim shepherded Aelfhild along to the stern before she could ask any more questions, but she stole a look back over her shoulder. The female raider was tossing another corpse over the side with the assistance of one of her fellows.

Necklaces of ears would have been less surprising, she thought, though so far there were none to be seen. But the Thrym let their women raid? And Jarngrim? In Earnfold, skin that dark would have had peasants fleeing in the street ahead of him. And woman warriors, well, that was only heard of in the wildest tales.

They came to the foot of the aft gangway. Aelfhild peered over the edge and regretted it. Foam crested on the waves between the hulls.

The two ships were fastened together with ropes now, as well as the boards, carried over by the Thrym. The vessels rode at different heights in the water, rendering the gangways sloped and uneven. Spray from the waves below added a layer of slick seawater. Both boats pitched and rolled in the current.

"No," said Ceolwen, leaning back after inspecting the path across. "No."

Aelfhild agreed. She stepped away from the churning gulf, shaking her head. Her feet were unsteady enough on the broad deckboards.

Rolf's brow furrowed as he watched them each balk. His patience seemed to be of equal measure to his chattiness. He waved at them to cross.

Jarngrim laughed and led the way. Stepping out onto the plank, steady and sure-footed, he turned around and directed an encouraging grin their way. The madman even shifted from one foot to another, doing a jig over the roaring water. Ceolwen shuffled forward, and took Jarngrim's extended hand.

"Slowly," she shouted over the waves, "Slowly, slowly." Then she squawked, windmilling her free arm as the raider dragged her bodily across the gangway and into the longship. Jarngrim received a royal slap across the face for his troubles as Ceolwen steadied herself on the deck. The gathered Thrym were weak with laughter by this point.

Bercthun made his way across unaided, drawing a round of cheers and hoots from the Northmen.

Then it was Aelfhild's turn. Some mad pride reared its head within her, and she waved away Jarngrim's offer of help.

You can do this, she told herself. You can do this.

Both her feet were on the board, and she shuffled forward. The wood bowed beneath her weight, and her stomach dropped with it.

No, you cannot.

The ships hit a deep trough between the waves, and the plank pitched sideways. She lurched forward, diving toward the longship. The landing would not be graceful, and she knew it. Bercthun threw his arms around her as her shoulder rammed his chest. They both dropped onto the deck.

Cheering carried over the waves from the other ship.

Bercthun brushed himself off and offered her a hand up.

"No, thank you," she replied, "I think I will just rest here for a moment." The burning in her cheeks was slow to fade. From her perch, she could see that the deck of the longship was covered with boxes and barrels. Where the slave ship had benches, the raider's ship had wooden chests arranged in rows up and down both sides. Supplies were piled around the central masts, which rose to the glorious red sails.

Aelfhild stared up, admiring the color. The cloth was tatty and weather-stained around the edges, faded and patched in some spots, but she had never seen a hue so beautiful in the bright sunlight. It was the color of a future free of chains.

After they had finished whatever work was left to do on the other ship, Eyvind and Rolf crossed over along with the warrior woman. Ropes were tossed back, the gangways lifted, and soon the two ships were drifting apart. Eyvind took his place at the steering oar in the stern, Rolf beside him. The rest of the crew tied off the sail and stowed loose ropes and boards.

Jarngrim led the Earnfoldings along to the ship's midsection in the shade of the billowing sail. He produced wooden cups from a nearby chest, and filled them from a barrel near the mast. Offering one to Bercthun first, he raised his own cup in a toast.

"He wants to thank you for saving his life," said the female raider. She wiped seawater from her hair and face with a cloth, leaving streaks of blood and paint behind. "Never let it be said that the Thrym are not grateful! I am Kolbrun. The others you know, I think. Maybe not Geir." She pointed toward the prow, and the outline of another man against the bright sky.

Ceolwen bowed. "Fine meeting, Kolbrun. I am Ceolwen, these are my servants Aelfhild and Bercthun. You speak very good Earnfolding, I must say."

"My father is of Earnfold, my mother's side is Thrym. Servants, you said?" She grunted. Kolbrun did not sound impressed.

Aelfhild was dumbstruck. She had never admired or envied any person in her life more than she did Kolbrun in that moment. The axe in the woman's belt, the warpaint smeared across her cheeks, the iron bands around her wrist. Here was a woman that no one could put in chains. Her voice came out a reedy squeak at first, and she cleared her throat. "I did not know the Thrym allowed their women to be warriors," she said.

Kolbrun seemed to consider this for a moment. "They do not." She walked off to the prow, carrying a drink to Geir who stood watching over the horizon.

Aelfhild and Ceolwen looked at one another. Ceolwen whistled softly and said, "I am glad she is on our side."

It was beer in the barrel; Aelfhild could smell it in her cup. She took a gulp, savoring the flavor. Jarngrim was still toasting Bercthun, who looked ready to collapse. So did Ceolwen, for that matter.

Kolbrun returned with food. It was bread and dried fish—no better than their previous meals, but it was something. They sat in a circle, gnawing away.

"That old *knarr* will take another week to get to Jarlstad at this pace. Even with a skilled captain, that old bucket is too fat for the waves," Kolbrun looked over her shoulder to the dwindling speck of the slave ship.

"Knarr?" Aelfhild asked.

"That boat was a knarr, for hauling goods. This is a *karvi*, for quick sailing and fighting."

"We are certainly glad you came to our aid," said Ceolwen. "How did you find us?"

"We left from Fornhofn a week ago, then saw the smoke down the south coast. Geir has eyes keen as a vulture and spotted your sails."

Something else had been gnawing at Aelfhild. "You said the slaves would be put to work in Jarlstad. Why will you not free them?"

Kolbrun stared back as though she thought Aelfhild might be simpleminded. "They are slaves." Her tone suggested that was all the explanation needed, but she continued. "They must work to buy back their freedom. That is the way of things."

No one argued, but Aelfhild brooded over the answer in silence. It was ill luck that had put her amongst those people, not her own failure. And it was nothing of her own doing that had plucked her from amongst them, but another twist of fortune. There was no virtue in keeping Sola and Runild in thralldom. But there were slaves in all the realms, north and south, and always had been. There were slaves in Cynestead, and Aelfhild knew some of them. It had never troubled her before today, just as it did not trouble Kolbrun now. It was a fact of the world.

Until you are in it, she thought.

She looked back at Eyvind at the steering oar. The man was deep in conversation with Rolf. What sort of plans they made, Aelfhild could not tell from their eyes. Rolf listened and nodded along.

Not yet free, Eyvind had said.

Aelfhild swallowed another lump of dry bread.

We may not be out of it yet.

1 9

THE WEATHER IN Thrymgard was fickle. Warm sun changed in a moment to pounding hail, then clear sky again just as quickly. The wind never slackened, and the clouds whipped across the sky above.

Ceolwen and Bercthun snored beneath sealskin wrappings. Not even the hail could rouse them from their exhausted torpor.

The Thrym showed off for their new passengers, or at least for the one that was awake. They displayed their prowess with a game played atop the oarlocks. Geir came back to join Jarngrim on the railing, where they jousted back and forth with the blunt end of boathooks. The goal seemed to be to knock the opponent off balance and onto the deck below.

Geir had the flushed cheeks and ample gut of a man who enjoyed more than the occasional horn of mead, and Aelfhild guessed that he and Cuthbert would have gotten on famously. But he was no less sure-footed than his compatriots, and his bulk made him hard to shift. Aelfhild applauded as Jarngrim fell to the deck. She had never cared much for such sport, but she thought it best to be polite. Kolbrun hopped up next and swiftly deposed Geir from his perch.

"Eyvind, you next," she cried, dangling from the rigging.

Aelfhild turned to find the captain standing behind her.

"Not now, *skjaldmaer*," he said, and sat between Aelfhild and her mistress' slumbering form. "Shield-maiden is what we call her, like in the old stories," he said, answering Aelfhild's unspoken question.

And there were such stories; she had heard them. Women rising up to protect the farms when men were at war, and even sometimes going raiding themselves.

Eyvind cleared his throat. "I have questions."

Aelfhild shifted beneath her blanket. The man's stare could bore through metal. "I can wake my lady Ceolwen, master, if you wish, but she is tired from the ordeal."

Eyvind shook his head. "Let her sleep. I will ask you."

Obeying some silent signal, Kolbrun and Geir departed for the prow, and Jarngrim for the stern. Suddenly, Aelfhild was very much alone.

"She is the daughter of King Osred?" Eyvind gestured to Ceolwen.

"She is."

"And you are her servant?"

"I am, master. My whole life."

He mulled that over. "Tell me how a servant came to be so far from home, then."

The sun was kissing the western horizon by the time she finished. Lines of vibrant pink and orange danced over the remaining clouds. Eyvind was silent for a time. His fingers played with the braids woven into his beard. He had broken in to ask questions once or twice, but for the most part let the words flow past.

"Some might not believe such a tale," he said.

"Do you?" Aelfhild snapped. She grew tired of the mystery. Eyvind seemed to be trying hard to be inscrutable, and it grated on her. Games were not something she had the patience for, not after the past week.

He chuckled. "Yes," he said. "Forgive me, I am not much good at chattering."

His Earnfolding was not wrong, but the phrases were awkward enough from time to time to remind Aelfhild that she was not speaking to a native. She softened somewhat. Perhaps she had mistaken awkwardness for manipulation. The man was difficult to read either way.

"I know Eorl Cuthbert," Eyvind continued, "I am of Trollsmork and those lands border his. He is a good man. Friends of his are worth trusting."

"Where in Trollsmork are you from?"

"Herjarsborg. Do you know it?"

She shook her head.

"It is a grand town, but does not have the sea," he said. "My father loves the trees and the forest there, but for me it is the sea. Wide, open sea." His outstretched arm swept an arc along the horizon.

"Open and free," she said. He nodded agreement, so she continued. "Free, just what you said we are not."

Eyvind paused in mid-nod and grunted. "Clever for a servant." Whether he meant that as a compliment was left unclear. "You must wait for when we come to Jarlstad."

"When will we reach Jarlstad, then?" Aelfhild asked. "My lady must see the Jarl."

"Two days with a fair wind. You have some luck, the Jarls will all be at the *Landsthing*. You can argue before them."

"Will they listen?"

Eyvind shrugged.

"You serve the Jarls?" she asked.

He nodded. "We are all sworn to Harald, Jarl of Trollsmork. I am a *huskarl*, as is Rolf, the others are *drengir*, like your man Bercthun."

She motioned to the bangles on his arms. Up close she could see each one was carved with interweaving knotwork patterns, and one of the silver bands was wrought in the likeness of a serpent eating its own tail. "Those are from your Jarl?"

"Oath-rings," he replied. "For battles we win, foes we slay."

"You must have fought many battles."

He shrugged again. It seemed to be his favorite gesture. They fell silent. The other Thrym were turning in for the night, settling down into piles of skins and furs. Rolf kept his silent watch from the stern.

Chill evening breeze tugged at the sail, the flutter of fabric and rhythmic wash of the waves a lullaby to the drowsy. Aelfhild's eyelids felt heavy over her dry eyes. And as abruptly as it had begun, the conversation was over. Eyvind stood, stretching his back, and sniffed the air.

"Storms tomorrow, I think. Sleep now, while you can."

2 0

IND TORE AT the sail and whipped up spray from the rolling sea. The morning sun hid behind clouds bruised blue and black, pregnant with rain. Drops had not started falling yet, but the grey line along the horizon pressing steadily inwards suggested the downpour was on its way.

Aelfhild had not found much sleep after Eyvind's warning. The breeze had grown steadily overnight into a gale, and the swells grew more frenzied by the hour. She sat beside her mistress, whose head hung over the railing.

"No more boats, Aela," Ceolwen moaned as Aelfhild patted her heaving back.

The Thrym had raised a cloth awning around the mast, giving some shelter against the rain and frothing waves. Kolbrun stood in the center, fussing with the ropes that bound cloth to mast.

"How much longer?" called Aelfhild over the din.

"Not long." The shield-maiden offered a toothy grin. "Just a passing squall!"

"If this is a squall, I do not want to see a storm," muttered Bercthun. His face was a pallid grey, but he had so far managed to hold on to his last meal. Aelfhild had too, though she was not eager to even see food anytime soon. Ceolwen had not fared so well.

The rain arrived, a single and unbroken wall of water. Looking back toward the stern Aelfhild could see Eyvind at the steering oar. Both he and Rolf looked bored beneath their dripping sealskins, so she tried her best not to jump whenever the boards creaked beneath them. The waters of the North Sea were famous for claiming the lives of unwary sailors, even in Earnfold. She tried not to think of the words *leak* or *sink* or *founder*.

Kolbrun tossed buckets over toward Aelfhild and Bercthun. The Thrym were already bailing rainwater from the sloshing deck, and the Earnfoldings joined in. It was a task well-suited to divert the mind from seasickness and contemplation of watery graves.

Somewhere toward noon—the sun still eluded them—the wind and waves began to ease. Rain slowed to a drizzling mist, and the Thrym ran up the sail again. Ceolwen flopped down onto the deck. "When I am Queen, there will be no more boats."

"We hear and obey, lady," Aelfhild replied with a grin as she returned another bucket of water to the sea.

Ceolwen kicked out at her servant in feigned irritation, but cracked a smile. She shouted back to Eyvind, "Land! I want to stand on solid ground once more!"

"Storm knocked us too far east," Eyvind answered. Beads of water cascaded from his beard as he spoke. "We could not come to land today with offshore wind. Unless you want to row for us."

Geir called out in the northern tongue from the prow. The Thrym rushed to the starboard railing, all peering into the distance. Aelfhild followed their stares.

In the distant rolling grey was another ship. It looked to be a longship of similar build but under dark sails, rendered black by the dim light. The sight had soured the mood aboard their vessel.

"What is it?" Ceolwen whispered.

Aelfhild shivered. "More raiders?"

"Ulfings," Eyvind answered. He had left Rolf at the steering oar, and come up for a better view. "Ulfings are one of the *Aettir*. We are all Thrym, but there are many Aettir. On this boat, we are all Leifings, and we feud with the Ulfings."

"Why?" asked Aelfhild.

Eyvind shrugged, the familiar motion. "An Ulfing stole a Leifing's daughter, or a Leifing burned an Ulfing's farm, who remembers? The Aettir fight, it is the way. They burn a hall, we take a ship. We fight because they fight, they fight because we do," he said, tracing a circle in the air with his fingers.

From behind, Rolf growled. It was the first utterance Aelfhild had heard from him. Eyvind looked over his shoulder and chuckled.

"My friend thinks I am not enough true to my people. Then we feud because Ulfings are traitor scum!" He thumped his chest with a fist.

Aelfhild had expected a more poetic answer; she loved the grand old tales of maidens trapped in rings of flame and songs of wyrms atop mounds of stolen gold, and had since childhood. This seemed petty. There was no heroic fire burning in Eyvind's eyes as he spoke, no storied grudge or ancient betrayal. He explained their fighting in the same calm and measured tones one might use to tell a child of the movement of the tides or the flowering of trees in spring. It was a fact of nature, inevitable and eternal.

"Will they chase after us?" Bercthun asked.

At least he has more pragmatic concerns, Aelfhild chided herself. Stories can wait.

Eyvind took longer to answer than was comfortable. He chewed at his bottom lip.

"Not before the Landsthing," Kolbrun said from the prow. "Even they would not dare break the truce."

The Thrym argued back and forth in their mother tongue, never taking their eyes from the outline of the other vessel.

"If they drift closer and want a fight, we put our spears in them." Eyvind concluded the conversation. "But we do not seek one out." This seemed pointed at Geir, who sounded eager for more axe-work.

Jarngrim lifted bundles of short throwing spears, rolled in sealskin against the damp, from a pile by the mast and tossed them fore and aft. All eyes tracked the other ship, though wisps of rain often obscured it from view.

"They go to this Landsthing as well?" Ceolwen asked, rolling the foreign word over in her mouth.

Kolbrun grunted. The shield-maiden sat atop a wooden chest, spear across her knees. "All the Aettir. Leifings, Ulfings, Skjoldungs, Eldings, and all the thanes from the far villages. There is always a peace before the council, but…"

But you never trust your enemy to fight by the rules. Aelfhild had learned that from Osric. Customs and laws and honor only held as long as they were convenient. And it was always the other side's fault when they were broken. She wondered how Osric had twisted the story to put the blame on Ceolwen or Cuthbert. He likely had the other Eorls eating from his palm by now. The thought made her grimace.

The Ulfings remained a shadow in the mist. Aelfhild imagined fell warriors lining the deck of the dark ship, gripping spears of their own. Perhaps these were the ones that took ears as trophies. They were ghostly quiet.

"Enough waiting," Eyvind snorted. "We row!"

He called to his warriors in the Northern tongue and they ran out the oars. Bercthun joined in, taking a place atop a sea chest, while Aelfhild and Ceolwen looked on from the prow.

Eyvind rowed them hard into the night. If the Ulfings gave chase, it was impossible to spot them in the murk.

The sun rose clear and bright behind the longship, casting its light over the Hlifseyjar to the north and west. After a short rest in the night, Eyvind had his crew rowing again.

"Heave!" Rolf shouted from his oar.

The Ulfing ship was still astern, distant but not yet out of sight. Grey sails billowed in the morning breeze as the pursuers raced to close the gap. Her knowledge of the Thrym tongue was shaky at best, but Aelfhild was sure Eyvind had shouted something about beating the Ulfings to Jarlstad that morning.

"Heave!" That, at least, was one Thrym word she now had etched in memory.

The captain's exhortation worked, and the Thrym set a blistering pace with their rowing. Aelfhild smiled to see Bercthun keeping pace. At least one of them was contributing.

"Heave!"

Meanwhile, she stood beside Ceolwen in the prow, fidgeting as others toiled. Her mistress seemed content to sightsee, but Aelfhild felt ill at ease when others did the work for her. She consoled herself with the thought that from her perch she could take Geir's place and keep watch for any oncoming dangers, which was a job in itself.

"Heave!'

Outcroppings of volcanic stone jutted from the sparkling waters all along the ship's starboard side, some towering in twisted, wave-carved spirals, others no more than a pile of boulders dotted with sun-bathing seals. Jarlstad was the largest of a handful of skerries and islets that made up the Hlifseyjar, the northwestern arc of the island chain encircling the great bay of Thrymgard.

Kolbrun had hardly even broken a sweat from the rowing, and as they cut through the waves she told the Earnfoldings how in distant years, before humans had settled so far east, a great volcano rose from the sea there; in its fiery dying throes, the mountain rent itself asunder, leaving behind a deep harbor protected on the east and west by wide arms of land. The northern slopes of the volcano remained, rising to a high peak bounded with sheer cliffs overlooking the port.

The Northmen had settled there long ago, carving a great fortress into the cliffs: the Klettirborg, where the Jarls gathered for their councils. That was the peak they could see, Kolbrun said.

As the ship drew nearer to land, gulls, gannets, and terns swooped down to check the ship's wake for discarded fish. The birds floated on the headwind, screaming at one another as they jockeyed for position.

Jarlstad dominated the horizon, its arms thrown wide to receive visitors. Aelfhild could see other ships to the south and west, a fleet of sails dyed every conceivable hue and all headed to the same place.

Eyvind swung the ship northwards into the mouth of the harbor. Fires burned in guard towers on either side of the channel, where lookouts stood at the ready.

Aelfhild clapped her hands to her ears as Eyvind raised a brass-bound horn to his lips and let loose two echoing peals. One of the watchers returned a single, sustained note, and the ship passed through the opening unhindered. She noticed a chain stretching from tower to tower, slack and mostly hidden beneath the water. Each of the iron links looked to be roughly the size of her head, and she guessed that it would keep out most any unwanted guest. The razor-sharp fields of lava rock above the beach would take care of any other intruders.

"The Thrym must not be scared of heights," Ceolwen muttered as she gazed upwards.

The city rose in layers up the side of the ancient volcano, one terrace stacked upon another and each teeming with shingled roofs. Thatched huts and ramshackle towers edged out onto platforms chiseled into the cliff face. Firelight flickered within the caves that dotted the ridge. Every crevice and ledge, no matter how precarious, sported some sort of shed or tent.

Flocks of seabirds nested in the jagged nooks and crannies of the cliff, many of them far below human houses. Long streaks of white on the red-black rock were testament to the birds' long habitation. Aelfhild noticed that the Thrym took care to close their mouths when looking up, and the stains above them hinted at the reason.

The docks of Jarlstad were a more familiar sight than the dizzying cliff dwellings, and put Aelfhild in mind of Haernmuth. The piers were abustle with life, other ships unloading cargo, and throngs of passengers who formed a column leading uphill and into the city.

Red-clad dockworkers met their ship as Eyvind guided them into an open berth. They tossed ropes down to Geir and Jarngrim, shouting back and forth in Thrym.

"So many people," Aelfhild said to Kolbrun. "Are they all here to see the Jarls?"

The shield-maiden shook her head as she sorted through cargo and tossed sacks onto the dock. "Only a few come for that. The Jarls only judge a few matters at a time. Most are here to sell and trade. Some are just here to celebrate—the Landsthing only happens three times a year."

There was a dog baying nearby, a sizable one if Aelfhild's ears served her, and the frantic howls seemed to be drawing closer. A mottled muzzle sailed over the edge of the pier, storm cloud grey and full of gnashing teeth. Golden eyes flashed from beneath dark stripes. Aelfhild reeled backwards as what looked to be a fully grown she-wolf came careening down into the hold beside her.

"Embla!" Eyvind called out. The beast bolted toward him, yipping and waggling its looped tail. The Northman bent down and allowed his face to be bathed by the exuberant, drool-laden tongue.

"Yes, play with that thrice-damned pup while *we* do the work." Kolbrun shouted as she shouldered a sloshing barrel up onto the pier. Eyvind flashed a grin Kolbrun's way as he rolled about on the deck with the dog; it was hard to tell who was happier to see whom.

Eventually Embla made the rounds to greet the rest of the crew, snuffling and pawing at Rolf, Geir, Jarngrim, and, finally, Kolbrun. Despite her tough talk, the shield-maiden bent low to cuddle the dog, clucking and making sweet nonsense sounds.

"Who is shirking now?" asked Eyvind as he brushed past, lifting himself up onto the pier with a bundle of weapons and armor in tow. He gestured for Ceolwen to follow, and Aelfhild and Bercthun came up in her wake.

Waiting for them on the docks was a Thrym noblewoman. She was the first of the northerners that Aelfhild had seen who had that air of brittle elegance so familiar from the court in Cynestead that suggested the very idea of dirt was offensive. She was tall and imposingly fair beneath her ruddy brown trestles. Something in her face, buried beneath the noble bearing, tugged at Aelfhild's memory.

Eyvind went to embrace the woman, and the resemblance clicked. They could only be siblings—twins even—so close was the resemblance. The man's flattened nose, scars, and flowing beard could not hide the identical eyes and cheekbones.

Aelfhild stood behind her mistress, waiting to be introduced. Someone had lifted Embla back out of the ship and the hound circled Aelfhild's legs, pushing a cold, damp nose into her palm. She stood stock still, worried that an untoward move might result in loss of limb.

Eyvind was speaking. "Eyrun, this is Ceolwen, Bercthun, and Aelfhild." He gestured to each in turn. "Our guests from Earnfold. This is Eyrun, my sister."

Eyrun bowed and smiled, greeting them in the northern tongue. After a brief exchange with her brother, she took charge of them.

"Please come with me, my brother has work to attend to." Eyrun's Earnfolding was as crisp and tidy as her spotless dress. She wrinkled her nose as she moved past the Earnfoldings, but made no comment—Aelfhild had not paid it much thought, but they all most likely stank to the heavens. They had been tossed about on the high seas for days without washing; sweating and lying in dirty hay, wrapping themselves in wet furs and seal skins.

No one on the longship had seemed bothered, as they were mostly in a similar state; but here, amongst washed company, their odor did stand out.

THEY FOLLOWED EYRUN through the docks and up into the city. Aelfhild breathed deep the smells of civilization, and relished the feeling of ground that did not pitch from side to side. Kolbrun and Geir followed behind the party, shields and studded jerkins thrown over their shoulders, axes hanging in loops at their belts.

"Not slaves, but not yet free," Aelfhild recalled Eyvind's words on the ship. It seemed they would be under guard, probably as much for their own protection as for the people of Jarlstad. The docks thronged with warriors carrying every manner of weapon from spear to billhook, shields slung across their backs, all making their way up into the walls of the town proper.

Jarlstad reminded Aelfhild of Cynestead, but as though her native city had been tipped on its side. Where Cynestead sprawled across the lakeshore, Jarlstad soared skywards. Narrow streets, a few covered in wooden planks but most of them mud and gravel, wove in between terraces of straw-roofed roundhouses, stables, lean-tos, and pens.

The town's outer wall was a flimsy palisade, made more to keep cows and pigs inside than any intruders out. As they went further up the hill, though, the walls turned to fitted red stone, the longhouses opened onto courtyards with sweeping views, and the press of people and livestock began to thin.

They wended up through a few levels of the city, passing by several courtyards set with wide rings of evenly spaced stones. Great halls with gilded doorways and glistening fresh coats of paint rose on either side of their path. In the center of one square stood a towering edifice, reed-covered roof split into multiple inset levels, engraved and ornamented beams stretching down from the eaves. Carvings of serpents, horses, wolves, and bears intertwined along the sides, filigreed with silver and gold, and wide arched doors were thrown open to reveal a murky interior, within which Aelfhild could just barely make out tall standing stones etched with countless lines. It was as grand a building as she had ever seen.

All three Earnfoldings stopped to stare. Kolbrun bumped into Aelfhild's back.

"What is that place?" Aelfhild whispered.

The shield-maiden shepherded them on without a word.

Eyrun led them into a vaulted hall where servants were busy at work preparing some sort of feast. She led them past a wide stone hearth, where fat crackled and sparked in the fire beneath spits heavy with game. Aelfhild licked her lips. The smell alone was more sustaining than a year's worth of dried fish.

Their guide waved them through into a curtained area in the rear of the hall.

Geir tapped Bercthun's shoulder, motioning for him to follow, and the two men set off in a different direction.

Eyrun found her guests new clothes to replace the tattered rags they had on, and then called in servants with buckets of warm water. "Enjoy, please," Eyrun said, closing the curtain behind her as she went back out in the hall.

And they did. Aelfhild did not think of herself as particularly fastidious—she bathed enough to stay presentable, but not so much as to upset the natural humors. The older women in the kitchens back home had always cautioned against excessive washing. But the steaming water felt divine, and she scrubbed until her skin was raw pink. She could hear Ceolwen's contented sighs from across the room.

Kolbrun splashed water on her hands and face, but seemed content to retain a layer of grime. Maybe it is a warrior tradition, Aelfhild mused as she wrung out her towel.

Eyrun returned with combs, intricate things carved of some sort of bone and inset with gems, to work the tangles out of their hair. A few of the worst ones had to be cut free with Kolbrun's beltknife.

They were given dresses made in the Thrym style: a woolen robe under a flowing rectangular overdress that fastened with copper brooches at the shoulder, cinched with a broad belt at the waist. Most of the women they had seen in the streets, including Eyrun, wore a similar garment. Pins and other ornaments, like earrings or bracelets, seemed to vary according to station and wealth, but the dresses were quite similar throughout the city.

The men wore tunics of dyed wool, some lined with fur or sewn with rich thread, others unadorned. Aelfhild's and Ceolwen's dresses were a deep rust red hue, which seemed to match some sort of theme in the hall—Eyrun wore a scarlet cloak around her shoulders, and the servants all wore some sort of garnet jewelry.

"Why red?" asked Aelfhild, holding up the thick fabric of her skirt.

"Red is the color of the Leifings. You know we are Leifings?" Eyrun asked. Aelfhild nodded, and Eyrun continued. "We wear it at the Landsthing so we know our kind from the others. Beware men in grey, they are Ulfings. They will not be friendly to you," she warned.

Kolbrun spat at the mention of Ulfings, earning her a withering sideways glance from Eyrun. Rolling her eyes in mock exasperation, Kolbrun wiped the spittle off the floorboards with the bottom of her boot, but a smirk lingered on her face.

"You will join my brother and I at table tonight, I hope," Eyrun asked Ceolwen, "we celebrate their safe return and the coming of the Landsthing."

"It would be our pleasure," Ceolwen responded with a small bow of the head, "but I would beg an audience with Jarl Harald as soon as can be arranged."

Eyrun chewed her lip for a moment, pondering the request. "My father is most busy now, meeting the other Jarls and their thanes. I cannot say when he will have time to spare for you."

Aelfhild and Ceolwen both stared, dumbstruck. Here was the daughter of the very Jarl they sought; by extension, the man they had traveled with, the man who had tracked them across the open ocean, was his son.

And the Gods continue to toy with us. Aelfhild could have screamed.

Surprise must have been clear on their faces, for Eyrun let out a delicate laugh. "Has he not told you? Of course he has not, my brother says nothing to no one," she said.

Kolbrun snorted, evidently not caring to hear her captain's character impugned, but Eyrun waved her off.

"I will talk to father and see when he has time. You are our cousin, after all," she said to Ceolwen, "and there is always time for family."

"Feast, feast, feast, feast," Aelfhild chanted, elbowing her mistress.

Ceolwen giggled beside her. Hunger, fatigue, relief, and a smattering of other emotions had swirled together to reduce them to children once more, peeking through a curtain as they watched servants load buckling tables with dish after heaping dish.

Guests were arriving at the hall, a steady flow of crimson tunics and dresses. There were eager embraces and a great deal of back-slapping; as Kolbrun had said, these Landsthings served as a sort of extended family reunion for many folk. Children scampered about underfoot, rough-housing and battling with wooden swords. Geir returned with a freshly scrubbed Bercthun, who looked dapper if somewhat self-conscious beneath a fresh jerkin and cloak.

Eyrun flitted about between the various groups, greeting new arrivals, speaking with guests, and keeping an eye on the flow of work. Benches and tables were carried in on strong backs, a line of them stretching on either side of the central hearth from the front doors of the hall down to the far end, where between two carved pillars sat a wooden throne atop a raised platform. The seat was covered in furs and hung with banners bearing the crest of the Leifings: a huntsman's horn hanging from a chain looped over the hilt of a sword, gold lines sewn on a field of red.

"Forgive me for saying so, lady," Aelfhild whispered, "but I am a little glad the Jarl could not see us."

"Me, too, Aela. I just want to eat. Hold me back, or they will not think me very ladylike."

Kolbrun appeared at the gap in the curtains.

Aelfhild's cheeks flushed as she straightened up from her vantage point. Ceolwen coughed beside her, and she could feel the laughter bubbling up. One look at her mistress and they both dissolved into chortling fits.

Looking thoroughly confused, Kolbrun stared down at her charges. "Are you two quite well?"

Ceolwen gasped for air and strained out a few words. "It has been a bad few days. Please forgive our madness." When they had composed themselves, the shield-maiden led them out into the hall.

Embla the wolf-dog arrived just before her master Eyvind, who swept in with Rolf and Jarngrim in tow. The three warriors wore fine armor for the occasion, tunics of ring-mail polished to a dull gleam, and they were the only men that kept axes at their side. All the other guests had made a pile of weapons by the door, keeping only their beltknives.

Eyvind made his way through the crowd, stopping here and there for an embrace or a brief greeting, and came at last to the throne at the far end. He stepped atop the platform but did not sit, calling out to his guests for silence. Eyrun, who had drifted up noiselessly beside them, leaned over and translated her brother's words for Ceolwen and Aelfhild.

"Brothers, sisters," he called out, "I welcome you to my father's hall on the eve of the Landsthing. Eat well but drink sparingly, for we will need our wits! The Ulfings have come in numbers, for they know they cannot face us in an even fight!" This comment aroused much murmuring and nodding from the crowd.

Eyes burning, Eyvind continued, "Do not start fights—I will brook no rabble-rousing, nor will my father!—but do not shrink from one, either. Our foes are not fools, they will taunt and trick you if they can. Be wary!"

He paused for a moment, letting the words sink in. "But enough of this unhappy talk—let us feast! Sit and be cheerful. We toast to spring's coming, to the Landsthing, and to the Jarl!"

With that he raised a cup, oath-rings clinking softly as they slid down his forearm, and a thundering cheer shook dust from the hall's rafters. Food was heaped on the tables and bowls passed around as the crowd jostled and elbowed for places on the benches, the room resounding with the scrape and clatter of knives on earthenware.

Eyvind and Eyrun sat across from one another at the table closest to the throne, each immediately to the right and left of the empty seat held for the Jarl. Rolf sat beside Eyvind, and Eyrun brought Ceolwen and Aelfhild to sit next to her. Bercthun disappeared to the other end of the hall, dragged away by Geir and Jarngrim to join the group of men by the mead-cask near the doors. There was hollering and no shortage of laughter from the crowd as Bercthun was put on display, the southern slave-warrior found lost on the waves.

"Some of the men were not happy to have Earnfoldings in the hall," Eyrun whispered to her guests. "Thrym do not always get on with foreigners."

Ceolwen mumbled something unintelligible through a mouthful of roast pork. Aelfhild could not criticize. Her bowl was piled with glistening mutton, turnips drowned in a lather of butter, and what appeared to be tiny lobsters baked in their shells. She had a leg of chicken in one hand and was eyeing the blackberries drowned in clotted cream further down the table.

Luckily, Eyrun seemed not to mind. "We live close to your lands, but that can mean trouble as well. Some of the older men remember raiding your villages. See that man across from us, beside Rolf? He says we should have nothing to do with your kind."

"Do not stare," she hissed, though her audience was far more focused on their dinners.

"My brother does not care for politics, but I take after my father," Eyrun shivered. She seemed giddy to discuss all the scandals. In conspiratorial tones, she told them who in the clan was not speaking to whom, which families were behind on their quitrent to the Jarl, and so on. The list of feuds was especially long. It seemed the Leifings got on no better with one another than they did with the other Aettir.

Cups were drained, belts loosened, and many a contented belch rang out to the rafters. Aelfhild found the lobsters to be particularly to her liking—they were small, tails barely as long as the palm of her hand, but sweet and tender. A swig of mead cleansed her palate, and she turned her attention to the purple-black berries that gave a delightful little pop when chewed.

Aelfhild glanced over to check on her mistress, who was applying herself to a joint of charred pork. A line of fatty juice ran down Ceolwen's chin and she smeared it aside with the back of her hand, any manners learned at the king's table long since pushed from mind.

Across the way, Eyvind pushed his empty plate around the table with a finger. His speech seemed to have exhausted the last of his social grace, and he sat in silence. Rolf was busy passing scraps from his plate to Embla, who waited beneath the table, grey snout poking out from beneath the boards.

By the mead-cask, Aelfhild could see the top of Bercthun's head in the crowd. Beside the young warrior was Jarngrim's dark, frizzy mane, which stood in stark relief to the fair-haired crowd.

"Where does Jarngrim come from?" she asked Eyrun. "He does not look like one of you."

Eyrun leaned in close. "His mother was a slave, you see. She was one of the *Imezliyen*, from far in the southern wastes. The Oescans take them as slaves when they conquer one of the tribes, and she was bought by a Thrym trader in the south and brought here."

"But he is not a slave?" asked Ceolwen between mouthfuls.

"No." Eyrun licked her lips, as though savoring the story. "His father was huskarl to my grandfather, Jarl Torfi. He fell in love with the slave girl, and bought her freedom. None of the men could believe he would be as mad as to marry someone like her. But he did. He gave up everything, his standing with the Jarl, his family title, to be with a foreigner. They live on a farm in Trollsmork, last I heard.

"When Jarngrim came of age, his father sent him to the new Jarl, my father. He became a warrior and now he fights with Eyvind. He has proved himself a true Leifing, even if he has southern blood."

Aelfhild nodded. "He fought well when he saved us from the slavers. But you said some of the men do not care for foreigners. Do they accept him?"

"No," Eyrun replied. "But they do not care for Kolbrun either, because she is…odd." She nodded toward the shield-maiden, who stood shoulder to shoulder with the other warriors by the mead-cask.

"But my brother takes to the odd ones, and my father knows better than to turn away a strong sword arm."

"Wise," said Ceolwen. She stretched her arms above her head and let slip a rattling burp.

Eyrun was too polite to comment on her guest's manners, and carried on seamlessly. "Perhaps. Sometimes I think they are both just stubborn."

2 2

CHAINS FEATURED HEAVILY in Aelfhild's dreams that night. She was back on Leofstan's ship.

You are not yet free, she heard, *you are not yet free.*

Wind howled through the sails, waves boomed and crashed on unseen rocks. Barefoot, she walked the deck of the gale-lashed ship, soaked by icy sheets of whipping rain in the twilight of the storm. Bowed, faceless figures surrounded her, all with palms extended in silent entreaty. Water ran in dark rivulets down their arms and dripped from the chains that bit deep into their exposed ankles. The outstretched hands begged for an offering she could not give.

She woke with a gasp. Sitting upright, deep breaths helped to steady her breathing as her heartbeat began to slow from its flat-out sprint. A shudder passed through her at the memory of those pale faces in the rain, flat and featureless as a child's rag doll. She rubbed at bleary eyes and swung her feet onto the cold floorboards.

A faint light shone around the edges of the curtain drawn about their beds; the fires in the hearth still burned. Aelfhild had no sense of the time in their windowless nook, but guessed that it was not yet morning. Her mouth was parched and her head still buzzed from the mead, so she wrapped a blanket around her shoulders and stepped out to fetch a drink of water. Ceolwen slept on undisturbed.

The doors at the far end of the hall were closed and barred, and the fires burned low. Sleeping forms wrapped in blankets lay dotted across the floor and atop the benches that lined the walls. Snores loud and soft drifted through the stuffy air. Aelfhild picked her way through the oblivious crowd, taking care not to tread on an exposed hand or foot as she sought a barrel or jar where she might find a drink.

Not far from the mead-cask, she found what she was looking for: a clay jug of cool, clear water. Pouring out a bowl, she took a deep draught, then cupped some of the water in her hands to splash over her face. Thus refreshed, she made the delicate journey back across the hall.

Embla sat near the curtain, wagging her tail as she tracked Aelfhild's progress back through the slumbering forms. Aelfhild knelt, taking Embla's broad face in both hands, scratching at the dog's cheeks and snowy white chest. The coarse bristles of the outer coat gave way to silky down underneath, and Aelfhild found it soothing to run her fingers through the layered fur. For her part, Embla made no protest, rolling over to expose a pink belly for scratching.

A movement from the nearby shadows made Aelfhild jump; someone had shifted on the closest bench. Eyvind lay there in the dark, and Aelfhild had not noticed him until now. He sat up, yawning and running a hand through his ruddy hair.

"Cannot sleep?" he asked Aelfhild, voice kept low to avoid waking those nearby.

She shook her head. "Dreams," she responded. "You?"

"Too many worries," said Eyvind, "I sleep little on these days." Embla stood and walked over to her master, sitting at his feet and setting a plaintive paw on his knees. He stroked the hound's ears. "What did you dream?" he asked, peering at her in the dim light.

"That I was on that ship again, in a storm," Aelfhild shivered at the memory of that frigid wind. She pulled the blanket closer around her shoulders.

He nodded, stroking the hair on his chin between finger and thumb. "The old women say you can spy the future from dreams." He could not mask the mocking smile that accompanied the words.

"Do you not believe it?" she asked.

Shrugging, Eyvind replied, "They are just dreams." After a pause, he added, "And I cannot remember mine. Do I have no future?"

His eyes pierced through her as they had at sea, and the intensity of the stare left her wondering if he actually expected an answer. Aelfhild forced a smile and shook her head.

As grateful as she was for their rescue, she still did not trust these people. They had been treated well, so far, and Eyvind seemed a fair man, but his words, the words that had echoed in her dream, still hung heavy in the air. *Not yet free.* The look in his eyes did little to set her at ease.

Rising from the floor, she bid him goodnight. He nodded in return, reclining on his bed as Embla curled up on the floor at his side. Aelfhild returned to her bower, where Ceolwen still slept peacefully. She lay down amongst the furs, and struggled for what seemed ages to get comfortable, tossing and turning.

They found Jarl Harald in his great hall the next morning attended by his warriors.

Harald was tall and lean, much like his son, but what little brown remained in his hair was falling to the tide of white. Deep lines were etched in his face, evidence of many cares and duties. He wore armor befitting a lord—fine mail, with gold links set amongst the rings of iron, beneath a fur-trimmed crimson cloak.

Silence fell in the hall as Ceolwen and Aelfhild left their chambers. The Jarl spun from his gathered huskarls to face the new arrivals, the silver thread in his cloak flashing in the light as he turned.

"And here is the cousin I have heard so much about!" Harald cast his raspy voice for all to hear, extending his arms to Ceolwen. "I welcome you to my hall!"

Ceolwen bowed low, then took the Jarl's outstretched arms in her own. They kissed one another on each cheek, a greeting common in the royal court of Cynestead. "I thank you, my lord, for your hospitality," she said. "We are deeply in your debt. May I present my maidservant, Aelfhild."

Aelfhild curtsied.

"And my servant Bercthun is…elsewhere, I fear."

The last time Aelfhild had seen him, Bercthun was deep in his cups and in very good company. If she had to guess, he was sound asleep in a ditch or pigsty along with Geir, Jarngrim, and possibly Kolbrun.

Harald led Ceolwen back toward his throne, where a servant brought a stool for her to sit by his side. The men in the hall gathered about their lord on his platform, while Eyrun appeared from nowhere and pulled Aelfhild off to the side. The women stood in the shadows to the side, where they could hear but would not get in the way, and so Aelfhild's world returned to normal order.

"We were pained to hear of the death of your father, he was a good man." Harald spoke the southern tongue without apparent effort, clearly at ease. His realm lay near to the border with Earnfold, thus knowledge of their language was a necessity. It made Aelfhild wonder if Eyvind might speak her language better than he let on.

"I did not know him well but our dealings were always fair. The death of your mother, though, cut me sharply. I knew her as a child," the Jarl said. Ceolwen's mother had been chosen from a Thrym house to marry King Osred, their marriage not a story of love or romance but rather a means of binding the two territories together.

Ceolwen nodded along, a study in demure patience.

"Under the watchful eye of the Gods, you have been brought safely to us," Harald placed a hand on Ceolwen's shoulder as he spoke. His tone and sweeping movements were reminiscent of Wictred's sermons in Cynestead—the Jarl was performing for his audience. "Surely it is fated that you come to us at this hour in such dire need."

From amongst the crowd, Eyvind sniffed at his father's words. All eyes turned toward the younger man, and those standing nearest him took a step away. He locked eyes with his father for a moment. Beside Aelfhild, Eyrun sighed.

"You must forgive my son," Harald spoke to Ceolwen but the words were pointed straight toward Eyvind. "He does not share my faith in the Gods of our peoples. But only the blind would fail to see their hand in this, and *I* do see it as clear as day. And we shall listen to the Gods and help you reclaim your birthright. No Oescan shall sit on the throne of Earnfold, not while I still draw breath!"

This last pronouncement drew cries of support from all gathered.

The warriors stomped their feet in approval, the thumping of floorboards echoing from the rafters throughout the hall. The Jarl stood from his seat, raising his hands to quiet the crowd. He switched to the northern tongue now, speaking to his men. Eyrun translated for Aelfhild as he spoke.

"Tomorrow, we go to the Landsthing. We stand across from our foes, the Ulfings, and we make our peace!" There was a chorus of groans and growls from the throng at these words, but the Jarl carried on. "Brothers, we will not stand by idly as our ancient enemies march up to our very borders. The Ulfings, they are poor and dirty folk, but the Oescans? Their cities flow with gold and wine, their lands are fat and rich. We will take back with the blades of our axes what they seek to steal with their schemes and forked tongues."

Harald paused, allowing his words to sink in. Murmurs coursed through the crowd as each man pictured the spoils of the south. The Jarl knew how to rule his subjects, clearly; the hook was baited, and had only to be set.

"It is long, my brothers, since we sailed south. It is long since Thrymgard went to war. The Oescans have grown soft. Let them quake at the sound of our horns once more; let them dread the coming of our longships." Throwing his hands in the air, Harald shouted, "What say you?"

The response was a roar, a physical wall of sound that shook Aelfhild to the bone. There was a rage rising in the eyes of these men, a thirst for blood and a thirst for plunder that was deeply unsettling.

These were the Thrym of the old stories, told to frighten disobedient young children: red-eyed raiders with wicked, hungry blades. She and Ceolwen and Bercthun, rode now atop a wild and uncontrollable wave; Aelfhild could only hope that they would not slip below as the wave broke.

Jarl Harald called for tables to be carried in, and breakfast was laid out. Ceolwen stayed by the Jarl's side, but Aelfhild was shunted down to the far end of the hall and forgotten. There was bread and butter, curds of cheese and bowls of whey to wash it down. The previous night's feast had not quelled her hunger, it seemed, and Aelfhild tucked in.

Looking up and down the table as she ate, she could see only one set of eyes that matched her mood. Eyvind sat at his father's right hand and picked at his food. His brow was furrowed and eyes pensive, but the Jarl paid his son little mind; Harald's attention was focused on Ceolwen and Eyrun beside her.

When Harald had at last turned back to his warriors, Ceolwen excused herself from the table, thanking the Jarl many times over for his kindness and saying she needed a breath of fresh air. Aelfhild followed her mistress out of the hall.

The terrace outside the door looked out over the waking city. Golden morning light bathed the rooftops below, and a steady breeze carried up the smell of the sea from the harbor. Aelfhild's loose hair fluttered around her face. She stood next to Ceolwen, and kept her voice low. "He has his own plans for you, lady. I doubt he holds your interests as dear as his own."

"I know, Aela, I can see it as well as you." Rocking back and forth on her heels, Ceolwen sucked in the chill air. "Maybe as queen I could tame them or channel them, but I have no power here, not yet."

"I think Eyvind may be an ally for us," Aelfhild said.

Ceolwen shook her head. "But he is not the Jarl, his father is. We must follow Harald."

"I do not trust him."

"Nor do I, but the list of people I do trust is short. Just you, now, Aela."

"And Bercthun," Aelfhild said.

"And Bercthun, if he yet lives. So we wait and see what luck the Landsthing brings us."

2 3

EYRUN ROUSED THEM before dawn the next morning, sending in servants with hot water and combs. Aelfhild and Ceolwen scrubbed and scoured until pink, then combed and wove their hair into long braids as seemed to be the local custom. They donned their dresses and went out to join the waiting crowd.

The previous day had been a whirlwind of feasting and preparation. Bercthun had never resurfaced; Geir and Jarngrim evidently still had him in their mead soaked clutches. Toward evening, Kolbrun had dragged herself back to the hall, looking pallid. They had all given the shield-maiden a wide berth. Aelfhild caught sight of Kolbrun again and she looked hale and healthy once more, if thoroughly miserable in her cleanest dress.

Every soul in the hall wore their finest clothes that morning, and all some shade of red. Eyvind's armor and cloak matched his father's, but with less gold on display. Rolf was there, too, amongst Harald's vanguard of greybeards who were armed for bear. Most of the other men wore just their cloaks and tunics and carried no axes or swords; Jarls and their huskarls were the only men permitted arms at the assembly, as it turned out.

Eyrun floated past, looking radiant despite the early hour. An ornate pin, whorls of gold around dark garnets, sparkled on her breast.

Servants hurried back and forth as final preparations were made and attendants had a few last hurried words with the Jarl. The hall thrummed with whispered conversations and the crackle of expectation. As the sun climbed above the horizon outside, Harald called for them to move out.

They were greeted outside the door by the rest of the Leifing's retinue, a crowd of red clad men, all bearing torches, who cheered their lord as he marched forth with his warriors.

A cloaking mist had settled in during the night, lending to the proceedings a suitably mystical air. The sun struggled in vain to pierce the fog to the east, and a gentle breeze blew sheets of wispy cloud up and over the cliffs.

As they walked up the hushed streets of the city, they were joined by other groups of Thrym, clad in various colors. Aelfhild saw men in blue, green, and white, and eventually a large group of men clad in grey cloth, her first sighting of the feared and hated Ulfings. There were pointed looks exchanged between those in grey and those in red, but no words or blows.

Following a switchback path from the highest terraces of town, they came at last to a great ironbound gate; doors thicker than Aelfhild's body and thrice as high were flung wide to allow the people in. These were the walls of the Klettirborg, the fortress of the Northmen, set atop the cliffs. Within was a broad courtyard set into the stone, dotted with longhouses for the guards and with ramparts that overlooked the harbor. Any view of the harbor below was obscured by the fog, but Aelfhild reckoned it to be spectacular on a clear day.

They followed behind Harald. He led them through the mouth of a tunnel and down into the very mountain itself. These were the veins where the volcano's molten lifeblood once had flowed, that the Thrym had taken and carved for their own purposes, building upon and reinforcing what nature had left them whilst digging a few new tunnels of their own. Wooden beams and pillars rose to support the curved ceiling as it snaked through the rock, and torches burned in sconces along the way.

They entered an echoing cavern, a globe with high vaulted walls of black and pitted stone. A large piece of the rock that made up the ceiling was gone, leaving a jagged hole that allowed light from outside to illuminate the chamber. The trickle of dew from the opening resounded from the curved walls. In the globe's center was a broad stone dais with five seats, and there were lines of benches radiating out in every direction from that central point.

The Landsthing. Aelfhild was no Thrym, but she felt a touch of awe at the weight of history in the sacred place. All the Aettir, the jarls and huskarls and thanes, had gathered here for generations untold to hold court, making laws and settling disputes.

The Leifings staked their claim to the rows of benches on the far side of the cavern, and the room sorted itself by Aett as the crowd streamed in. The Ulfings, looking dour in their grey tunics, sat opposite; other clans in green, white, and blue spread out in between. The mood between the other Aettir seemed friendly enough, men in different colors mixing together to greet and converse with friends and acquaintances. Red and grey were the only two colors that remained starkly divided.

There were few women at the assembly, Aelfhild noticed, and they were mostly relegated to the benches furthest in the rear. A man's station could be told from his nearness to the center of the room—huskarls sat on the front benches, the thanes behind them, with freemen and women at the outer edge. Eyrun and Kolbrun sat along the outer ring beside Ceolwen and Aelfhild, explaining the customs and goings-on of the day, and pointing out important persons.

As the flood of people into the chamber slowed to a trickle, a lone, ancient man limped onto the central stone platform, leaning heavily on a wooden staff. His robes were as snowy white as his beard, and his skin bore the constellations of veins and liver spots that came with a burden of years. Straightening himself, the elder rapped the end of his staff thrice upon the stone. Conversations stopped, and men took their seats.

"The Lawspeaker," Eyrun whispered, "recites the law of our Aettir."

The old man's voice rang out in the silent chamber, swelling with the echoes. He started from a drawl, chanting the laws of Thrymgard, but his voice increased in pitch as he rocked from side to side in a sort of rhythmic trance. Eyrun did not translate, and Aelfhild was inwardly glad. She understood it to be a key part of this seasonal ritual, but the Thrym seemed to have many, many laws.

After the Lawspeaker finished his recitation, he called forth the Jarls. Three men stood, Harald included, but Aelfhild was stunned to see them joined on the dais by a woman. She stood a head taller than many of the men, with a mirthless face beneath white-gold hair. Armor shone in the torchlight beneath her blue cloak, and a short sword hung in a gilded scabbard at her side.

Eyrun must have anticipated their surprise, for she said, "Hafdis, Jarl of Rifstrond. Her husband died, and she became Jarl." Her voice hinted that there was another story waiting to be told.

"Jarl Runar of Nordeyjar is the one in green," Eyrun continued, pointing to a bald man in a padded vest, which Aelfhild suspected was chosen to mask a spreading midsection. The flab around the cheeks and chin was harder to hide.

Coming to the last man, Eyrun spat the words to clear them from her mouth as quick as could be. "And Sindri of Ulfseyjar."

With a wolf's hide wrapped about his shoulders, Sindri cut an impressive figure. He wore a tunic of silver brushed chain; he was the only one of the Jarls that wore no gold, for it would have spoiled his colors. The pommel of his sword was carved into the maw of a howling wolf, as was the broach that secured his tunic. He was younger than his peers and, enemy or no, Aelfhild found him quite handsome.

The Jarls spoke out when called upon by the Lawspeaker, listing their grievances and what cases they brought before the Landsthing. The exchange was civil and measured, any animosity between the men and woman on the platform buried beneath layers of ceremony.

Aelfhild then learned that fishing rights were of the utmost importance to the Thrym. The entire morning was devoted to the question of who could fish in which waters, and punishments for men who had fished where they had no permission. It was agony—torture by tedium. A thane or freeman would stand before the assembly to seek justice, and the Lawspeaker would keep order between the Jarls as they passed judgment. Eyrun translated only when Ceolwen or Aelfhild requested, which was seldom.

The sun had already reached its zenith, scalding the dark walls of the cavern with its rays, when Jarl Harald at long last rose to bring the matter of Ceolwen and Earnfold before his people. Harald waved for Eyrun to bring Ceolwen to his side. The chamber filled with expectant silence as men strained for a glimpse of the outlander.

With a deep breath, Ceolwen stood, squared her shoulders, and strode up the aisle next to Eyrun. All eyes followed her. She took her place beside the Jarl.

Harald explained all that had transpired to bring the Earnfoldings to his hall. Tidings of Osred's death drew out little reaction from the crowd, but news of the Oescans and their designs on the kingdom had a marked effect. The audience seethed as whispers coursed outward in tendrils through the assembly.

Jarl Harald arrived at his point: the Thrym could scarce afford losing influence with their southern neighbor, and he would do everything in his power to prevent that. If the other Jarls would join with him to put his cousin, Ceolwen, back upon her throne, both Thrymgard and Earnfold would benefit from a closer bond.

Rising from his seat, Jarl Sindri, the Ulfing, broke in to Harald's speech. Kolbrun translated his words for Aelfhild.

"And why, brothers," he shouted, "should we spill our blood to put a lost waif upon a throne so very far away? We had little good from Osred in his time, I see no cause to put faith in another of his line." He tipped his head toward Ceolwen.

There were stomping and calls of approval from the gathered men, especially those in grey.

"Jarl Sindri is perhaps too young to remember our battles with the Oescans of old," Harald replied, taking no pains to hide his disdain, "but I know his father would never have flinched from a chance to meet our old foes on the field."

The Leifing side of the cavern erupted in jeers.

And so they dance, thought Aelfhild. The Leifings and Ulfings couched their dispute here in civil words, but there was little doubt that this was just another skirmish between the two clans.

Sindri's counterblow was swift. "And glad I am that my father is not alive to see such a barefaced, greedy play for land and power." He pointed an accusing finger at Harald as his voice grew steadily louder. "For surely we would not be blamed for thinking the Leifings would put one of their own blood on the throne, only so their Jarl could rule all the lands from the Trollsmork down to Suthscir?

"For surely we would not be blamed, brothers, for asking which lands such a man would turn his gaze to next?" Rising to a fever pitch, Sindri spun to face each other Aett in turn. "Would he come for your lands then, or yours, or ours?"

Shouts rose with the Ulfing's words, drowning out any further speeches. Men in red and grey were on their feet, howling and shaking fists. The Lawspeaker was forced to hammer the stone platform with his staff repeatedly before order could be restored.

Harald spoke once more. "Those of us old enough to grow hair on our chest remember the bitter quarrels we had with the Oescans in years past," he cried out, "and some of us cannot run and hide to our own little islands when the enemy marches upon us. When Fornhofn burns, when the walls of Herjarsborg are pulled down, what then will you do? Watch over the waves as their legions pick us off, one by one? Hide in the cliffs, squabbling over the last fish in the sea?"

Harald turned toward the other two Jarls. Now he was quiet, the reasonable man, older and wiser than his opponent. He shook his head, and sighed.

"How heavily the crown weighs upon me." Aelfhild could almost hear the line. She grinned, for she had seen this act before; old Osred had been a master of it and many a headstrong nobleman had been taken in.

"You know I have no more lust for power than any man here. We act as one in this, or not at all. Now is no time for trifling feuds. I call for a vote." With that, he took a seat next to the other Jarls.

Sindri lingered for a moment, looking suddenly uncertain, then sat down without response.

That was the trap, and he had fallen headfirst into it. If he continued shouting, the others might think him petty to so bully an old man. But ceding the last world to Harald was equally unwise. With more experience, Sindri could have sidestepped, but youth did have its pitfalls. Aelfhild fought the urge to stand and applaud her Jarl's performance.

Jarls Hafdis and Runar withdrew to their respective huskarls and thanes to hear council. Harald, bathed in the calm of the ever-graceful victor, sat beside Ceolwen atop the central platform, while Sindri set to pacing back and forth in front of his men. The boy had much to learn.

And so they waited, and waited. The shadows in the cavern lengthened as the sun continued in its fiery arc across the heavens.

Hafdis was the first to retake her seat.

Runar was arguing with a pair of his huskarls in a flurry of waving arms and pointed fingers. He stamped his foot to end the discussion, then hurried back onto the dais.

The Lawspeaker hobbled to the platform's center. "Jarl Hafdis, what say you?" the old man called.

Hafdis stood, armor clinking. "The Skjoldungs stand with the Leifings," she said.

Those in red nodded in approval, letting slip a few sighs.

"Jarl Runar, what say you?" the Lawspeaker called once more.

Rising from the bench, Runar tugged at the end of his vest. He was silent for a long time as the sweat beaded on his bare pate. "The Eldings stand with the Leifings."

Cries of dismay rang out from those in grey.

The white-robed elder turned to Sindri. "Jarl Sindri, what say you?"

Sindri sat with his hands upon his knees, face a grimace. He did not look up from the floor as he spoke. "The Ulfings will stand with the Leifings, but with one condition."

The Lawspeaker nodded for the Jarl to continue.

"Our feud with the Leifings is not yet finished. We demand a *holmgang*."

The crowd erupted at these words.

Aelfhild asked what the word meant, but Kolbrun hushed her as the Lawspeaker rapped his staff once more upon the stone.

In the ensuing silence, the white-bearded man, sagging upon his staff, faced Harald. "A challenge is made. Jarl Harald, what say you?"

"The Leifings accept."

2 4

S THEY RETURNED to the Leifing's hall that evening, the mood was mixed. The decision had been made, and it was the outcome they had sought; the Thrym would support Ceolwen in her bid for the throne. The news of this challenge, though, had set the Earnfoldings' hosts on edge.

Jarl Harald went off with his huskarls for a private council. Eyrun stayed to explain to Ceolwen, who had understood only a fraction of what was said, all that had happened. Aelfhild listened in, keen to learn more about this holmgang.

"It is a fight between two men, to settle a dispute or answer some slight. The men stand within a circle and fight until one yields or dies," Eyrun told them. "Now each Jarl will pick a warrior; they will not fight themselves. It will end the feud honorably, according to the law."

"Who will fight for the Leifings?" asked Aelfhild. The prospect of a duel stirred the romantic inside her.

Eyrun sighed. "I fear I know who it will be. My brother is fool enough to offer himself, and my father fool enough to allow it."

Aelfhild asked, "You do not agree?"

"I helped bury my mother, and I have no wish to do the same for my brother. I would have one of the others fight. But my father will say that there is less honor in it." Eyrun brushed a stray strand of hair from her face with a growl.

Ceolwen hesitated before she spoke, and Aelfhild was glad of it; her mistress did not always choose her words with the proper care and this well of resentment clearly ran deep. "Do you not think he will win?"

"I think it is far from certain. And I think honor means little to the dead," their hostess replied.

"What can we do?" asked Ceolwen.

The answer seemed to tumble from Eyrun's lips unbidden. "Go home."

Aelfhild's ears burned with shame. Beside her, Ceolwen coughed and kept her eyes fixed firmly on the ground.

Eyrun's cheeks had flushed to match her dress. "Forgive me, cousin! You are family and family will always have a place among us. Your being here is not your fault, I know that, and I was wrong to take it out on you."

"There is nothing to forgive," Ceolwen mumbled, "I understand."

Eyrun stammered another apology before sweeping off into the hall.

Aelfhild put a hand on her mistress' shoulder, and saw the glint of tears. The strangled whisper was barely audible. "Was she right, Aela? Is all of this my fault?"

"No, lady. This is Osric's fault. And Harald's. We never had a choice."

Ceolwen wiped at her eye with a sleeve, and inhaled sharply. "We could just…stay. Here in Jarlstad."

Aelfhild reeled back. It felt as though she had been kicked by a mule. Give up? Live as an exile in a foreign land, at another lord's sufferance? That was the easy path, surely, but not the *right* one. Osric had to be punished, and she was more certain of that fact than anything else in her life.

She was saved having to answer by Bercthun's arrival. He staggered through the door followed by Jarngrim and Geir. Aelfhild and Ceolwen stared at their long lost and mud caked companion. He beckoned to them.

"Come outside and see!" His breath was still awash with mead.

They found the streets of Jarlstad decidedly changed from their trek that morning. The first day of the Landsthing had passed, and the Thrym made merry once more. Doors were unbarred and thrown open to reveal hearthfires burning high and bright within. Singing and the beat of hide drums carried up from the lower tiers, and revelers walked the streets.

They stood atop one of the ledges carved into the mountain's flank and looked out over the town below. Aelfhild sat between Ceolwen and

Bercthun as they watched shadows dance around bonfires in the evening twilight, feet dangling in the air. Firelight reaching up toward the emerging stars painted the wooden walls and thatch roofs in flickering hues of yellow and orange, and they could hear the drumbeats and fragments of song that drifted up from below.

"There are worse places, Aela. We have seen some of them." It sounded as though she was asking permission.

"Yes, lady, but it is not home."

Ceolwen nodded and said no more.

"It is a grand sight, though," said Bercthun. He remained oblivious to the mood of his companions.

"Yes," Aelfhild replied. And it was. But grander still would be the sight of Osric on his knees.

They could not afford to falter.

Runners came and went from the hall throughout the night. Plans were being made across the city, and Eyrun listened in on all of them. The woman sat amidst a veritable spider's web of rumormongers and informants that came to her with any little tidbit of news. She kept a bulging purse handy, and pressed coins into greasy palms as her spies divulged their secrets.

Ceolwen was sulking. It was her way. The others were back to drinking, for Eyvind had arrived at the hall after dark. Harald had made his choice just as Eyrun predicted, and the Thrym were hard at work toasting their champion. Aelfhild, with her horn of mead in hand, wandered over to the Jarl's daughter.

"When will the holmgang be?" she asked.

"Tomorrow at midday. He fights a man named Olaf. I wish it were earlier—I want to have done with it. But the Jarls do need their show." Eyrun's voice cracked from overuse.

Unsure of what to say or do, but wishing to comfort the woman who had shown them such kindness, Aelfhild reached out to touch Eyrun's arm. The intrusion startled Eyrun. Her eyes flashed and her right hand darted toward her belt, but her face softened as she understood the intent. She patted Aelfhild's hand and gave a slight, weary smile.

"Thank you," Eyrun said. "I was too short with Ceolwen earlier. How is she?"

"She will recover. My lady has always been sensitive, but there is royal strength inside her."

"You must think us all so foolish."

"Lady?" This was a turn Aelfhild had not expected.

"Looking after the highborn, cleaning up our mistakes and waiting for the next. I can see it from where I sit, so much foolishness. So much wasted time and work."

Aelfhild paused to consider her reply. "For what it is worth, lady, I think you would make a fine Jarl."

Eyrun threw back her head and laughed, though hoarse as she was, she suffered for it. Aelfhild handed over her mead horn, and Eyrun drained it between coughs.

"One day, perhaps. My cousin is fortunate to have you. Come, Aelfhild, I need more mead to get me through the night."

On the way to the mead-cask, they passed Eyvind. He was the only sober soul at the table, drinking bowls of whey instead of mead. The others were hard at work on his account, though; Kolbrun was doubled over with laughter, Geir's tunic was stained with drink, and Jarngrim kept the mead flowing from a deep pitcher.

Eyvind nodded to his sister and to Aelfhild as they drew up a bench. "Enough of frowning, sister," he said. "Enjoy life, and let father do the worrying."

Eyrun grinned and raised her horn. "For luck!" she shouted.

"For luck!" The resulting howl set the walls of the great hall ashake.

2 5

ELFHILD SQUINTED AGAINST the sun, regretting her
last few horns of mead. It was nearly midday, but it still felt as
though there was wool packed between her ears. Bile lurked
at the back of her throat and threatened a hasty return.

The Leifings were assembling outside the great hall and Aelfhild
already suspected mischief. This was not the dignified crowd of yesterday,
this was a mob that coursed with barely repressed rage.

Eyrun was shouting at her fellows in what seemed a vain attempt to
drag them to order. Kolbrun and Jarngrim were trying to keep the peace
as well, but they were out of their league.

"Some of them have clubs," Bercthun had to shout over the din. He
was trying to shield Ceolwen and Aelfhild with his body, but the throng
of red tunics continued to swell from all sides. "And I saw a few lifting
stones from the street."

At some point, Eyrun lost patience and led her people down through
the levels of the city.

Aelfhild clung to Ceolwen's arm as they were swept along; they could
not have fought the motion of the crowd if they wanted to. Bercthun
stayed as close as he could, hoisting himself on the shoulders of those
nearby to track his charge's movement.

After a few twists and turns the Leifings spilled out into a courtyard.
The press of bodies deposited Aelfhild and Ceolwen alongside a tumble-
down wall at the end of an alley heavy with the smell of pigs. Ceolwen
climbed up and tugged at Aelfhild's shoulder.

"You can see from up here, Aela."

Within the courtyard was one of the rings of lime-stained rocks that Aelfhild had seen upon her arrival to Jarlstad. The white stones marked out a circle in the dark soil, no more than twenty paces across. Fires burned in low braziers set outside the ring.

Eyvind stood there with his father and the other huskarls, awaiting the arrival of their foes. Three round shields of the traditional Thrym style—varying designs with the clan's colors painted around the central metal boss—lay on the ground beside Eyvind. He wore no armor, clothed only in his woolen tunic atop breeches and foot wraps of linen. An axe hung from his belt, edge flashing in the sunlight.

Harald shouted his Aett into submission. He roared until the veins bulged from his neck and forehead, and an uneasy silence fell. Aelfhild could still feel the nervous energy around her, though, as fists tightened around clubs and reached into pockets for stones. Sweat slicked the palms of her hands.

The other Jarls arrived with the Lawspeaker before the Ulfings showed. Jarl Runar and the old white-robed man stood away from the Leifings, but Jarl Hafdis walked over to Eyvind. She put a hand on the side of his head before ruffling his stubbly hair; Eyvind grinned back. Hafdis patted Harald's arm as she passed by to rejoin the Lawspeaker on neutral ground.

As the Ulfings arrived, Aelfhild's heart fell. Sindri dragged another mob along behind him. Their approach was quieter, but all the more intimidating for it. The burnished silver of the Jarl's arms and armor sparkled as he approached the ring, his champion close behind.

Olaf was the tidiest man Aelfhild had ever seen. His head was shaved smooth and shiny, his whiskers trimmed and sculpted into fussy lines. The man looked as though he ought to be weighing out coins into neat little piles from his master's coffers, not striding over a battlefield. The eyes were the only part of him that gave any hint of danger—they were keen and never still. He stood at the edge of the ring, looking over his opponent, as Sindri and Harald met in the center.

The Ulfings took up their position across from the Leifings as final preparations were made. Grey painted shields were laid down for Olaf as he gave his axe a few testing swings. Eyvind stood across from him, head bowed and perfectly still.

The Lawspeaker stepped forth, laying out the rules in the northern tongue for all to hear, even though every man and woman of Thrymgard knew them by heart. But the ritual had always to be followed, the traditions maintained.

Kolbrun had explained the custom earlier. "Each man has three shields, but no more. If one steps outside the stones, he is a coward, and made a *nithingur*, beneath the law's protection."

Each combatant stooped to pick up a shield and hefted their axe before turning to face the old man once more. He spoke again, then the combatants turned to face one another. With the ringing crack of the Lawspeaker's staff against stone, the battle began.

Olaf moved with serpent's speed across the ring, closing the gap in a heartbeat and striking toward his opponent's left thigh. Eyvind was ready, though, and met the slicing blade with the edge of his shield, knocking back the Ulfing's attack before pushing forward with the shield's iron boss. Blows rang out against wood as the two men sparred, probing for any weakness.

Aelfhild ducked as the first rock flew overhead. Another followed, lofted from within the Ulfing side, and fell further back in the Leifing's sprawling crowd.

Harald's people were evidently not the only ones spoiling for a fight. She tried to split her attention between the fight in front of her and the threat above.

With a splintering crack, Olaf's first shield was cleft from edge to boss by Eyvind's axe. The two men separated to their respective side of the ring. When the shield was replaced, the Lawbreaker called for the fight to start anew.

The crowds bristled, and both Sindri and Harald turned to yell at their followers.

More rocks flew over the arena, and this time Aelfhild saw some from both sides. There was shouting as the projectiles found marks.

Ceolwen cried out and fell to the ground from her perch. Dropping beside her, Aelfhild could see a gash on her mistress' forehead.

"The bastards hit me!" She sounded more indignant than injured. There was a touch of blood, and the bruise would be a sight to behold, but Ceolwen was fine.

"Just a scratch." Aelfhild had to yell to be heard.

Suddenly, the wall of bodies surged forward. Shouts came from every direction, and Aelfhild bent over Ceolwen's body to shield her from the stones that rained down.

Bercthun was behind her, pulling at the back of her dress. "We need to go, now!" he cried. Then the crowd shifted, and he was gone.

There was fighting nearby, whether it was axe on shield or club against club was impossible to tell. There were writhing red tunics in every direction, countless flailing arms and fists and boots to trip on. Aelfhild tried to pull Ceolwen through, but the press was suffocating. She fell, losing her grip on her mistress, and scrabbled on the rough ground for footing.

"Aela!" She could pick out Ceolwen's scream.

Getting back on to her feet, she pushed her way through the Leifings. She saw a flash of bare skin through the heaving wall of chests around her. There was a shirtless man in front of her, all sweat and tattoos, whom she did not recognize from before. A blade flashed in his hand.

Ceolwen screamed again. "Aela!"

There was no time to think. She snatched a stone from a nearby hand, shoving away its owner, and hammered the tattooed man in the back of the head. He dropped like a punctured waterskin.

Another one appeared, bearing different tattoos and a curved dagger. She lashed out with her rock, but someone in the crowd jostled her to the side.

Screaming surrounded them as more folk noticed the knives. Not all the Thrym were as courageous as their raiders, it seemed. Feet lashed out left and right in the scramble to escape as men attempted to climb overtop one another.

Aelfhild hefted the stone with both hands above her head and launched herself forward.

The man stepped forward as he stabbed, and she clipped him across the jaw with her balled fists. They both fell, and she landed on top.

Blood filled her eyes faster than the first time, in a cloud of writhing wisps, and she brought her hands down over and again where the attacker's face had been. Time slowed, and there was only the fight.

The man had stopped struggling long ago.

Someone tackled her from the side and she hit the ground.

Someone fled, sending loose gravel skittering.

Bright sky opened before her eyes as the madness passed. She was on her back in the dirt, the remnants of the red and grey clad rioters fleeing in all directions.

"Aela!" Ceolwen was close enough to hear her voice over the war drums pounding in her ears.

Kolbrun's face appeared above her, followed by Eyvind.

"You lived," said Aelfhild. Her own voice seemed far away.

"Hold still," Eyvind commanded.

She lifted her head from the ground. Gore covered the front of her dress, and had splattered up along her sleeves.

That dress is ruined. The thought drifted lazily through her mind.

Ceolwen was crying.

"She is hurt, we must move her! Out of the way!" Kolbrun shouted.

It is not my blood, she wanted to say. *I am fine.*

As hands lifted her from the ground, her head lolled sideways. The hilt of a dagger protruded from the side of her dress, wedged in between her lower ribs.

I am fine, she strained to say one last time.

She fell backwards into silken oblivion.

2 6

ELFHILD OPENED HER eyes, and she was back in the Leifing's hall. People hurried around her.

She could hear Embla whimpering.

Pain lanced through her side as hands pressed against the wound.

She slept again.

"They have done as much as is able. But if the wound festers, or she bleeds within…" It was Eyrun's voice, pulling her back to consciousness.

"Tell me that the men who planned this will pay with their lives." There was Ceolwen. "They were hunting me in that crowd. If not for Aela, I would be dead. He must pay!"

Harald spoke next. He sounded unmoved. "Who?"

"Sindri! You know it was his men!"

"It does have Sindri's scent about it, true enough. And he always has, what is your phrase, many irons in the forge? You may think he was behind it. *I* may even think he was behind it. But can you prove this, cousin?"

"What?" Ceolwen was screaming again.

"Those men were not Ulfings. I think Sindri had one of his men slip coins into the right hands, but it is our word against his. Nothing will happen."

"Find the other man, then! There were two, she only killed the one. The second escaped through your men!"

"I can promise you one thing with the Ulfings—the other man will be floating in the harbor with a knife in his back by morning."

"So you will do nothing?"

The Jarl thought the question over. "Welcome to Thrymgard, cousin."

The assembled Thrym laughed as Ceolwen stomped off into the recesses of the hall. Each footfall shook the boards beneath Aelfhild, sending out fresh bursts of fire through her side.

"You, boy, did you know the girl was a *berserkr*? Some might think it rude not to tell a man he was sheltering a madwoman."

"Forgive me, lord, I did not know," said Bercthun. "One of the slavers said something about her going wild in Haernmuth, but I did not see it myself."

Harald grunted.

Off to one side, Eyvind was shouting at Kolbrun and Geir, who mumbled their replies toward the floor.

A new set of feet stomped past, and the pain dragged Aelfhild back under.

This time, when she opened her eyes, there was silence. Not silence— embers of a fire crackled and snores rose from nearby benches. Nighttime, then.

Her side throbbed. Furs and blankets were piled around her, and the heat was stifling.

Gingerly, she pulled a blanket aside. It took more than one attempt, but she found that if she moved with only her right side and slowly, the pain from her ribs was tolerable.

"You are a hard one to kill."

A hand pulled away a roll of fur beside her face, revealing Eyvind seated alongside her bower. Embla's nose snuffled its way into the gap from the floor below.

"We did not know if you would wake."

Aelfhild's tongue was bone dry. "How long?" was all she could manage.

"Two days, now. Stay flat, just lift your head."

He lowered a bowl to her lips, some sort of broth that stank of rotting grass and barn stalls and tasted no better.

"Sip," he chided.

She could have downed the whole reeking bowl, but did as ordered.

"Your mistress was here with you for a long time, until we sent her away. My sister and Kolbrun, too, and Jarngrim and Bercthun both. You made some friends here."

Embla licked Aelfhild's cheek as she lay back to take a breath.

"And my hound wanted to sit with you, so I joined her." He seemed pleased with his little jest and chuckled.

The broth had helped. She had enough strength for more questions.

"Who won?"

Eyvind raised an eyebrow. "I should say you won, but the thing of it is not to be stabbed. Try for that the next time."

"No," she rasped. "Olaf."

"*That* fight. I held my own. It did not count much when the Aettir all went wild. Sindri seemed calm about it. And father is never happy, so no harm there." After a pause, he added, "He is very not happy with you, though."

"Why?"

"A berserkr is ill fortune wherever he is found. And a woman berserkr, too." Eyvind whistled through his teeth in mock amazement.

Aelfhild felt a tear run down her cheek. Now they all knew her shame. "The Gods cursed me," she whispered.

The webwork of compresses and bandages that swathed her midsection shifted as her shoulders shook, sending forth fresh pangs from her wound. She focused on the pain as she tried to wrestle back composure.

At the sight of tears, Eyvind became engrossed with his thumbnail. He fiddled with the ragged edge in silence.

"Maybe," he said as she calmed, "maybe. But it kept Ceolwen alive, and it got you here. What if it is no curse?"

Through gritted teeth, she replied, "You do not even believe."

"Fah!" He swatted the accusation away with a hand, oath-rings jangling. "So my father says. The old men here say not to take stones from the shore, because elf spirits live in them. Could be, but I have not seen one."

Elves? Aelfhild still felt woozy, and he was rambling now.

"And they say that we must pray, because the Gods live above. Could be, but I have not seen them. If they are there, they do not much bother with us. So I say, save your breaths. But there is a...place or a part for all of us, I think. Call it Fate if you like. And maybe yours is to keep your mistress safe."

He lifted her head once more and tipped the bowl against her lips.

"And to talk too much," he added.

In spite of herself, she snorted.

Whether it was something in the drink, or just fatigue from the ordeal, her head felt like a lead weight pulling her back down into the furs. She yawned, which proved a mistake and left her wincing again.

"Sleep," Eyvind said. "Kolbrun will see to you tomorrow."

2 7

WEAT DRIPPED DOWN Aelfhild's forehead, stinging her eyes. She dropped down onto one of the rocky cairns that marked the road out of Jarlstad.

"Come on, girl," Kolbrun called from ahead, "a few steps further than that! Show some backbone!"

Aelfhild tried to ease her breathing so that her chest did not swell enough to tug at the rent in her side. The jabbing pains had eased through the days into a constant ache, but had yet to fully take their leave. Her world since the holmgang had consisted of a set of steadily widening circles. At first, she could wobble only three or four unsteady paces from her bedside. With practice, she could reach the hearth. Then, eventually, the door. And Kolbrun had been the unyielding taskmaster.

That afternoon, they were just outside the city's palisade. Away from the cliffs surrounding the harbor the slopes of the volcano trailed down into fields of crushed rock and ashen soil. It was a harsh landscape, and foreign to Aelfhild's eyes. Little grew there but clumps of grey-green lichen.

"A few more steps, Aela," Ceolwen said. She was the balm to Kolbrun's whip, ever sweet and supportive. "Lean on me."

The Jarls had spent a week locked in council, doubtless hard at work dividing Earnfold up amongst themselves, and had no time for outlanders. So Ceolwen had been left free to help her servant along.

With her mistress under one arm, and crutch beneath the other, Aelfhild dragged herself further down the path.

Over generations the Thrym had reclaimed patches of farm and pasture from the burnt soil. As they crested a ridge, rectangles of verdant green spread out in a wide patchwork before them, each divided neatly from the next by precise stone walls.

"The soil is loose, so the farmers build walls to hold it back from the sea," Kolbrun pointed down into the dell. "To ease the wind, as well. Less staring, now, more walking!"

And blow the wind did; it never ceased on the island. They were buffeted by gusts on their way down the hill.

"Horses, Aela!" Ceolwen raised her free hand to point.

Thrym horses were a sight to behold. Ceolwen seemed to fall in love with them on the spot. They were squat, nearly equal in width and height, and had thick, fluffy coats. Their stubby legs gave them a clipped, scurrying gait that was chipper and endearingly awkward.

Kolbrun let them rest in the lee of one of the pasture walls out of the worst of the wind. Ceolwen wandered along to stare at the animals while her servant recovered.

The shield-maiden handed Aelfhild a waterskin.

"Drink."

Aelfhild took a swig while making a decidedly unladylike gesture at her tormentor. Luckily, Kolbrun's attention was elsewhere.

"Queenling, would you stop laughing at my people's horses!"

Still beaming, Ceolwen shouted back, "They are as adorable as you are, skjaldmaer!"

As she handed back the skin, Aelfhild remembered. "Did you ask about those two slaves I told you of?"

"Yes," said Kolbrun, "but no one remembers them passing through. Boats have been coming and going with the Landsthing, so no one can say for sure."

"It was a mother and young girl, someone must have seen them!"

"How many slaves do you think come through here this time of year? Hundreds or more. No one remembers them. And why are you so concerned?"

"Because it was a scared woman with her child! They helped me, helped us, survive the worst of the slavers."

Kolbrun did not appear impressed, but Aelfhild pressed on.

"And they deserve to be free."

"What does *deserve* have to do with it? That is life. You are so free to leave your master?"

It took Aelfhild a moment to answer. She opened her mouth more than once, but the words seemed false. She settled on an answer, though she knew it to be a feeble one. "Not the same."

"No? She can have you caned like some wayward dog. You were never once whipped?"

There were memories. Ceolwen's tutors had not been allowed to strike her for disobedience, so Aelfhild had born those beatings. And Ceolwen had been a headstrong child. Though, in her defense, the Aethling had always begged forgiveness afterwards.

Kolbrun did not wait for an answer this time. "Some lead, some are lead. So goes the world."

"It is not—"

"Fair? Right? I wager two weeks ago you thought nothing of it. You go on waiting for the world to be fair, girl. The rest of us will get on with living."

"You sound like your own master," Aelfhild replied. It had come out with more acid than she intended, but she was in no mood to back down.

Kolbrun sniffed. "There are worse things. Eyvind is cleverer than he looks."

She stood and brushed the grass off her back.

"Up you get. We have a ways to go yet."

They gathered up Ceolwen, and continued their slow journey.

Rows of turnips and cabbages stretched out along either side of the gravel road. Sheep bleated in a paddock up the hill. The elfin horses cantered along beside the intruders.

But Aelfhild could focus on nothing but the thought of Runild and Sola. She hoped they were alive and sailing homeward. Hope was all she had, though the dour Thrym were working hard to take that small comfort, too.

2 8

YRUN TOOK THEM aside at breakfast the next morning.

"I have word from my father. The Jarls will gather today to make plans for your return to Earnfold," she told Ceolwen, "and would speak to you."

"And we are, what, expected to smile and swoon for Sindri when he comes to our aid?" Ceolwen asked.

"You know the way of things by now, cousin. Bite your tongue and take your place. But never forget. Your chance will come one day." And there was a glimpse of the spider plucking at the strings of her web. Eyrun was no mere ornament, and woe to any who thought of her as such.

The Jarls arrived with their guards soon after.

Harald was first. He swept his cousin up in the crook of his arm as he strode over the threshold. "Ceolwen, my dear, we speak of you and your future kingdom today. Happy tidings!"

Aelfhild locked eyes with Harald as he passed. Though the Jarl said nothing, the twinge at the corners of his mouth hinted that she was spoiling the view. She had noticed many of the other men seemed tense around her, as well, particularly the greybeards.

Eyvind's attitude was unchanged, though. He motioned for her and Bercthun to join him behind his father.

Jarl Hafdis arrived, flanked by her bluecloaks. Aelfhild's estimation of her only increased on closer viewing. Hafdis made no attempt to hide the streaks of grey in her hair nor the wrinkles that radiated from her eyes with dyes and powders, as some aging women did. She wore her age with honest grace.

The remaining Jarls arrived together. Runar sagged and sweated his way in, making Sindri look even more elegant in the process. It was hard to imagine that the Ulfing had not chosen his companion for that very effect.

Sindri took a bow in Eyvind's direction.

"Eyvind," he said, "you look pretty as ever." He spoke in Earnfolding, and clearly for the whole audience's benefit.

Aelfhild's eyes darted to the scar that puckered on her rescuer's cheek. From the sound of it, that was Sindri's work. She and her mistress were not the only ones with cause to curse the man, then.

But without hint of anger, Eyvind replied. "Many thanks, my lord. And how is the Jarl's hand this morning?"

The grin remained plastered on Sindri's face, but his stare was pure, molten hatred. He spun away and strutted off to join his peers.

Aelfhild strained for a glimpse of the man's hands, but both were hidden beneath gloves.

The others would know, but that was a question for later.

The Jarls gathered around a cloth map of the eastern lands unfurled across a tabletop.

"The Oescans send a legion north from Hibernum, most likely toward Cynestead," Harald told Ceolwen, drawing a line with his finger atop the map. "We have word also that Eorl Cuthbert raises his warriors in Wynnthwait to keep enemies from his borders."

"Cuthbert lives?" Ceolwen's breath caught as she spoke.

Bercthun flashed Aelfhild a triumphant grin as she squeezed the young warrior's arm.

"So we hear," continued Harald. "But he can only hold his ground against an Oescan legion, not fight through them to take back your throne. He would need many more warriors."

"And the other Eorls, where do they stand?" asked Ceolwen, pointing to the various pieces of Earnfold.

Jarl Hafdis spoke haltingly in the southern tongue. "We know little, but the others do not look to be fighting Osric, not in open."

In her native language, she spoke at length to Harald, who shook his head. Jarl Sindri broke in angrily, and a heated argument ensued, ended only by Runar pounding a fist into the table.

Silent in her confusion, Ceolwen stood by and waited for some explanation. At last, Harald turned to her and spoke.

"What do you know of Aettirheim, the city of our forefathers?" Harald asked, his voice hushed, each word endowed with a somber weight.

Aelfhild had heard the name before in old tales, an ancient place whence had come the people that settled first in the lands of Thrymgard and Earnfold. Orn, the first king to rule from Cynestead, was said to have been born in Aettirheim.

"Only stories," said Ceolwen, looking confused by the sudden change in topic.

"It is the old home of both our people. The brothers Vignir and Orn, the sons of mighty Sigurd, came here and made their kingdoms. In these very lands." Harald's eyes were focused on a place far, far away as he spoke.

Nodding, Ceolwen opened her mouth to ask further questions, but was interrupted by Jarl Hafdis.

"Do you know of the Oath-Stone? *Eid-Stein*, we call it." The golden-haired Jarl sounded less awed than Harald.

Ceolwen shook her head.

With an indignant glance at Hafdis, Harald resumed his fervent explanation. "The kings in Aettirheim swore on the Oath-Stone before they could rule. It chose the ones who were worthy and marked them as king."

"How?" whispered Ceolwen.

Everyone in the hall leaned closer to hear the answer.

Harald, however, seemed to be less certain of this. "We do not know, but the stories say clearly—"

"It is a myth!" Sindri cut in.

"It is truth!" Harald thundered, rising to face his rival. Hafdis put a hand on the man's quivering chest to calm him. "It is truth," repeated Harald, veins bulging as he struggled to reign in his temper.

Hafdis explained the Jarls' intent. "The Thrym are not eager to fight for an outlander, and Osric has a claim to the throne as good as yours.

This is not a strong fight for you. But if you were marked as a queen—if there was maybe some sign—they might believe and follow."

Hearing this, Ceolwen stood with jaw dangling. Aelfhild felt much the same. This was their plan? To chase ghosts and half-remembered legends while the Oescans marched an army most real into the heart of her homeland seemed the height of foolishness.

Ceolwen stammered to find the right words.

Seeing her reluctance, Jarl Harald stood and motioned for her to follow. "Come, I will show you."

Harald led the procession through the streets to the high walls of the building that had so fascinated Aelfhild upon their arrival to Jarlstad.

Gilded carvings of coiled serpents and lunging wolves adorned the walls, and Aelfhild could see upon closer viewing that the jutting roof beams were engraved with ravens. The peak of the uppermost roof, curved like a pair of bull's horns, strained to pierce the clouds.

The other Jarls remained outside with their warriors as Harald kindled a torch and led the Earnfoldings in. Eyvind lingered in the arched doorway, watching from afar.

The interior of the great hall was murky, lit only by the torchlight and what little sun spilled in through narrow windows above. Motes of dust danced through the reedy light before disappearing back into shadow. Slabs of grey stone, taller than a man and twice as wide, stood in rows that ran the length of the hall. The lines Aelfhild had been unable to make out from a distance were runes; hundreds upon hundreds of spidery runes covered the surface of each stone. Here was found the history of the Aettir, stretching back into ages long forgotten by most, cut into the bones of the world.

Time lay heavy over this place, and she understood the reverence with which the Thrym treated it. It was a holy site, not out of some connection to the Gods, but from the sheer, overwhelming presence of collected memory.

Holding his torch aloft, Harald led them to one specific stone at the furthest end of the hall. It was ancient, pitted by exposure to rain and wind and ice, presumably in the long years before it had been carried to Jarlstad. A deep crack ran down the center of the slab. There were pictures carved amongst the runes, faint and faded, but just visible beneath the torch's glow. One image was a man, sword in one hand, the other held overhead. A circle was carved around the raised fist, with thin lines extending outward from it.

"Sigurd," Harald whispered, voice brimming with wonder. "In his hand was carried the light of the sun." He searched through the runes for a particular section. "Here."

None of them could read, not even Ceolwen and Aelfhild with their more privileged childhoods, so the gesture was somewhat wasted. The best they could do was to stare at the graven lines, twisting and indistinct.

"Eiðursteinn, it says. Oath-Stone, the old word." Harald's finger hovered over the tablet. "And here is written Aettirheim. It is no myth."

It felt hard to deny the force of the past, so strong was it here. And Aelfhild had to admit there was a twinge in her breast, something primal that stirred at the sight of the carvings. But it did little to allay her doubts.

"Let us go out, my lord," Ceolwen said to Harald, "I have much to think on."

Harald led them back out into the sun, where they stood blinking in the light. He turned to face them. "I am sure it was the Four that brought you to us. Think of it—had my son left from Fornhofn one day, one moment later, he would have missed your ship in the sea and you would be lost to us forever. We are meant to walk this path together, you and I, by the Gods themselves." The old man's eyes gleamed as he stared at Ceolwen. "I will wait for your answer. Do not take overlong." With those words, the Jarl gathered up his warriors and set off uphill with the other lords, cloaks swirling in the breeze.

Eyvind stayed behind, his shoulder propped against the doorway. There was a long silence before he spoke.

"If you go to Aettirheim, I would go with you."

Aelfhild raised an eyebrow. "I heard you scoff at the Gods. Do you believe in such stories now?"

Eyvind shrugged, and pointed toward the sinking orb of the sun. "Since I was a boy, I wanted to sail west, to see where we come from. Stone or no Stone. To go where there are no maps, that is what I want." With that, he set off after his father.

Throughout the walk back, Ceolwen was silent, seemingly lost in thought. Aelfhild fell in next to Bercthun and asked him for his thoughts.

"I know the stories, and I am of the same mind as Eyvind. I would see it all for myself." There was a dreamy quality to Bercthun's voice, but that soon faded. The young man shook the fanciful visions from his head. "But taking the queen is too dangerous. Better to head south, back to Eorl Cuthbert."

In her mind was the same answer, and Aelfhild knew that the wiser path, or at the very least the safer path, lay to the south. But her heart spoke otherwise. The stirring in her chest told her to turn westwards. It was a fool's fancy, she knew, but the desire for such an undertaking nagged at her.

Her side throbbed, and she took a rest at the foot of yet another set of stairs carved into the mountainside. Jarlstad was not a city for the weak-legged. Ceolwen dropped down beside her.

"I heard what Bercthun had to say, Aela, and now I would know what you think." Ceolwen's eyes implored her for help, and it was clear that she was cast adrift upon unfamiliar waters.

Aelfhild considered how much she ought to share with her mistress, and chose the truth. The old trappings of rank had mostly disappeared between the two over the last few weeks, lost amidst the blood and tears. She held nothing back, and told all about the warring of her head and heart.

"I feel the same, but I fear the choice is made already," Ceolwen said with a sigh. "What Jarl Hafdis said is the truth. Most Thrym will not follow me without some proof. Cuthbert needs us, but if we go south now, how long can we fight the Oescans alone? Even with Harald's help, the outlook is not good."

She rubbed at her brow. Weariness showed on her face, not so much of the body but more of spirit. "You said to me that we rode a wave, Aela. I think that wave now sweeps us west."

2 9

"ARE YOU CERTAIN he is alive?" Ceolwen asked, peering down at the sprawled body.

Geir lay atop a pile of netting along the dock, covered with flies and oblivious to the world. Broken mugs and chicken bones were scattered around him, evidence of his latest debauch.

"He is, though he may regret that before long," Kolbrun replied. She poked the slumbering form with a toe and got no response.

"We need some water, maybe? Is there a bucket nearby?" Aelfhild looked up and down the pier, while Bercthun and Ceolwen joined the search.

Kolbrun's approach proved more direct. With a glance over the edge of the pier, she shoved with her foot against Geir's shoulder. Trailing fishnets and empty tankards, the warrior dropped into the muck left by low tide.

The Earnfoldings rushed to the edge of the wooden boards and peered into the morass of kelp and sea-salt ooze below.

Geir stared up from his puddle, face full of questions.

"Eyvind needs you," Kolbrun called down.

Ceolwen had given her decision to the Jarl that morning, and Harald had been most pleased to hear it. The offer made by his son, on the other hand, seemed to be far less pleasing to the old man and he had spent a good while in private with Eyrun and Eyvind.

Raised voices had echoed throughout the hall, which were politely ignored by servant and guest alike. Harald's stubbornness ran deep, and his children had inherited the same trait in equal measure; all that wore the Leifing's red were well accustomed to turn a deaf ear to the quarrels.

Eventually, Eyvind had emerged to seek out a crew for the westward voyage.

Rolf made it clear from the start that he had no intention of leaving his captain's side, with Kolbrun and Jarngrim joining in soon thereafter.

Geir had been next on the list. He shook brackish sand from his boots as the shield-maiden filled him in. Then Kolbrun led them all to meet back with Eyvind.

The northern quayside was a boneyard of old ships, some still half-built on sawbucks and others stripped to skeletal keels and left to warp in the sand. They found Rolf and Eyvind beneath the upturned hulk of a derelict barge, talking to one of the salvagers. The man was caked from head to toe in wood dust, and dragged a bowed two man saw along behind him.

"Vidar has a ship for us," Eyvind said.

"Yes, a ship!" Vidar continued. He spoke the southern tongue for his new visitors, with a trace of Haernmuth accent. "And a fine ship she is. Little and nimble, like that lass over there."

Kolbrun scowled. Vidar already had a puffy bruise around one eye, and Aelfhild fancied such free talk might earn him another before long.

"But she is right for what you want. Short, shallow, and sturdy is what you need for the North Sea fjords."

Ceolwen glared. "What do you know of our journey?"

"Begging your pardon, lady," the boatbuilder winked with his good eye, "but all Jarlstad talks of you. They say you sail west to the old lands. And I know what you seek." Vidar leaned in close to his new conspirators and whispered, "Gold. They say there are hordes buried in the old cities. Gold, silver, and gems past dreaming!"

"The old drunks say?" Eyvind grunted. "So it must be truth. But what is the price for your boat? The Leifings will pay well if she is what you tell us."

"I am not after the Jarl's coins. No, no. You need my boat and you need my hands, so let me come hunting with you! I get a share of the gold—much as you like, lord—and the fame!" He stretched the last word, clearly savoring the prospect.

Eyvind pulled his crew aside. "What say you?"

"I know the man," said Kolbrun, then noticed their questioning stares. "From drinking, nothing more! He goes a bit mad for the skalds' tales, but he is harmless. I say yes."

"And he is right, we could use a man who knows how to fix a leaky hull so far from home," Bercthun added.

"Agreed," said Ceolwen. She glanced over her shoulder. "And it looks as though he does not eat much."

Aelfhild nodded. Rolf rolled his eyes but nodded, too.

Vidar applauded when given the news, sending out a cloud of sweet-smelling oak shavings, and scampered off to gather his things.

When they returned to Harald's hall, one of Hafdis' huskarls was waiting.

Rolf tipped his head toward the blue-hooded stranger. "Onund."

"Rolf." Onund returned the nod.

According to Kolbrun's translation, Jarl Hafdis had sent her man to keep eyes and ears on the endeavor. Rolf knew the man of old and approved. Eyvind needed no other recommendation. Thus Onund became the tenth and joined them at table that evening.

Jarl Harald was also well acquainted with the Skjoldung, as it turned out, and Eyvind's father regaled all gathered for supper with stories from their youth, tales of shield-walls and dawn raids, broken spears and burned longships.

Onund, cloak thrown back to reveal hair long and silver to match his whiskers, had a quick smile and catching laugh. He and Rolf chuckled and raised toast after toast as the Jarl recounted adventures the three had shared as boys at Landsthings many years past, and how they had left mayhem in their wake as they scampered about Jarlstad.

Ceolwen called Aelfhild and Bercthun aside from the feast.

"I am ashamed, but I never thought to ask either of you if you would join me in this. You have both done more than a Queen could dare ask. If you do not want to take this next leap, I will think no less of you."

Aelfhild stole a glance at Bercthun, who looked ready to burst with laughter, before she replied. "You will not be rid of me so easy, my lady. I go where you go."

His brow set in grave creases, Bercthun squared his shoulders and puffed out his chest. "I have not yet been freed from my oath. A poor protector I would be to let you go alone on this path."

Ceolwen pulled her companions in tight, sending scarlet blood rushing to Bercthun's face. And the matter was settled.

The mead-casks were spared that night; even Geir sipped rather than guzzled from his drinking horn. There was a journey ahead, and they would need their wits. But the food was spread forth in buttery, gut-bursting splendor, for they would need their strength, too.

As dark fell and the tables were cleared, Eyrun led Ceolwen and Aelfhild back to their bedchamber, where two pinewood sea chests sat atop the benches.

"A gift from my father and me," Eyrun said, bowing to each of them in turn.

"I wish we had more to repay you," Ceolwen replied, "but I can make only promises on an uncertain future."

"Repay us by returning safe, and bring my brother back with you. Here you will always be welcomed, whether as a queen or just as a kinswoman." The slender Thrym's eyes turned from her cousin to Aelfhild. "Both of you will be welcomed, regardless of what my father has to say."

With that Eyrun left them to examine the contents of their new chests.

The tang of pinesap lingered still on the untreated boards, and swirled about them as they pried up the lids. Within were fresh clothes—wool trousers and tunics, knitted for heavy wear and tear, and traveling cloaks of dark, rusty red. There were leather boots and belt-pouches alongside wraps for hand and foot, and beltknives for use at sea. A dress was, after all, a fine thing to wear to the Landsthing, but there was little use for skirts and trinkets at sea; this was the clothing of a wayfarer.

Sorting through the clothes, Aelfhild found an axe at the bottom of the chest.

It was a stubby, short-handled thing with curving blade, like the one that most Thrym warriors carried. It was a commoner's weapon—lacking the elegance of the jarls' swords and without the brutish heft of the huskarls' great-axes, but quick to forge and simple to wield. The haft was bound at the bottom with leather straps, and a loop of rawhide dangled from a ring at the base to be fastened around the wrist of its wielder.

Aelfhild did not touch hers, but covered it over with wool once more.

Ceolwen gave her new weapon an awkward swing before sliding it in her belt, grinning at Aelfhild.

"Will you not try yours, Aela?"

Aelfhild shook her head. Memories of the rock in her hand, and the dagger, and the feel of sticky hot blood splashing her wrists stirred at the sight of the weapon.

"Do you think they will teach us how to wear them? It sticks in my ribs a bit." Ceolwen fumbled with her axe's handle. "I will be the Warrior-Queen of the North, who sailed in savage longships to forgotten lands! Think of the scandal back in Cynestead!"

Her mistress was in a raring mood, and for good reason—there was adventure ahead! Aelfhild pushed the memories down and set her face in a smile. The axe could stay in its hiding place until it was needed, if it ever was. Best for all involved if it was not.

"Yes, lady," she said. "What stories they will tell of you!"

3 0

HE NEXT MORNING, they wrapped cloaks around shoulders, tightened the bindings on boots, and tucked knives snug in their belts before they carried their sea chests out to join the others.

Harald and Eyrun accompanied them down to the docks with a crowd of Leifings and blue-clad Skjoldungs in tow. Toward the back of the throng was a single green tunic, a man sent by Jarl Runar. Sindri doubtless had eyes in the crowd as well, though he would not deign to grace them with his open support.

Aelfhild set eyes on their ship for the first time, and saw that Vidar had been true to his word. It was small for a longship, about half the size of the one that had rescued them from the slavers. There were gaps for eight rowers on a side, and the deck was just wide enough for a man to lie flat across with arms extended. But this one was not meant for war; with its narrow prow and shallow draft, it would dance across the waves. The slender oaken beams swept into elegant scrollwork at the prow and stern, and the mast was carved with runes.

Dockworkers were loading barrels of drink and foodstuffs, stacking crates on the deck with the oars and sailcloth. Vidar was there, hard at work with mallet and chisel in search of any flaw in his workmanship.

From a passing barrel, Aelfhild caught the unmistakeable whiff of dried fish.

She sighed. In her mind, she knew that it was a food fit for long journeys, since it weighed nothing and never spoiled, although as far as she was concerned that was only because it already had. In her heart, she despaired to think of all the dried meat and tasteless, mealy crusts in her future.

The old stories never talked about *that*.

Eyvind stood waiting for them, watching over the final preparations of the ship, with his faithful hound Embla alongside. Geir and Jarngrim carried over bundles of spears and sticks, and set shields along the pegs of the boat's railing, while Kolbrun and Rolf helped the others carry their chests aboard.

In the prow, Vidar was chiseling lines into the exposed keel.

"He says it is an ill omen to have a ship with no name," Eyrun said. "So they named her *Unn-marr*. In your language, it means Wave-steed."

Rolf placed Aelfhild and Ceolwen furthest forward, where they would be the least nuisance to the rest of the crew.

Though it irked Aelfhild somewhat to be treated as dead weight, she admitted grudgingly to herself that she was in no hurry to pull an oar. Her wound was much improved, but still stiff and sore.

Bercthun, meanwhile, was lined up with the other warriors and got no such special treatment.

At last the ship was ready to sail and the mooring lines untied. Eyvind was last to drop down from the pier, lifting Embla down after him. She wagged her crooked tail madly as she scampered about the deck before settling down on a bed of straw made up for her by the steering board.

"A safe journey to you, cousin! We will await your return and curse the days you are gone from us!" cried Harald.

"We shall return to you, I promise!" answered Ceolwen. "I have every faith that the Aettir's strength will carry us through!"

This received a cheer from crew and crowd alike.

Eyrun did not join in. She stared at each of her brother's companions as though committing faces she might not see again to memory. When her gaze turned to Aelfhild, their eyes met.

Bring my brother back safe, she had asked.

Aelfhild saw the same prayer repeated in Eyrun's expression that morning. She smiled at the Jarl's daughter, but received only a nod in return.

The crew pulled in the ropes and pushed back from the dock, and their journey was begun.

In the stern, Eyvind stood at the steersman's oar with Rolf by his side. Kolbrun and Jarngrim sat furthest aft, across from one another, then Onund and Geir, with Vidar and Bercthun closest to the other Earnfoldings; they ran out their oars, and set to rowing at a cry from Rolf.

Back on the docks, the crowd shouted their farewells. The Jarl raised a hand in parting, while Eyrun stood unmoving beside her father. The two stayed and watched for some time; even as the rest of the crowd dispersed, they lingered on. Aelfhild watched them dwindle from sight. She bore no great love for the Jarl, and Eyrun deserved better comfort. Eyrun deserved many other things besides, in her estimation.

As they passed between the twin guard towers at the harbor's mouth, Eyvind raised the brass-bound horn to his lips once more and let forth two long peals. Another horn was blown in answer, and the ship glided forth from the harbor atop the falling tide.

Swinging around to the east, they rowed along the island's coast into the open ocean and raised the sail upon the mast. Wind billowed through the crimson cloth, and the gold lines flashed in the sunlight.

"Red sails, lady!" Aelfhild shouted over the booming surf.

To her credit, Ceolwen looked to be handling the swells better this time around. "Red sails mean Thrym, Aela!"

"Red sails mean freedom!" cried Bercthun.

Though the rest of the crew did not know where the words came from, they whooped along with the Earnfoldings.

Klettirborg, high atop the dark cliffs of Jarlstad, faded gradually into the distance as the breeze bore them along.

Aelfhild heard odd splashing noises to either side of the prow, breaking the rhythmic crest of waves against the keel. She caught the flash of a silhouette out of the corner of her eye, but nothing was in the water when she turned.

Suddenly, a huge fishlike creature leapt from the waves beside *Unnmarr*'s keel. Aelfhild squawked in fright.

There were sharp, swept wings along its sooty back and white belly, and it cut through the water with astounding speed. More of the monsters followed, weaving and cavorting through the waves. One tilted on its side as the flock swept past Aelfhild's perch, as a single round, soulful eye turned upwards to meet hers.

Ceolwen and Bercthun joined her at the railing, staring with mouths agape. Embla barked at the intruders, but could do little from within the confines of the ship.

"Sea pigs!" called Eyvind from the rear.

The crew joined them to watch the animals at their sport, though the Northmen were more familiar with the sight. These new beasts followed with them for a time, enjoying the wake stirred up by the ship.

Kolbrun laughed, a rare sound. "A good omen! The Gods smile on us!"

"WE SAIL WEST from Jarlstad for another day until we meet the coast. After that, north."

Eyvind had to raise his voice to be heard over the waves. It was a fresh, windy morning, and he sat in the prow with the Earnfoldings. He traced the route on a cloth map spread before them.

"Then we cross through the Ormsund into the North Sea."

A sea serpent, drawn to impossibly large scale, reared its snarling head above one of the icebergs by his finger. Between the northern ice floes and the horn of Thrymgard, the thinnest sliver of ink marked the strait linking the North and East Seas.

"Then south and west along the coast, and, after many days, north again toward Aettirheim."

Aelfhild saw the Grimbergs on the map, the mountain range that hemmed in Thrymgard and Earnfold on the western borders. From the northernmost mountains sprouted fire and smoke. Volcanoes!

She saw that their route would take them past the erupting peaks, and fought back the urge to jump about with giddy squeals. As much as she yearned to see every fresh wonder on this adventure, she was keen to be as gruff as her companions. The Thrym treated the journey with the stoic disinterest befitting heroes found in the skalds' tales.

Except for Vidar, whose eyes watered and knees quivered at any mention of Aettirheim. Aelfhild could practically see the piles of plunder dancing through the man's head.

"There is a small village not far from the Sund." Eyvind pointed to a dot on Thrymgard's northeastern coastline. "They will know if the ice is broken. We go there first."

The Aettir were sailors without rival and could make their way by sun and by star with ease. When the sun had risen well into the sky, Eyvind took from his sea chest a small wooden board carved with curving lines and with a crooked flange at its center. Holding this flat in his palm, he somehow could tell their distance north by the shadow cast across the board's surface. Eyvind seemed satisfied and called back to Rolf to hold course.

Toward evening, swept-wing terns and gulls flocked out to meet them, and they could see the surf crashing against the crags of the shoreline. Rolf guided *Unn-marr* along the coast as they searched out a spot sheltered from the worst of the breakers in which to make land.

Keen-eyed Geir spotted a cove in the arm of a rocky cape, and they ran out the oars to bring the ship in.

Aelfhild's boots sank deep in the squelching sand as she dropped down from the prow and strained forward on a tar-stained rope with the others. Once the ship was above the tide mark, Onund and Rolf hammered wooden pegs into the sand and secured the lines.

Ceolwen and Aelfhild carried sacks of food over the dunes and through the clumps of prickly sawgrass, where Eyvind and Kolbrun were busy making camp. The crew scoured the beach for dry driftwood and broke up some of the sticks they had brought with them, and soon had a roaring fire to warm their hands and dry their feet.

As she wandered just outside the edge of the dancing light cast by the bonfire, Aelfhild strained up onto a boulder to get a better look at the countryside. To the west, just barely visible in the distance, she saw bright specks of fire and white smoke against the night sky.

"Is that the village nearby?" she called out to her companions. "I see lights."

Eyvind joined her, looking out as he chewed on a crust of bread. "Oddsbaer, yes. We go tomorrow."

"Why not tonight?" Aelfhild asked, "It is not so late."

"If we come in the dark, they will think us raiders and attack," he replied. "This is hard country. The Jarls do not have much hold here, and there are outlaws. We will let them see us and invite us to come in."

"Horsemen coming!" Jarngrim called from the rocks above, shading his eyes against the dawn light.

"How many?" asked Eyvind.

The watchmen held up two fingers.

"Just scouts, then." Eyvind turned to the others. "But be ready."

Kolbrun tossed a shield over to Aelfhild. "Where is your axe, girl?"

Blood rushed to her face. Fumbling with the strap on the back of the heavy boards, she mumbled, "In the ship."

"And much good it will do you there." The shield-maiden shook her head and stalked off to join the captain.

Aelfhild watched as Ceolwen slipped axe into belt with trembling hands.

Moving out from the fire, they stood in a loose formation behind Eyvind and Rolf on the sand. The Thrym kept their weapons sheathed but near to hand. Beside Eyvind sat Embla, her ears perked up and snout to the air. Vidar had brought a hunting bow along with him which he carried up onto the scarp beside the cove. His hand hovered by the quiver of arrows slung at his hip.

The horsemen made good time across the plain that stretched from the coast back to Oddsbaer. Aelfhild recognized the clipped, bouncing gait of her mistress' beloved Thrym horses, a sight that made the advancing men a good deal less imposing.

One of the scouts stayed back at a distance as the second advanced.

As the rider drew closer, it became clear that Eyvind's crew had little to fear. Atop the horse was a fresh faced boy, not yet a man, with thin whiskers on his chin and a panicked light in his eyes. He wore an ill-fitting helmet cinched down with a leather strap and a dented breastplate that showed flecks of rust; the white knuckles gripping his spear told Aelfhild that he likely knew as little of warfare as she herself did.

To his credit, the young man cried out in a steady voice that gave no hint of his fear. "Who are you, and why do you come to these lands unbidden?"

A simple message, and one Aelfhild could understand without a translator's aid—she grew more comfortable with the Thrym's language day by day.

Eyvind lifted his palms to show he held no weapon. "We come from Jarlstad with open hands. I am Eyvind, son of Harald, Jarl of Trollsmork. I wish to speak with your master."

The young man rode back to his companion, who turned and rode off toward the village. Their minder returned but kept a cautious distance.

"Wait there," he called.

Standing down the alarm, the crew turned back to their breakfast. Embla ventured out to sniff the young man and his horse, returning to her master when she had decided for herself that the boy was harmless.

They stoked the fire and broke their fast with bread and cheese—and fish for whoever was in the mood. Aelfhild could see their watcher lean forward in his saddle at the sight of food. His cheeks were hollow and skin pallid, evidence of meager rations and a hard winter.

She was not the only one that noticed. Onund took pity, calling out, "What is your name, boy?"

"Birgir," replied the horseman after a pause.

"Will you not break bread with us, Birgir?" The silver-haired old man beckoned the boy over.

A fearful glance toward home hinted at Birgir's divided loyalties. His duty was to watch over the invaders, not mingle with them, but a meal was sore temptation.

"You can watch us better from over here, boy," said Onund with a laugh.

In the end his hunger won out, and Birgir dropped from his horse and joined them by the fire. The boy wolfed down everything handed to him, paying heed to little else, but he blushed and fidgeted under their gazes once finished. Sheepishly he thanked them before returning to his horse as the warriors settled back in the sand to await his companion's return.

The second horseman, another rail-thin youth, returned and spoke with Birgir.

"Thane Kjartan welcomes you, and bids you join him in his great hall in Oddsbaer!" With a grand sweep of the arm, Birgir gestured for them to follow.

Eyvind left Rolf with Vidar, Geir, and Bercthun to guard *Unn-marr* in her berth. The rest followed along behind the two lads on the path back to Oddsbaer.

As they walked, Aelfhild took in the countryside. The land was even and patchy green, but the soil was all sand and pebbles, hard for farming. Nothing grew taller than a shrub, as there was nothing to break the biting winds. Cattle grazed in the distance, herded by men with black-spotted sheepdogs.

Oddsbaer was painfully quaint in Aelfhild's eyes. A wooden palisade which would scarce have passed for a fence in Cynestead circled a collection of a sod-roofed huts, barns, and sheep paddocks. The great hall, its roof newly-thatched and doors thrown open, stood proud in the center of town across from the lone well.

Outside the threshold stood a lanky man with a golden beard and great bushy eyebrows beneath his fur cap; he wore a studded leather jerkin on his chest, and a short sword hung from his belt. Behind him stood a handful of warriors in tattered and rusty armor, holding spears with notched edges. Here was Thane Kjartan with his men, such as they were.

"I welcome you, Eyvind, son of Harald, to Oddsbaer! Join me in my hall!" Kjartan opened his arms wide in welcome as he shouted his greeting.

Eyvind bowed low. "We thank you, Kjartan Thane, for such welcome. I bring you gifts from Jarlstad and from my father." He opened a small wooden chest that Onund had carried along from the ship, producing pelts and precious stones from within. "Hides, amber, and garnets from Trollsmork. May they do you well!"

Onund handed the chest to one of the Thane's men, while Kjartan beamed with delight. Such respect paid to him in front of his men, and from a Jarl's son no less, did him great honor. He clasped Eyvind's forearms, and beckoned them into his hall.

The roof was low and there was little light from the small windows. The sweet springtime fragrance of clary sage hung from the walls and rafters in bushels of purple cones and broad leaves struggled to mask the of smell of hay from the floorboards and smoke that gathered around the narrow gap in the ceiling.

Meat crackled on a spit over the hearth. Benches were laid out around rickety tables, with a few barrels pulled up to make extra seats. Kjartan's wife Saeunn met them inside–a greying woman in an embroidered dress which had clearly been left to the moths at the bottom of some chest for many years. She greeted each of her visitors in turn, bidding them to be seated and take their rest.

Mead was poured and bread set out, and Kjartan stood with Eyvind at the head of the table to raise a toast.

None of the folk in Oddsbaer looked any better fed than young Birgir, and that included the Thane, much to his credit. Kjartan and his warriors restrained themselves with visible effort when the roast mutton was laid upon the table along with curds and bowls of whey. They took care to serve the guests more than they gave themselves, but the way each bone was carefully saved after being picked clean revealed much to Aelfhild's eyes.

The Thane asked many questions about the Landsthing, eager for tidings from the assembly, and Eyvind and Onund told him all that they knew. Kjartan shouted his approval as Eyvind recounted the holmgang, his audience hanging on each word. Quick to prove the courage and skill of his own men, their gold-bearded host told them of a wicked band of outlaws that had preyed upon them over the winter, and how his men had driven the brigands off with spear and blade.

Kolbrun translated for Aelfhild and Ceolwen the parts they could not quite make out, though Kjartan's dramatic gestures and hand-waving were most helpful.

When they came finally to the matter that brought *Unn-marr* to Oddsbaer's shores, the Thane shook his head gravely at mention of the Ormsund. "The winter was a cold one, and the ice has lingered long," Kjartan explained. "Only now is it breaking. Mist is thick over those waters, and the ice has broken many hulls. That is a dangerous path you take."

"But there is no shorter way to the North Sea," said Eyvind, "and we must get through."

"Go south, my young friend, through the mountain passes by Earnfold; that is my council," the Thane said, his voice near to pleading. "The bottom of the Sund is strewn with the bones of ill-fated ships."

Eyvind explained the trouble in the south, about Osric and the Oescans and troubles in Norholt, but skipped over any mention of Ceolwen and her claim. "The passes are no safer," he finished.

Kjartan thought on this for a while, clucking softly as he stroked the locks of his beard. "Sail north, and see the ice for yourself. If you cannot pass through, return to my hall. Wait here with us for the summer, and the ice will surely be gone. Strong backs and steady sword arms are always needed here, and you will win much praise and silver keeping the bandits from our lands."

Nodding his agreement, Eyvind extended a hand to the Thane. "So it shall be," he said.

3 2

EAVING TOGETHER, THE crew pushed *Unn-marr* back into the chilled water, and clambered aboard as she drifted out. The warriors stowed their oars and ran up the sail once the ship had nosed out into the waves.

Kjartan and Saeunn watched and waved from the point overlooking the cove as the ship departed. Though Saeunn had insisted they stay overnight in her hall, none of the crew could bear the thought of stealing more morsels from the folk of Oddsbaer. So they had camped under the stars, and the Thane and his wife had ridden out with the sunrise to see them off.

As the ship passed the rocks where the onlookers stood, Kjartan removed something from around his neck, and with a mighty heave sent it flying toward the longship. Ceolwen snagged the item and tossed it back to Eyvind, for whom it had been intended. It was some sort of rock or bone on a leather cord, worn as a talisman.

"For luck!" cried the Thane, thumping a closed fist over his breast. Eyvind looped the string around his neck and raised his hand in farewell as he steered them out to sea.

With her shallow draft and smooth lines, *Unn-marr* cut a swift trail through the water. The jagged coastline wended north and they followed along its bends and breaks. There were no settlements this far out in the wild; Oddsbaer was the edge of the tamed world. Seabirds and the occasional troop of rotund seals sunning on the beach seemed the land's only occupants.

They spotted one single sign of human passage—a broken keel and barnacle encrusted mast wedged between boulders along the beach. Sails and ropes had long since been lost to rot, and no trace was left of the sailors. The Thrym fell silent as *Unn-marr* swept past the wreck.

By mid-afternoon of the second day, they came to the northeastern horn of the coast, where the land fell back and began its long, westward journey. Here was the mouth of the Ormsund, their passage through to the North Sea. Evidence of the thawing icepack drifted past them, small chunks of white and blue bobbing in the waves and bumping harmlessly off the keel.

They had lost their favorable wind, and the unusual calm of the day proved a two-fold hindrance; not only were they forced to row rather than sail, but there was also no breeze to sweep away the fog.

Mist clung tight the ice, obscuring most of the strait, and the sun did little to burn away the wall of cloud. Keeping as close to the rocky coast as he could, Eyvind steered the ship into the mist. Rolf stood in the prow, peering ahead, while Aelfhild and Ceolwen stood at the railing with long spears to push away any threatening chunks of ice.

Cracking and groaning filled the air, the ice jostling as it warmed and split. They sailed blind, unable to see more than a boat length ahead, and at a snail's pace.

Sweat stood out on the faces of the crew despite the chill, as all eyes and ears strained in the fog. Suddenly, something unseen but sizeable grated against the hull. The hollow grinding stilled every breath on the ship.

Visions of cracking wood and rushing, icy-black water filled Aelfhild's mind.

"Hold! Hold!" Eyvind shouted.

They floated there for a moment, silent and still, waiting.

Rolf turned to his captain, eyes wide, and shook his head. Flicking the sweat from his brow, Eyvind snorted as he stared off into the fog.

"Back!" he called.

Carefully, painstakingly, they turned the ship, its keel grating at one point off the gravelly bottom of the shallow channel. Returning the way they had come, Eyvind steered them out of the fog bank and back into the sun's welcome embrace.

No one spoke.

The taste of defeat sat bitter on all their tongues as they turned south once more and sought a berth for the ship. On a wide stretch of black sand, they came ashore and dragged *Unn-marr* up behind. Vidar bustled about the exposed hull, checking the damage.

Eyvind stood brooding, his gaze fixed northwards toward the Ormsund, as they made a fire and laid down their blankets.

The mood was sour that evening. Aelfhild knew that they all struggled with the question of if they should or even could push onwards. It was writ in the lines of each face. But she knew just as well that none would willingly be the first to back down, and waiting another month or more in Oddsbaer felt too much like admitting defeat.

Eyvind plopped down amongst the crew with a grunt and put his hands to the flames. His crew looked anywhere else to avoid their captain's stare.

Aelfhild met his gaze. His eyes dared her to speak, challenged her to suggest turning back. He looked to be spoiling for a chance to vent his anger. So, instead, she asked, "What was it that Thane Kjartan gave you?"

He lifted the talisman from his chest and shrugged. "A lump of rock. Some damn fool charm or spell on it, no doubt."

"Let me see that," said Onund. Leaning closer, he peered at the stone and rolled it about in his hands. "Troll bone!" The old man whistled in surprise.

The words were greeted by puzzled stares from his companions.

Onund scoffed. "Young folk," he muttered, then launched into a story.

"Long ago, in the time of my father and your grandfathers," the old man began, waggling his grey whiskers, "there were trolls all about these parts. In the forests and in the mountains they waited, to devour unwary wanderers or steal lost sheep. Wicked creatures, they were, but stupid."

"Like an Ulfing!" shouted Geir. His outburst garnered a few chuckles from the Thrym.

"My father, and your grandfather, and yours," Onund continued, pointing to Eyvind and Kolbrun, "were troll hunters, and there were many such men in those days. With dogs and spears and fire they gave chase, for a troll was a threat to one man but easily tricked and trapped by many. Long years ago, the last troll was felled in these parts. They linger on only as bones now, these rocks that a wise eye can see."

"And bring good luck," Onund crooked an eyebrow in Eyvind's direction, "to those that remember their roots, and listen to their elders... and betters."

Smiles shone once more around the fire.

Cupping the troll bone in his hand, Eyvind ran a finger over its smooth surface. He nodded to Onund, then spoke for all to hear: "And tomorrow it shall bring us good fortune, I am sure of it. The fog will lift, and we will pass through the Sund."

Unable to sleep, Aelfhild lay beneath her blanket and stared up into the night sky. There were sparse clouds, and she could see the stars quite clearly. The Anvil, with the North Star at its tip, moved higher aloft each day as the journey brought them ever closer to the crest of the world. Other constellations barely rose past the line of the horizon now, where back home they would float well overhead this time of year.

Back home, she mused.

Cynestead's high walls had girded her whole world for as long as she could remember. She and Ceolwen had ventured out on occasion, but no further than an afternoon's journey. Everything within those confines had seemed so terribly important, while news from the outside, of the death of some jarl or king, of the marching of armies or sailing of fleets, had counted for nothing at all.

Do they still think of us? She wondered if anyone in Cynestead spared a thought for her or Ceolwen's whereabouts.

Doubtful. Whether it was King Osred's son or daughter that took up the throne was of little concern to most Earnfoldings as they went about their lives. It was tempting to think their disappearance would be keenly felt and long remembered, but the truth of the matter was less romantic.

With all that had happened in the short span since their leaving, folk would scarcely even recognize them when they returned.

And they would return. Osric would be dealt with, and Ceolwen would be Queen. In Aelfhild's mind that was fact, with the particulars to be filled in along the way. But what happened afterwards, that was less certain.

Embla must have noticed that one of her humans was awake, for the hound trotted over and settled onto Aelfhild's blanket. Aelfhild scratched at the dog's velvety ears and stared skywards.

Here she lay, on a beach strewn with the bones of trolls, at the far, icy edge of the world, and watched the ghostly bands of the Northern Lights dance their spectral greens and blues across the sky.

The horizon stretched out in every direction, unbound and alluring. Aelfhild understood now what Eyvind had meant when he talked of the pull of the open sea. Endless, unwritten possibility stretched out before them now. That thought might once have frightened her.

Ceolwen snorted and stirred in her blanket nearby. Aelfhild watched her mistress settle back into whatever dreams troubled her.

The Aethling had a royal future waiting for her back in Cynestead. For herself, Aelfhild saw only the past there; a Queen's servant was a servant all the same.

She had tasted freedom beyond those walls. It was bought with danger and pain, beyond a doubt, but she was loath to give it up now.

Surely Ceolwen would understand. Once she was Queen, she would free Aelfhild to go back into the world. That much was owed.

Embla wagged her tail, and offered her belly for rubbing. Aelfhild obliged.

The stars shone above, figures of myth standing out in eternal, fiery relief. Aelfhild drew in a deep breath.

I cannot lose this, she thought.

3 3

THE GROAN OF the creeping mass of icebergs was their constant companion, an unrelenting reminder of the danger lurking in the lightless depths; it called to mind the gnashing teeth of some giant monster, grinding wood and bone without effort in its frozen jaws.

Slowly they rowed through the dark channels of the Ormsund, winding their way westward through the maze of bays and rivers and dead ends in the ice field. No words passed between the crew, as each mind was turned fully to the task at hand.

Aelfhild pushed a slab of splintering ice from their path with her spear. Looking back, she could no longer make out where they had entered; the strait shifted and changed to mask their passage, constantly opening new routes before blocking them off again. If the Sund were indeed a great beast, then they had been swallowed through its maw and drawn down into the roiling belly.

She shivered at the thought, but there was nothing to be done. Turning back now would be as treacherous as pressing forward.

For hours they went on thus before Eyvind called for a break. They drifted on a narrow inlet atop still, black waters, chests heaving from nerves as much as from the effort of rowing.

Aelfhild and Ceolwen joined Kolbrun and Jarngrim to relieve the first set of rowers. There were no waves to fight and the pace was unhurried, so it was easy at first. The long oars turned easily in their holes in the hull, and Aelfhild focused on Kolbrun's shoulders as they moved forward and back, forward and back, always keeping in time.

After the first hour, her side was sore. By the third, every movement drove nails of fresh agony deeper into her ribs. The skin on her hands was raw, even beneath the linen wrappings, and muscles that she was hardly aware she possessed cramped into acid knots. Drenched in sweat and with lungs burning, she focused only on the movement of the oar, following her leader, forward and back.

Beside her, Ceolwen labored in the same wretched state, but sympathy was a luxury long since abandoned.

The pain dragged on for what must have been days. In her mind, Aelfhild saw the sun set and rise anew overhead.

She hated Eyvind for not calling a stop to their toil.

She hated the ice for its endless sprawl.

She hated the oar and the ship and all aboard it.

They were hopelessly lost, of that she was certain, doomed never to find escape from the snaking waterways. Each dip of the oar felt like it would be her last, and only by sheer will did she muster the strength for the next.

Show them you have worth, she repeated with each stroke. Prove you are not a burden.

Finally, mercifully, Eyvind stopped.

Slumping forward, Aelfhild grunted wordless relief.

A reedy, pitiful groan from across the ship told her that Ceolwen stilled lived, but that she might regret that fact. Kolbrun, slick with sweat but gallingly unruffled, helped Aelfhild up and sat her down in the prow.

Ceolwen sprawled next to her servant, and the two lay panting. Any other day, Aelfhild imagined their Thrym companions would have gotten a good laugh from the two young women: broken by a mere half-afternoon of rowing. Today, they all had their own concerns.

"You did well," Bercthun said as he brought them each a drink of water. "We must be close to finding the way out."

It sounded more like a wish than a promise, though, and Aelfhild understood why when she raised her head up from the deck.

The sun dipped lower and lower in the sky, but there was no end in sight to the ice field. A good part of the morning and all afternoon they had spent rowing, but there was only white and blue to the west. Kolbrun and Jarngrim took up watch, leaving Aelfhild and her mistress to rest, as the others went back to the oars and quickened their efforts. Spending a night out on the Ormsund was not an option.

Aelfhild dragged herself upright and took up a pole alongside the others. Kolbrun patted her shoulder in approval before shunting a pillar of ice away from the hull.

As the edge of the sun began to kiss the horizon, uncertainty gave way to fear. Sweat beaded on foreheads, breathing quickened and grew ever more ragged. They stole glances westward in hope of a glimpse of open sea. But each turning in the ice gave way to another, one waterway leading into the next in that spidery web-work of channels.

Oars clattered behind her and Aelfhild spun.

Vidar had ceased rowing and curled himself into a ball, rocking back and forth with hands over his ears.

"Vidar," Eyvind's voice started as a warning growl, but rose when the man did not respond. "Vidar!"

"No, no, no, no," they could all hear the craftsman chanting.

"Row, Gods damn you!" Rolf's voice was a thunderclap, drowning out the buckling ice for a moment.

Vidar screamed back. "We are dead men! Trapped, trapped! He led us straight into death!" He raised an arm to point toward Eyvind, but never completed the gesture.

The spear shaft made a resounding crack as Kolbrun clipped Vidar across the back of the head. He crumpled onto the deck. Bercthun grabbed the man's feet as the shield-maiden lifted his shoulders, and they dumped him in the prow. Kolbrun took up the trailing oar.

"Forward," Eyvind said, as flat as though nothing had happened. The crew obeyed.

The screaming still echoed through Aelfhild's ears. *Trapped, trapped!* She pushed the voice down as far as possible, but her heart raced at the thought.

Trapped!

In the west the sky was changing from blue to orange and pink as more of the sun disappeared from sight. Ice came at them faster now, the oarsmen churning with growing speed in a last bid to be free of the strait, and Aelfhild set her mind solely to clearing the path.

Piece after piece that drifted toward the hull she pushed back, taking solace in each small victory.

Vidar was folded up at her feet. She ignored his whimpering as best she could.

She caught a glimpse of Ceolwen's eyes and saw only whites.

Even Kolbrun's breathing had quickened noticeably.

Trapped! The echoes remained.

But the icebergs seemed to be shrinking. She looked ahead—the waterway was wider here.

They rounded a looming island of white and sky blue, and she risked a glance up and westward.

"Open water!" she shouted. "I can see open water!"

"Row for me, now! One last charge!" cried Eyvind.

Rolf took up the call and set the pace. "Heave!"

"Heave!"

"With me, you sniveling curs! Heave!"

Twilight was upon them when they finally broke from the floe.

Aelfhild looked out across the wide horizon, speckled with a handful of listing icebergs. By the starboard rail Jarngrim lifted his spear overhead and howled. Embla lifted her muzzle skywards and joined in. The rest of the crew followed suit.

It was joy, raw and primal, the thrill of survival given wordless voice.

Even Rolf grinned from ear to ear.

With what little light they had left, they sailed southwest along the coast, and found a place to berth the ship. The grey sand of the beaches was strewn with melting fragments of the floe, trophies from a battle hard-won. *Unn-marr* was pulled ashore with tender hands, and lavished with much praise for her strength and resilience as they tied off the ropes.

Feet on firm ground once more, Aelfhild dropped to her knees to kiss the earth.

Eyvind ordered for a cask of mead to be carried up from the ship, and they built a roaring fire along the dunes. Though they were all exhausted and sore—Ceolwen and Aelfhild resembled doddering crones as they limped about with stiff limbs and bent backs—they drank and danced around the fire, calling out into the darkness.

Raising a drinking horn above his head, Eyvind cried for silence. By this time, they were all well in their cups, and feeling little pain.

"Earnfoldings, hear me!" He wavered as he spoke, holding a charred stick aloft in his other hand. "Today you have done a great deed. Few dare to sail these waters, and fewer yet pass through with their lives. But we have beaten the Ormsund!"

The crew whooped and hollered incoherent insults back at the strait as they drained their cups, but it seemed that Eyvind was not yet done. When silence had returned, he continued. "Today you have become one of us. Ceolwen is already Thrym by blood, but you two," he pointed to Aelfhild and Bercthun, "you two, I name Thrym by deed. Come forward!"

Accompanied by much hollering and clapping from the rest, Aelfhild and Bercthun stood before their captain. He gave them each a sound thump on the head with his makeshift scepter.

"You are Thrym, and Leifings, too! The best Thrym!" He slurred ever so slightly as he spoke.

There were cries of agreement from all sides. Onund snorted, but Rolf was quick to push him over in the sand.

Bercthun knelt before Eyvind, and raised his hands for silence. "Lord, now that I am Thrym," he paused to burp, "I wish to swear my loyalty to the Leifings!"

The Thrym applauded, and Bercthun continued. "I swear to be true to the Jarl, and to all in his line and household! I will do my duty to the Queen, and to Thrymgard."

Eyvind slipped one of the arm rings off his wrist, and pushed it onto Bercthun's outstretched arm. "I accept your oath, young Bercthun. Stand now as one of the Jarl's warriors, and our oath-brother!"

Aelfhild clapped as her friend rose to embrace the captain, and Ceolwen whistled through her fingers. They both grabbed Bercthun by the shoulders and shook vigorously when he dropped back down beside them.

As the crew toasted Bercthun's new oath-ring, a shadowed form dropped over the side of the boat and slunk into the firelight. Vidar stood before them, tears in his eyes.

"I failed you all today," he whispered to the bristling audience, "I was weak. I beg of you to forgive me, and let me work away my shame."

Eyvind tossed his stick into the fire as he stood to face Vidar. He put a hand on either side of the woodworker's scrawny neck.

For a moment, Aelfhild feared the captain might throttle the smaller man.

Then Eyvind spoke. "Fear is the mark of a wise man, not a weak one. But the coward lets it rule him."

Vidar sniffed and nodded his head. He made as if to turn away, but Eyvind pulled him back into a shoulder-snapping hug.

"You will learn," said Eyvind as he pounded Vidar's back. "Now, sit and drink amongst friends!"

Aelfhild had never seen eyes so grateful. Vidar joined them and raised a horn, the tear stains on his cheeks shining in the light of the campfire. She raised hers as well.

"We lived!" she shouted, then threw back her head and howled once more into the night sky.

3 4

T TOOK ANOTHER day to be rid of the ill effects of the mead, but their luck stayed true and gave them a strong, southerly breeze to carry them west away from the Ormsund and into the deep waters of the North Sea. The wind filled *Unn-marr*'s sails and spared them from rowing as they recovered from the revels. There were a few smudges of cloud on the distant horizon, but the weather was fair and sunny and the days grew longer as Spring stretched her warming tendrils across the land.

The coast dropped sharply to the south after leaving the narrow strait, and they followed its course to avoid errant icebergs. It was a barren landscape, boulders and crushed rock interspersed with yellowing grass, free of trees and with only the occasional patch of malnourished bushes growing from crevices in the stone. In the distance, to the south and west, the snowy peaks of the Grimbergs jutted skywards.

This was Örland, the Scar-Land, Eyvind told Aelfhild. He sat in the prow with her and Ceolwen, pointing out the sights in the distance.

There were her volcanoes in the distance, some dormant and others very much awake, and all of them crowned by glaciers and decades of snowfall. Whenever they spewed forth their fire, the ice melted and sent ashen floods rushing out over the plains, scouring the land of any and every living thing.

Shifting his gaze westward, Eyvind nodded at the grey smudges on the horizon which Aelfhild had taken for clouds. "Ash," he said, "from the Eldfjoll. They burn and smoke all year long. We will pass under their clouds in a day, maybe two."

"Is it dangerous?" Ceolwen asked.

The Thrym shrugged his broad shoulders. "Safer than the Ormsund, but we must still go carefully. The air is bad, and the ash can set fires," he answered. "But we will pass through. Do not fear, little queen." Eyvind tousled Ceolwen's hair and walked off toward the stern, chuckling to himself.

"I did not say I was afraid." Ceolwen muttered loud enough for her servant to hear as she straightened her hair. Aelfhild held back laughter of her own.

Abruptly, there was a great deal of commotion from the starboard side of the ship. Geir and Vidar had been trailing lines for fresh fish to bring a little more variety to their diet. Geir had hooked something and yanked his line in hand over fist. He shouted as he produced a large prickle-finned fish with opaline scales from the water, lifting the thrashing bounty up above his head for all to see.

Evidently they had run across a school of the creatures, for Vidar soon had one on his line as well. It did not take long for the men to fill a barrel with fish, promising hearty suppers for the crew and for the gulls alike. Seabirds had already begun to circle the boat, following the sun's glint off the scales, and jabbered frenziedly as they waited for guts to be tossed overboard. With practiced hands, the fishermen cleaned the catch and left the birds to squabble over the cast-off innards.

The flaky, white fish proved delicious when roasted over their camp-fire that night, and they were all glad of the change from dried rations. Bones and scales crackled in the fire while, not far away, a blissful Embla worked through a pile of fish heads, filling the air with her crunching and slurping.

Kolbrun belched and patted her belly. "Onund," she called, "Give us a story!"

"A story!" Bercthun cheered.

The glow of the dying embers played across Onund's craggy features as he pulled his hood low over his brow. He thought for a moment, searching for the right tale, then cleared his throat.

"Long before mighty Sigurd led our people to Thrymgard, when he was still a young man, he wandered the land as an outlaw. For Sigurd was a great warrior—they say that he could split a shield with a single blow—but brash and quick of temper, as is often the burden of youth. On the road one day near Aettirheim he met two young men a-horseback, both finely dressed and clad with shining swords."

"Sigurd was not born to wealth. His clothes were dirty, his shoes muddy, and his axe was worn and rusty. The young men mocked him for his ragged clothing, and asked him what he hoped to do with such a paltry weapon. Now a wise man would have known to let the insult pass, but Sigurd still had much to learn. He told the men that he had this axe from his father, and his father's father, and though the edge was notched, it would cleave shield and helm with ease, and that they were fools to think that the blade mattered more than the hand that held it.

"And so they fell to boasting of their deeds and insulting one another, as boys will, and finally one of the foolhardy young men challenged Sigurd to a fight. His ire raised, Sigurd struck the man down with two swift strokes of his axe. As ill fortune would have it, though, it was the son of a Jarl he had slain, and the other man, his servant, was there as witness. And so Sigurd fled to distant parts; he lived off the land, and found what work he could as a warrior. There he gained some fame and wealth, for those were hard times and a strong sword arm was always in need.

"Sigurd had an older brother, Breki by name. Breki was a berserker, a shield-biter as they are called, for such is their madness and rage that they gnaw at the edges of their shields before battle. At that time, the holm-gang was a common thing, and fought always to the death. The winner could take the slain man's belongings, and there were some, like Breki, that used this to win much wealth. None could stand against Breki and he killed many men, some of them nobly born. The jarls feared him and hated him, but could never catch him. Time and again he would slip from their grasp, for he knew the old magic and was a shape-changer."

"As Sigurd's fame grew in the outlands, the freemen and thanes would oft seek his council in matters of war or in disputes, for he grew wiser and more level-headed with each passing year. Though he was an outlaw, he was counted as a good man and gave fair judgments. Sworn to no master, he went only where he was welcomed, and always earned his keep.

"Fleeing the wrath of all those he had wronged, Breki came riding into the southern parts where Sigurd was lingering at that time. They say that the eagles followed Breki wherever he went, for he always fed them well on the corpses of the men he killed. Folk in the outlands were easy prey for one such as he, as the law was only weakly kept at the edges of the realm. Breki took from them freely and none could stand against him."

"The thanes and farmers gathered together to seek out Sigurd, the only man thought strong enough to stand against Breki, and begged his help. 'Your brother takes what little we have,' they said, 'and kills any who deny him. You will have great fame if you slay him, and surely the jarls in Aettirheim will reward you for his head.' Sigurd's heart was heavy when he heard this, and he furrowed his brow and would not speak. He did not answer them but went up atop a high mountain, where he sat for many days and nights, unmoving."

"Some say the Gods spoke to him in a dream, others that he took council from the singing of the wind in the trees and the birds in the sky; none know for certain what passed there. On the ninth night, he returned, and said this to the waiting men, 'I have little love for Breki, but it is a wrong and evil deed for a man to slay his own brother. I will go to Breki and speak with him, and send him from these parts. If he will not hear my words, only then will I raise a hand against him.' All thought this fair and praised his wisdom."

"And so Sigurd sought out his brother, and they talked for long hours. Sigurd told Breki all that had happened, and all that he had done for these people, but Breki would not be moved. Sigurd offered to Breki all of the treasure he had won in the outlands as a ransom, but Breki would have none of it. Breki called his brother a coward, and told Sigurd that he had grown soft living amongst farmers and doing their bidding. There was only one way to settle the matter, said Breki."

"Brother and brother stepped into the circle of the holmgang, and such a fight had hardly been witnessed between men. They broke their shields and their weapons against one another, grappling with hands in a contest of brute strength. The blood rage and battle lust consumed them both, and they howled and bit one another like wild beasts. Unable to overcome his brother, Breki changed his shape; now a bear, now a wolf, now a serpent. Whatever form he took, Sigurd would best him—he pinned the roaring bear to the ground, clamped the wolf's snapping jaws shut with his fists, and tied the thrashing serpent in knots around itself. Once more in the form of a man, Breki traded blow after blow with his brother, but could not overcome him. As his strength failed him for the first time, Breki bowed before his foe."

"Such was his rage that Sigurd could not stop himself, and raised his brother high in the air, throwing down his body and crushing it against the bones of the world. As the frenzy left him, Sigurd wept bitter tears over the broken corpse of Breki. When the other men came to reward him with rich gifts of silver and gold and praise for his valor, he would accept nothing, such was his grief. 'By this deed I am cursed,' he wept, 'Kinslayer, I name myself. I will have none of your gold nor do I want your kind words. Burn my brother's body and cast the ashes to the wind, raise no mound or stone for him, so that this evil may be forgotten.' With those words he rose and went into the forest, and was not seen or heard of for many a year."

All eyes were riveted on Onund as he finished the tale. As his voiced trailed off, they followed Sigurd along forest paths in their minds' eye.

Aelfhild wiped a tear from her eye; the story had struck a little too close. "Do the stories of berserkers ever end well?"

But she knew the answer before she asked.

Onund chuckled. "No Thrym story ends happily, lass."

3 5

"E NEED MORE water by the mast, before it burns through!"

Aelfhild dragged her bucket through the waves once more, and splashed the smoking sail.

Ash from the Eldfjoll swirled around her in billowing clouds, collecting in drifts and mixing with the saltwater to form jet black sludge. Where cinders gathered in unquenched piles, they sparked and sputtered against the wood of the hull and cargo.

She refilled the bucket as, beside her, Ceolwen emptied a pail of ashen slush over the side. They were all of them ghosts beneath cloth masks, two watering eyes poking from a blank face and body coated in pale dust. The ash stuck to every surface, rendering their entire world in grey hues. *Unnmarr* cut an inky line through the sea as she sailed, though it was soon plastered over again.

Embla whined from beneath a wadded blanket. The air was thick with brimstone's reek and the ashfall tore at the nose and throat, so Eyvind had swathed her in wool for their journey through the shadow of the mountains.

Aelfhild shook ash from the rigging, and her eyes followed the line of the mast skywards. High above, lightning arced in stark blue lines through the churning clouds.

The Eldfjoll themselves were spectacular. Three peaks vomited columns of smoke and soot forth into the heavens. At the root of each one glowed an immense crater, shimmering malevolent red with heat. It was the only hint of color on the dead landscape. Steam burst from the shoreline as molten rock poured from fissures along the mountainside and cascaded into the sea.

There was a distant boom, and flecks of liquid fire sprayed from the nearest caldera.

"Ivar is stoking his forge-fires today!" shouted Onund.

And for a moment, gazing at the burning earth, Aelfhild could imagine the Smith sending sparks from his great anvil in the world's heart.

"More water here!"

The cry broke her from the daydream, and she swept back into motion.

Eyvind kept the ship a safe distance from the coast; the Thrym said that the gasses from the mountain would scald the lungs of those foolish enough to draw too close. Rafts of pumice drifted atop the waves, scraping and scratching at *Unn-marr*'s hull. The porous stones were no threat to the sturdy oaken boards, but the way the rest of the crew kept an eye cocked skyward hinted these were not the only weapons in the volcanoes' arsenal.

An ember sputtered in the sailcloth before Aelfhild could quench it and left a thumb-sized hole behind. The red wool was splotched brown with ash and charred in a dozen places now.

"Let us hope the Smith does not stoke his fires any more today," she said to Ceolwen, who was pouring another load of mud over the side.

Ceolwen flexed her shoulders and winced. "You wanted to see volcanoes, wild girl. I hope this will cure you of that madness."

Aelfhild watched the fell glow of lightning flicker within the whorls of ash overhead. Not even the pinkest Cynestead dawn or shadiest Ealdorscir meadow could compete with the furious, primal beauty of this skyline. It was glorious.

Not cured yet, was the only response she could think of.

The further they sailed from the fuming peaks, the higher the ash cloud rose above them. Color began to return to their grey world as they passed from its clutches in the afternoon. Blue water and bright sun greeted them.

Aelfhild pulled down her mask and savored clean air. Looking back, she caught sight of Ceolwen's face and snorted laughter. A straight line across the cheekbones split her face—and all their faces—in two; half caked grey, half clean and dripping with sweat. Washing the jagged grains of dust from their hands and faces left the skin raw and flushed.

Embla emerged from her covers and shook indignantly. She sniffed at the dark slurry left on the deck before marking it as her own.

"The ash got into all these barrels, here," Kolbrun called over her shoulder. Cupping a palmful from their water supply, she took a sip, then spat it out onto the deck immediately. "What filth! Tastes of charcoal and old eggs."

Meanwhile, Vidar was fussing with the sail. He pressed a finger through the cloth in some of the burned patches. His frown did not promise good tidings.

"Can you patch it?" asked Eyvind from the steering oar.

"Not in the wind. If we make land, I can. And we must check that nothing burned into the hull."

"Geir! What do you see?"

Geir, straining up over the prow, shook his head.

The wave-battered cliffs that marked the western bounds of the Grimbergs were not welcoming to travelers. It was the edge of civilized lands, and the mountains seemed keen to keep any that strayed outside those borders from returning.

So *Unn-marr* continued southward, and they kept watch for a cove or bay.

Ceolwen plopped down beside Aelfhild and yawned. "I would pay my weight in gold and silver to sleep in a real bed again," she said. "Beneath a roof, snuggled into furs after a hot meal. Imagine it, Aela!"

Aelfhild scrambled for a reply, but her mistress was already rolling onward.

"Once we are back home I shall bathe and sleep for a whole fortnight. We will feast and ride horses wherever we wish to go. If I never walk anywhere on my own two feet after this, I would be well satisfied. Streets to walk on and walls and curtains to keep the men from staring at us every minute."

"What do you miss most about home, Aela?"

Tell her the truth. Tell her you miss none of it. Tell her you will not stay.

It was a sore temptation, but the pleading look in those eyes told her this might not be the time and place for that argument. Ceolwen needed support; she needed a friend, and happier memories. So instead, Aelfhild replied, "Walking in the market like we used to."

It was not a lie. But neither was it the whole truth. Evasions and half-truths were a time-honored tool for all servants, but that did not mean Aelfhild's conscience would not jab at her as she tried to fall asleep that evening. Ceolwen's smile was payment enough to cover that inconvenience.

"Yes! And we will, we will!" She leaned back against the hull, her eyes unfocused as she pictured distant futures. After a long silence, there was another question. "What do you think we shall find out west?"

"What do you mean?" Aelfhild asked.

"Do you believe in all this?" Ceolwen waved a hand vaguely around them. "Sigurd and Breki, the Smith at his anvil, the Oath-stone, Aettirheim. Will we find anything, when we get there?"

Aelfhild fidgeted for a moment. "They seem to believe it all very—"

"—I am asking you, Aela."

"I think..." Aelfhild bought herself time.

I think what? She thought of the conversation with Eyvind at her bedside. She thought of Harald and his hunger for devotion. She thought of Bercthun's tales beneath the moons, and Onund's stories, and how they stirred her heart. She thought of the northern lights and the flaming calderas and all of the world's wonders she could never explain. And oddly enough, she thought of dried fish and how no skald ever thought to mention it.

"I think that there is some truth buried inside it. All the stories start with something true, and that gets buried a little deeper and twisted all around each time someone tells the story again. So I suppose I believe in the heart of the story but not all the little bits...if you can make any sense of that."

Ceolwen gaped back at her.

Aelfhild backpedaled. "It was foolish, do not listen to me."

"No, no, I just never knew you were so...wise."

Unsure if she should take that as a compliment, Aelfhild nodded.

"Do you believe in the Gods? Just one last question, Aela, I swear!"

"Yes." And that was the truth; the question had not been if she loved the Gods, though.

Ceolwen rubbed her palms into her eyes. "As do I. The Gods are toying with us for their own sport, I think. If we find nothing in the west, then this can all be over. If there is something to it all, though…" She left those words dangling. "Harald said it was fated, and that is what frightens me the most."

3 6

N COLDER TIMES, glaciers had carved the shores along the North Sea into fjords wide and deep. Sheer stone walls rose from sapphire water and ended in crowns of trailing juniper, where flocks of ravens flitted about and argued in their croaking voices.

At long last, after days spent with bitter water and flapping sails, Geir spotted a promising looking fjord for them, and they sailed inland.

The sheer lines of the cliff face gave way to rolling, grassy slopes, studded with copses of rowan and yew. Whitewater rushed through rock-strewn courses between the hills and cascaded down into the waiting sea. Rolf steered them through the narrowing waterway, and Aelfhild rowed with the rest. With each passing day she found she could pull the oar longer and keep time easier with the crew. They beached *Unn-marr* at the base of a hill and carried their supplies up the slopes to make camp.

An unbroken canopy of leaves, cones, and needles stretched off into the distance to the south. The grass was lush and soft here, the soil black from years of falling ash.

Listening as Cuthbert had taught her so long ago, Aelfhild could hear birds and bugs of all manner rising in chorus.

Eyvind divided them into groups. "Vidar will see to the ship. Rolf and Geir, find us a spring to fill these barrels. Should not take long, from the look of things."

The pair hefted water-skins and set off into the brush.

"Jarngrim, Onund, Bercthun, with me. Set snares, find roots and berries, whatever provisions are out there."

"Kolbrun, Aelfhild, Ceolwen." He pointed to the women. "Firewood."

Aelfhild felt her chest deflate. Back to the old ways.

Embla was already on the scent; her tail wagged furiously as she snuffled around in the leaves. Eyvind followed along with a bundle of throwing spears as the other men set off into the woods.

Kolbrun was not pleased with her task and took no pains to hide it as she led her charges into the forest.

"Kolbrun, guard the outlanders. Kolbrun, pick up sticks," she muttered, kicking up leaves. "Kolbrun, tidy up the camp."

The shield-maiden spun on her heel to face the Earnfoldings. "He is better than most but he is still a damned fool some days. I am going hunting. You two, find dry wood and do not die, or I will never hear the end of it." With that she stormed off toward camp, presumably to fetch her spear but possibly to find rope with which to throttle her captain.

"We will be fine without you," said Ceolwen to the shield-maiden's retreating back. She looked toward Aelfhild, and they burst into giggles.

Embla barked in the distance.

The work was far from exciting or glamorous, but necessary. Aelfhild felt right at home. She daydreamed as she wandered about, enjoying the cushion of moss and loam underfoot. Onund's telling of the fate of Breki and Sigurd was still fresh in her mind, and she wondered at the age of the trees. Had they been saplings when Sigurd wandered in these forests, grieving the death of his brother? She brushed a hand along the gnarls and ridges of a moss-draped oak. Generations had passed since humans had lived west of the Grimbergs, but some of the trees might yet remember their passing.

She stooped to gather a few branches that looked fit for burning and paused. There was another sound in the wood, not her footfalls and not Ceolwen's either. She listened.

Something was snuffling through the loam nearby. Something heavy.

Aelfhild waved to get Ceolwen's attention. She ceased her humming and squinted in her servant's direction.

Carefully, Aelfhild lowered her bundle of firewood. She took care to place her feet on moss rather than in the leaves as she stepped toward a nearby bush. With finger and thumb, she pulled one of the branches aside to peep through.

A hulking boar, a lump of bristles and mud on four bone-crunching hoofs, was rooting through a bank of fallen leaves on the other side. Its ears swiveled back and forth as the shovel nose carved ruts through the earth.

It has not seen you, Aelfhild thought. Just step back.

She let the branch fall into place and crept backward.

Behind her, Ceolwen was wide eyed and ghost white. "What is it?" she mouthed.

Aelfhild waved for her to back away. As Ceolwen turned, her foot caught a root in the ground, and she crashed into the dry leaves.

Scrambling to lift her mistress, Aelfhild did not look back over her shoulder. The rustling of their own feet drowned out most noise, but she imagined a pair of mad eyes and piercing tusks emerging from the bushes behind to inspect the intruders.

She heard a grunt and whispered "Run."

There was a bent yew tree, perfect for climbing, about fifty paces ahead of them, and Aelfhild closed the gap faster than a heartbeat. Ceolwen was at her heels the whole way. They sprang up the base and launched themselves into the tangled branches, scampering up and out onto the overhanging limbs. Flakes of dry bark rained down beneath them.

The boar sniffed along their trail at an easy trot. It circled the base of the tree, snorting and squealing at the foreign scent.

"What do we do?" whispered Ceolwen.

At this point, Aelfhild was not sure which direction they had come from. She turned to face in what she hoped was a camp-ward direction, and shouted.

"Help!"

They both took turns yelling, but got no response. Noise did not seem to perturb the boar, which had now returned to foraging below their roost. It did not look angry, but Aelfhild was in no hurry to drop down and test matters.

"We could run, Aela," Ceolwen hissed across the tree.

"I do not even know which way camp is."

"We could throw something."

"Unless you are hiding a spear somewhere, I would not."

Ceolwen scoffed.

"Wait, did you see that?"

Aelfhild turned to look. Something had shifted between two distant trunks.

Vidar's head appeared around the side of an oak.

"What is it?" he called.

"Boar!" Both Ceolwen and Aelfhild shouted back.

The woodworker emerged from behind his tree, bow in hand. He crouched and surveyed the scene.

Do not try it alone, thought Aelfhild. Go for help.

Vidar seemed to be debating the same question. He stole a glance back the way he had come. He looked at his feet, then back over his shoulder toward safety.

Then he seemed to reach a decision. With a deep breath, he crept forward.

"Be ready to run," Aelfhild whispered to Ceolwen, as the bowman nocked an arrow.

The first shot hit the boar in its meaty shoulder. It bellowed in surprise, but showed no ill effects, and thrashed about in search of the attacker.

Vidar got another arrow in its side before the beast spotted him and charged.

"Run!" Aelfhild called, but Ceolwen was already sprinting away.

Another shaft whistled through the air, and a fourth, as Aelfhild raced through the trees.

There was a heavy thump behind. The boar had reached Vidar.

But there were no screams.

She turned, expecting carnage.

Instead, the bristled carcass lay at Vidar's feet, a pair of arrows sticking from its skull.

Aelfhild walked over to Vidar. He stared at his kill, panting. It looked as though Vidar had not expected this outcome either from the size of his pupils.

"Thank you," she said, slapping his shoulder.

Vidar's words failed him. He wheezed back what Aelfhild took for a reply.

"Grab a leg and we can drag it back," she said. He nodded.

As they pulled the boar behind them, Ceolwen emerged from the woods with Rolf and Geir in tow. The men lowered their spears when they saw the carcass.

"Aela!" Ceolwen pulled Aelfhild into her arms.

Geir peered down at the boar and chortled. "Just a little thing."

"Be silent!" Ceolwen shouted. "It was not charging *you*!"

They carried the beast back to camp and left Rolf to dress it for cooking. They had to return to their piles of firewood, but went under guard this time. The others were waiting when they returned. Eyvind and Bercthun held a bundle of roots and berries between them and looked embarrassed. Kolbrun carried one skinny rabbit and looked angry.

"I leave you two alone in the woods and this is what you find," the shield-maiden muttered.

Vidar did not seem to be prepared for his newfound glory. Though the boar did look decidedly smaller on a spit over the glowing coals, everyone was quick to slap his back for standing ground.

"I said you would learn, Vidar," Eyvind cut the heart from the roasting carcass. "And learn you did. All hail the huntsman!"

Vidar took a bite of his trophy as Thrym and Earnfolding all cheered.

3 7

ND KOLBRUN WAS right, she never did hear the end of it.

"Since I cannot depend on the skjaldmaer to keep you safe," Eyvind said to Ceolwen and Aelfhild, "we shall have to teach you how to fight for yourselves. Go and fetch your axes!"

The pair exchanged nervous glances as they went back to the ship to retrieve their weapons, and found Kolbrun and Eyvind armed and waiting upon returning to the crest of the hill. Each of the Thrym had their axe and shield at the ready and bid Aelfhild and Ceolwen do the same.

"Your most important weapon is here," Eyvind began, tapping a finger to his head. "Watch every move of your enemy. The way he stands, the way he walks, the way he swings and turns. Listen to his breathing. Small things can turn the tide. Watch us."

He turned to Kolbrun and they squared off, showing how to stand and how to circle an opponent in low, guarded gait. With deliberate sweeps of his blade, Eyvind taught them how best to hook an enemy's shield, or swipe away an incoming axe-blow. Aelfhild and Ceolwen mimed each stroke as Kolbrun walked behind them, nudging wayward feet or elbows with the haft of her axe.

"Now for some real practice!" Kolbrun and Ceolwen broke off to one side, and Aelfhild stood before Eyvind.

Aelfhild's heart hammered as she clenched the haft of her axe. The leather straps of her shield bit into the soft skin on her forearm. She drew in a deep breath and released the air slowly through her nose.

"Ready?" asked Eyvind.

She nodded, afraid to speak lest her voice tremble.

Slowly, he stepped forward until they were but a pace apart. His first swing was low, looping toward Aelfhild's knee; she threw out her shield arm to block.

With an overhand blow, Aelfhild hooked the edge of her axe over Eyvind's shield and pulled it forward with all her strength. He did not budge.

"Break," called Eyvind. "Again."

This time, Aelfhild watched his advancing feet. She did not notice her shield drop, nor did she have time to dodge his axe blow. Her arm went numb as she stumbled beneath the impact.

"Shield up!" he shouted. "Learn to see it all at once, not just the one thing!"

Stepping back in, Aelfhild raised her shield, peering over the edge. Her chest was heaving. They circled, eyes locked.

With every heartbeat, she feared the coming bloodlust. It lurked at the edge of panic and she knew what it brought. The glinting edge in her hand promised only woe. She wrestled her breathing back under control.

Eyvind must have noticed. "Good," he whispered. "There will always be fear. Use it to stay sharp, but control it. Do not let it rule you."

He darted forward and swung, but she danced out of reach.

There was a sharp breath, a little gasp of air, right before he attacked. She listened for it again.

They circled.

Then suddenly, there was the noise; she launched herself to the right with every ounce of strength in her legs and lashed out at Eyvind's shield. The blow struck home, and he hollered as he rocked back on his heels.

"A fine hit!" cried Rolf.

The greybeard had come to watch this new spectacle and shook his fists in approval. Ceolwen and Kolbrun continued their sparring nearby.

Eyvind grinned. "Better."

They practiced stance and swing until Aelfhild's arms ached from repeated shield blows and her hands blistered on the axehandle.

"The axe is a tool," Eyvind said as he strode between the two Earnfoldings. "It is as worthy or weak as the hand that holds it."

Aelfhild repeated that to herself over and over. The hand that wields it. She ruled the axe and not the other way around. Trust the Thrym to hide their most profound teachings in the shield-wall. She could protect Ceolwen with it. She could kill Osric with it. She could help.

This was something new she could offer.

"Take the anger, take the pain and the hope for tomorrow," continued Eyvind. "They are tools you use to make sure you live and your foe dies. But keep them in hand always."

He spoke to them both, but Aelfhild had little doubt the words were for her benefit. Ceolwen had not so far proved an eager or apt pupil. She held the axe away from herself at arm's length and sagged under her shield.

Aelfhild was keener. Her stomach no longer turned at the weight in her hand. There was, she found, a primal thrill in the axe blow: a tremor that drifted along the wooden handle and coursed outwards through her whole body and tugged at instincts long buried and tucked away. As the feeling ebbed, it left her calmer, soothed. This was no real battle. She had no illusions about that. But one day, with practice, she would be able to stand beside her companions rather than behind them. And if the control Eyvind offered was a way to temper her curse, then she would seize hold of that chance with all her strength.

Wolves howled in the nearby woods that evening. The crew had made no effort to mask the smell of their roasting pig, and the aroma had carried. Aelfhild knelt beside Embla at the edge of the firelight, staring into the trees. The hound shifted side to side, growling at every snapping twig and stirring leaf.

Geir, Jarngrim, and Bercthun were busy picking over the remains of Vidar's boar, though by now it was down to just hooves and bones. The three were determined to let no scrap of pork escape. Onund napped beneath his hood. Vidar and Kolbrun were playing a game of knives, throwing their blades into the dirt to see whose aim was sharper.

Ceolwen sat atop a log watching Rolf and Eyvind polish the sea salt and dirt from the iron studs in their leather armor. As Aelfhild wandered over, she heard her mistress interrogating the Thrym.

"Will we know it when we reach Aettirheim? All this land looks the same to my eyes."

Eyvind did not look up from his work. "We are still sailing to the south here, following the line of the land. From the Ormsund it dips south and west, curving like a bowl. When the land starts to rise to the north once more we will be close."

"How much longer?" asked Ceolwen.

"Hard to say, cousin. Maybe ten more days, if the winds favor us."

"Will there be anything left after so long?"

"Some old stones and little more would be my guess." Eyvind lifted his armor in the firelight, checking the shine on each bit of metal. He seemed satisfied and laid the armor tenderly atop his blanket.

"The tales say the city was built atop a high hill with a view of all the lands around," he said. "The harbor was filled with sharp rocks that rise up from the water like teeth, and only those that knew the safe course could sail through them."

"So we look for those rocks in the sea."

Eyvind nodded. "And there may be something left of the walls. But it may take some searching." He clucked his tongue, and Embla came over to join them. She sat close to her master's leg and chuffed as the wolves set to howling again.

"Keep the fires high tonight," he said. "The pup smells trouble."

Aelfhild looked out into the dark. "Do you think they will come close?"

"Not if they have sense. My Embla knows just what to do with a thieving wolf."

Embla growled her agreement.

3 8

FTER TWO MORE days of sailing, the coastline ceased its southward slope as they came to the bottom of the curving bowl that Eyvind had described. They made good progress with fair winds and fine weather.

The morning of the third day was bright and clear with a strong southerly breeze that whipped spray from the sea and kicked the waves up into white peaks. *Unn-marr* leapt from trough to trough with graceful ease and left a trail of foam in her wake.

Ceolwen and Aelfhild stood in the bucking prow as water splashed up onto their faces and wetted their hair, voices raised to the breeze. Any trace of seasickness was long gone, even in the high swells.

Jarngrim stood at the port-side rail and stared at a spot along the coast. Something had caught his attention. Rolf and Eyvind both raised a hand to their brow as they scanned the shoreline; Aelfhild did as well, but could see nothing.

"What do you see?" hollered Eyvind over the booming of the keel.

Jarngrim shouted back, "Cannot be sure. On the bluff there, south and west."

"Stone walls," cried Geir. "Vines on them, but handwork beneath."

Rolf angled the ship in the direction of Jarngrim's outstretched hand. The move brought them head-on into the wind, so their sails were of little use.

"Oars!" Eyvind called, as the crew scampered to their places.

Aelfhild's view was rather limited with her back to the prow of the ship. She focused on keeping time with the shoulders in front of her, though such a mundane task did free her imagination to wander.

He said ten days, and the details are all wrong, so it is not Aettirheim. Maybe it is one of Vidar's long-awaited treasure hordes.

In her mind's eye, piles of silver and gems glittered in underground vaults. There were always traps in the stories, spiked pits, hidden rooms, and rings of fire. And wyrms.

A wyrm atop a mountain of gold!

They would need their spears.

By the steering oar in the stern, Eyvind and Rolf pointed and peered at whatever Jarngrim had seen. Her curiosity was truly piqued now, and Aelfhild struggled with all her will against the temptation to turn and look; her task, though, was to pull the oar, and if the rest of the crew could resist looking, so could she.

Rolf changed course to the southeast, moving them along the shoreline, which afforded the rowers a better view of the clifftops. High above, perched on the rocks and cloaked by the undergrowth, was the unmistakable shape of stonework. The joints between stones, all sharp angles and level edges, stood out even at a distance. Oars knocked against one another as the rowers stared upwards.

Though the forest had tried its hardest to reclaim the bluff, part of a wall remained.

The cliffs here were too sheer to scale, rising straight from the water to dizzying heights atop which the wall stood. But a fissure split the rock face and snaked inland, and they followed its course.

Rock hemmed them in on both sides, and they rowed in darkness lit only by the sliver of sky overhead. The channel was narrow, not twice as wide as the ship; if they stretched the oars out to full length, they could scrape the canyon walls. The splash of oar blades and the sound of their breathing echoed in the tight space.

The canyon emptied into a small cove.

Aelfhild watched Eyvind's eyebrows rise as they passed back into sunlight. As she turned to look with the others, she heard Ceolwen gasp.

The cove was perfect. A stream tumbled down from the cliffs and through a sluice of boulders to mix with the saltwater of the sea. Tall pines dotted the bank above and cast dancing shadows over the shell-strewn sand of the beach. The water below was perfectly clear, revealing swarms of iridescent fish that darted and hid amongst the seaweed strands.

Over the ship's starboard side, a path rose along the cliff and disappeared into the upper crags. There were wide steps carved into the steeper sections of the trail; even the ancients had not wanted to spoil the inlet's beauty, it seemed, and the carving had been done only where necessary.

It felt crass to spoil the pristine beach with footprints. Aelfhild tried to step lightly as they pulled *Unn-marr* ashore.

"Geir, Vidar, with the ship," ordered Rolf, slipping an axe into his belt-loop and a shield over his shoulder. "The rest with us."

Embla led the way up the path, with Eyvind behind. Years of rain and ice had worn the stone smooth, so they placed their feet with care. The way was steep and winding and they were out of breath when they reached the top. Aelfhild stood bent over at the waist, hands on her knees, sucking in deep breaths full of cloying pollen. Kolbrun and Rolf beside her were in no better state.

Emerging from the rocks at the trailhead, they found themselves on a carpet of dry needles and cones beneath a stand of spindly evergreens. Ravens croaked and cawed at the intruders. Black wings beat the air as the birds swooped off from their roosts, spouting indignation.

The wall that Jarngrim had spotted was little more than a half circle of fallen stones at the edge of the bluff. Vines and bushes wrapped themselves around the bottom of the masonry and sprouted from every exposed crack. At such a height, the site commanded an unmatched view of the coastline for as far as the eye could see, and they all stood for some time admiring the scene.

"A watchtower, maybe?" said Bercthun.

Eyvind agreed. "Most likely. There would have been many along the coast to spy out raiding ships. And they would burn fires in the mist to mark the shoreline for wayfarers."

"So does this mean we are near to Aettirheim?" Ceolwen asked.

"No. We are still too far south. This is just some small outpost, but it means we are at the edge of the lost lands now," Eyvind replied.

Ceolwen nodded.

There was a mix of disappointment and relief on her mistress' face; Aelfhild could tell because she felt the same, just for different reasons. She knew Ceolwen wanted the journey to end but feared what they might find. In Aelfhild's case, it was the opposite.

"Spread out and look for more," came the order.

They fanned out inland under the watchful eyes of the ravens.

Just a short way from the tower, a steep bank sprouted up from the ground, breaking the downhill sweep from the cliffs. It curved off in both directions and looked artificial despite the thick mat of sawtooth grass that grew up and over the lip. The deep roots of the grass provided solid holds for hand and foot and made climbing easy, although the blades scraped at exposed skin.

From atop the ridge it was clear that this was some sort of earthwork circle around a central bowl-shaped depression. Weeds grew thick and unruly in the center, but along straight pathways that marked out rectangular tracts covered only by moss.

"A ring-fort," said Rolf, and the others nodded their agreement.

Seeing the question in Aelfhild's eyes, Eyvind explained. "A wall of dirt around longhouses where the warriors lived. They would have watched from the tower, and kept their ships in the cove below. It is in a good spot—clear views and easily held against attack."

The other warriors nodded in approval.

They slid down the steep walls into the center and wandered about. Hidden amongst the shrubs and coated by lichen were carved stones—the remains of foundations, walls, and hearths.

Aelfhild kicked something up as she walked and bent down to find a smooth piece of flint, sides chipped evenly to a sharp edge. A striking stone, if she had to guess; it fit the contours of her hand quite nicely, and she slipped it into her belt pouch for later inspection. They found more artifacts strewn about the ancient fortress, pieces of carved stone or badly rusted iron, but there was little left that could be of any real use.

As Aelfhild knelt to brush the grass and dirt from some foundation stones, she heard a sharp crack and a yelp from nearby. Ceolwen, who had stood close at hand just a heartbeat earlier, had disappeared.

Standing up to get a better look, Aelfhild saw the gaping hole in the ground that had swallowed up her mistress. She screamed for the others.

The crew sprinted over to the spot and peered down into the murky pit.

"Ceolwen!" Aelfhild shouted.

There were groans from below, and the clank of shifting debris.

"I am alive," Ceolwen called back, "Just some bruises. I cannot see a thing, though."

"Stay there, do not move."

Kolbrun had brought a length of rope. She unwound it from her shoulder as Rolf set about making a fire to light some torches. Aelfhild's new flint proved most useful, striking sparks from an axe blade into dry grass, and soon they had flames flickering and torches kindled. Rolf and Bercthun wrapped the rope about their shoulders to belay the others as they slid down. Embla sniffed frantically and whined at the edge of the hole as her humans disappeared.

Ceolwen's nerve held out, even alone and in the dark, and Aelfhild was proud of her; never once did her voice crack as the crew set about affecting a rescue. As soon as Aelfhild's feet touched the floor, she squeezed her mistress' arm.

"I am fine, really," said Ceolwen. Brave words, but Aelfhild could feel her trembling.

With an ill placed step, Ceolwen had dropped down through ancient planks into some sort of cellar. It was dank and cool under the soil, the air stuffy. Their torches revealed lines of clay jars filled only with dust or mold, and piles of decaying wood now turned to splinters. They followed the passage forward. Rolf swept his torch across the floor as they went.

Traps, thought Aelfhild.

The walls and floor were set in unadorned flagstones and the chamber was maybe ten paces across at widest. There were no traps. At one end of the hallway was a set of stairs covered over with more flimsy boards. With little effort they were back in the sun.

Ceolwen grinned at Aelfhild. "Let us not do that again."

Both sighed with relief.

Onund had stayed behind to explore the rest of the cellar, and called them back in. Ceolwen sat in the fresh air with Embla, but the others returned to sate their curiosity. The hole made by the unplanned royal entrance was roughly in the middle of the cellar's ceiling, the stairs at the south end. Back to the north, Onund showed them a plinth rising up from the floor upon which rested an ornate stone casket, runes etched atop the lid.

Holding his torch close to the inscription, Onund deciphered the words slowly. "Arinbjorn, Thane of Skelborg."

"Does old Arinbjorn have aught else to tell us?" asked Kolbrun, peering at the carvings in vain.

"Skelborg," Eyvind repeated. "Not a name I have ever heard."

A ring of shrugs and blank faces said that none of the others had either.

"There is more," said Onund.

Behind the tomb were more bones. Four bodies, the flesh long since crumbled away, rested in an even row along the far wall. Their arms had been folded across their hollow chests. Onund held his torch over a fifth skeleton which lay slumped in the corner.

"This one laid out the others," he said.

Kolbrun walked along the wall. "What do these runes say?"

This section of the tomb was paneled with granite slabs, and each was carved with spidery writing.

"All names." Onund squinted as he read. "Buri fathered Borr, who fathered Ve, who fathered Vali, on and on. The Thane's lineage, I would guess."

"But how did these five die?" Aelfhild asked.

The crew was silent.

"Our friend here may tell us," said Eyvind from beside the fifth body.

The most recent runes were scratched rather than chiseled; where the others were neat, clean cuts in the stone, these were a mess of shallow scrapes made by a knife or spear tip.

It took Onund a moment to decipher. "*Thurse above*, that part is clear, but the next..." He pursed his lips. "*Burn root, vines wither*. That is all there is."

Thurse above. Aelfhild's skin prickled at the thought. Even wyrms paled in comparison to the Giants' Bane.

"I thought they were just a story," she whispered.

It was the constant refrain of nursemaids to misbehaving children, "Behave, or the Thurse will come for you." There were a dozen other geists and ghouls that could be substituted in for the Thurse, and none of them real. That was one story that Aelfhild hoped did not bear a seed of truth.

"No," said Onund. "They drove our people from these lands. Sigurd gave himself to drive them back. They are real enough."

"Like your trolls, though," Eyvind broke in, "they are gone. They have been gone for an age."

Onund sucked at his whiskers. He did not reply.

"They starved down here," Kolbrun sounded queasy, and Aelfhild had to agree that the image was not a pleasant one.

"Leave the dead to rest," Jarngrim said from behind. "We should not linger."

They followed him back into the sun.

"What do the other words mean? Burn root, vines wither?" Aelfhild pondered aloud.

Eyvind shrugged. "Imagine how the mind must play tricks on a starving man. Sounds like madness to me."

3 9

HEIR CAMP WAS peaceful that night, with the stream bab-
bling away nearby and the distant rhythm of waves against
the cliffs. Aelfhild stared into the fire.

Onund was telling the others what they had found in the
crypt. "For some reason, they stayed behind. Maybe they were too old or
sick. Most of the folk left out of these parts when Aettirheim fell to the
Thurse and went east with Sigurd and the rest."

"Tell us of the Thurse," said Aelfhild.

The Thrym grumbled.

"Ill luck," she heard Vidar say.

Ceolwen shushed them. "I would hear it, too," she said.

"You know that human and Jotunn made war on one another, yes?"
Onund asked.

The Earnfoldings nodded.

"It begins there. Jotnir were too few to last against our kind. So they
took the arts taught to them by Ivar the Smith, upon whose Anvil all are
shaped, and twisted them. Those are the Thurse, cursed spawn of Giants.
And the Thurse were fierce and drove us from Mannaheim, but the victory of the Jotnir was brief."

"The creatures turned on their makers and hunted them to the end.
They drove our people out into the world, and all the tribes scattered.
Some wandered to Aettirheim and made a city there—our ancestors."

"But the Thurse found them. And the Aettir defended their lands and
cities for long years, but the tide was not to be stemmed."

"Sigurd rose to gather the people, and they fled east. It was in the passes of the Grimbergs that they had their last battle. Sigurd fell, but the Thurse were broken. And the surviving sons of Sigurd, Vignir and Orn, went on to settle lands of their own—our lands."

The Skjoldung spat as he concluded. "A foul tale!"

Silence hung over the camp.

"Cheer us up, old man," Geir tossed a pebble toward Onund. "Give us something joyful!"

"What?"

"Tell us about Thane Arinbjorn."

"I am not so old that I knew him, you wag."

The tension had broken and the others joined in.

Jarngrim shouted, "Make it up, like you always do!"

Aelfhild could already see Arinbjorn in her mind. She said, "I picture him with a great belly and a long black beard. He smiles and laughs easily."

"Like Eorl Cuthbert," said Bercthun. "I like it."

"A thane would have chainmail. Does he fight with a sword?" asked Jarngrim.

"No, a spear," Eyvind replied. "He is humble, not vain."

Onund stood before the crackling embers and let his blue cloak swirl around him. He raised his voice to the stars. "And so with flashing spear and shining mail Thane Arinbjorn of Skelborg strode out to meet his foes. Battle was joined atop the Grand Stair, and one by one he cast his enemies down to their ruin. They parted like breaking waves around his tower-shield and fled before his flaming gaze."

The old man mimed the spear strokes and counterblows.

"He needs a monster to fight!" cried Bercthun.

Vidar rubbed his hands together. "More gold and silver!"

"Beautiful women!" was Geir's suggestion.

Kolbrun kicked the man in his protruding gut. "What would you know of beautiful women?"

Onund continued. "And then came the troll, the rock eater spewed from the vile depths of the earth. Arinbjorn held the line! His men quailed from the beast's foul breath, but the Thane stood tall. He matched blow for blow, until his spear broke on the obsidian hide and shield shattered beneath the leaden club."

The audience held their collective breaths.

"All was lost! But as the troll reached to devour Thane Arinbjorn in its reeking maw, the Gods sent him one final burst of strength. He seized his broken spear point and skewered the creature through the mouth, up into its pebbly brain!"

Aelfhild whooped for Arinbjorn along with the others.

"Arinbjorn took the troll horde—the buried gold and silver!—but not for himself. He spread it around to his people, and was loved by all. He lived on many years to raise a toast with his sons and his sons' sons!"

"Well put, Onund," said Eyvind when the cheering had died down.

The skald took a bow before settling back into his blanket. There were smiles around the campfire once more.

But the wheels turned as they always did.

Aelfhild found herself thinking of a neglected tomb in a forgotten hole. She thought of nameless bones and walls that guarded mere foundations. That took some of the glimmer from the story, and she saw her thoughts mirrored in eyes around the campfire. Will they remember us? Remember me? It was a hard question to avoid.

"Servants do not get tombs."

She realized she had spoken the thought aloud.

"You are a hard one to cheer up, girl," muttered Kolbrun. The shield-maiden rolled onto her side and put her back to the fire.

"Kings do. And Queens," said Ceolwen. She stared into the heart of the fire, oblivious to the baleful stales directed her way from all sides.

The girl would always be a royal. Even without a crown, there was no curing her of that upbringing. Still, Aelfhild was taken aback by the callous comment.

"Such gloom!" Eyvind called. "Why waste your worries on what sort of tomb you will have? You will not care much when it comes time to lie in it. Live, and let your deeds be your mark on the world!"

Rolf grunted; evidently the grey-beard agreed.

"That is what Arinbjorn would tell you, if he could," Eyvind said. "Now sleep, we have a ways yet to row and this talking helps no one."

4 0

STRONG WIND BLEW up from the west for several days and slowed the ship's progress. They rowed but could make little headway against the force of the waves, and tacking against such a wind proved slow and fruitless work. The crew labored hard for little return and came ashore exhausted each night.

Unsympathetic to sore arms and tired backs, Eyvind had Aelfhild and Ceolwen practice their axe work every evening before turning in. Each of the Thrym had advice to give, and each a different style. Kolbrun fought defensively, always deliberate and measured in her movements; Rolf was wild and aggressive, his blows unpredictable. One warrior gripped his axe in just such a way, another differently, while one placed his feet closer together, another further apart.

At first Aelfhild found the mess of conflicting instruction overwhelming, but she soon realized that the Thrym were merely trying to give her a range of choices. There was no single path, and tactics that suited one warrior might cost another his life. It would be up to her to find what fit.

She tried them all, ducking and shuffling and swinging until her limbs turned to lead and could move no more. Then she would flop down on her blanket and snore until roused to stand watch.

They woke one morning to find good fortune had delivered them a southeasterly wind. Rolf set a westward course under billowing sails, and the crew took their ease.

The first clouds did not appear until midday. They began as distant dots along the horizon to the south and east.

Aelfhild noticed the Thrym starting to stir. Kolbrun went back to confer with Rolf. They pointed toward the storm front, and whispered back and forth.

The clouds were bruised purple-grey, but Aelfhild saw little to worry about. *Unn-marr* had passed through ice floes and cinder storms, and a little rain would be no more than a break from the tedium of sailing. She remembered how her companions had brushed off the squall on their first day together, and felt no fear.

But the wind grew and the sky darkened. Lightning lanced through pregnant thunderheads along the storm line, though the thunder was still just a murmur in the distance.

When Geir leapt to the prow to scan the shore for a landing place, Aelfhild began to fret.

They were well out to sea and the wind was against them. The coastline was different here than near the Grimbergs; limestone pillars and islets rose to block easy passage to the narrow beaches beyond.

White froth appeared atop the waves as the gale whipped higher, and the deck rocked wildly beneath their feet.

Eyvind and Rolf came to a decision in the stern and turned the ship out to sea. They rode the breakers away from the storm, but even Aelfhild with her limited seamanship could see that outrunning it was not a possibility.

"Lash down the oars and chests," Rolf bellowed. "Stow the sail and set lines for running off."

A few of the words Aelfhild did not recognize. She knelt beside Kolbrun as they fastened ropes through slats in the hull.

"What is *running off*?"

"We cannot row and the wind will break the mast clean off with sails. So we float bare and let the storm carry us along."

"And the ropes?"

"We toss them over if we need to slow. Too fast, and we plow into the wave in front of us. Too slow, and we fall into the one behind."

Neither choice sounded good. Aelfhild's throat felt suddenly narrow, and she swallowed hard.

"But Eyvind knows what to do?"

Kolbrun looked up at her. There was no hint of jest in her eyes. "Anyone can hold the oar and pray. Now is the time for praying."

They pulled the cloth awning up around the mast and huddled beneath it. Eyvind and Rolf stood at the steering board, watching the waves.

Vidar was chanting to himself; the words were hard to make out, but the tone was pleading. Kolbrun crouched with her hand atop one of the coiled running lines and waited for a signal. Geir and Jarngrim did the same. Their eyes did not drift from Eyvind.

Aelfhild sat beside Ceolwen and Bercthun. She had no prayers for the Gods. Instead, she reached out and held both of her companion's hands. Her mistress did not look up. Bercthun merely nodded.

Rain began to fall, a pitter-patter at first, but building as the sky above blackened.

Thunder crashed around them in ear-shattering clamor, and the sea boiled under the assault of rain and wind. Hail pummeled *Unn-marr*, drumming at the wooden boards and tearing at the stitches of their woolen shelter.

The deck heaved. Aelfhild wedged her feet into the hull and pressed her back against a sea chest.

"Line away!" She could not tell if Eyvind or Rolf had yelled it.

Kolbrun dropped her coil overboard, and the boards of the railing creaked as the rope snapped taut in the waves.

Twilight engulfed them beneath the shroud of storm clouds. Lightning flashed, illuminating Rolf and Eyvind as they wrestled the steering oar into place.

It was too loud to speak, or at least too loud to be heard; Vidar's lips were in constant motion. Wind, surf, hail, and thunder roared over any words. Aelfhild kept a tight grip on her friends. In the flickering light, she could see white eyes.

"Line away!"

Geir tossed his rope over the side.

A splintering crack shook the deckboards, felt as much as heard. The mast bent and snapped, breaking halfway up and ripping away the awning as it careened out into the waves. Torn from its moorings, a cord scythed past Aelfhild's face with a high-pitched wail. All of the crew dropped face-down into the water sloshing the deck as debris whipped overhead.

Unn-marr lurched to starboard. Ropes still bound to the mast dragged the ship over, and Kolbrun sprang to the railing.

"Cut it free!" she howled to the Earnfoldings.

Aelfhild fumbled for her beltknife and sawed into a nearby line thrumming with tension. It frayed and snapped beneath her blade, and she was flung sideways as the anchor dropped away and the ship rocked upright once more.

She had lost her hold of Ceolwen and Bercthun.

Hail pelted her face and shoulders, and the rain was numbing cold down her back. Her feet and fingers were frozen.

Lightning spread searing cracks through the clouds and left her blind and blinking in the murk.

"Line! Line!" came the cry from the stern.

In another burst of light, she saw Jarngrim scrabbling to get his coil of rope over the rail.

There was no end to the storm in sight. The darkness sprawled toward both horizons.

The ship's prow dipped wildly into a trough and hooked the back of the next wave. A wall of water roared across the deck. Aelfhild watched as a man's body, she could not tell who, was swept over the railing and out into the sea. Water slammed against her chest and pulled her feet out from under her. She hooked an arm through one of the ropes across the deck and pulled herself out of the wave's clutches.

Unn-marr shuddered, her hull screaming as it bent beneath the added weight. Aelfhild could feel boards fracturing beneath her.

Lightning. This time it shimmered through the air at a snail's pace; the glow skittered across the water's roiling surface.

The world was suddenly still.

Rain drops hung suspended in the air.

Aelfhild looked up.

Another wave towered over the prow, paused in mid-break.

She took a deep breath.

Then she was in the sea.

She thrashed to stay afloat beneath the sopping weight of her clothing. The waves drove her forward. There was no controlling direction, so she kicked and flailed just to keep her head above. Light and thunder, and she saw a beach. The waves that crashed upon it were mountains. She tried to turn, but the current was stronger. She was borne onward in the dark.

The sea lifted her body into the air before slamming back down against the shore. Sand scraped at her face and arms. As the surf rushed back, it seized her legs to drag her out once more.

She gasped air whenever her head broke the water and cast around for a handhold in the shifting grains.

Teeth sank into her shoulder. Jaws closed, vice-like, around her arm. Something was pulling her up from the waves, the tear of fangs a welcome relief from the battering tide.

Embla. A single thought raced through her mind. Embla has me.

She had paid no mind to the dog in all the chaos.

Aelfhild tried to stand but was knocked once more from her feet by the waves. Embla kept dragging her bodily up the shore toward rocks above.

It took Aelfhild a moment to clear her lungs once she was out of the water. She clutched at Embla's sodden fur.

Another lightning flash revealed a struggling form in the surf not far away. Barking wildly, Embla ran toward it.

Eyvind, battered bloody beneath his torn clothing, staggered up from the waves behind his faithful hound. He grabbed unsteadily at Aelfhild and they stumbled up the shore in the darkness, unable to speak over the waves and howling wind. He retched seawater and sagged onto her shoulder.

In the lee of rocks higher up the beach they sheltered, clinging to one another in the gale as they shivered and shook.

Embla huddled close for warmth.

The storm raged on outside their cave.

4 1

ELFHILD'S EYES WERE crusted with salt and swollen shut.
She heard the wind still howling. But there were cracks
of daylight through her eyelids now.

Time had passed but she did not know how much. She
had drifted in and out. At least once she had lurched awake to vomit up
stinging hot seawater and reeking bile.

A cold nose pressed against her cheek, and she heard Embla's whine.

"Good girl," she croaked and ran her fingers through the hound's
salt-bristled fur. "Good, good girl."

Gingerly, she rubbed a palm against her puffy face. Sand, salt, and
flakes of what she guessed to be blood fell away as she rubbed in slow circles. Beneath the swelling she could feel bruises spreading along the bone.

Every thread of muscle in her body ached. Every joint was creaking
stiff. Her tongue had swollen to push her jaws apart.

Little by little, she worked an eye open. Sunlight split cracks in her
skull, but she was still glad to see it.

The storm was over.

They had sheltered in the mouth of a cave along a narrow, sandy
shelf. It looked as though the tide was high now, and the waves washed up
to the edge of the boulders at her feet.

Joints in her back popped as she turned. It was less a cave than a
tunnel, sloping up to a shining circle of sky above. The wind whistled at
the edges of the hollow as it swept through.

Eyvind was in rough shape. What little of his skin was left unbruised was pallid and clammy to the touch. His breathing was shallow. Embla lay at his side and whined.

Aelfhild risked standing. It took more than one attempt.

There was nothing outside their cave, little wreckage besides a few floating boards and some sailcloth. And no other survivors.

Her swollen throat could produce nothing over a whisper. Yelling for help would have to wait.

She imagined Ceolwen nearby, hurt and alone.

Her mistress needed her.

Shaking Eyvind's shoulder got no response. His lips were chapped bloody and broken.

Water. Find water, then find the others, she thought.

Ceolwen is alive, Ceolwen needs water. She chanted to herself as she limped into the cave. Ceolwen is alive, Ceolwen needs water.

The tunnel ran at a steep angle toward the ground above. She shimmied along the rock face despite her protesting muscles. The exit was narrow, but she wormed her shoulders through one at a time. Her hips stuck, and she swung in mid-air for a moment.

Ceolwen is alive, Ceolwen needs you.

Her fingernails cracked as she pulled at the earth in front of her and dragged the rest of her torso onto the ledge.

The chalky, sun-swept limestone of the cliffs was too bright for her smarting eyes, and she shaded her face with both hands. Delicate bridges of the white stone arched amongst the columns, islands, and canyons carved from the coast by eons of rainfall.

There were pits and caves all around, but she saw no other life from her perch besides the algae coating the rocks. And no water save for the sea below.

She stumbled into a puddle left by the storm. Dropping to her knees, she took a sip. The water was sweet and cold. She slurped until there was nothing but a stain left on the rocks.

She found another pool at the bottom of a shallow crevice. Eyvind needed water, but she had nothing to carry it. Lifting him through the tunnel was out of the question.

She cast her eyes around.

You are dead, girl, and you know it. This is all just wasting time.

She tried to push the voice down.

Look at the grand adventurer now! How could you ever think you were more than a mere servant?

"Not now," she hissed. She shook away the tears that blurred her vision. "Think!"

Her gaze dropped to the hem of her tunic. It was torn along the lower edge.

She had an idea.

What she could not tear, she cut with her beltknife. When there was a sizable enough ball of wool in her hands, she dunked it into the water. It emerged sodden and dripping.

She slid back down to Eyvind and squeezed the cloth over his lips. Much had been lost along the way, but she was able to wring out a trickle of freshwater. The Thrym sputtered as drops fell on his tongue, and she propped a foot under his back.

It took her several trips up and down the cliff, but eventually he opened his bloodshot eyes. He sucked at the damp cloth before speaking.

"The others?"

"Not yet," she said, ramming confidence behind every word for her own sake as much as his. "We will find them. Rest."

He nodded and lay back.

She went back up to the clifftop and gazed out across the empty landscape.

We will find them, she repeated to herself.

Then she turned her eyes skyward.

"You will not beat me!"

It would have been easy to have died. To have lain on that beach and sobbed and waited and shriveled into nothingness. It would have been easy to let them win. "They" were a loose weave in Aelfhild's mind, everyone and everything—Osric, Leofstan, Sindri, nobles, the world, Fate, the Gods.

But she stood on that thin spit of land washed by an uncaring ocean and vowed that they would not have an easy victory.

It had taken time, but Eyvind had his feet beneath him now and together they hoisted Embla through the tunnel's mouth. Aelfhild had to brace both feet against the earth and yank Eyvind's arm to get his broader frame through the gap. They had no destination but shuffled along the ledges and clambered around gaps in the stone in search of any sign of life or wreckage. The wind snatched any and all cries for help out to sea, so they relied on their eyes.

Eddies below them swept around pieces of *Unn-marr*. Fragments of the deck, barrel staves, ropes, sailcloth; all were evidence of the ship's death. But mourning the vessel would have to wait until they had found the rest of the crew.

Embla ran to the edge of a deep pit in the limestone and set to barking. Aelfhild and Eyvind ran over.

Rolf looked up from below. He sat along a ledge in the crater, his feet dangling just above the pounding surf. It looked as though he had rescued supplies from the water; beside him sat a barrel along with rope and wood bundled in tattered cloth. But he could not reach the ledge above, and so he had waited.

"Hail, brother." Eyvind wiped at the corner of his eye as he spoke.

"Brother." Rolf smiled. It was the first time Aelfhild had ever seen his teeth. "Sister." He nodded toward her.

He tossed up his equipment first, then shimmied up the rope that Aelfhild and Eyvind anchored. The barrel was packed with dried fish, and they ate as they continued the search.

Aelfhild led the way across a soaring causeway between the island they had washed ashore on and the mainland. The ribbon of pitted white stone looked impossibly brittle between the great cliffs, and she tested her weight on it first before her heavier companions.

She looked out over the shore below as the men crossed after her. To the west, the setting sun cast long shadows along the bay. *Unn-marr*, or what remained, reared from the shaded water. The scrollwork prow jutted up from the waves, but the broken hull disappeared into sand beneath.

Nothing was left of the aft section; everything behind the stub of mast was strewn through the surrounding rocks.

Eyvind and Rolf stood beside her in silence. Their shoulders fell at the sight. It looked as though Eyvind might say something.

Then Aelfhild spotted a speck of fire. It flickered up the beach from the wreckage.

"Fire!" She was already running as she shouted.

Eyvind and Rolf called out to her from behind, but she did not listen. Pebbles scattered beneath her feet as she shimmied along limestone sills and leapt over fissures. She jumped and landed on soft sand, then sprinted toward the light.

Embla dropped down and kept pace beside her, baying the entire way.

Figures shifted at the edge of the firelight at the sound the dog's barking.

Aelfhild saw Ceolwen. She did not stop her sprint.

She hit her mistress head on and wrapped her arms tight around boney shoulders. They fell to the sand. Aelfhild could feel Ceolwen's tears on her shoulder, and wept plenty of her own.

"I found you," she whispered. "They did not win."

If Ceolwen heard, she never asked what those words meant.

Eyvind and Rolf caught up. Kolbrun and Jarngrim were both there to greet them, standing beside the Earnfoldings entwined on the ground. Embla spun in frantic circles around the reunited group.

Aelfhild stood, eventually, and brushed sand off herself.

The Thrym all gazed toward the shipwreck. Not far from *Unn-marr*'s grave a damp blanket clung to the outline of a body.

Her smile faded, and she wiped the joyful tears from her face.

Eyvind asked the question. "Who?"

"Vidar," Kolbrun answered. Her voice cracked.

The captain ran a hand through the hair over his forehead. "Anyone else?"

"Not yet."

That means Bercthun, Geir, and Onund still have a chance, Aelfhild thought. We will find them, too.

4 2

WE MOURN HIM later." Eyvind turned his back on Vidar's corpse. "We have to find fresh water—this is all for nothing if we die here. Aelfhild, Ceolwen, you two keep the fire burning, maybe search the beach for what you can find. Jarngrim and Rolf together, Kolbrun with me, we look for water and dry wood."

The Thrym set off toward the ridgeline, while Aelfhild and Ceolwen went to work. They used the last few hours of dusk to make a pile near their camp of anything that might prove useful.

The pickings were meager.

Ceolwen levered open the swollen lid of a sea chest. She laid out the sodden clothing to dry, and added the axe within to the stack of weapons. Aelfhild kicked up a bundle from the sand—something thin and heavy swaddled in linen. She unfurled the cloth and found Rolf's great axe beneath. The long, swept handle bore a hooked blade; she ran her finger along the interweaving knotwork set into the iron. He would be glad to see it.

She laid it beside their two unbroken shields, three hand axes, and solitary spear. It was not much of an armory. The wrapping she measured against her shoulders.

Let the warriors worry about the weapons, she thought. Cloaks and foot-wraps are more use than spears to us now.

Ceolwen, who had been rooting around the north edge of the beach, darted up to her servant. "Someone is coming, Aela!"

"One of ours?'

"I cannot see in the dark! Grab a blade until we are sure!"

Whether it was Onund's stories of the Thurse, or the effects of too much sun and salt, or just plain fear of the dark, Aelfhild's heart quickened. It must be one of the crew, she thought. But what if, on some twisted whim of the Gods, it is something else?

She hefted the great axe while Ceolwen grabbed hold of the spear.

A lopsided figure dragged itself along the beach toward their fire from the north. The sun was nearly gone in the west and the cliffs shaded the intruder completely.

"Who goes?" shouted Aelfhild, hoisting the axe over her head.

"Just a weary old man," the shape replied. Onund shifted beneath his sailcloth blanket and pushed aside the spear he had been using as a crutch. His outline was clearly human now, and Aelfhild was glad the darkness hid her burning cheeks.

She helped the Skjoldung over to the fire.

"Are you hurt?"

"Only scratches," he replied, but dropped down near the flames with a groan. In the light, Aelfhild could see his face was smeared with blood.

"Let me see." She took Onund's face in both hands, and tilted his head back into the campfire's glow. "Your brow is split. Let me clean this off."

While she wiped the wound clean with a rag soaked in seawater, she told her patient what had unfolded in his absence. "And you have not seen Geir or Bercthun?" she asked.

He shook his head. Then, after a pause, said, "Poor Vidar. The lad had promise."

Aelfhild was spared having to think on it any further by Eyvind and Kolbrun's return. The pair's conversation carried into camp ahead of them. It sounded as though Eyvind was reasoning with the shield-maiden. "I hear what you are saying, but we cannot waste rations just waiting. Two days at the most, then we move on."

"Geir has stood with us more times than I can count," Kolbrun replied. "We owe it to him to at least search."

"And we will tomorrow; more than that I will not promise you." The captain caught sight of the new arrival. "Onund!" he shouted.

"You see? We should not give up so quickly—he could yet live," said Kolbrun, but Eyvind seemed to be finished with the matter.

"Water?" asked Aelfhild. Talking had made her throat raw and scratchy.

"Not even a trickle," Eyvind muttered. "We will look again tomorrow, unless the others have better luck."

Rolf returned with Jarngrim in tow not long after. The pair had fared no better.

They spent the next day scavenging and searching but found no sign of their missing friends.

At sunset, they buried Vidar.

Eyvind and Rolf took hold of the blanket upon which the body lay and they carried him uphill to a spot looking eastward over the ocean. Trailing behind them with her grey head held low, Embla whined softly. Ceolwen and Aelfhild followed with the others.

There were no tools with which to dig a grave, so with bare arms they scraped out a shallow pit in the sandy soil and lowered the body down into it. Kolbrun placed Vidar's hands atop his breast and brushed the hair back from his pale face. They built a cairn of loose stones over him and stood for a moment in silence when the work was done.

Eyvind spoke first. "Vidar was brave…"

He stopped. The speech must have rung as false to his own ears as it did to Aelfhild's. He cleared his throat but could not find the words to continue.

"He was a foolish boy who dreamed of treasure." Kolbrun broke the silence. "But he had a good heart. He pulled his own weight. He tried to be better." Around the grave, heads were nodding. "And he deserves more than we can give him," the shield-maiden finished.

What it was that prompted Aelfhild to raise her voice then, she could never say. Maybe it was that she felt the crew's strength flagging, hers not least of all. Maybe it was for her mistress' benefit, or for whatever fragment of Vidar's spirit lingered on. The hows and whys eluded her in the moment, but she said the words that seemed to be needed.

"Not with gifts, but with our deeds we must honor him. If we fail then he has truly died for nothing. So we must do what we set out to do, and carry his memory with us."

All of her Thrym companions turned their eyes toward her, and for a moment she worried that she had spoken out of place. But Rolf and Eyvind nodded in silent agreement. A faint smile tugged at Jarngrim's lips.

Kolbrun reached over to touch Aelfhild's hand. "Well spoken," was her response.

Ceolwen said nothing but stood and would not lift her eyes from the grave. If she heard the conversation around her, she made no sign.

Kolbrun knelt and ran her fingers over the stones.

"Farewell, Vidar Tryggvason."

One by one, after taking their leave of the fallen, the other Thrym followed her back to camp.

Ceolwen was the last to turn away, and Aelfhild waited just down-hill. The Aethling had confided little in her servant since they had been reunited. What pain her mistress had seen on the day of the storm, Aelfhild could only guess. But she knew one thing: this undertaking was, in the end, all at Ceolwen's behest, and it would have been inhuman not to bear a great deal of guilt for this new turn.

Aelfhild tried to reach out. "It may take him some time but Bercthun will find us. He has not let us down before," she said.

Ceolwen's features creased into a frown. "After the sea took us, when it was just me and Kolbrun, I was sure you had survived, Aela. I just knew, I felt it, that we would see each other again. But I do not feel that now. What if Bercthun really is gone?" She stopped to tug back a stray strand of hair. "Vidar is dead because of me, and if Bercthun is—"

"No, stop!" Aelfhild tried to sound firm without being harsh. "That helps nothing. All of us agreed to come of our own will. I knew the risk, as did Bercthun, as did they all. Now you need to be strong. This guilt will break you if you let it."

Holding back tears, but only barely, Ceolwen lowered her head. "I am trying. Truly. But my dreams give me no rest. I hear the thunder and see their faces beneath the waves, and though they say nothing, I see the blame in their eyes—I cannot shake it."

These words, and the weariness with which they were spoken, sent a shiver up Aelfhild's spine. She tried her best to be consoling, but the words seemed false in her mouth. The path ahead of them was a hard one, and nothing she could say would ease the journey.

If she is not strong enough to do this, then perhaps she does not deserve to be Queen. The thought ran unbidden through Aelfhild's mind, and as ugly and distasteful as it was she could scarce drive it out. Time and again it returned, a gadfly lodged within her skull.

No! She drove out the niggling words with a new chant.

Ceolwen will see this through and Osric will fall. There is no other choice.

Back at camp, the Thrym looked to be having an argument of their own.

Eyvind announced his decision as the Earnfoldings arrived. "We have waited long enough. Tomorrow we break camp and set out, but we leave a trail behind us easy for Geir and Bercthun to follow if they yet live. We notch trees, break branches, and make whatever marks we can as we pass."

Kolbrun did not look pleased. "We tried," she said, patting Jarngrim on the shoulder.

Eyvind hooked both thumbs into his makeshift belt of knotted rope as he turned to face the others. "The plan is the same as before. We stay as close to the coast as we can and make our way north. On foot it will take longer. Weeks, a month maybe. We travel light and fast and hunt as we go. There should be food aplenty in the forests this time of year.

"We just need to find it. And soon."

4 3

"HALT!" CALLED ROLF.

They clattered to a halt in a meadow of bracken.

Jarngrim passed over the one surviving waterskin, and Aelfhild choked down a mouthful. The only spring they had found so far dribbled down the cliffside in rust brown runnels. The water left a syrupy slick on the tongue and tasted of nothing so much as blood. Going thirsty was almost preferable.

"Small mouthfuls," Rolf ordered. "We march again soon."

The greybeard drove them hard. He seemed to need almost no sleep; he hollered at their backs until dusk then kicked them from their bedrolls the next dawn. And each day grew noticeably longer, with summer's onset compounded by their northward progress.

Aelfhild cinched her rope belt tighter. Life at sea—the rowing and ship's rations—and now the marching had burned off any excess fat from her frame. Any curves she had once had were replaced by wiry muscle, so her breeches sagged around the waist. Ceolwen, who had always been more richly endowed in that respect, was in much the same state.

She joined her mistress in rummaging through the brush in search of berries. Her stomach growled. The strip of dried fish at breakfast was a distant memory and even just a handful of wild strawberries were worth scraped knees and a stiff back.

The Thrym pulled up stalks of a tall, golden-crowned herb wherever they found it, munching on the raw stems and roots for the water as much as anything.

"*Hvonn*, it keeps you strong," said Onund as he split a stalk between the two Earnfoldings.

It had a sweet musky smell and was eye-wateringly strong when undiluted, but it yielded a dab of moisture and cleaned Aelfhild's tongue of the iron stain. The others squeezed a few muddy drops from the roots.

"Enough rest," Rolf shouted. "March!"

Embla ranged out ahead as they tramped onward, and true to Eyvind's words they made no attempt to hide their passing. Like some marauding army, they twisted branches, flattened shrubs, and scored marks on the bark of trees. In such remote lands there was little worry of a foe picking up their trail, and with any luck Geir and Bercthun might be able to follow.

"March!" The pace never slackened, and Rolf was quick with the lash if any of his charges lagged.

Knobbly birch trees broke up the sprawl of heather and and evergreen sprigs. Spring was already well underway; the flowers bloomed pink, white, and purple, and the bugs were hard at work.

"No dawdling, queenling!" Rolf prodded Ceolwen onward with the butt of his axe.

In several thickets the crew had stumbled upon swarms of bloodsucking insects rising from the ground and twice they had to make a sprinting retreat from the maddening, thrumming clouds.

They crested a hill and saw the glimmer of sun on flowing water.

"Water!" shouted Eyvind, though he was late.

Neck and neck with her mistress, Aelfhild was already leaping and sliding down the slope. The other Thrym were close behind.

It was a swift-flowing stream that pooled in a stone depression at the valley's edge before falling as fine mist to the beach below. The water ran muddy through the hills, but tasted better than the dregs they had found so far.

Aelfhild immersed her entire head in the bracing flow. Layers of grime caked atop sand and salt peeled away from her skin. There came a splash from the side as Jarngrim disappeared into the rippling pool. He emerged, covered in goosebumps but with a wide grin slapped across his face.

Any sense of modesty had disappeared long ago, as they had all been cooped up together aboard *Unn-marr* for days on end with nothing but barrels to hide behind. They dove and splashed in the water. Even their taskmaster seemed content to just float in the pool.

"Rest well tonight," Rolf said, "for we march twice as hard tomorrow."

Dew sparkled on every stem and frond the next morning, and the dawn light spread across the meadows in wildfire hues.

Embla stood atop the crest of the hill overlooking their camp; the hound's ears trembled as she tilted her head to and fro. Aelfhild knelt by the dog's side and strained to hear whatever sound had Embla so fixated.

Every manner of wren and wagtail raised its voice in the cool morning air. It was a striking choir of chirps and whistles, but Aelfhild had never known the dog to be interested in birdcalls.

"What does she hear?" Ceolwen asked. The Thrym all stood with heads cocked to the side as well, listening for any sound.

"Grab your packs," called Eyvind. "We follow the pup's lead!"

They followed Embla's snuffling nose along the stream bed. The water seemed to grow muddier as they went, and soon Aelfhild could hear the noise. It sounded almost like thunder, a muffled rumble pulsing through the earth. As they made their way closer, she could make out the individual strains—grunts, clicks, and hundreds, even thousands, of footfalls upon mossy soil.

Using a stand of willow bushes to screen their movements, the crew fanned out along the edge of a broad meadow cut by the stream. Aelfhild peeked over the leaves and saw reindeer.

A herd, too vast to count, stretched an endless column across the flowering sward. The beasts milled about, munching at shrubs and slurping at the stream.

It explained the mud, and Aelfhild tried not to think overly hard about what it meant to be downstream from such a herd. She had taken a deep drink and washed her face in those same waters upon waking.

Flies and midges swarmed the deer in a swirling blanket of grey and black, and the smell of manure, sweat, and mud was palpable even at some distance.

Hunting was at the heart of both Thrym and Earnfolding culture, be it as a sport for the nobles or as a necessity of survival for the commonfolk. In the northern forests, game was a mainstay of the diet, while furs and animal bone were vital trade goods. But taking down a deer—especially a larger reindeer—required tools, tools they did not have.

Vidar's bow and quiver were lost in the sea, there were no horses to ride down prey, and they had but a single hound. Fierce though she was, Embla could do little without a pack to aid her.

The animals were calm for now, drifting slowly but steadily north-ward as they grazed. Occasionally one would raise its great, shaggy head to survey the meadow, ears twitching at the biting gnats, and then bend back down to graze.

"Back," whispered Eyvind.

The crew ducked down and snuck out of sight of the herd.

"We need more spears." Eyvind kept his voice low as he drew lines in the dirt with a stick. "There were some birches further down, we need branches from those."

"Then we flank the herd, or try. We cannot hope to get behind them, but we do what we can. Three from one side," he pointed with the stick, "four from the other. We may be able to drive a youngling or a weak one from the pack."

Aelfhild nodded along with the others. The plan was as good a one as they could come up with given the circumstances, and there was little choice but to try. Even a single reindeer would give them all enough strength to march a fortnight.

First came the spears: Rolf hewed down the longest, straightest branches he could find; Jarngrim trimmed them to size; Aelfhild joined the others in whittling down the ends into wicked points. The birch wood was hard, forcing them to grunt and scrape until their beltknives were dull. Most of the spears were stout and about as tall as Aelfhild, but a few they made lighter and shorter for throwing.

Not a single one of the branches was perfectly straight, though, lend-ing the weapons a shabby appearance—more children's playthings than deadly arms. Eyvind frowned as he hefted one to test the balance, but held back any remarks.

Spear in hand, Aelfhild split off with Onund and Kolbrun. They settled down behind a screen of ferns and waited for the signal.

The sun was high overhead now, and the day had grown rather hot; sweat ran down their faces, soaking shirts and plastering down hair. Not content only to harass the deer, the gnats bit them without mercy.

A sharp whistle rang out across the clearing, two short bursts, and Kolbrun replied with a single whistle.

They set out at a steady creep, staying low in the undergrowth.

Hot sun baked Aelfhild's neck and back. Her thighs, unaccustomed to the low gait, bunched into knots.

The humans' movement had not gone unnoticed. Some of the reindeer had ceased grazing and stood with heads held high, eyes and ears turned toward the trespassers. A few of the animals snorted and stamped in anticipation.

She could see little over the matted bracken, but Aelfhild knew they must be drawing close. Sweat coursed down her brow and stung her eyes. Beside her, Kolbrun raised spear to shoulder, and she did the same.

With a yell the others rose from their hiding spots and charged.

Embla cut a growling whorl across the meadow as the deer scattered. The herd split in every direction under the assault, but so great were the animals in number that deer in the center piled against one another, ramming against the backs of their fellows who were slower to flee. The hunters headed for this tangle.

Eyvind and Jarngrim let fly with short spears as they ran, but the warped sticks flew wide and Aelfhild did not see any strike a target.

An aging buck, crowned with a magnificent rack of antlers but unsteady on his feet, was snarled in mud by the bank of the stream and slow to turn from Embla's pursuit. The buck made a last bid for freedom, surging from the mire and limping across the field. Its panicked eyes darted about and froth gathered about its braying lips.

Embla latched onto the deer's hindquarters, but her teeth could make little dent in the thick hide. The deer arched its shaggy back and sent the hound flying into the underbrush.

Aelfhild raced to help the others encircle the old beast.

Hooves tramped and flailed at the hunters.

Something in the meadow snagged her foot, sending Aelfhild tumbling. Snags tore at her as she rolled upright and ran on.

Breath came in short gasps.

The reindeer must have known that it was trapped, but the fight was still far from over. Bellowing and grunting, the towering animal swiveled and kicked with its stout legs at the humans that darted in and out as they probed for weakness.

Rolf was the first to get in front of the buck. He slipped in and jabbed with his spear, but found no purchase.

"Watch the head!" someone cried.

Antlers swept the greybeard to the side and Aelfhild heard him yell in pain.

"In front!"

Next came Jarngrim, leaping and thrusting. His spear stuck into the reindeer's chest. The blunt end of the carved stick caught the ground, snapping under the weight; the reindeer's bulk drove the point home with deadly force, and its front legs gave out.

"To the side!"

Onund came in beside Kolbrun, driving cruel points into the buck's flank. The beast collapsed, and a final blow from Eyvind ended its suffering.

Aelfhild watched the life drain from the deer's wide eyes. Her unused spear trailed along through the dirt. Around her, the Thrym howled in victory.

Embla bounded back up from the bushes to sniff at the steaming carcass.

Rolf groaned.

The thrill of the hunt faded as the crew rushed to his side.

Blood stained the greybeard's breeches along his right leg where the antlers had driven home. He pressed both hands against the wound.

Kolbrun tore strips of cloth from her cloak, and Aelfhild helped the shield-maiden to bind the wound. They pressed their weight against the bindings, though the blood was only a trickle now.

The others stood by, panting and dripping sweat.

"Can he walk?" asked Jarngrim.

"I am not dead yet, boy," Rolf growled back. "I can walk fine."

Eyvind put a hand on the wounded warrior's shoulder. "Rest now, we will see to the kill."

Rolf lay back. "Takes more than a deer to put me down," he muttered.

Soon they had a fire going, and smoking brands to drive away the eager flies. By nightfall they had a feast.

There was no salt and no herbs for seasoning the meat, but Aelfhild had never tasted such splendor. Back in civilization, it would have been judged gamey and tough, but in the wild there were no such lofty standards. Grease stained her cheeks and her belly panged as it swelled beneath the weight of venison.

Grimacing, Rolf made a few test strides with his birchwood crutch.

"Need a few days to rest, old man?" called Onund. He received a warning growl in reply.

Aelfhild leaned back and let her belch waft out toward the stars. She relaxed while she could, for she had an inkling that the scrape would do little to keep Rolf from the crew's heels.

4 4

ELFHILD DROPPED ONTO her blanket, exhausted.

It had taken Rolf no time at all to recover. He still winced when he thought no one was looking, but seemed to drive them on all the harder for his pains.

The march that day had been long, and she was asleep almost as soon as her head kissed the ground.

She dreamed.

The shifting walls of the grey hallway loomed around her again, just as they had on the night of the hall-burning in Cynestead. Every detail was the same, down to the damp odor of mold and stone dust. She felt the familiar twinge in the palm of her hand as she stepped through the shimmering doorway.

The mass of vines was there to greet her. Tendrils writhed and wriggled, thorns glinted from amongst the snarl. This time, though, the coiled brambles parted layers to reveal the white glint beneath. Bones, a jumble of ribs, splintered femurs, spines, and jawbones, made up the center of the orb. Gauzy roots spread in webwork across the cracks and breaks in the ivory.

She felt no fear. The sight was repulsive, but she was detached from the feeling—more that she knew it ought to disgust her, but emotion was remote and slippery.

Then there were the whispers, countless and on all sides.

Listen.

This time, when she woke, she wasted no time worrying or wondering. The previous warning had saved Ceolwen and Cuthbert both.

She listened.

And heard only the usual nighttime sounds. Bugs scratched and shifted through the brush. The embers of the campfire popped. Ceolwen snored to her left. But it was only Ceolwen that snored. She heard no other breathing.

Rymr hung in the sky overhead, illuminating the camp with his ghostly blue glow. Valr was just rising from the horizon.

The other blankets were empty.

Aelfhild looked all around, but saw no sign of the Thrym. Some bushes on the edge of camp shook, and she caught what might have been a flash of Embla's tail.

Something was happening. She wrapped her blanket round her shoulders and set off on what she thought was the dog's trail. There was a voice, faint in the distance, and she followed the thread.

The Thrym had gathered in a small copse of spruce trees.

They were arguing.

"You know, all of you, that I am no coward. That is not why I asked to speak," Jarngrim was saying.

"We know, brother," Eyvind replied. "None here doubt you. Say what you will."

Aelfhild placed each foot with painstaking care. She huddled down at the edge of the trees, and peered through the branches. Kolbrun's feet were visible, and little else, but she could hear the warriors speaking.

"It has been weeks and we have still not come to Aettirheim. I only wonder if it is wise to press on with this. So far, we have been lucky to find water. That will not last forever," Jarngrim continued. "The venison is long gone, what rabbits we have seen are all skin and bones, and roots are nothing to live on. And we have already lost more than any of us wanted."

"We do not know that Geir is lost," said Eyvind.

"I think we do," was Jarngrim's reply.

Rolf broke in. "Watch how you speak!"

"No, old friend, he is right. If we meet Geir on the journey back my heart will be well glad, but I do not hold much hope for it."

"That is why I asked to speak tonight." Jarngrim's voice once more. "I do not care which royal polishes a throne in Earnfold. That is not my worry. I care for each face in this circle. Two—no, three—are missing already. I count Bercthun as one of ours. And I do not wish to lose more. That is all."

"You all know I will hear you out," Eyvind said. "Jarngrim has spoken. Tell me now what you think. Onund?"

Aelfhild heard the Skjoldung suck at his whiskers. "Stories are not worth dying for. I am of a mind with Jarngrim."

She winced at this new betrayal.

"Kolbrun?"

The shield-maiden shifted from one foot to the other. There was silence.

The answer was slow in coming. "I do not know. Truly. I swore to see this through, but I do not want to throw our lives away for nothing."

The old man sounded frail. Kolbrun's voice was anxious. And Eyvind had tossed aside the power that was his birthright and called for a vote. For the first time, Aelfhild saw, or heard, true uncertainty in her Thrym rescuers. They were stripped of their armor and without a ship to sail, and their spirits wavered.

They were suddenly so *human*. Disappointingly human. Aelfhild needed them to be more. She wanted them strong and steadfast, not whinging about and waiting for rescue. These were not the bold heroes that had swept her up from the grips of slavery.

"Rolf?"

"My oath is to the Jarl. I will take the girl to Aettirheim or die along the way."

Aelfhild could have applauded. Here was the strength they needed. But the tally so far was grim.

Eyvind sighed. More than anything she wanted now to see his face, see some clue to his decision.

"Let me think on it. I will make my decision tomorrow. But I will tell you this now—I free each one of you from your oath to my household.

Any man or woman who wishes to turn back may go without shame. No one goes further but of their own will."

Over her shoulder, as she turned to sneak back to camp, Aelfhild heard one last snatch of conversation: "still one to ask."

She was settled in next to Ceolwen by the time the Thrym returned. They muffled their footsteps carefully, but Aelfhild could hear the change in breathing. Sleep was far away. Her thoughts raced.

It was a betrayal. How many midnight meetings had she and Ceolwen slept through while the Thrym plotted? She cringed as she remembered her plans to sail off with the raiders after Ceolwen was made Queen.

She bore all of Ceolwen's weight on her shoulders. The Gods were no help, so up to now she had relied on the Thrym to carry hers.

Now that support crumbled, and she felt herself teetering.

Aelfhild gritted her teeth and swung at Eyvind. He sidestepped and parried the blow with his spear shaft.

"Better," he said, "but when you lead with your foot I can see the strike coming. Try it again."

She stepped back and hefted her birch staff in both hands.

They were alone in the clearing. The other Thrym had gone off to forage and check the snares set the previous night, while Ceolwen slumbered on under Embla's guard. The Aethling's training at arms had proved a vain effort, and Eyvind no longer bothered.

This time she feinted with her left foot, but drove in with a rightward swing. It worked, and Eyvind was on his heels as they locked weapons.

Aelfhild put every ounce of her weight behind the stick, but the Thrym was more than a head taller and heavier than his lean frame suggested.

She staggered back.

This had been their dawn ritual since the shipwreck, but the first time she had real cause to strike the man.

Tell him you heard everything. Tell him you know.

Instead, she blew back stray hair from her face and attacked.

They dodged and parried, trading hits.

He danced back as the butt of her staff scythed past his nose.

"Easy!"

Her chest heaved with the effort, and she stood glaring at him from across their shrub-strewn arena.

He met the stare. "What has come over you?"

"I heard you."

She spat the words, then spun to strike while he was still dazed by the impact.

But he did not seem to be. He hooked his spear shaft behind her twirling foot and sent her sprawling.

"Leave the flourishes for the skalds and their stories. Never show your back to a foe."

Slamming against the hard soil drove the breath from her lungs.

"Do you remember when I told Vidar that only a fool feels no fear?" There was no anger in his voice. He appeared as unfazed by her eavesdropping as he had been by her ambush.

"No," she lied. She pulled herself onto one knee.

"I would set my warriors against any challenge, any enemy, and be sure of victory. There are none finer. Each one has a heart as true as any of the heroes of old."

He swung again as she stood, and she reeled backwards to block the blow.

"But they fear. They doubt. You think Sigurd never had one moment of weakness?"

They circled.

The anger was still there, simmering in her breast. But she knew there was truth to those words. That she had built the Thrym into something more than they were. That they could not be everything she needed, and it was wrong to blame them for failings not of their own making.

But the expression Eyvind wore was too close to a smirk, and she would be thrice-cursed if she was going to admit fault to that face. She rolled forward and swung high. He blocked, but she drove her staff into the back of his left knee. He sagged but stayed upright, and their weapons locked once more.

Face to face now, he asked another question.

"What is your vote?"

"You know what it is!" She strained to push him off-balance.

"Why?"

There was no shifting him, so she leapt back out of reach.

"What do you mean *why*?"

"Do you go on just because your mistress tells you to, or is there something else?"

Revenge was the first word that popped into her mind. Or to obey Fate, or to spite the Gods, or to see the storied lands of her ancestors. To see justice done. Any would have made a fine answer, and all rang true to some extent. But she chose a simpler reply.

"I need to know that I can."

He leaned against his spear and stared back at her.

"So do we go?" she asked.

He drew a deep breath. "Yes." And exhaled. "We go."

"Now be on guard." Hefting his weapon, he said, "I will not hold back this time."

And they fought on.

ONE LATE AFTERNOON found Aelfhild pressed against a lichen-stained rock face, fingers and toes probing for holds. A rope was tied around her waist, trailing down to the outcrop below where Eyvind and Ceolwen stood fretting.

The fjords of the northern coast, beautiful though they were to look upon, had been a great hindrance on the journey to Aettirheim. A few were shallow and ran only a short distance inland, making for an easy crossing over soft, grassy ground. Many, though, were less welcoming—these were yawning rifts, carved deep into the earth by vengeful glaciers, with sheer rock walls plummeting into the black churn of waves. Entire days the crew spent following these chasms west in hopes of finding a suitable crossing, only then to make the painstaking climb down the rocks to pass over a half-submerged sandbar in water cold enough to numb the legs and freeze the toes.

Just a stone's throw to her left and slightly below, Kolbrun pulled herself up onto a ledge. The servant and the shield-maiden had turned out to be natural climbers—or at any rate more natural than the rest. Their nimble feet and strong fingers gave them the dubious honor of being first up, bearing ropes to fasten once they reached the top.

Heights were not something Aelfhild was particularly keen on.

The higher she climbed, the more she regretted this newfound talent.

You wanted to pull your weight, a voice within her head chided as she wedged her toes into the next crevice, *and here you are.*

Her left hand sent some loose rock and gravel raining down on the onlookers, and she could hear in the swift intake of breath below. But her hold did not falter.

Only one more ledge to go.

With bruised fingers, Aelfhild dragged herself up onto the upper lip of the bluff, then rolled over to give Kolbrun a hand. They emerged onto a wide stone shelf, polished smooth by the elements and bare of vegetation save for specks of moss in a few sheltered cracks. Forgetting the ropes around their waists momentarily, the two women turned to absorb the view.

The ocean stretched out in endless aquamarine to the east. With the sun at their backs, their shadows danced in stark black relief atop the swells. To the south the pale crescents of the twin moons cleared the horizon side by side, and beneath the heavenly orbs stretched the jagged coast, the hills through which the Thrym and Earnfoldings had toiled for days.

Aelfhild turned north to see what was still to come.

A lump rose in her throat at the sight, and she recalled words Eyvind had spoken weeks before: a harbor filled with sharp rocks, like teeth. Stretching out before them was an oval bay nestled within a deep basin between the ridges that dominated the coastline to the north and south. The mouth of the bay was filled with dozens of jutting boulders and narrow skerries, some bare but some sporting thickets of greenery. The surf erupted in foaming towers around the spits of rock and fell back in whirling eddies.

Aelfhild could see where some of the rocks been shattered into jagged pieces, and others worn down by the sea to lie hidden just below the tides. How any boat could sail through that sieve without foundering she could not even fathom.

She looked over at Kolbrun, who stared with equal wonder. "We found it," whispered the shield-maiden. "I did not think…"

Calls from below and a tug on the rope around her waist brought Aelfhild back to the task at hand. There were no easy places to tie down the rope, so she and Kolbrun would have to use their own weight to belay the other climbers. The two women sat side by side, feet wedged against the ground and held tight to the lines as the others came up to join them. Going was slow, but pair by pair the crew emerged over the ledge.

Rolf and Eyvind stayed down with Embla, who had to be lifted in a harness woven of some spare lashing. It took four strong backs to pull the poor dog up the cliff, but Embla put up little struggle, only whining softly as she bumped and scraped her way up the rough wall. The hound's master followed, leaving Rolf to bring up the rear.

With both Aelfhild's and Kolbrun's lines tied around his waist, Rolf made the climb, cursing loudly as he slipped and slid. His burly feet and hands did not serve him well on the cliffs.

Only once did he fall. The rope bit and sawed at Aelfhild's waist and shoulders, while gouts of cursing and wheezing from below told the waiting crew that Rolf yet lived. When he finally hauled himself over the edge, blood streaked the greybeard's face, but he waved off any attempt to examine the wound and continued to curse everyone and everything in sight.

The old Leifing fell silent, though, when he stood to look north.

They all did. It was an odd mixture of awe and relief and shock that crossed her companions' faces upon seeing that distant harbor, and Aelfhild marked each one. Ceolwen stood and blinked, not seeming to trust her own eyes. Eyvind grinned. Jarngrim rejoiced at the sight, lifting his arms high in victory; he grabbed Kolbrun's shoulders and shook. Onund tugged at his beard as he laughed.

Rolf was the hardest to read. Fear was not the proper term for what she saw in the old man's eyes, more a sort of reluctance. The creases in his forehead ran deep.

"Two days' journey, I think," Eyvind said in response to a question no one had asked, pulling them all back from wherever their minds had wandered. "We can cut inland from here and stick to the hills, avoid climbing through any more of these wretched valleys."

Rolf spat and rubbed his head. He agreed.

Shading her eyes from the sun, Kolbrun peered off into the west. "There is a gully leading down from here, should be easier going."

"I want us down from here before nightfall, then we make camp. No time for dawdling! Take in the view tomorrow, cousin," he said as he jabbed Ceolwen in the ribs. The Thrym chuckled as they shouldered their coils of rope and wool-wrapped bundles and shuffled down from the rocky crest in single file. Aelfhild lingered.

"After everything, we are almost there. Some part of me thought it was all a lie. I can scarce believe it, Aela." The voice came from far away, but it seemed steadier and more confident than Aelfhild had heard in a long while.

"You sound more like yourself," she replied. The uncertainty that had been building in Ceolwen's voice of late had caused her no end of worry. Learning of the crew's reservations had not helped, either, but that seemed to be behind them. None had challenged Eyvind's decision, nor shown any resentment. Not in front of the Earnfoldings, at any rate. "It is good to have you back," she added.

"Just two days and I will be Queen. And then we can go home."

Stronger by the minute, Aelfhild marveled.

"First we have to get there, your lordship. One step at a time. Down we get." She curtsied mockingly before pulling Ceolwen, who still seemed lost in a daydream, along by the belt.

The two Earnfoldings followed the Thrym down through the gully.

"Think of it. We can sleep in a bed again, under a roof. Wear clean clothes," Ceolwen droned on from behind. "Ride a horse instead of walk. Grow big and fat."

"Eat something other than dried fish and unripe berries," Aelfhild joined in, "wash with warm water."

"Shoes for our feet. Combs for our hair," Ceolwen suggested, as they caught up to the Thrym.

Eyvind seemed less keen on the little game. "And a rest for our ears," he called, leaving Aelfhild and her mistress to snort with laughter as they jogged along at the rear.

4 6

THUNDER RUMBLED OFF to the west, and Eyvind called for them to quicken pace.

Aelfhild puffed at the steady stream of rain that flowed from the tip of her nose as she pulled her threadbare cloak closer around her shoulders. The squall was stifling—they marched, hemmed in on all sides by translucent walls of water, seeing little but an outline of a person ahead, and hearing nothing but the pounding rainfall. The rivulets streaming down her face probed for a way into her mouth and nose with every breath. Sodden ground squelched underfoot and more than once she feared she might lose a foot wrap to the sucking mire.

Eyvind led, and Rolf brought up the rearguard, while the rest trudged along and tried their best not to tread on the heels of the indistinct figure ahead.

The ground turned from mud to sand as they came nearer to the coastline, and soon they could hear the cresting whitecaps of the sea once more. Somewhere in the mist nearby was the roaring, rocky mouth of the bay, and whatever remained of Aettirheim in the cloud-covered hills beyond.

They got a respite from the worst of the rain as the deluge eased, but the swelling thunderclaps hinted it would be brief.

A low knoll rose up at the southern edge of the ancient harbor, dotted with spruce trees and overgrown with shrubs. Something about the shape of the hill's crest looked odd from a distance, with lines too straight and angular to be natural. As they drew close, it was clear that there was stonework of some kind beneath the vines and brambles, a wall not unlike the one they had found by the ruins of Skelborg.

It was a ring of stone about the height of a man, with a hole for a door at one end—another watchtower over the southern approach. Wooden beams had long since rotted away and any upper floors collapsed down, leaving only the lower level behind. Moss and lichen grew up from the mulchy dirt to cloak the masonry in a green fuzz.

"We shelter here tonight," Eyvind declared, with an eye on the approaching storm.

Rolf and Jarngrim trimmed branches from the nearby pines, which the others wove into a makeshift roof. It was a crude piece of work and unlikely to keep out much water, but better than sleeping bare. They propped a few stouter logs under the sagging center and spread their blankets around the outside edge of the room to avoid the worst of the leaks.

A fire was unworkable. All their tinder was soaked and there was not a patch of dry grass or wood for leagues. Sparks spluttered and smoked on the damp earth but would not catch, and any hopes of warmth were dashed when the storm arrived. The ceiling leaked like a sieve and doused everything below, so they sat in the dark and shivered up against one another. Distant bolts of lightning would cast dancing light through the doorway and the cracks in the roof, while the thunder took its time to catch up.

Aelfhild sat with her back against the stone, puffing into her clasped hands. Ceolwen had settled in and lay swathed in a blanket with her head on Kolbrun's shoulder. Rolf sat to her right, staring with unfocused eyes through the doorway across from them. All the others were either asleep or hidden beneath their cloaks, but Aelfhild had offered to take the first watch and the stolid Thrym had joined her.

The image of the greybeard looking out toward Aettirheim had lingered in Aelfhild's mind, and time and again on the day's dreary march she had returned to it. She could read her mistress easily enough, and the other Thrym had reacted in much the way she expected.

Imposing a figure as her fellow watchman was, Aelfhild's curiosity conquered her. "I saw your face yesterday on the cliffs, when we climbed up," she said.

Not able to make out her words over the clamor of the storm, Rolf leaned in and she repeated herself.

Continuing, she explained, "You looked unsure. The others were all glad, but you were…different." The final word was a little slow in coming, for it was hard to find the right Thrym word for a thing when she could hardly even put a name to it in her own language.

His eyes narrowed into an appraising stare. With a nod of approval, he said, "It is a wise thing to watch faces. You can learn much."

That seemed to be all Rolf was willing to say, but Aelfhild was not yet satisfied with an answer. She kept her eyes trained on his face, illuminated only now and then by the flashing storm, and waited. For a moment they sat in silence, each testing the other's will. The Thrym cracked first and chuckled.

Rolf let out a dramatic, shoulder-arching sigh, so she would know that he continued only under protest. Then, weighing each word with care, he spoke.

"When I was a boy, I wanted more than anything to fight for the Jarl. This was Harald's father, Torfi—Eyvind's grandfather. My father fought for the Jarl, my uncles, my brothers. In my eyes Torfi was like a Jotunn, so strong and brave. We loved the Gods in our house"—he raised a hand in the air—"but only a little more than we loved the Jarl." The hand dropped just slightly; the contest had been a close one.

Aelfhild had not expected so much from the warrior, who only broke his studied silence to shout orders at lazing crew members. Rolf's voice was rough and his manner less practiced than Onund's tale-telling, but his seemingly unguarded honesty was far more moving.

"So I trained every day, and fought all the boys in my village, even the ones bigger and stronger than me. And when I was old enough, the Jarl took me in to his hall and gave me an oath-ring." The Thrym's eyes gleamed as he rubbed calloused fingers along a band of iron on his wrist. "And I grew to know the Jarl, over the years. He was a great warrior, truly without match. But he was not a kind man. Greedy, and always hungry for power. His sons and his wives feared him as much as his foes. I learned much in Torfi's hall."

The sound of rain dripping through the paltry roof filled the ensuing pause.

"Those that knew him, truly knew him, did not mourn overmuch for the Jarl when he died. To the end he was the greatest of warriors, and for that I still honor him. But any love I bore for him was lost when I sat near and saw that he was not a god, just a man.

"We love all of Onund's tales, and we love Sigurd and the Gods," he said as he drew a long breath, "but they are far away from us. Now we go walking into the old stories, and I wonder if we will be glad of what we find up close."

A greying eyebrow crooked in her direction as if to ask whether that would suffice.

Aelfhild nodded. "Thank you," was all she managed, not certain how to reply.

Rolf settled back into his cloak and resumed watch over the empty doorway. He stretched his leg out before him, rubbing at the hunting wound.

Wisdom could be found in the most unexpected places. Aelfhild recalled long ago some aged teacher in the king's hall at Cynestead trying to give that same lesson to a young and disobedient Aethling and the Aethling's daydreaming servant-girl. It had seemed little but the prattle of the elderly then, along with so much else.

I suppose that's the way of it, she mused, the important things seem useless until you need them, and the useless seem so terribly important.

Rolf's words set her to thinking about old King Osred, Ceolwen's father, whom she had given little mind since his death. When he passed, people had spoken of him in glowing tones—as a giant amongst men and a benevolent ruler.

Aelfhild could remember a man remarkable only in his blandness, trapped between crown and throne and ringed by an equally forgettable crowd of followers and flatterers. She had grown up in his presence, but meeting him for the first time would likely have been a hollow experience.

I watched a King die, feeble and bed-ridden, she thought. I have seen the future Queen of Earnfold soil herself as a child, and as a grown woman heave her stomach out over the side of a ship. Aelfhild snorted. There is no grandeur left in royalty for me.

But that had only been half of the old Thrym's point and she knew it.

None of them knew what was to come and tomorrow was uncertain, that was true. But every tomorrow had been since they sailed from Jarlstad, and even long before that.

Lightning flickered and thunder boomed above her, as if to drive home the thought.

If the legends were false, so be it. If the Gods proved as callous and cruel as she suspected them to be, so be it.

Coming this far is a victory, for which we have fought and suffered, and I will not let doubt strip me of that, Aelfhild decided.

4 7

MBLA WOKE THEM all with frantic, dripping kisses the next morning. The last watch had fallen to Eyvind, and at dawn he had taken the hound for a stroll along the beach, so Embla returned drenched in saltwater and filled to the very brim with energy.

None were fortunate enough to escape the drool and lashing tongue.

Sunlight streamed through the cracks in the roof in place of rain—a change most welcome—and Aelfhild could hear gulls crying over the sound of waves.

Every piece of her was soggy and pruned, so she rushed out into the morning air to dry. Off to the east the sun was already well clear of the horizon, meaning they had slept in.

The tide was on the ebb so the seabirds were out in force to scavenge the leavings of the sea. Sandpipers ran up and down the sand, staying just ahead of the surging water. Gulls skimmed the ocean's surface in raucous, careening flocks.

A tremor of nervous excitement spread through the camp as they bundled up their meager supplies in blankets and shouldered shields and weapons. The long-awaited day had arrived. They set off toward the featureless hills beyond the disused harbor, where they hoped to find the ruins of Aettirheim and an end to their seeking.

Her clothes and assorted worldly possessions dried out as they walked; Aelfhild could only guess at how she, and all the rest, must have reeked, with their dirty bodies in damp and filthy clothes, but luckily there were few passersby to meet in these parts, and they had all grown used to one another. She bent to remove the wrappings from her feet and sighed at the feeling of sand beneath her toes.

They took advantage of the low tide and followed the line of the beach at a more pleasant pace than the forced march of recent days. There were shells of every imaginable shape and size scattered around, some even that sprouted legs and skittered away from the crew's trampling feet. Embla ran back and forth investigating the countless smells. Eyvind wore a look of serene contentment as he strode bare-foot through the edge of the waves.

Aelfhild watched Ceolwen, not far ahead, as she basked in the sun. If any doubts still festered in her mistress' mind, she was doing a fine job of hiding them—she walked with eyes closed and face tilted skywards.

Kolbrun could be heard whistling as she rambled along behind and kicked up the sand.

A merry band of castaways out to stretch their legs, thought Aelfhild, picturing the sight. Their thin bodies, tangled hair, and ragged clothes gave one impression, but the axes tucked in the Thrym's belts, the shields slung over backs and rough spears in hand offered another. If there were any brigands in these lands, they would think twice before tangling with such desperate-looking newcomers.

The sun was straight overhead as they left the beach, crossing over the dune line into the sawgrass beyond after a pause to bind cloth wraps back around sandy feet.

Onund was the first to find signs of the old settlement. Sickly dwarf birch grew in the sandy soil past the dunes, and in a clump of spindly grass and yellowed leaves the Skjoldung saw something the others had missed.

Aelfhild had walked right past, but her brief shame was eased by the fact that Eyvind and Kolbrun had also failed to spot it.

Onund and Jarngrim called them back, as the two men tore away the plants and brushed off the sand that hid an oblong chunk of hewn stone. The sandy soil had swallowed up almost half of the pillar, while wave and wind had chipped and smoothed it down. As the dirt fell away, faint etchings stood out on the stone's face, calling up a now-distant memory in Aelfhild.

Months ago it seemed, when she and Ceolwen had fled down the Swiftea in their little boat, Cuthbert and Bercthun along with them, and found three stones like this one on the riverbank.

Runestones.

The thought of Bercthun pained her; other things had kept her attention since the shipwreck, but she held out little hope for the young warrior when her mind drifted in that direction. He had been a good friend, to all of them.

Not now. Aelfhild pushed the feeling back forcefully. There will be time for all that later.

"Can you read it? What does it say?" Eyvind was asking, but Onund shook his head.

"A warding stone, to drive off enemies and wild beasts," the old man said, pointing to a few indistinct lines. He frowned. "I cannot make most of it out, but it means there must be something here worth guarding."

With greater care they pressed on into the hills. Beyond the first ridge the grass grew thicker and greener with each step. Sea breeze rippled along the feathered blades. At the base of the hill beyond, the remains of a wall ran in a long half circle, disappearing into a gully to the west and ending abruptly to the east where a chunk of land had tumbled down into the ocean below.

The stone blocks had been laid by skilled hands, clearly, for the joining was close and even. Lichen and vine rose up to choke the structure and little by little undo the work, but the masonry had lasted for generations without upkeep. Grass sprouted in a few spots where the mortar had cracked, the probing roots a herald of slow but inevitable decay.

It seemed a paltry sort of defense, Aelfhild thought, for at the tallest point the stones rose only as high as her nose; feet flat on the ground, she could look over the top. Thinking back to Jarlstad, though, she realized that this was only the foundation of the outer bastion, which would have been built with a stockade overtop—logs sharpened to points, lashed together, and coated with pitch.

There were gaps between the stones in a few places, smaller ones evidence simply of the weight of time, while the more sizable holes hinted at assault by ancient foe. What would have been the southern gate was long cast down, but in her mind's eye Aelfhild could see it clearly.

She shouldered past farmers driving their longhorns to market and fishermen carrying the day's catch. Women with baskets at their hip or slung over their backs pulled along horses burdened down with shorn wool. The ironclad gates stood open under the watchful guard of the Jarls' spearmen, and the folk thronged at the entrance as they waited to enter the city. All the sounds and smells were the same ones she could recall from a trip through Cynestead on market day.

But the vision faded, and now Eyvind led them through empty and silent streets, long overgrown and lost to time.

Here and there bare rock gave hint to settlement, the occasional hearthstone or in one spot a little chimney that Rolf guessed to be the ruin of a blacksmith's forge. But it was hardly different from any other glade they had walked through on the journey.

Ceolwen and Aelfhild stood side by side atop the hill, quiet and deep in thought.

The land beneath what had once been Aettirheim rose upwards from the sea in a series of rolling hills and dales leading into rougher scarps beyond. In the glen below the Earnfoldings there was an overgrown jumble of stones amidst the grass and a few clumps of scraggly shrubs, but little else of note.

"Is there nothing left?" Ceolwen asked of no one, and there was no answer.

Did you truly believe it would all still be here?

Bitterly and silently, Aelfhild chided her mistress, her companions, and herself most of all for allowing themselves to be swept up into chasing the fancies of an old man.

Harald stirred our hearts with fair words and sent us to the far end of the world to chase ghosts. But in cursing him, she cursed her own gullibility. The excitement of the morning, born from tall tales and childish wonder, had begun to sour, and she could see it on the others' faces, too.

"Forward. Keep searching," Rolf barked, falling back on his natural skill at calling layabouts back to work.

Aelfhild had to admire the steadfast greybeard. She thought back to the previous night's conversation. How right Rolf had been to temper that half-crazed hope, which so often in this world was followed close behind by disappointment.

As they wandered on, she again drifted off into imagining how the faded city would have looked. The pile of stones became a temple, built with highest reverence to honor gods and ancestors and enduring long after the builders had gone. Aelfhild pictured nobles in their finest threads bringing white ewes and geese to the priests for sacrifice, trying to win favor with the Four for their own petty causes.

Chickens pecked in the streets, dogs barked, and children ran about with stick and stone, locked in boisterous battles. Treading the same ground as the Aettir of old did strike a chord deep within, a rightness that tugged at long-buried, ancestral memory.

Not far away, Embla began to bark. She burrowed into a patch of loose dirt, flinging mulch out behind her, and the crew converged on the growls.

At the bottom of the pit Embla had scraped there was a smooth, greyish circle etched with cracks, the top of something larger. Eyvind stooped to brush away the dirt as the others looked on expectantly. Slowly, delicately, he unearthed more of the object, and Aelfhild felt her gut tighten as it took shape.

Even before the hollow arc of the eye socket emerged, they had all guessed what was buried there. Standing and brushing the earth from his hands, Eyvind pushed dirt back over the skull with his foot.

Onund was first to break the silence. "Not all of the Aettir fled when the Thurse came. Some stayed to fight and hold the enemy back"—he grimaced into his silver whiskers—"and others could not make the journey."

"May they find peace," Jarngrim said before turning away.

The Thrym repeated his words, while Ceolwen and Aelfhild said the same in the southern tongue, and left the bones to rest.

A less pleasant image played in Aelfhild's eyes now of warriors putting up a bloody final defense of falling walls, while the old and feeble and infirm sat helpless outside an empty shrine that would offer them scant protection. Smoke and blood hung heavy in the air. Clenching her eyelids tight, she shook her head to drive away the vision.

Their normal roles reversed, Ceolwen touched her servant's shoulder tenderly. "Aela, are you with us?" The familiar voice cut through the half-heard screams and the muttering of desperate prayers that seemed to drift up on the breeze.

"Just a daydream," she replied and forced a reedy smile.

In truth, it had seemed like something more. In Jarlstad, in that great, dark hall, she had felt memory collected around her in such weight that it could almost be touched with the outstretched hand. Here in the ruins of the old city lurked something similar, moments of such strength and clarity that they lingered on, waiting patiently in the emptiness to be called to mind.

Ceolwen seemed poised to ask something else, but the Thrym called to them from a nearby hillock.

"Come now!" Eyvind shouted. "Kolbrun found…something more."

By his tone of voice, he did not fully trust whatever his eyes were seeing, and bid them make haste before the mirage faded.

4 8

CLIFFS OF DARK granite loomed over the far side of the next dale and continued out of sight, stretching off into the eternally ice-bound wastes at the top of the world.

This rough terrain had shielded Aettirheim from attack on the northern edge, for no sizable force could have scaled and passed over without notice, while the treacherous, toothed coastline was a natural barrier to any foes from the east. The remains of the fallen ramparts ran along the city's southern and western bounds before ending at the sheer rock face, thus completing the defenses.

Aelfhild could see that the nearest bluff was cut in the middle by a narrow cleft which snaked back into the rocks and disappeared into darkness. Leading up to the shadowed opening was a broad and grassy road, lined on either side by domed mounds swathed in green.

There were eleven of them in all, five to the east and six to the west, spaced evenly and with exquisite precision. Round boulders ringed the base of every mound in a circle broken only by a single, square slab placed at the point nearest the central path, one facing another across the way. A thicket of brambles had taken root somehow atop one of the domes. Gnarly roots pushed aside the carefully placed markers. The other mounds were clear of any growth save for grass and wildflowers.

These were without question barrows, the tombs of honored warriors and wealthy nobles, where the deceased were laid to rest along with their treasures. Many a fireside story which had kept young Aelfhild awake late into the night began with a barrow trespassed upon; curses and strong magic were said to linger over such places, and could cause untold evil if disturbed by those greedy for gold and silver. For a moment, she thought of Vidar and his fevered longing for treasure.

He would be near to bursting with glee if he could see them now.

These mounds, though, were serene and beautiful—sun streamed down atop the emerald crests to cast ten perfectly matching shadows, one spoiled by the curling vines.

"No carvings," said Eyvind, nodding his head toward the smooth stones, "I want to know how the mounds are still so clear as much as who is beneath them."

Kolbrun did not sound her usual bold self. "There is old magic here."

Eyvind's brow furrowed and he opened his mouth to speak, but evidently thought better of any snide comments and kept quiet.

Rolf had made his way along the path between the barrows and stood before the gap in the cliffs, peering into the murk.

"Stairs here," he called back to the crew, beckoning them over.

What once had been a natural gully in the rock, the Aettir's craftsmen had carved into a winding staircase by chipping steps into the tapered channel. The walls were close—Aelfhild could stretch from one side to the other without fully raising her arms—and twisted and turned as they cut steeply upwards. Boulders blocked the way in a few places, forcing them to clamber over or under to pass by.

As they climbed higher, Aelfhild noticed that her palms grew slick with sweat, and her mouth felt suddenly cottony. Her heart quickened and her breathing along with it. The climb was not an easy one, to be sure, but there was some other unfamiliar feeling that nagged at her.

It grew worse further in.

Jarngrim was just ahead of her, and she could see dark stains spreading across the back of his tunic. Heavy breathing echoed within the tight space. It seemed she was not alone in her weariness.

Over her shoulder Aelfhild looked back to check on her mistress. Ceolwen's skin was pale and damp, her face haggard. When the two Earnfoldings finally emerged back into the sunlight, they found the Thrym leaning against one another or kneeling as they struggled to catch a breath.

Embla growled as she paced a circle around her humans.

There was no grass atop the cliffs. Thorny brambles grew in great, tangled clusters. Alongside the verdant meadows below, this land looked somehow ill. The cloying pungence of overripe mushrooms drifted up from the thickets.

Aelfhild's lungs burned, and it felt as though a great foot pressed down on her chest.

"Something is wrong about this place," Jarngrim spoke in hushed tones, as though there might be some hidden listener. He gripped his axe tight.

The others seemed to instinctively clutch at their weapons as well; Rolf's knuckles cracked around the haft of his great axe, and Kolbrun picked at the edge of her shield.

Eyvind, spear over his shoulder, stepped forward. "We must be clear of here by sunset; this is no place to be after dark. But while the sun is still up, we keep moving. Be wary, though. Jarngrim is right."

Hackles raised, Embla trailed behind them at a distance. The hound shied away from each snap or rustle heard within the thicket.

The thorns tore cruelly at their feet and legs though the vines themselves were brittle and crumbled underfoot. It was as though something had poisoned the earth. What that something was, Aelfhild could not begin to guess.

From the center of the plateau rose a building, clearly unnatural despite its cloak of brambles, set into a wide crater in the rock. Whether it had always been open to the sky, or if there had once been a roof that had since rotted away was unclear, but two bare stone arches crossed above a high, circular wall that enclosed an unseen central courtyard. There were no visible breaks in the stone, suggesting the structure had either been carved from the very bedrock or the masonry hidden by some profound artifice.

It was from here that the feeling of dread seeped, setting their teeth on edge and stealing the very breath from their throats. There was a terror here the likes of which not one of them had ever before come across.

Aelfhild could feel her hands trembling as she followed Eyvind and

Kolbrun over the edge and down into the hollow; she squeezed the haft of her makeshift spear for the modicum of comfort it offered.

Another seamless arch, cut into the outer wall, opened into darkness.

The crew clustered around the door and stared inside. There was no sound but their labored breathing, though Aelfhild doubted she could have heard much over the blood pounding inside her ears.

Eyvind spat, trying to clear the taste of the foul air from his mouth, before giving orders. "Jarngrim, Onund, stay back with Ceolwen. If we do not return, take her away from here. Rolf, Kolbrun, Aelfhild—with me."

Both Jarngrim and Ceolwen raised their voices in protest at being left behind, but Eyvind silenced them with a raised hand. "Do as I say. No questions." It was no longer the voice of a friend. It told the pair that their captain would brook no dissent.

"Hold," Eyvind pointed to a spot on the ground outside the doorway and Embla planted herself there. The hound barked plaintively as her master walked away.

Axes raised, Rolf and Kolbrun led the way, Eyvind and Aelfhild behind.

As Aelfhild passed by, Ceolwen touched her servant's hand. Their eyes locked, and wordlessly they bid one another farewell.

Then Aelfhild stepped through the arch, leaving daylight behind.

It took a moment for her eyes to adjust to the darkness, but once they did she found it easy to see. Light crept in from the doorway behind and through a few cracks in the walls and ceiling, illuminating a long hallway that opened to the left and right and followed the curve of the outer wall. The floor was dusty, the air perfectly still. Rolf led them to the right, probing the floor in front of him with the long handle of his axe; beside him, Kolbrun kept the shield raised to her chin.

Pace by agonizing pace they made their way through the hall, which Aelfhild felt must have run the entire length of the structure, accompanied only by the sound of their shuffling feet and ragged breathing. The walls were featureless and smooth, rising evenly to meet the curved ceiling; there were no straight lines to be seen in the entire place.

Another bark from Embla echoed through the tunnel, but the sound was grown faint by the time it reached them.

It grew increasingly difficult for Aelfhild to swallow, so dry had her mouth grown, and her gut felt as though it had abruptly liquified. With a shaking hand, she wiped at her burning eyes, and drew in as deep a breath as she could manage.

Eyvind must have sensed her growing discomfort, for he reached over and put a hand on her shoulder. Though it was clear he fared little better than she, Aelfhild drew strength from the gesture. Even the slightest human touch helped drive back the panic that threatened to take hold of her feet.

At last they came to another door, this one cut from the inner wall. It threw a wide ring of daylight into the dark hallway. Rolf peered around the corner before stepping out and Aelfhild followed, holding her breath.

Sand covered the floor of the round courtyard. The crossed arches hovered overhead in sharp relief against the haze of sky beyond. On this side the wall was carved with countless intricate lines and patterns, all meaningless to Aelfhild's untrained eyes, running along its entire length. A dais, carved of the same unblemished stone as the rest of the building, stood in the room's center directly beneath the intersection of the arcing pillars.

At the foot of the dais sat a figure, vaguely human but curled in upon itself. The stench of death hung heavy in the air, and the feeling of dread was overpowering—this, Aelfhild gazed on in terror, was the source.

A grinding hiss emerged from the hunched form, as though it sensed the sudden intrusion, and the twisted horror began to unfold.

In lurching movements, accompanied by a crackling like the breaking of twigs, a helmeted head rose on a neck of blackened flesh and rotted sinew, while arms bound by ancient, tattered leathers appeared from a coat of tarnished chainmail. What had once been a man stood from agelong rest on decaying limbs; a nightmare made manifest.

Draug the Thrym named them, *lich* in Earnfolding.

Aelfhild knew the words. She had heard the legends of spirits torn from the grave by black and unspeakable rites, filled with bloodlust and blind fury. Bound to tombs or to places of great power, the wight lingered, dead but not dying, until destroyed or released from whatever terrible chains tethered it to the living realm. Never, not for an instant, had she believed that such monsters truly darkened the world.

Rust coated the pieces of the draug's armor that had not yet rotted and fallen away, the gaps revealing twisted flesh and bare yellowing bone beneath. With a rasping scrape, it drew a sword from the frayed scabbard on its hip. Silently, patiently, the monster stood and waited for the humans to move.

Aelfhild quailed at the sight. Not only was the specter itself more terrible to look upon than anything she could possibly have conjured to mind, but its presence shook her understanding of the world to the very center.

Unmoving she stared, helpless, all thoughts of flight or survival scattered in fear. The crude spear fell from her limp fingers but her ears did not even hear the noise it made hitting the sand.

The Thrym were no more used to dealing with such foul aberrations than Aelfhild, but they had at least been tested by battle and years of training. Struck dumb by the sight of what all had thought a mere children's tale, for a moment they faltered.

But then Eyvind took a deep breath, raised spear to shoulder, and let fly.

At such close range it was impossible to miss. The iron blade broke through the timeworn mail covering the monster's breast and drove deep.

A scream wracked the draug's body, rattling through hollow chest and bare jaws, but the creature did not fall. It stepped forth and swung with vicious speed at its attacker.

Kolbrun was ready, and met the falling sword with her shield. The force of the impact sent the shield-maiden careening backwards, and she rolled toward the edge of the room.

"Leifings to me!"

Rolf's shout split the air as he sprang upon the distracted lich from the side, swinging the great axe in long powerful strokes. Such unholy speed did the wight possess that it parried each blow, hissing as it was driven back.

Eyvind scrabbled about in search of a weapon, while Kolbrun sought an opening for her next assault.

Slowly, Aelfhild gathered her senses. Her wits returned and she shook the blood back into her fingers.

"Eyvind!" she cried, stooping to grab her fallen weapon.

The Thrym turned and caught the spear as she tossed it over.

With a leaping thrust he drove the sharp point deep into the monster's leg, drawing its attention away from Kolbrun. The woman's shield lay in splinters on the ground as she crawled away on hands and feet.

Glittering in the light, the great axe swung, but the draug turned aside Rolf's blows time and again.

"Face me!" the greybeard howled.

Blindingly fast, the beast lashed out with a twisted, reeking leg. It connected with Rolf's wounded thigh and the warrior stumbled. He had time to raise his axe in defense, but the cursed blade split through the wooden haft and bit down into the man beneath.

A wordless scream tore from Eyvind's throat. He rushed in and wrenched the spear from the wight's chest, swinging it away from his wounded friend.

Aelfhild, not realizing she too was howling in rage, ran to the stricken warrior's side. Blood foamed through Rolf's grey-streaked beard as he wheezed, and stains spread from the gash in his chest.

There was nothing she could do for him.

She grabbed the upper half of the Thrym's broken axe and turned to face her nightmare.

The battle-lust rose within her. This time she knew it, coaxed it, called it forth.

Red pulsed inwards from the corners of her eyes.

Kolbrun came from behind and chopped into the lich's sword arm, wrenching at her trapped axe. Eyvind clutched at the imbedded spear shaft. Unable to strike at the humans with its blade, the draug snapped its jaws behind the rusted faceplate of its helm and scraped at the Thrym with bone claws.

"Strike now!" Kolbrun screamed.

The splinters in the broken handle pricked Aelfhild's palms as she charged in, swinging for the wight's neck.

Over and over she struck. She felt flesh and bone give way under each blow, and did not cease until the corpse fell twitching and headless to the floor.

Eyvind was first to Rolf's side. He cradled the dying man's head in his arms.

Try as he might, the greybeard could not speak through the blood; he coughed and retched, straining to whisper some word in his captain's ear. Kolbrun held one of his writhing hands, Aelfhild the other. Both women's faces were stained with tears.

Bending close, Eyvind strained to hear the dying man's words, and drops ran down his cheeks to stain Rolf's brow.

Long after the old warrior had drawn his final breath, the three of them remained, weeping. When their grief was spent, they lifted his body and carried him out the way they had come.

4 9

ELFHILD'S EYES WERE red, her cheeks washed in long lines by tears, when she returned to the bloodstained sand of the courtyard. It was dark out now and she carried a torch with her.

They did not have enough wood to build Rolf a fitting pyre. Instead, they had raised a cairn of stones over him. He lay alongside the Jarls of old, clutching his broken axe.

Ceolwen, Onund, and Jarngrim came with them this time, Embla as well, and looked upon the wight. The hound growled and would not approach the carcass; the rest drew back in silent loathing. Eyvind and Kolbrun retrieved weapons scattered during the fight as the crew fanned out to examine the room. None of them, not even wise Onund, could understand the carvings along the wall, though their state of mind was hardly the best for such studies.

The central dais was what held the most interest for them now.

The lich had sat on the edge of the stone platform, whether left to stand unending watch by the fleeing lords of Aettirheim or merely drawn by some fell will to haunt a place of power.

Aelfhild knew, in her heart, that this was what they had set out to find.

Vidar. Geir. Bercthun. And now Rolf—she pictured each one. Good men had died for them to come this far and now the journey was at an end, but what should have been a great triumph rang hollow.

Atop the platform were more carvings, and these were similar to runes that they had seen before. In the center was fitted a chunk of black, volcanic glass, larger than any piece Aelfhild had ever seen. The facets were chipped smooth, but curved inward in a way that twisted the light, making the crystal seem to shimmer from within.

The Oath-Stone, she marveled.

Onund bent close to peer at the marks on the platform, but took care not to lay a hand upon it. The others held up their torches at a cautious distance.

Ceolwen made as if to come over as well, but Eyvind waved her back, shaking his head. "We do not know what will happen," he said.

She swallowed hard, and remained by the doorway.

Muttering to himself, Onund pursed his lips. "Here is the word for Jarl, here is *oath* and *fire*. This is all old and beyond my ken." He straightened. "The girl should touch the stone. That is how it must be."

"Wait," Kolbrun spoke, "I saw the draug myself. There is some dark magic in this stone. A curse. Leave it be, I say, while some of us still have our lives."

Jarngrim nodded and muttered his support for the shield-maiden.

Eyvind looked from face to face in the torchlight. "Much has been lost on the way here. If we walk away from this it has all been for nothing. I say let her try—"

At that point, Ceolwen snapped. "Do not speak of me as if I am not here!" she thundered.

The Thrym were taken aback.

Aelfhild felt her face flush, for even she had for a moment forgotten that her mistress stood nearby.

"I am the Aethling and the heir to the throne of Earnfold," Ceolwen roared with every bit of authority she could muster, "and for once I will choose my own fate."

Eyes cast to the floor, Eyvind began, "Cousin, I—"

"Step aside, *cousin*." She twisted the last word. "It is my choice. I do not belong to your father or to you or to anyone. No longer will I be a slave to the Thrym." Stepping forward, Ceolwen extended a hand to her servant. "Aela, will you stand beside me?"

Aelfhild hesitated only briefly before taking the outstretched hand.

I have been with her at every step, she thought. I cannot falter now.

The Thrym all moved away from the dais, and Aelfhild could feel the expectant stares. She followed Ceolwen to the center of the room, and stood one step back and to the side.

Ceolwen's newfound confidence faltered when she reached the Oath-Stone, for there was no clear ritual, no chant or spell or gesture. Gingerly, she reached out to touch the carvings on the table.

Nothing changed.

She knelt on the dais, reaching out for the crystal set within. In the palm of her right hand Ceolwen cupped the black gem, but without result. Placing her left palm on the other side, she bent to look into the murky glass.

A twinge of shame, for herself and for her mistress, ran through Aelfhild's body. Her ears burned under the steady gaze of the crew.

Then the Oath-Stone began to glow.

At first Aelfhild thought it was just a glint of torchlight off the glassy surface, a trick of the eye, but steadily it grew into a bright, pulsing orange light.

Ceolwen gasped in wonder. Slowly she stood and extended a trembling hand as ethereal tendrils, flickering thin flames, reached out from the stone to caress, embrace her.

Without warning a shriek split the hushed air in the courtyard, an ear-splitting scream that came from everywhere at once. Ceolwen seemed momentarily to float in the air, before a searing pillar of light erupted from the dais and lanced into the night sky.

Aelfhild was thrown backwards by a wall of heat and thundering sound; blinded and deafened she flew. Her back struck the distant wall, driving all the air from her chest. Her ears rang and her vision went pure white.

For some time she lay in the sand, senseless, fading in and out of wakefulness. Her head and limbs seemed impossibly weightless, yet would not move. Shimmering white light filled her vision. There was no pain, just a sense of distance, as though mind and body were separated by an immeasurable rift.

Floating in that void, Aelfhild began to hear voices. Quiet at first, they rose gradually in strength as the ringing faded into the background.

"Eyvind! Jarngrim! Onund!" Kolbrun was shouting, calling desperately for her companions.

Jarngrim spoke up first, sounding frightened: "I cannot see anything."

"Keep blinking, it will fade," the shield-maiden said. "Eyvind! Answer me!"

A groan came from somewhere to Aelfhild's left. "Here," wheezed their captain.

"Still alive," croaked Onund from across the room.

"Aelfhild! Ceolwen!" cried Kolbrun.

Aelfhild stirred as the whiteness burned into the back of her eyes faded into swirling spots of vivid color, and tried to straighten her body which was wedged up against the hard stone of the wall. Pain shot up and down her back and raced along her ribs when she moved. Coughing, she answered. "I am alive."

"Ceolwen!"

Silence.

Again, after a pause. "Ceolwen!"

There was no reply.

Their coughs and moans echoed from the walls as they waited for the blindness to pass. Eyvind whispered gently to whimpering Embla.

Aelfhild's arms and legs still felt numb, so she sat clenching fists and toes to regain some feeling.

Pieces of the room drew back into focus little by little. What Aelfhild thought at first were fragments of her impaired vision, dots of burning orange that floated across her field of view, proved to be real; like the embers of a fire blown on a gale wind, pinpricks of light danced in the air, drifting slowly upward toward the stars in a loose spiral. All of the torches the crew had carried with them had sputtered out in the sand, but the ghostly glow cast by the wisps lit the room enough for Aelfhild to see the others.

She shifted onto her knees, ignoring the protests of her aching back, and stood slowly to her feet. To her left, Embla pawed at Eyvind's prone form. To her right, Kolbrun offered a hand to Jarngrim to help him off the ground, and on the far side of the courtyard Onund sat upright in the sand, rubbing his eyes.

"Ceolwen," Aelfhild whispered, begging the darkness to answer.

Dust hung heavy in the air and stuck in her throat, making her cough again. The spasm shook her body, sending a cloud of fine dust out from her clothes and hair. Puzzled, she wiped a finger across her face, which was caked in a layer of the same powder. She stared at the grey on her fingertip.

It looked like ash.

Ash.

Ceolwen.

Bile rushed up in her throat, and she doubled over to retch into the sand. When her stomach had emptied, she straightened, shuddering, and began in a frenzy to brush the dust away from her skin and clothing.

The Thrym looked on bewildered by her sudden turn of madness. They peered at the ash that covered them all until, one by one, the same realization dawned.

Aelfhild dropped to the floor, pulling her legs to her chest and hanging her head between quaking knees. Back and forth she rocked, sobbing.

She cannot be gone.

No.

No, she repeated endlessly.

Silence fell. Eyvind knelt beside her and reached out to touch her shoulder. "There was nothing you could do," he said, his voice consoling. "None of us knew what would happen."

Aelfhild screamed at him to leave her be, the words bursting forth half-formed, and swiped at his outstretched arm.

The Thrym took a step back. Kolbrun gasped.

"Aelfhild," the shield-maiden called.

But Aelfhild would not answer.

Let me die so she can come back. Take me in her place, she prayed to the Gods as grief boiled over into rage within her chest. She turned upon the heavens. Why would you let us suffer, just to do this? Why do you torture me?

"Aelfhild!" This time it was a command, from all the Thrym.

She lifted her gaze from the floor. The others stood around her in a half-circle, staring intently down, not at her face but at her right arm.

Never had Kolbrun's voice sounded so timid. "Look at your hand," she whispered.

Confused, Aelfhild lifted her arm.

On the palm of her hand glowed a rune, one long line running from fingers to wrist that crossed through two corners of a hollow square. The marks shone from within, yellow-gold like sunlight, and seemed to pass through her skin into the flesh beneath. Turning her hand over, she found the same design on the back. When she made a fist, faint trails of light slipped through the cracks between her fingers.

She gaped at the mark. Nothing felt different about her palm, no cuts or scarring, as she ran the fingers of her left hand across the rune. There was no pain or burning.

Her four companions were struck dumb. Slowly, Onund sank to his knees. The old man bowed his head. Jarngrim did the same, and Kolbrun followed.

Shaken from stupor, their captain turned to face them. "What are you doing?" Eyvind cried.

Onund's eyes did not lift from the glowing rune. "The Eid-Stein chose her. She has been marked by the Gods. You see it with your own eyes. It is fated."

Eyvind did not kneel, and for that one kindness Aelfhild was thankful. The eyes of the other three warriors were fixed upon her hand and glinted with fervent hunger. It terrified her to see them so possessed.

Something snapped within her mind in that moment and she scrabbled to her feet.

Without looking back, she ran.

At a dead sprint she rounded the door and headed out through the passage, wanting nothing more than to be under the night sky. Behind her came startled cries and Embla's barking. Once outside, she did not cease, nor pause to think why or whither she fled.

She ran until her legs gave out. A grassy meadow rose up to embrace her and she fell face down, panting, and stayed there until the sound of rough footpads drew close. Snuffling at her face and hair, Embla nuzzled Aelfhild's neck.

Not far off, Aelfhild could hear Eyvind ordering the other Thrym to build a fire and make camp. Someone draped a blanket over her back but she did not turn her head to look.

She could not hold on to a single orderly thought. She wanted to weep. She wanted to laugh. She wanted to scream, run, bleed, howl, to hide away. She wanted to die, to walk into the waves and sink into the darkest abyss.

Overcome with exhaustion, her eyelids closed and Aelfhild slept.

5 0

STRAY LOCK OF hair lay across her face when she awoke, festooned with morning dew. The grass all around her was damp, and water beaded on the blanket covering her body.

Aelfhild sat up. Every bone creaked as she stretched.

Not far away the coals of a fire smoked, and three figures lay around it wrapped in cloaks. Closer to her sat Eyvind, blanket hitched up over his shoulders and with his legs drawn up to his chest. The ruddy mane of his beard spilled down to cover his knees.

He held out their waterskin.

Aelfhild drank deep.

The Thrym did not lift his eyes from her once, but it was her face he watched so closely and not her hand.

"I do not know why I ran," she said, breaking the silence.

Eyvind snorted. "I would have."

The answer surprised Aelfhild, and she stared back without reply.

He continued, "It is madness, just madness. Yesterday we saw nightmares made real. The monster, and Rolf…" His voice faltered. "Then Ceolwen, and this." The Thrym balled his right hand into a fist and she took his meaning.

"No one is that strong. It would have been inhuman not to run," he finished.

Aelfhild shuddered, "I never wanted this. I could never have dreamed… I did not ask for it." She pleaded with him as though he had accused her of planning the deed, but the warrior sat shaking his head. Her voice fell to a whisper, "I do not want it."

Eyvind pulled his blanket tighter against the chill of the dawn air. "Maybe that is why you have it. While you were sleeping I sat here and thought. All night long I thought. I am no wise man, and no priest"—at this he grinned—"but I do know how those three looked at you."

With a nod of the head he pointed toward their sleeping companions.

"My father is not a fool. Ceolwen was always just a way for the Leifings to gain land and power. I do not think even he believed the Stone would be so real. But it was a good story to tell the warriors, to stir their blood for battle. But this," his voice trailed off.

Aelfhild stared at the shining rune, its brightness lessened in the light of day. Taking her cloak in both hands, she tore a rough strip from the bottom and wrapped her hand to cover the mark.

Eyvind nodded as he watched her tie it off. "Now it is not just about thrones and crowns. What you saw in their eyes is a taste of more to come. Kings, Queens, Jarls, Eorls, they are here and gone. Men know when to listen to them, when to follow them, and when to pay them no heed. But one chosen by the Gods? That is no trifling thing.

"Of all the hands that could bear that mark, then, I would only trust those that did not seek it out. That is what I thought."

They fell silent for a long time.

Aelfhild turned the question over in her mind before she asked, "What if I keep running?"

"You would be mad not to," he answered, "Fate be damned."

There was a strong charm to that notion, to turning her back on the schemes of men and Gods, spurning fate and simply walking away. Within her the argument raged and would rage forever.

"I cannot do this alone," she said finally.

Eyvind shook off the dew as he stood. He crossed over to Aelfhild and offered his hand. With a grunt, she lifted herself to face him.

"You will not be alone, not ever. That is my oath." From around his neck he pulled the lump of troll-bone that Thane Kjartan had thrown him from the shore of Oddsbaer.

She had not spared it a thought since then, assuming it lost in the waves with so much else. Eyvind looped the string over her head.

"Whatever comes, I always stand by my friends."

Aelfhild's face flushed, and hidden though they were beneath his beard, she saw that his cheeks reddened as well.

Then Eyvind turned and walked over to wake the others. "And so do they," he added over his shoulder.

Kolbrun yawned as she stirred the fire back to life. Onund doled out a bit of dried fish to each of them for breakfast, and they ate in silence before breaking camp. Jarngrim hummed as he slung the shield over his back and rolled up his other belongings in a blanket.

Returning from her morning hunt, Embla licked at red stains on her jaws. The day had begun well for her. Eyvind knelt to scratch at her neck and the hound wagged her curly tail.

"Home," he said, and Embla trotted south in her master's wake. The remaining Thrym followed.

Aelfhild took one last look at Aettirheim, the green hills and dark cliffs washed by the morning sun as it rose above the bay. She bid farewell to Ceolwen, and to the others. She bid farewell to her old life, everything she had known.

With a deep breath, she straightened her shoulders and set off.

AUTHOR'S NOTE

Thank you for reading!

This is a self-published novel. Self-published novels and authors rely on word of mouth and reader reviews to succeed. If you enjoyed this book, please consider taking a minute to post a short review on whatever website you purchased your copy.

If you would like to receive a notice whenever I release a new book, click here to join my mailing list:

http://eepurl.com/da0ZCf

This list will only be used for notifications of any new titles I publish.

NOTE ON PRONUNCIATIONS

The language of Earnfold is based (loosely) on Old English. The stress in all Earnfolding words will always fall on the first syllable. Here are some of the names with a guide to pronouncing them:

Aelfhild – ALF-hild
Bercthun – BERK-thun
Ceolwen – CHEH-ul-wen
Cuthbert – COOTH-burt
Cynestead – COON-eh-steh-ud
Ealdorscir – ALD-ur-shir

Earnfold – ARN-fold
Leofstan – LEH-of-stan
Leohtmere – LEH-ot-mer-eh
Osric – OS-rich
Suthscir – SUTH-scir
Thrydwulf – THRID-wulf

The language of Thrymgard is adapted, again liberally, from Icelandic and Old Norse with simplified spelling. Stress will always fall on the first syllable of the word.

Eyrun – EY-roon
Eyvind – EY-vind
Hlifseyjar – HLEEFS-ey-yar
Jarlstad – YARL-stad
Jarngrim – YARN-grim
Jotunn – YO-tun

Kjartan – KYAR-tan
Leifing – LEYF-ing
Ormsund – ORM-soond
Saejunn – SIGH-oon
Skjoldung – SKYOLD-ung
Ulfheim – ULF-haym

Oescan names, places, and words are adapted from Latin. They are heavy on vowels and should be a little easier for speakers of English to read.

Oesca – oh-ES-ka   Imezlii – i-MEZ-lee-ee
Hibernum – hi-BERN-um   Lucianus – loo-SEE-ahn-u

All errors and inconsistencies, in any language, are my fault and mine alone

ACKNOWLEDGEMENTS

I'd like to thank Andy Meisenheimer for his invaluable editing. I never realized how much collaboration is involved in the publishing process, but his input made this a far, far better book. It also taught me more about writing than 13 years of English classes.

Thanks to Rick Britton for his great work on the map of Heimgard.

Thanks to Evelyn Edson and R. D. "Doc" Larrick for their beta reading and feedback.

A special thank you to my brother, Mike, and sister-in-law, Teresa, for their encouragement. And for all the beer.

But most of all, I want to thank my parents for their support and unending patience.

I could not have done this without y'all.

ABOUT THE AUTHOR

Ander Levisay is an author of fantasy stories featuring faraway worlds that still, somehow, have Vikings in them. He has lived in Iceland and Russia, but currently resides in Virginia with his dogs and cats. Whether it's writing, reading, or gaming, Ander can always be found in front of a computer screen. He probably should get out more.

His debut novel is *Runes and Red Sails*, the first book in the *Queenmaker* series.

You can learn more about the author and his novels at:
www.anderlevisay.com

www.ingramcontent.com/pod-product-compliance
Lightning Source LLC
Chambersburg PA
CBHW020259200626
46816CB00001BA/375